1st

Nelson McKeck
No 1458

ANOTHER PAMELA

ANOTHER PAMELA

or, Virtue Still Rewarded

A Story

BY UPTON SINCLAIR

New York

THE VIKING PRESS

1950

PRINTED IN THE U.S.A. BY
AMERICAN BOOK–STRATFORD PRESS, INC., NEW YORK

To the memory of
LEWIS BROWNE:
scholar
and loyal friend

FOREWORD

Two hundred and ten years ago there was published in London a four-volume collection of letters entitled *Pamela: Or Virtue Rewarded*. They caused an immense sensation and started a new form of literature known as the English novel. A middle-aged printer named Samuel Richardson became, overnight, a celebrity and the darling of London society, especially the female half.

Recently it came to my knowledge that Pamela Andrews had experienced a reincarnation and was living in Southern California. I sought her out and obtained permission to edit and publish the letters which she had written to her family over a period of several years. I have made no changes except in the punctuation and occasionally the spelling; for Pamela had only a grade-school education, and while she is very bright she could never be called learned. Let no one make the mistake of underestimating her on that account. I quote the words which the old-time printer wrote concerning her former incarnation:

"From the low opinion which she everywhere shows of herself, and her attributing all her excellencies to pious education, and her lady's virtuous instructions and bounty, let persons even of genius and piety, learn not to arrogate to themselves those gifts and graces, which they owe least of all to themselves; since the beauties of person are frail, and it is not in our power to give them to ourselves, or to be either prudent, wise, or good, without the assistance of Divine Grace."

The old-time English printer went on to list the many virtues of Pamela: "her signal veracity, which she never forfeited; her obliging behaviour to her equals, before her exaltation; her kindness to them afterwards; her forgiving spirit, and her generosity; her meekness in every circumstance where her virtue was not concerned; her charitable allowance for others; her maiden and bridal purity; her signal affiance in God; her thankful spirit; her grateful heart; her diffusive charity to the poor; the cheerful ease and freedom of her deportment. . . ."

Who can possibly fail to profit from reading about the possessor of such qualities, no less astonishing in the twentieth century than in the eighteenth?

UPTON SINCLAIR

ANOTHER PAMELA

Dear Sister:

This will be the most exciting letter I ever wrote to anyone. I have a job! Oh, how I wish I could see you and tell
you about it! I shall write very small to save paper; but
soon I shall be able to buy more, for I am to have forty
dollars a month and my board and keep, and even uniforms
and laundry. Such a wonderful thing has happened to me,
I can hardly believe it; but here I am, and no matter how
hard I pinch myself I do not wake up. I have been picked
up and carried away to a palace; Mother has money to get
tar paper for the roof before the rains come; you will
be able to go on at the college. You too will have to pinch
yourself, but I assure you it is real. I was expecting to have
such a hard time finding work, and I was afraid even to try;
but I prayed and prayed, exactly in the way that Rev.
Strayker told us—not telling God what to do, but telling
Him that I was sure He would take care of me and that He
would know exactly what was best for me. And of course
He did, but what a strange way He has of working—to
break a connecting rod in the engine of a big automobile!
Surely as wonderful a case of providential action you ever
read in the Sabbath Lessons.

It was the day before yesterday, the hottest day we have
had this summer—and you know what our heat can be.
Grampa gave out and couldn't stand to work; he was lying
on the bed indoors, Mother was doing out a wash in the
back shed, and I was carrying water to the onion patch.
You can see me, barefoot, with the work dress that has
given way in a dozen places and been patched the best I

can, and with the big straw hat that is tied with string. I look up for a moment, and there I see somebody coming up the path, walking very slow, a heavy lady with fine clothes which I don't know how to describe. There is a man in uniform following behind her, and I look down to the highway and see a big black car standing.

First I think she has seen our sign and has come to inquire about washing; but then I decide No, she would have driven up the road close to the house, and the man would be the one to get out. I guess that the car must have some trouble, so I go to her, and when I get near I see that she is out of breath. I say, "Can I help you, ma'am?" And she says, "I see you have a tree." I say, "Yes, ma'am, the only tree for a mile around." So many times we have thanked God for the chinaberry tree and its thick shade, but never did we guess what He meant it to do for us.

Well, the lady says, "I think I can make it," and I do not offer to help her because I am so very dirty, and I guess that if she wanted help it would be the man's business. She stops twice to get her breath coming up the slope. I offer to get her a chair but she says never mind, she has a lap robe, and I see the man is carrying a very elegant one, and I am glad because I know our chairs are old, and I am not sure there is one that would hold all of her. When she gets under the tree she says, "Spread the robe, Pietro." I want to tell her that the chinaberries will ruin it, but I suppose she can see as well as I can, and I am afraid, for she is such a very grand person, in a dark dress of some fine stuff which I guess is silk because that is the only name I know. She is heavy but holds herself very straight, even when she is tired and breathing hard. She is about fifty, I would guess, and has brown hair and lovely dark eyes; her face is kind, but I would hate to make her angry, and I surely mean to not.

Well, there she sits on the lap robe, and she says, "How

far is it to the nearest garage?" I say, "About six miles, in Mesa Seco." She says, "Go down, Pietro, and stop the first car you can, and drive in and get help. Then hire a car and come back for me." He says, "Yes, my lady"—he is some sort of foreigner, but the lady doesn't seem to be. The man goes back to the highway, and she looks about, and you know the things she sees. The house is even worse than when you were here, for the last santa ana took off about a quarter of the tarpaper on the roof, and a lot of it is still hanging because the ladder is broke and Grampa has been too tired to fix it. You and I know that if you have true religious faith you can be happy even in a shack that is half old tin and half unpainted boards; but unbelievers don't know that, and it is a part of our faith not to let them make you ashamed of the lot to which the Lord has called you.

The lady looks about her and I can see that she is being polite and not showing too much of what she thinks. "You have lived here all your life?" she asks, and I tell her not quite all, and how we bought this place after Daddy was killed on the railroad. She wants to know why we didn't get more damages, and I tell her about how he signed away his claim while he was in the hospital. She puts me through a questioning and I suppose she is passing the time, which may be long because the garage at Mesa Seco isn't much. She asks what we are growing and I tell her onions, and that I was carrying water from the spring. She wants to know can't we dig a trench to the onions and I explain that it is a small spring and we would lose the water in the ground, so we dip it out and carry it. Then she says, "But you can't live on onions," and I explain that we have three goats tethered out on the hillside, and that Mother earns cash money by taking in washing. "But who is there out here to wash for?" she asks, and I explain about Uncle Zebulon in town who comes twice a week and brings and takes. I tell her, "So we get money to pay our taxes." She answers, "There ought not to be any taxes on poor people's homes." I had never thought of that, but it would be nice, and I so said.

She looks out over the hills and says, "I suppose you get rabbits too," and I explain that our faith does not permit us to eat flesh. She wants to know about our faith, and when I use the word Adventist I see that it doesn't mean anything to her. When I explain that Jesus Christ is coming to earth again, she asks if I really believe that, and I assure her that He has definitely promised it in Scripture. She looks about and says, "Then I suppose it doesn't matter what sort of house you are living in when He comes." I say, "Yes, ma'am, exactly, it only matters that you believe in Him and have a clean heart. If your feet are muddy from working in the fields He will not hold such a thing against you." She has invited me to sit beside her, and I am sitting sideways, keeping my feet off her lap robe.

She wants to know the rest of my faith, and I am glad to explain, as one can never tell when a seed may fall on good ground, and how could I know what God meant when He caused her car to break down? Perhaps it might be in order to give a rich lady her chance at salvation. I explain that we keep the seventh day literally, and she asks, "But then you have two rest days?" I answer that we keep only the Sabbath. She pins me down, "You mean that you work on Sunday?" And I explain that perhaps we work a little harder on Sunday, because we have just had a day's rest, and have had the word of the Lord preached to us, or at any rate have read our Bibles. She replies that she never heard of such a practice as keeping Saturday, except for Jews. "It could be convenient," she says, "because in a large household most of the help want Sundays off."

I realize then that she is looking me over. She asks how

old I am and I tell her sixteen. She says, "You are tall for your age, but you are thin, and it is your diet." I assure her that I do a man's work six days in the week. She says that I am not bad looking and I tell her that I hope not too bad, but it is better to have good behavior than good looks. She surprises me by asking if my yellow hair is genuine, and at first I don't know what she means—imagine, she thought maybe I had dyed it! I explain that our church would hold that for a sin, even if I had any idea how to do such a thing. She asks about my education and I tell her how the school bus passes here taking the children to school and bringing them back again; I tell her about my sister who is working her way through college and wants to become a doctor. Imagine, she lives only about twenty miles from our wonderful college and our hospital and she does not know that they exist! I told her plenty, and I hope she was impressed.

So it came out what she had in mind—that she would teach me to be a parlormaid. Of course I told her that I would be very happy and would try to serve her to the best of my ability. She said I could have the Sabbath off and do my hardest work on Sunday, when they had a cold supper in the evening and let nearly all the help go. She did not tell me what faith she belongs to and I could only pray she was not a Papist. She told me I would have to keep clean, and I assured her that I took a bath every Friday before my worship began. She said that wouldn't be enough, I would have to bathe every day, and I said I would be willing if she did not mind my taking so much time off.

Then she looked at me very hard and said, "I suppose that your religion has taught you to be honest?" I answered, as quick as I could, "Oh, indeed, you may be sure!" She said, still solemn, "We have jewelry, and our guests sometimes are careless and leave it lying around." I felt my cheeks getting hot and I told her, "I am quite sure it could never cross my mind to take anything that did not belong to me. I could not be happy to work for you if I thought you doubted that." So she said, "That is all right and I will trust you." But for the first time I began to doubt if I would care to work in that place. I do not like the thought of jewels, and still less of people suspecting me. If it had not been for you and Mother I might have said No.

She asked, "Have you a dress that is fit to travel in?" and I told her, "I have the dress that I wear to church when I have the chance. It is old and too small for me but I keep it clean." She said, "That will do. While the car is being repaired, you will have time to bathe and pack your things." "Oh, am I to go now?" I asked, and she said, "Why not? My parlormaid has left me and married; it is something they are always doing, and I hope you will not." I told her I was far too young to think of any such thing as to git married. She said, "You must not say 'git,' or people will think that you have no education." I said, "Yes, ma'am," and she said, "You will call me Mrs. Harries, and call any lady by her name, never ma'am." I said, "Yes, ma'am, Mrs. Harries."

Well, then I felt the tears coming, and she said, "Why are you crying?" I told her, "I am not crying, it is just that I cannot stop the tears from running down my cheeks." She said, "You must not have your feelings hurt when I teach you things." I said, "Oh, it is not that. But I have never been away from home in my life and it is all so sudden. I will have to ask my mother." So I called Mother and she came, wiping the soapsuds off her hands and arms, and surprised to see a great lady sitting under the chinaberry tree. You know how Mother is when she has been working on a hot day, her face is as red as the wattles of a turkey gobbler and the cords of her thin neck stand out like ropes. She stands and hears what I have to say and doesn't say a word till I am through. I know that she will not be afraid of any rich person, because she knows that we are all equal in the sight of the Lord and that those of us who have the true faith are better; also that we can keep going so long as one of the nannies is fresh.

She says, hard like, "It must be understood that this child will keep the Sabbath strict." Mrs. Harries says, "That has been agreed to, Mrs. Andrews." But that doesn't do for Mother. "You must know," says she, "our Sabbath begins at sunset on Friday, and she lays down her work at that moment, and her time belongs to the Lord until sunset on Saturday. 'Six days shalt thou labor and do all thy work: But the seventh day is the sabbath of the Lord thy God; in it thou shalt not do any work, thou, nor thy son, nor thy daughter, thy manservant nor thy maidservant, nor thy cattle, nor thy stranger that is within thy gates.' " Mrs. Harries answered, "I will respect her beliefs. But how does she know the moment of sunset, since we live in the mountains, and especially when it happens to be raining?" Mother explains that we have an almanac that tells us the moment, and we have an alarm clock which is all right when it is working.

So that is settled; but Mother isn't through yet. She asks, "Do you happen to be a Romanist?" Mrs. Harries says, "Oh, dear, no!" Mother says, "We do not go for Popery," and then asks what faith Mrs. Harries holds. Mrs. Harries says, "I belong to the Brotherhood Group," and Mother has never heard of that, nor have I. "Do you follow Scripture?" she asks, as if she was the one that was doing the hiring. Mrs. Harries says that they preach the Fatherhood of God and the Brotherhood of Man, and Mother says that may be all right, but she don't want no notions taught to her child, the plain word of God is enough, and William Miller has explained it clear. Mrs. Harries promises very solemn that she will let my faith strictly alone; and Mother says, "I have brought her up proper and you will find that she is an honest and decent child." And so it is a bargain.

The man came with a car and drove Mrs. Harries to the hotel in the village, which I fear she will find no cooler than the chinaberry tree. A tow car takes the sick car away, and I go in and give myself a scrubbing and put on my best clothes and tie up my things in a bundle. Then I sit and wait and perspire all over again, and wonder can it really be or will this rich lady think it over and decide that I am too lowly to be taken into her grand home. Of course I don't know what is the matter with the car, and when it is almost night and nobody has come I am in despair. All that time Mother is talking without one stop, telling me how Satan rules the world, and how most of the people in it are damned souls who will be gathered up like chaff from the threshing floor and cast into everlasting fire. Of course I know it is true, but that does not make me want to hear it so many times. I have to promise in the presence of Jesus that never, never will I permit any trace of false doctrine to find lodgment in my mind, and that never will I go to bed without having read a chapter in my Testament and prayed for help in understanding it. I promise; and then tears come into my eyes and I say, "Oh, Mother, she has gone without me!"

But no, when it is dark I see the lights of the car; and then I fall to boohooing like a baby because I am leaving my tarpaper home and going to live in a great house full of damned souls. Mother has to call me a booby and lead me down to the car and push me in; and there I sit by the foreign man—he is from Italy—and I gulp and choke and try to listen while he tells me about connecting rods, and how it was the heat that caused it to break, and the engine had to be taken apart and a man had to drive all the way to

Riverside to get a new part. The Italians are very sociable, I learn. There is a glass wall between us and Mrs. Harries, and she does not speak on the whole trip and perhaps is asleep.

Anyhow, I am here; but I have used up all my writing pad. I promised Mother I would write and tell her everything about my new home, so I will write next to her and she will forward it to you. I will only tell you that God has indeed given me a sign and I will strive to grow in His grace. Your devoted Sister

Pamela

LETTER II

Dear Mother:

I have had so many duties that I have not been able to write until the Sabbath. First let me tell you that last night I read Revelation 14 and studied every word of the First Angel's Message, and checked every word of its prophecies by the interpretations in "The Great Controversy." This morning I have said my prayers, and now I suppose it is a proper observance for me to write my beloved Mother. It is not work but a pleasure, and since we are told to honor our parents I hope it is proper, but please to ask Rev. Strayker about it, as I have no one to ask here and our nearest church is so far away that I do not know when I shall be able to attend service. If I am doing wrong in so writing I hope that my good intention will be an excuse.

Well, I am here, and it is the most wonderful place that anybody could imagine. You must picture a great canyon, wide at the mouth and coming together at the top, where there is a pass that explorers came through in the old days, I am told. At the entrance to the pass is a sort of high shelf, and there stand the buildings, high enough so that they are safe from the floods which may come rushing down the canyon in winter—it sometimes happens that the road is washed out, but the telephone line runs along the side of the mountain so that it is always safe. The view is wonderful; you see below you for I cannot guess how many miles. The valley is planted in barley, which is now a bright yellow stubble, just after the harvest; the orchards are a shiny dark green, being irrigated by wells with windmills. The cultivated land extends right to the edge of the mountains on both sides and the effect is very strange, as if it was a pattern cut out by a tailor—a cover of yellow and green cloth fitted neatly to the bare brown edges of the mountain slopes. The valley opens to the west and the sunsets are so beautiful that I think God is surely painting his warnings of hell below.

The mansion is of some sort of red stone, and is three stories high, but they call it two and a half, because the top story is low with small windows, and that is where we women help have our rooms. We do not have to climb there, because there are little elevators that run themselves, and there is one called "service" in back, that is for us. At first it scared me but already I am used to it. Our windows face the mountain, where we sometimes see deer and foxes. I have a little room all to myself, and it is so neat and clean that it took my breath away when I saw it; I was told I must always keep it so, and this I will surely do.

On the place are many other buildings, including a long garage with many cars, and rooms above for the men help. Also there are guest houses, it is like a little village all laid out in a park, but it all belongs to one man, or maybe it is to her. I have not yet found out, but I shall, because the help all talk. So far I have had so much to do that I have not had time to listen; I have trouble remembering all my duties, for it seems that I am sort of substitute for everybody, and when they have a day off or are sick, I come in handy and have to do their work the best way I can. It keeps me jumping but I don't mind it so long as nobody scolds me, and so far I have managed it that they don't have to. My boss is the housekeeper who is Mrs. Jessup, and she is large and stout and very strict; but I soon saw that she is kind, and I told her I would do my very best and would she please to excuse my ignorance at the start. She said she would, if only I would try to remember; it is, she says, the curse of her life that nobody will carry any responsibility, and I promised her I would do my best in that way.

As you know, I was hired for a parlormaid, but it seems there is no parlor; it is called the drawing room, but I have never seen anybody drawing in it. It is long and high and has the most wonderful furniture; I did not know that such things existed in this world. The bookcases are what is called French walnut, and whoever carved them had no mercy on parlormaids, for they are all over flowers and leaves and wriggly stems, and I have to take a soft rag with just a little oil and carefully wipe every crack and crevice. You know how the dust is in our California summers, and here it is worse because there is even more wind than at home and it drives the dust in under doors and windows; so every day I have to dust everything in this great room and in the dining room next to it. Mrs. Jessup will pass through and stop and run her finger along a bit of polished wood, and then hold it up and look at it, and if it was wrong I should be so ashamed, but so far it hasn't been.

The trouble is that in the midst of the work Miss Bascom will come—she is the secretary and a very fashionable young lady. Perhaps I oughtn't to say it but I can't help thinking that she has put something on her cheeks to make them more pink. Her clothes are very smart, I am sure, and she has little black things hanging from her ears and a shiny piece of jewelry at her throat, and perhaps this is what she may someday leave lying around for somebody to think of stealing. I don't doubt that she is very superior to me, but I am trying to practice goodness to all and hope that sooner or later it will win their hearts. She says to me, "Pamela, will you phone Pietro and tell him to bring the car in ten minutes." Miss Bascom does the shopping for the family, and there is a phone to the garage, so that does not take long; but then she says, "Oh, I have forgot where I put my handbag, will you help me to find it? Have a look in my room." So I run upstairs quick—the elevator is too slow—and her room is so lovely, all with pink flounces and things I never saw before, I am afraid almost to touch anything. I find her handbag on a table underneath a tray that has had ice tea on it—at least I hope that is what it is. Alongside the bag is a tiny little gold watch with a bracelet-like that goes on her wrist. I think she cannot have meant to leave it there so I take it to her, and she says, quite offhand, "Oh, thanks, Pamela," and I am glad that I took the chance but it scared me terribly.

So you see that I have many errands and have to be ready for everything. You can see me in a pretty black dress with snow-white collar and cuffs, cap and apron. Miss Bascom took my size and bought them for me the first day, and Mrs. Jessup taught me manners and how I am never to speak unless I am spoken to and then to say no more than is needed. "Important people do not want their attention distracted," she said, and I said, "Yes, Mrs. Jessup," as meek as could be. But I listen and find that many of these people want to talk and not to a dummy. Miss Bascom said to me when she was getting my measure, "You will surely have a hard time making anybody believe that your hair took that bright color by nature—is it really so?" And I can't see that that was exactly a needed remark.

I am glad that you met Mrs. Harries, so you can imagine her. She is curious and wants to know about everybody, even a humble parlormaid. Yesterday morning while I was having my breakfast—we help have a dining room of our own next the kitchen with lovely smooth blue walls and blue table smooth and hard as glass—well, I heard a buzzer, and cook said, "Oh, dear, that is Mrs. Harries, and I am frying the master's breakfast bacon, will you take my lady's orange juice?" I jump up, and she tells me to get the glass of orange juice out of the huge white icebox—only it has no ice, it is frozen by electricity, can you imagine—because I thought that electricity was hot! Anyhow, there must be a silver tray and a paper napkin—they say that is not fashionable but it is the way here, because my lady is economical in small things and extravagant only in great ones. Two slices of toast, and I put the butter on quick and then walk fast because they say that she counts the seconds after she has buzzed, which she does the moment she opens her eyes.

Well, I am on time so she does not scold. She is lying in her bed that has a pink silk spread, and she has on a jacket all lace with pink ribbons, and she is very elegant looking but much too plump between you and me. She says, "So it is you, Pamela," and I say, "Yes, Mrs. Harries," as proper as can be, and I set down the tray. Oh, how I would love to look at that lovely room, all in pink silk!—but I start to bow myself out because I have been told not to stop and watch her drink and eat; she will buzz again when she wants the tray taken. But she says, "And how do you like your work?" So I say, "Oh, everyone is kind to me and I am very happy."

She says, "Will you write that to your mother?" I tell her how I am planning to write, and that I hope it will not count as work on the Sabbath; she says she would think not. But how could she know anything about our doctrines? She asks, "What is this about half your money going to your mother and the other half to your sister?" and I explain. "But," says she, "you will have to have pocket money. What will you do for a stamp and paper to write to your mother?" I say I have not thought of that. She asks, "Why does your sister have to have exactly twenty dollars a month?" and I tell her how hard Rachel has to work and how every dollar that she has to earn is time taken from her studies, and I want so to have her make good grades and perhaps get a scholarship. My mistress asks is she older than me, and I tell her two years older and ever so much smarter, and of course she has a long way to go to be nurse and maybe doctor.

So I forget my own breakfast and stand while she sips orange juice and eats toast and asks me questions about Rachel and the college and all my family, and where we lived in Oklahoma, and when we came to California, and who built the house, and couldn't we have it fixed, and how do we live, and what do we eat besides onions and goat's milk, and how many years did I go to school, and what did I learn and so on—it must have been fifty questions. Never did I hear so many or so persistent. I have nothing to hide so I tell her everything. I think it must be that she never had a chance to meet very poor people and perhaps didn't even know they existed. I suppose she is just as curious about the poor as I am about the rich—and how many questions I would ask her if only I dared! Of course it is not the same, for she is the mistress and I am the servant, and you told me to study Ephesians 6 and I have done so. "Servants, obey them that are your masters according to the flesh, with fear and trembling, in singleness of heart, as unto Christ." I don't have any trouble about having the fear and trembling, and am only in danger that I may have too much and lose my wits entirely in the presence of master and mistress and their elegant guests.

But this lady has a most kind heart, and when she is through hearing the story of a poor ranch girl she says, "Since you assure me that your sister is a good girl I am glad to be the means of helping both of you. I will tell Miss Bascom that your salary is to be fifty a month, and that will leave you ten dollars to buy yourself pins and needles and whatever you please." I say, "Oh, Mrs. Harries, that is too much!" I cannot keep the tears from gushing into my eyes, and she says, "You must not be too emotional, Pamela; that is a way to prepare unhappiness for yourself. It is a sad lesson that I learned long ago." I said, "I thank you, ma'am—that is, Mrs. Harries," but I could not stop the tears and I was in great confusion. "You are too good," I say.

She goes on, "You are to have half a day off in the middle of the week, and if anybody is going to town you may ride with them, and you will have money to go to a show." "Oh, thank you again," I say, "and I will buy pins and needles and paper and stamps, but as for the show, that our faith does not permit."—"You mean," she says, "you have never seen a movie?" I say, "In our church we have them often on Saturday evening. I have seen educational pictures and travel scenes from all over the world. But we are not permitted to see the theater shows which I am told are full of sin and wordliness." "Well," she says, "perhaps it is just as well, for they do show a lot of trash. But now and then I go when I am in town, and I take whoever is with me. Someday it might be you." "Oh, Mrs. Harries," I say, "you honor me and I beg you to forgive me. I would love to ride with you and wait upon you, and while you see the show I would wait in the car and be perfectly happy to read my Testament. It is what I promised Mother." Says she, "It has the advantage that it is cheaper." I dare to reply, "Yes, the Gospel is free, Mrs. Harries, and has been all through the ages. So also is Salvation." I say no more, because I realize that if I talk religion to her I am inviting her to tell her ideas to me, which she has promised not to do. But I think that possibly I have planted a seed. She tells me to take the tray—she has finished sipping and nibbling her breakfast, and I say "Thank you" once more and go out. Your loving Daughter

Pamela

LETTER III

My dear Sister:

You will see the letter that I wrote Mother and learn about this place where I am living and the good news that I have received a raise in pay in the first week, which almost took my breath away. So you do not have to worry about leaving me with nothing. I know that every dollar will mean two more hours of study for you and I am happy every time I think of it. How good to us Providence has been! Truly, "the words of God shall be fulfilled!"

You ask me to tell you about the people here, and this I can do now, because I have become friends with the old lady who is called Miss Lucy and has been the sewing woman in this family since it began. She is lonely and loves to talk, and I spent some time helping her to cut some cloth, I holding it straight while she cut, and that earned her friendship and she tells me all she knows. She tells me that nobody in this household is ever turned off; they are given light duties and there is a row of rooms with baths under one roof on the edge of the walnut grove where they live and take care of each other, and Miss Lucy said, "Maybe fifty years from now you will be living in one of them." This is more of the kindness of our mistress; but I am sad to learn that she never goes to church and seems to have no faith at all, and of course I know that goodness without faith is barren. "Not according to our works, but according to His own purpose and grace."

I will tell you about the master. He owns oil wells in Texas and has retired and has nothing to do but amuse himself. Most mornings he goes to a board room, as it is called, that is a place where the prices of stocks are put up on a board and he buys or sells them; some people call it gambling, and perhaps I would if I understood anything about it. In the afternoon he plays golf, which is knocking a little ball around a field, and it seems that men spend a lot of time learning to do that exactly right, and they bet money on who can do it best. They put on special pants that are short and baggy and are called plus fours; they look very funny. Between times he is at his club, so he is not often at home. I have seen him pass through the room, but he has never spoken to me, and I have dared only a tiny glimpse of him out of the corner of one eye. He is a big man with a red face and he has a loud voice when he is angry, so I am told by Miss Lucy, but I have not heard it and hope I may never. He manages the help, but gives his orders only to the top ones. Mr. Carmichael the butler has gray hair and a very mild voice, and he bows and says, "Yes, sir, yes, sir," and I think that he is obeying the advice to obey them that are his masters according to the flesh with

fear and trembling. Everybody in this place is afraid of Mr.
Harries and yet he has never done any harm that I can hear
of or even threatened it.

The sad thing is that he and his wife are always in a quarrel. Miss Lucy says that she never raises her voice but is
quietly stubborn; she can have her way, because she is much
richer than he is—her family owns great shipbuilding plants
near Philadelphia and in the war they paid fortunes. The
husband and wife differ about politics and all their ideas
and the people they like and everything; they have no children of their own, but have an adopted nephew, and she
has a much younger sister, and the too kind lady gives them
everything in the world they ask for. The man insists that
she ruins them; years ago he would fly into a rage about it
and beat the boy, and for that she has never forgiven him.
He still loves her but she forbids him her room, and that
unhappiness has been going on for ten years or more and
getting worse.

"What a dreadful sad story!" I cried when I heard it,
and could not keep back my tears, try as I would. What a
difference it makes in the way you look at a palace and the
wonderful things in it and about it, knowing that those
who own it have nothing but torment in their hearts! I tell
you, Sister dear, when I heard that I went to my room and
fell down on my knees and thanked God for the revelation
He has given me of His Holy Word. More than ever I cherish my Testament and my faith. Never, never will Satan or
any of his emissaries be able to take these treasures from me!

To go on with the story, the two younger people are
grown up and both are away, so it may be some time before
I see them. She is a grand young lady and is with friends in
the Canadian Rockies, of which I never heard before, and
he is in Paris. At the table where we of the help eat our
meals they talk all the time about the family; they pick up

bits of conversation and put this and that together. I keep
still because I am so young and so new and curiosity would
not become me; but oh, you may be sure that both my ears
are busy, and I miss nothing of the stories and comments.
The young lady, Miss Yvette, is rather cold and self-centered,
I gather. Master Charles is hot-tempered and reckless, also
divinely handsome with wavy golden hair. It is the kitchen
maid, Mary, who tells me about him, and she says he has
most elegant manners, and that he is kind when he is sober,
but, alas, he is melancholy and he drinks, and Mary, who is
an Irish girl and a Papist, says, "You watch out for him!" I
ask, "What will he do to me?" and she says, "Plenty, if you
let him."

This makes me hope that he may get the position in
Paris for which he is hoping. The people here are all full of
gossip about it. He wants to be in the Embassy there. His
grandfather is a man supposed to have great influence; but
Mr. Harries refused any help. He has been heard to say that
he wouldn't recommend the boy to be a dogcatcher. Mr.
Harries favors his sister-in-law, while his wife adores the
very ground that her nephew walks on; so they are always
pulling and hauling against each other. The mother of
Charles was her sister; both the parents were killed by an
avalanche in Switzerland, and he was adopted when he was
very young. A sad, sad tale; I never knew there was so much
sorrow in the world. If people only knew how little joy
great wealth would bring them, they might pay more heed
to the blessed Gospel. I have pity for this proud family, and
more so when I think of the fate they will meet at the
Judgment Day. It is dreadful to have to think this about
people you know, but it is God's will.

I have told you about the family, and I could tell you
more about the help. They are all kind to me, I suppose
because I am young and so strange to this great world, and

I show that I am trying to be obliging. Mrs. Bodger, the cook, is a devout Methodist, and her assistant, called Anna, is a German Lutheran, about which I do not know much. Mary, who washes all our dishes and peels all our potatoes, is a Papist, as I told you; she is very humble and good-seeming. Pietro, Mrs. Harries' chauffeur, is also a Papist; he and his family have a cottage, and there are three Portuguese families who have attached cottages and who work the great ranch, mostly with tractors. Mr. Harries was once in business in Portugal, I am told, and he speaks their language and gives them orders. They all drive off to mass very early on Sunday morning, and I suppose they think it does them good. They drink a great deal of wine; the family also has wine on the table, but we help do not, I am glad to say. Mr. Carmichael is very strict about keeping it locked up, and there was a great to-do one time when Master Charles broke into the wine closet, so Miss Lucy tells me.

I am telling you the gossip that I hear. I am learning to keep my thoughts to myself, and I am taking your advice and not letting anyone see the letters I write. I have made myself a little flat bag and I put the letter in it and pin it inside my bodice and so it is safe. When I find myself in town I drop it in the mailbox and no one is the wiser. Poor people, they cannot help believing what they have been taught; I don't think any member of the master's family ever enters a church, and except for the Romanists the help go rarely. I shall not tell this to Mother, for it would worry her to think of me living among heathen and infidels. This is for you only, from your devoted Sister

Pamela

LETTER IV

Dear Mother:

You must not think that I neglect you; but my many duties keep me busy, and sometimes I am tired at night, and I have to choose between my Lord and my Mother. I know which you would rather I put off. Be sure that I am well and happy in my work; that is, I am as happy as I let myself be. It is hard to decide how to feel in a world which as you say belongs to Satan. I forget myself in friendship for the people around me, and then suddenly I think, but these are lost souls! and then I am sad. I must not be self-satisfied in that I am more fortunate than they; that is the way of the Pharisees. All I can do is to pray God keep me humble of heart.

I prayed, and I believe the answer is coming. Dear kind Miss Lucy, the sewing lady, is asking me questions about our faith. She has been with the Harries family since before my lady was born and is a very good soul. She was brought up an Episcopalian, which she says is a somewhat worldly sort of church and she has let her interest lapse. But she was curious about our Sabbath and asked me about it, and of course I explained and showed her the words of Jesus and what they mean. I gave her "The Great Controversy" to read and she talks about it when we work together, which sometimes happens. She would be a brand plucked out of the fire, and how happy I should be if I should be able to think that I had done it, of course with God's help.

You surely need not worry about the Papists; they do not bother me. They seem to be perfectly satisfied with their

own ways and do not even think about mine. All they have
to do is to go through their ceremonies, cross themselves
and bow and mumble, and they are sure they are all right.
They do not read Scripture, and I do not think they even
have it in their homes. They are not taught to make converts, they leave that to the priests, and I am surely in no
danger of meeting any priest. If Satan has set such traps for
my feet it will be in vain.

Thursday is my lady's luncheon day, when her friends
are invited to Casa Grande, as this place is called. That is
a very busy day, and I asked Mrs. Jessup if I might watch
and learn how the table is set so that if anybody is sick or
anything I could do it; that pleased her greatly and she
said, "I see you really have your mind on your work." Indeed I have, and I said, "I don't want you should ever tell
me anything twice." I learned how to place the different
knives and forks and spoons, for it seems they have to be
just so and the one farthest to the outside is the one you
take first, and if you do not know about anything you watch
and see what your hostess does and that will be the thing
for you to do.

Mrs. Jessup says people will judge you by such things,
and if you are wrong you are an outsider for always. She
says that the way I hold my knife and fork is bad and she
showed me, and I have learned, but it seems very queer at
first; when I see Sister again I will tell her, because if she
should ever come to be a doctor she will meet important
people and they must not think she was brought up in a
shack, even if she was. Mrs. Jessup herself it seems was a
rich lady and was in boarding school with Mrs. Harries, but
now she is "in reduced circumstances," that is her words,
and I wonder what she would say if she could see the circumstances of my dear Mother. But don't you worry, because we have heard some words that tell us we shall take

no heed, saying what shall we eat and what shall we drink
and wherewithal shall we be clothed.

I try to obey this command literally, but it is not easy for
the reason that I have to give so much heed to what other
people are eating and drinking and wearing; I have to learn
the names of many kinds of foods that I never heard of before, because someday I may have to wait table, and what
a mess it would be if I did not know the names of what I
had to serve. When my lady says, "Go and get a bottle of
seltzer," I am not to stand like a dummy, but to know that
it is in the icebox which is called the refrigerator and that
when you press the handle the seltzer shoots with a noise,
as if there is steam in it even when it is cold. I have to learn
that cashew nuts are little things that are curved like the
joint of your finger, and they are salted; I ask Mrs. Jessup,
"May I taste just one?" and she says, "That is very bad
form—but just one." I learn that artichokes are like big
green rosebuds, and you peel off one leaf and dip it in a
sauce and then sort of scrape it off with your teeth. It takes
a long time to eat things like that, but the ladies all have
the time; they came, a dozen of them—they call themselves
the Thirteen Club, because it is supposed to be bad luck
and they make fun of it. They are very elegant ladies, and I
look out the kitchen window and see that they have fine
cars waiting and some of them have chauffeurs. Afterwards
the ladies play a game of cards which is called auction
bridge, and that I know is very wrong, but do not worry because I shall never let myself be tempted.

We help do not have the expensive foods like the ladies,
but we have a plenty such as I never dreamed of in my life.
There is meat three times a day, and people cannot get
used to the idea that I do not want it; they pity me when
there is no call to. I assure them that when I have milk I
have no chance of starving. Indeed I fear that I eat too

much and am gaining weight. Old Mr. Carmichael looks at me in his kind way and says, "You are getting to be very pretty, child." That makes me blush, and I say, "You know, sir, handsome is as handsome does." He says, "I do not see that you do so very bad, my dear. And you should look in the mirror and see what is there." I do not want to become vain, but of course I cannot help looking in the mirror which is over my dresser, for it is my duty to keep myself neat, and Mrs. Jessup is very fussy that I should have no strand of hair hanging loose which she says is disreputable, and collars and cuffs must not have a speck on them. I am not to try to save on laundry, because there is one on the place and everything is taken twice a week and comes back in two days, and expense is no consideration where cleanness is concerned, Mrs. Jessup tells me. I talk with Miss Lucy about it and she says that this great ranch which I thought so wonderful is just small change to these people who have immense incomes from outside, millions and millions that nobody knows about and that they never tell, it is all handled in Texas and the East.

Well, that is enough for tonight, I am living in a world that is a strange mixture of good and evil, but you are not to worry, because I have the key that unlocks the secrets and tells me all I need, and I will cleave to that which is good and spew the evil out of my mouth. It is you who have given this key to your beloved Daughter

Pamela

LETTER V

Dear Sister:

You ask for a report on my observance, and here it is. I realize that I am living in a world very far from the Lord's grace and so I must not neglect to fortify my soul. I inquired and learned that we have an Advent church in the town of Junipero, which is not too far away; so I got up early on Sabbath morning, and as I did not want to ask any favors I walked four miles to where the highway passes the mouth of this wide canyon and there I waited for the bus. It was full with a holiday crowd, but I did not mind standing up. So I attended service and heard a refreshing sermon; afterwards I introduced myself to the pastor, Rev. Tucker, and he was very kind, and I promised to attend when the weather permitted. I had bread and milk and a salad in a little cafe, and rode back and it was hot by then, and I did not enjoy the walk to Casa Grande, but my heart was light because I had done my duty.

I see all the work of Satan about me, but it does not trouble me. We have learned from a great example that temptation does not matter if one has power to resist it, and this by the grace of God I have. I assure you that I could be perfectly happy to come back and milk the goats and help to prepare the onions for market; I stay in this place of worldly glory because I am able to help Mother and you. I wish you both to be at peace about me and sure that I am not letting myself be in any way changed. Your devoted Sister

Pamela

LETTER VI

Dear Sister:

The short letter enclosed is the one that you are to send to Mother, who will be expecting this of you. What I am writing now is only for you. I would not tell Mother a falsehood for anything in the world, but there is no need to tell her all the details of the life here, which would alarm her and perhaps cause her to order me home. I am sure that you, living in a college and reading many books, will not be surprised to hear about the wickedness of what is called the smart world. Young people understand each other better, I think, and I trust you to keep my secrets and give me your advice. Mother would have no peace in her mind if I told her that after the luncheon the rich ladies most of them lighted up cigarettes, and that some of them smoked while playing cards. I can testify, because it was my duty to empty the ash trays and wipe the tables clean and fold them up and put them away in the big telephone closet.

What I have to tell you is what happened on Sunday, which I think was the most amazing thing I ever have seen. My mistress never goes to church, alas, but often on Sundays she will invite a lecturer and pay him; she will send out cards to everybody she knows, and that is a great many. The sending out of the cards was early in the week and that was the job of Miss Bascom; but Sunday is my sure-enough workday, and believe me, I was a tired girl that night. There was dinner at one o'clock and there was company and a big turkey and no end of fixings such as I never saw. I worked all morning getting the rooms in order; all the time the master was in the smoking room, and he left the door open, and there were men discussing politics, which I do not understand, but I suppose we are Republicans because Mother is and Daddy was.

We help had our dinner at noon and then most of them went away, but I didn't, you can be sure. I helped the cook and I helped Mary dry the dishes, and I waited on Mrs. Jessup and Miss Bascom and Miss Lucy, because when there is important company they have their dinner separate from the family. The big dinner was served by Mr. Carmichael, dressed in his black suit with tails, very hot I guess; he carried in the turkey on a big silver platter—he had carved it all up into slices. The dining-room girl helped him serve and I helped cook get things ready. I was told that the lecturer was at the table and that he had just come back from Russia, which is now called the Soviet Union, and he is going to tell about what is called the revolution. He is a Jew and his name is Goldman, and he has written an article in a magazine, which is how Mrs. Harries came to invite him. Mr. Harries is not here—when things like this are going on he gets into his big fancy car and drives far away. This is what Miss Lucy tells me, and you must keep these letters locked up and let nobody ever see them.

Well, then my real work begins, for I have to clear the table and get it ready for the afternoon guests; it will be loaded with food, and after the lecture they will come in and help themselves. There will be coffee and Miss Bascom will serve it, dressed very elegant. There will be a big bowl of fruit punch that is waiting in the refrigerator, and I am happy to hear it will not be liquor. There will be piles of plates and paper napkins, and every kind of food that you can pick up and eat, little sandwiches, crackers, slices of cheese, olives, celery, little onions, several kinds of nuts including those funny cashews, and chocolates and other kinds

of candy. All that has to be placed just right, and Mrs.
Jessup guides me and helps, and I listen and learn.

Pietro and one of the Portuguese men are bringing folding chairs and placing them in the big room, and the people begin to come; all sorts of people, many of them rich,
and some of them working people, I am told, but all of
them neat and proper. They have come from long distances,
but I suppose they don't mind driving on a Sunday afternoon. There is close to a hundred, enough to fill all the
chairs in the big room; and when the table is set and everything ready, it is proper for me to stand behind the door
and listen, for it is educational for all. This Mr. Goldman
is a stoutish round-faced man with dark hair and glasses; he
is a businessman and has been to the Soviet Union on business, and Mrs. Harries introduces him very proper. She
says it is important that we should learn the truth about
the Soviet Union and not believe all the terrible things we
are reading in the newspapers. The Russian people have
made a revolution, and it is a very good thing because their
old government was wicked and cruel, and we sent our
soldiers to Russia, fighting them and trying to put the revolution down, and what business was it of ours? We said we
went into the war to put the Kaiser out, but now apparently we are trying to bring back the Czar.

So then Mr. Goldman talks, and I am curious about him,
because I don't think I have ever heard a Jew before, and
of course they were the people in the Bible, and I wonder
what they are like now. He talks very quiet and says he will
just tell what he saw with his own eyes. He tells that the
people are having a hard time, because the country has been
ruined by the long war; but the workers and peasants now
feel that they are free and that their country belongs to
them. They expected help and understanding from the
American people and could not understand why American

soldiers invaded their country and fought them. He says it is not true that the people are treated cruel, but only those are arrested that are fighting the new government and trying to sell it out to the foreign enemies. He tells how the people live and what they told him—he can speak Russian, and he makes you feel that President Wilson was deceived and made a great mistake.

Well, when he finishes Mrs. Harries asks for comments, for that is her custom always. And up there pops a little man, another Jew, it seems; his name is Mr. Isaacs, and he is a journalist, and very excitable, and it seems he hates the Bolsheviki, he says they are terrible men, and murderers, and he tells the most awful things that they have done. He pours it out without stopping, until when he is getting his breath my lady asks Mr. Goldman what he has to answer. And so they go at it, hammer and tongs, back and forth, and nobody else has a chance to be heard. Mr. Isaacs has been to Russia too, and had a hard time getting out with his life. They work themselves into a passion and shout at each other, and I wonder if they are going to have a fight; but Mrs. Harries doesn't seem to mind it a bit; she sits there large and calm and comfortable and lets them go to it. Even when Mr. Isaacs calls Mr. Goldman a bootlegger she doesn't interfere and doesn't seem to be shocked. I ask Mrs. Jessup about it later and she says that Mrs. Harries has the idea that everybody should have a chance to say what he pleases and that way the truth will come out and maybe they will agree. But I am sure those two Jews are never going to agree about the Bolsheviki.

As to the bootlegger business, which sounds so awful, Mr. Goldman says that he bought a lot of sugar in Cuba and sold it in this country, and maybe it was used to make rum but that is none of his business, he was dealing in sugar. And that has nothing to do with the question whether

the Russian people are to be free to choose their own kind
of government and whether American boys should have
had to pour out their blood in the snows of Archangel. So
they go at it some more, and then I don't hear them because Mrs. Jessup whispers that it is time for me to plug in
the coffee urn to start it working and to bring in the punch
and put a chunk of ice in it and other duties. When I come
back Mrs. Harries is telling the company that this has been
most enlightening and that now that they have heard both
sides they can make up their minds. As for her, she has long
ago decided that all war is wicked and that no excuse for
it can be found; also that poverty is wrong and is the cause
of wars and of revolutions too—if people would do simple
justice there would be no need of killing anybody or over-
throwing any governments. All that the governments should
do is to print plenty of paper money and give it to the poor
who need it; that would start up purchasing right away and
the making of more goods and there would be plenty for
all. She said, "You know what I always say, bread and
butter first."

I am so glad I heard that, because it seems to me such a
wonderful idea. I had never thought of it and I wonder if
you have. You know the Year of Jubilee that you read
about in Scripture, and how the land and goods were dis-
tributed every fifty years. I am wondering if that is the way
the ancient Jews did it—for it seems to me that would be
an easy and convenient way. I wish you would look up the
words "paper money" in your Concordance and see what
you find about it. I am saving up my money to buy a Concordance of my own, for I am going to need it since I am
living among unbelievers and will have to be prepared to
answer their arguments. Don't let this story worry you too
much. Your devoted Sister

                                        Pamela

LETTER VII

Dear Mother:

This is first to tell you that I am well, and very busy, but not so that I have neglected my religious duties. I am sad indeed to hear that Grampa is not well; this must make things harder for you. Be sure that I will so perform my work so as to keep this position and you will have the money every month. Miss Bascom kindly offered to make out separate checks for you and Sister and mail them to you; in that way I do not have to make a trip to the post office to get money orders. In this place everything is done regular. I think it is because we are all scared of Mr. Harries; even if he does not find fault with us we are scared that he will. I think he is a kind man, but he likes to have everything just so and is irritable. He has never yet had to rebuke me, and I hope he will not.

Everybody here is talking about Master Charles, because he has sent his aunt a cablegram that he is coming. He did not get the appointment to the Paris Embassy that he wanted and he must be vexed about it. He is on a steamer, and when he gets to New York he will drive here; he has his car in the steamer, Miss Lucy says; he took it to Europe—can you imagine such a thing? I suppose if you have so much money you have to find ways to spend it. He will be here soon because he drives fast.

Everybody here talks about him a lot. They agree that he is naughty, and why that should make him interesting I do not know; it certainly does not make him so to me. Some of the help smile when they speak of him to me, and they look knowing; it seems they have the idea that I might fall in love with him, but little do they know me. Tell Grampa that I have not forgotten the poem he taught me, "The lips that touch liquor shall never touch mine." Of course it might be that I could speak some word of admonition to him and do him good. Rev. Tucker preached on the subject of the duty to admonish; he says that we should never give up the worst sinner as hopeless, but should give him the chance to hear the word, and not to be shy or apologetic. I asked him if that applied to servants, and he said it did, but of course with due regard to propriety. The command to servants to obey masters does not hold where moral questions are involved, because the laws of God are everywhere superior to those of man.

There is a photograph of Master Charles standing on the big piano in the drawing room, and as I work there a lot I have many chances to study it. He is tall and very handsome in a cadet uniform, and it is easy to see how a girl being untaught and unwarned might fall in love with him; but I am neither of these things. I study his rather sad face, and I know that he is a victim of the struggle between a too indulgent aunt and a too severe uncle. I try to imagine some way it might happen that I would have a chance to point out to him the error of his ways. Be sure that if the chance comes I will not shrink from my duty, and also that you will hear about it from your devoted

Pamela

LETTER VIII

Dear Sister:

Well, the great event has happened, the young master has returned. It is touching to see how my lady adores him, and how the whole place takes on new life because of his coming. I was dusting in the big room when he came in and ran upstairs to see Mrs. Harries; he went two at a time, not stopping for the elevator. I saw that he was wearing a white shirt that they call a polo shirt, and linen shorts which are too short but I suppose are all right when you get used to seeing men's legs. He was upstairs a long time and no doubt was telling her his adventures, at least such as are fit for an aunt to hear.

I had supposed that he would treat me as the master has done, to be unaware of my existence unless there is an errand he wants; but no indeed! He comes downstairs and I am dusting for dear life but shaky a little inside. He sees me and stops and says, "Why, what's this! A new girl?" He makes some exclamation which I take to be French, but of course I can't spell it. He says, "Turn around," and I suppose that is a proper command since it would be very rude to keep my back turned to him. He exclaims, "A pretty one!" and asks, "You weren't here when I left, were you?" I say, "No, sir" and I am trembling now in my knees. He says, "Where did you come from?" and I tell him, "From Mesa Seco," and he says, "Where the devil is that?" I would like to say, "Oh, sir, you must not use such language to me," but I am not sure it is bad enough to deserve an admonition.

He stands there and looks me over as if he were about to buy a filly or a heifer. "Why, you are a sweet thing!" says he. "How old are you?" And I tell him, "I was seventeen last week, sir." He asks, "And did Aunt Maggie give you a birthday party?" I say, "No, sir I did not tell her." Says he, "What a shame!" and then, "You shall have a party, this very day. Come and take a drive with me and we will have a lovely party!" I say, "Oh, sir, I could not do that! I have my duties." So he says, "All right then, this evening. Say nothing to anybody, but come away and we will have a party to end all parties!"

I had not supposed it would be anything like that, so very sudden, and I am at a loss what to say next. I think fast and say, "But I have duties in the evening also, sir." "What?" he says. "They work you at night, too? But this is wage slavery! It shall not be permitted in my home! I will speak to Aunt Maggie about it and have it stopped!" But I say, "Oh, sir, it is not her duties that I have in the evening. It is my duties to God." "What?" he cries again; and then, "Oh, my God!" I say, "Yes, sir, your God and mine too." Says he, "Tell me what is it you do in the evening?" and I say, "I read a chapter in my Testament, and then I read a chapter in one of our books of interpretation." At this he exclaims, "Well, I'll be God-damned!" and I know that that is the time for real admonishment. I say, "You may be indeed, sir, if you persist in using language like that."

I am in fear that this will anger him, but no, it is quite different, he seems to be overcome by surprise. It may be that nobody has ever spoken to him like that before—and surely never a servant. He is staring at me and says, "What is your name?" I tell him, and he says, "Here, Pam, sit down," and signs me to a chair. I would not sit in his presence, but he bids me to, and I suppose there is no law against it, so I obey. He takes the next chair, and there he sits, resting his hands on his bare knees and leaning forward, staring. "Now," he says, "tell me about it." I am so confused, I ask, "About what, sir?" "I mean about your religion, and why you have to work at it so hard that you never have any time for fun."

So there is the chance that I have been dreaming about—but truly I never dreamed it might come so quick. I tell him our faith, and he listens close, and he says, "Then you believe that Jesus is coming back to earth again?" I say, "He has told us so and therefore I know that it is true." "And when is this to be, kid?" he says, and I tell him, "That has not been vouchsafed us to know, but we are told to be instant in prayer, and to watch and wait, for we know not in what hour the Son of Man cometh." "And where do you think He will come from?" "He will come from Heaven, where He reigns with the Father." "And that is somewhere up in the sky?" "So we are told." "But up in the sky there are billions and trillions and quadrillions of miles of empty space that is cold beyond imagining, and suns millions of times as big as ours, and they are hot beyond measuring; how can there be a heaven there?" I say, "That I do not know, sir, but we are told in Scripture that it is there, and so we are bound to believe it."

I am neglecting my dusting, but I suppose the housekeeper cannot blame me for obeying the orders of the young master, especially since he has just come home. He is willing to listen, and we are enjoined to be ardent in our cause, so I talk fast and tell him all I can, what a wonderful man William Miller was. He says, "Oh, you are a Millerite! I have heard the word. People used to sell all their belongings and put on white robes and go out and stand in the fields waiting for the Judgment Day!" I say, "Some did that, but somebody had misinterpreted Holy Writ. There are many who presume to interpret for themselves."

All this time he is listening, but I see that also he is look- ing me over, and it makes me embarrassed. I have looked in the mirror enough to know that my cheeks have filled out and have good color in them, and it is different from what Miss Bascom has in a jar on her dressing table. The people here have told me that I have a nice figure, but I am not pleased to have it studied by a young gentleman so very close. His kind of shirt has a wide collar and is open at the throat and I see that his neck is brown; I know that he plays golf, and maybe he did even in Paris, I don't know. He has lovely blue eyes, and his golden hair has a nice wave. I think that I have never seen anybody so handsome, cer- tainly not that I have spoken to. He is quick and eager in his manner, and seems interested in what I am saying, or maybe it is in me, I cannot be sure.

"Listen, Pam," he says, "all this is new and strange to me, but I want to know more about it. Won't you come for a ride after dinner and tell me about it?" So there is a problem for me. I say, "Oh, sir, if I thought you really wanted to know about my faith—" and he breaks in, "Of course I want to know. Nobody has ever talked to me about religion in my life, and this may be my great opportunity." At that my heart gives a bound, for I see that another of my prayers is being answered. But I cannot be sure what to make of him, and I say, "Oh, Master Charles, I am a poor country girl, and I have never talked with a gentleman like yourself. I am trying so hard to do what is right in your aunt's home." Says he, "What harm can it do to take a drive with me?" I manage to say, "I think I should ask her permission—" but again he breaks in, "Nonsense, when your work is done you are free and have a right to go for a walk in the evening and no one will question you. Meet me by the big live oak tree at eight o'clock." And since it is God's work, now I decide that I dare not say No.

From that time on I am in a state of excitement over the wonderful thing that has happened to me. I pray for guidance and try to think of all the things that are likely to impress such an elegant young gentleman. I have talked to his aunt and have an idea of what impressed her, the great college and the hospital which we have built, and which she did not think that poor and plain people like us would have the sense to manage; so I will tell him first about these, and I will not speak about his sinful ways until we have become better acquainted, and perhaps he will bring up the subject.

The family has dinner in the evening, you understand, and I do not eat much; when the others ask about it I tell them that my lady gave me some candy, and that is true, for when I took her the mail she had a box of chocolates by the bed where she lies and reads, and she offered me a piece and I took one. I do not want to criticize her, but I cannot help noticing the many kinds of candies and fruits that she has in her room, and she says that she cannot understand why she grows stout, because she eats so lightly. So she does at the table, but nibbles all the time between meals, and if I dared I would tell her that that is the reason. She has taken me to town with her, and I have done the shopping, so I have had to learn the fancy names of all the different sweets and perfumes that she buys; she is very particular about getting exactly the right kind and will drive a long way to find the place where she can get it. She had a friend with her, and of course I was all ears for their fashionable talk; she said that the last time she had traveled she had counted up the number of things she had to collect and take along, and there were fifty-four. When I got home I looked up the place in Isaiah 3 where he rebukes the fashionable ladies of his time, "the chains, and the bracelets, and the mufflers, the bonnets, and the ornaments of the legs, and the head bands," and so on. I counted them up and he names only twenty-two articles; so you see how the world has got more complicated.

Well, I have wandered from the story of me and young master. This is a long letter and I am tired, so I will finish it tomorrow night. This will tell you that I am alive and not harmed, but much hurt in my feelings and flustered. Your anxious Sister

Pamela

◄∙∙∙►

LETTER IX

Dear Sister:

Well, it is another evening, and I am taking it to tell you the things that happened to me. It is awful but it is not as bad as it might have been and as I can guess. "Yea, though I walk in the valley of the shadow of death, I will fear no evil, for Thou art with me."

I go for a walk—it is just getting dark, and parked by the oak tree is young master with the car, which is long and low and has the top down so that we are in the open. It must have tremendous power, for it goes like the fastest wind, and with just a faint little purring sound. It is a foreign car, he tells me, Merseedys or something like that. There is a half moon and an evening star, and it is all so lovely that I am breathless. Once or twice he lays his hand on mine so that I will not be too frightened at the speed. There are hills and the road winds and I see the lights of the car flashing here and there over the trees, and it is so wonderful I can hardly keep from crying out.

Then he comes to where there is a smooth place by the road and there he stops, and turns off the car lights, and says, "Now, then, you will tell me about it." So it is the chance that I have been hoping for; I will tell him first about our college and our hospital, and then I will tell him about our faith and prove it to him by Scripture. I begin, and he sits quite still, and I talk fast, and am so happy because it is going so well I hardly notice that he has laid his hand on mine. I tell him how many students are at the college and that my sister is one of the best; I tell him about the hospital, and how many rooms it has, and about our great sanitarium in Battle Creek that is known all over the country. I am just starting to tell him about William Miller and his discovery of the Bible prophecies, when I realize that he is taking up my hand and holding it in his; I have a warm feeling and realize that my heart is pounding and that I am very much confused so that I hardly know what I am saying. He is such a wonderful person as I have never talked to in my life before. I have heard people say "losing your head," and I think maybe that is what is happening to me, so I stop and say, "Oh, Master Charles, I think you should not do that!" "What is it that I shouldn't do?" asks he, and my common sense should have told me that he knew, but I have lost my common sense. "Hold my hand," I say. "But," says he, "I am already holding it," and holds it tighter. I see that he is teasing stupid me, and I say, "Please don't, Master Charles, you frighten me." "But," says he, "what are you frightened of? I am not doing you any harm." "But it could be harm," I say, "and I fear it is not right." "Don't you trust me, Pam?" he asks. "I assure you I mean you no evil." "Oh, sir," I say, "please spare me. I am a poor country girl and am not used to the ways of rich gentlemen." "But you could soon get used to them," says he, and I know he is laughing again, and I want to laugh too, but also I want to cry and I am all undone. I try to draw my hand away, but he holds it, and I am afraid to jerk hard because that would be rude, and my duty to my master and my duty to myself are all mixed up, and my heart is pounding as if I had been running a long ways uphill.

His hand is bigger than mine and very firm. I am telling you the truth, Sister, that I am shocked to discover: I like for him to hold it; so then I decide that I am a wicked girl, and the tears come into my eyes, and I think it is dark and he cannot see them, but I cannot keep from a little sob. "Pam," he says, "you are being a silly child. Don't you realize that you are falling in love with me?" I say, "Oh, sir, you must not say that! You are so far above me in station that I could never think of such a thing." "But," says he, "station has nothing to do with it. If it happens, you have to face it and so do I. You are a lovely sweet thing, and it would be easy for me to fall in love with you." You can imagine then what a tumult I am in. I am choked for words as I say, "But, sir, it makes no sense to talk of love, for you do not know me at all." "I am coming to know you right now," says he, "and I have made sure that you are a darling and can make me very happy." With that he puts his arm around me; I am horrified, and at the same time I know this awful fact that I like to have him do it. I protest, but when I look back upon it I fear that I did not protest enough, and he takes me in his arms and kisses me; he kisses me again and again, and first I think I am going to faint dead away, which is something I have heard about but surely never did. Then something rises up in me, there is a warning voice as if it were God speaking to my soul, and maybe it was. I cry, "Oh, no, sir, it is not right!" and I push him away, and the moment I do so I lose my self-control and burst into tears. I have never been in such a state; I feel that I have been disgraced and that I am a lost soul, and I cried so that I thought I could never stop and I almost choked myself.

Well, he seemed much surprised and he let me go, and he said, "What is this, what is the matter with you?" He became alarmed and cried, "Stop it! Stop it!" And when it went on he said, "You are being a silly fool. Since when is it a crime to kiss a girl?" He went on, growing angry, so I began to remember my position, that I am servant in his house, and that maybe I have been rude, and that I may have done wrong to come with him to this place and have led him to misunderstand me. "The devil!" he exclaims. So I make an effort and get control of myself, and I say, "Yes, sir, that is it. The devil is working in our hearts, both yours and mine, and is leading us into temptation." He asks me, do I believe that literally, and I say, "Of course I believe it, for it is in Holy Writ. Have you not read how the devil took Jesus up into an exceeding high mountain and showed him all the kingdoms of the world, and the glory of them, and saith unto him, 'All these things will I give thee if thou wilt fall down and worship me.'" "Good Lord, she really believes that!" he cries to the air, and I say, "I know that it is God's Holy Word, and if I do not believe it my soul will be lost in everlasting hell fire." "And you think that mine will be lost also?" "Indeed, yes, Master Charles, that is why I consented to take this ride with you, so I might have a chance to plead with you and do what I can to save you from being among the lost souls when He comes again to judge both the quick and the dead."

So again it is the chance which I have been dreaming of, and I start to explain; but alas, he will not take it as I have hoped, far from it. He resists the Word, and in such a dreadful way that I hesitate to put his speeches on paper. But you and I both have to learn to understand the devil's wiles, and to meet and overcome them, and this I am surely having a chance to learn. Says he, "The story is silly on the face of it, Pam. For if Jesus was God, as you say, how could He be tempted? The devil offered Him the kingdoms of the world, but in the first place they don't belong to the devil, and in the second place, what use would God have for them? If God wanted them, He could take them, couldn't He, and why the devil would He have to go to the devil for them? Can't you see that it's a meaningless story?" "Oh, Master Charles," I tell him, "I cannot listen to such talk! Who am I to probe into the mind of God, or of Jesus either?" To that he says, "But you have a mind and you know what it is like. You know that it is impossible to know something and at the same time not know it. If you are God, and know everything, how can you at the same time be a man and know only a few things? The essence of being tempted is that there is something you want; but if you are omnipotent and can have whatever you want, who can offer you anything or threaten to withhold anything from you?"

I am ashamed to say that I was in confusion, because I had never heard such an argument and I could not answer it. "I am only an ignorant girl, sir," I said, "and I cannot dispute with an educated gentleman like yourself. But I know that Jesus came to earth to wash away our sins with His blood, and that if you believe in Him you will be delivered from the power of Satan." "But who is this Satan," he asks, "and how does he get all this power? Did God make Satan, and if He did, why didn't He know what an evil cuss he was going to be? If He did know, why make him and give him power to torment mankind? If God doesn't want young girls to be kissed by lovers, why does he turn Satan loose to tempt the lovers to kiss and the girls to want to be kissed?" "Oh, sir," I cry, "you are talking blasphemous!" But he says, "I am not doing anything of the sort. I am trying to use my mind, and if God doesn't mean me to use it, why does He give it to me? If He wants me to believe something, why does He make it look like nonsense?"

By then I am ready to cry again, and I say, "Oh, sir, I have never heard such talk in all my life!" To that he says, "That is because you are an ignorant person, just as you say; but you don't have to stay that way. If you would read the history of religions, you would know that every race and tribe of humans has had stories about their gods coming down to earth and fathering demigods. If you were a born Hindu you would believe one set of legends, and if you had been an ancient Greek you would have believed a different set. What I can't make out is why an American girl should pick out the legends of ancient Hebrews and decide that they are what she has to accept." "Oh, sir," I cry, "it is the word of God, and I have had the hope that I might convince you of it and so help you to lead a happier and better life!" "Well," he says, "I have not had a very happy life, it is true, but who can have it in a world like this, where men torment one another, and lie and steal and kill as I have seen them doing in many parts of the earth? It needs something more than old holy books to help them."

There is such sadness in his voice that I am beginning to tremble again and can hardly keep from sobbing. I say, "Oh, Master Charles, I honestly thought that I was going to make you happy!" At which he replies, "You still might, if you did not have so many foolish notions in your pretty head." Whereupon he catches my hand again; but I am warned now, and I know what Satan is doing, even if I do not know why God allows him to do it. I draw my hand away and say, "No, sir, you must not do that!" "You are determined against me?" he asks, and when I delay to answer for fear of being rude, he asks, "If I kiss you again will you start crying like a crazy creature?" "What I will do," I

say, "is to get out and walk home." "Silly child!" he says.
"Don't you know that you are fifty miles from home?" "I
will walk fifty miles if I have to, Master Charles, in order
to keep myself from evil-doing." To that he answers, "I am
not a heel, and I have never yet made a girl walk home."
He meant those words to be reassuring, and I think he had
no idea how he shocked me, for it was telling me that I was
one of many, and how near I had come to falling into the
nets of the tempter. "It is getting late, sir," I said, "and you
had best take me home."

So he turned on the lights, started the car, and we drove.
Now it was no longer beautiful and I was no longer happy,
for I saw that I had failed entirely. Tears ran down my
cheeks and I tried to wipe them away without his knowing
it, but somehow he knew. He asked, "Have I hurt your feelings that badly, Pam? I assure you, it is not such a wicked
thing to try to make love to a girl. It is a compliment, if
only you would take it so." "Oh, sir," I answered, "it is not
that. It is that I had hoped to bring the peace of God to
your heart, but I am too ignorant and cannot answer your
questions." "For that you need not be ashamed," says he,
"for the wisest men that have ever lived have not been able
to answer the questions I have asked you. How can God be
both all-powerful and all-good? For if He is able to prevent
evil, why does He not so do? If He allows it to happen, it
must be that He does not care, and if so He is not good.
Millions of men are good enough to try to stop evil—why
not the omnipotent God?" "To that I know the answer,"
I say. "God is leaving men free to accept or to reject his
Holy Writ." "Yes, my dear," he says, "but billions of men
have lived on the earth and never heard this Hebrew Writ,
and they have suffered all kinds of torments which they
have not deserved. A devil might have contrived their fates,
but surely not any good God." At that I am terrified and

tell him, "Have you never thought that God might send down a thunderbolt to punish you when you speak such words?" He says with a laugh, "I hope He will contrive it that the bolt may miss you, who are surely not to blame for any of the words I am speaking. You have done your godly duty, as I will testify before the Judgment Throne."

Nothing happens, and he drives me home. He says, "Let's not make a quarrel of this, Pam. Let us be friends." I say, "Indeed, I do not wish you any harm, sir," and I add, "I will not tell your aunt." He says that I am a dear. He lets me in and I steal up by the back stairs and feel that I have been doing something very wicked, and wonder if I have been missed in the house and what the people will be thinking about me. But God knows that I meant right, and you, dear Sister, will think no evil of your devoted

Pamela

LETTER X

Dear Mother:

I am glad to hear that Grampa is getting better. I am well and haven't much news except that I work hard and try to please my mistress, and now the young master has come and is very polite to me. I am meeting a great many people here. At home we had a lonely life, but I did not know it because it was all I had. Now I am in a busy little world and watch the people and listen to them talk and it is a new sort of education. All the life centers about the family, the rich people; they are supposed to have everything, and yet I have decided that they are the least happy

of all; they all want things they cannot get, and I sometimes think they do not know what they want. It is too
much to write about but someday I will tell you. Everybody here goes out and talks about the family to the people
they know, so there is a whole world watching them and
thinking about them. It is just as if it was a king and queen,
a prince and princess, such as I read about in the history
book.

My lady is a kind and generous person, but she is sad, because she has discovered that so many other people are unworthy. She gives away great sums of money to people, with
the only result that they all want more. Her mail is full of
begging letters, and people come to ask her for money for
all sorts of causes. Miss Lucy tells me how it has been all
her life—for Mrs. Harries has had these great sums of money
since she was a girl. On the wall in the pingpong room—
that is a game—there hangs a big photograph of the Pennship
plant, that is the shipbuilding company; it is made of a
dozen photographs pasted side by side and the place must
be a mile long. So everybody knows about the money, and
they go off and think up schemes to get it. They pay her
compliments, and how can she know what to believe?

Miss Lucy says that she has two kinds of friends: the
rich ladies who were her friends before she got interested in
what is called social reform, and those she has met in the
different kinds of "movements" she now helps to support.
She keeps the two kinds separate for the most part. The
ladies come to lunch every Thursday, and she gives them a
fine lunch and then quarrels with them because they do not
agree with her ideas but are satisfied just to have their
money and spend it on themselves. On Sunday afternoons
comes the crowd that is interested in her ideas, and they
get only the pickup food, and they quarrel among themselves over whatever ideas are brought up by the speaker.

The master likes the rich ladies and sometimes comes and greets them, but he has agreed to stay away from home on Sundays; several times he has got wild about the people she invites and has ordered them out of the house. Being that it is her house, she has never forgiven him for it.

I saw a funny scene the other day; at least it was funny after it was explained to me, but at the time it scared me. Mrs. Harries was sitting out on what is called the loggia, a big paved place that is in front of the mansion and has a wonderful view. (That is the way they spell it, but they call it lojja.) It was late afternoon and the sun was low and she was playing a game of cards that you play by yourself, and maybe cheat yourself, so Miss Lucy says. I brought her the afternoon paper and the mail, which they send a man into town to get. She took it from my hands, and at that moment Miss Bascom came running out and whispered to my lady, and up she jumps, which is very unusual for her, for usually she rises slowly and moves with dignity. But this time she knocks the chair over backwards and fairly runs into the house. Of course it is not for me to look surprised or to ask questions; I am supposed to go on with my assigned work and I do, but out of the corner of my eye I see coming around the corner of the house a tall gentleman in a black suit, and I have seen him before and know that he is some kind of reformer, and I can guess that he has come to ask for money. Later Miss Lucy tells me how she heard our lady say, "He has had enough." But why did she not write him and tell him that, instead of letting him take the long trip from Los Angeles, perhaps a hundred miles each way?

It is a strange world, and I am watching it and learning things that may be useful. I keep quiet, trying to make no enemies, for I have made sure that all is not the love and peace that I imagined when I first came here. I am sure that

if I told Mrs. Harries that Grampa was sick, she might offer
me some money to send to you; but I think it wiser not to,
because the others would be sure to hear about it and then
they might be jealous, they would be sure that I was one of
the designing ones and had been paying her compliments. I
think it better to do my work and make sure of the regular
money. I note what you tell me, that your share means ten
or a dozen washes that you do not have to do out every
month, and it is better to be sure of that and give thanks to
a kind Providence, which is done every night by your loving
Daughter

Pamela

LETTER XI

Dear Sister:

I have read your long letter twice, and be sure that I shall
study it until every word is engraved upon my soul. (So
Rev. Tucker says we should do with the words of Our
Lord—not that you would wish me to compare them.) I
note Rev. Strayker's answers to the young master's questions about the struggle between God and Satan; they satisfy me, but of course I do not know that they will satisfy
him. I do not even know if I shall have a chance to tell
them to him. I am grateful for your warnings about the
dangers to which I exposed myself. Naturally, studying to
be a nurse and perhaps a doctor, you have to learn more
about men than I ever expect to know. Thank you again
and again. I have been shocked to discover the possibility

of sinful thoughts and feelings in my mind, and you may be sure that I shall not again forget the lesson.

Master Charles got into his car next morning and drove away, without so much as a smile for me. That is the way of all four of the members of this strange family, I learn. Each one has a fine car, and they go their own ways; they tell Miss Bascom where they are going, for she forwards their mail, and she tells Miss Lucy—each person here has to have somebody to talk to. So I learn that Master Charles has gone to Hollywood; he has an apartment there, and pays rent for it all the time. He likes the ladies there, the night clubs and the smart restaurants; I suppose he would have taken me there if I had let him, and wouldn't I have fitted in beautifully! Miss Lucy says that with all his money he cuts quite a swath. That is her word, and I looked it up in the big dictionary which I have to dust. While I am at it, Mrs. Jessup comes in, and she says, "What are you doing, child?" and I tell her I am looking up a word. "My sister is going to college, and I do not want to grow up an ignoramus. I hope it is not presuming." "Not if you don't take too long," she says. "What is the word?" So I am caught, and I do not want to tell what they call a fib, even a little one, so I tell, and she asks, "Where did you hear that word?" I say, "Someone told me that someone was cutting a swath in society," and she answers, "Take my advice, child, and don't let anybody cut a swath through you." So I know there has been talk about me, and I say, quick, "I want you to be sure, Mrs. Jessup, that I was brought up decent and I mean to stay so and I hope you will believe that." "Well," says she, "take my advice and do not go out at night with men above your own station." I answer, "It is kind of you to warn me."

She goes away and I go on with my work, but I am not

so happy, because I want people to love me and to think kind things about me; but I hear sly remarks and see laughing glances from the help, and I know what they are thinking, and it makes my ears burn. Later I am helping Miss Lucy, and I suppose that Mrs. Jessup has talked to her, and maybe told her to find out the story from me. Anyhow, Miss Lucy wants to know what really happened, and I decide to tell her, because the truth is always better than a falsehood, and here it has to be one or the other. I am not bound to secrecy that I can see, so I tell, all but the kisses, of which I am so ashamed; I just say that he took my hand. She is absorbed in the story as if it were a novel, of which she reads all that she can get hold of. She plies me with questions, and I do not tell her about his arguments against God, for why should I help Satan by passing such things on?

Well, she talks, and tells me that it is an old story; the young master is very free with the women, is the way she puts it. He is so handsome and so elegant and so rich that none can refuse him, and she doubts if anyone did ever refuse him before; in fact, I think she had trouble in believing that I did, but in the end I convinced her. It seemed to her quite wonderful and made me more important in her eyes. Being a maiden lady, she does not know much more about such matters than I do, but she confided to me that she had been in love once and had her heart broken when the man preferred a rich girl. We had a heart-to-heart talk, and I have been told a lot more about this family and its affairs. It seems that this being free with the women began when the young master was in what is called prep school, and the drinking began there too, and that was why his uncle beat him. My lady could not refuse him anything. She sent him away to Europe with a tutor, and there he gambled away great sums of money, but she paid his debts and kept the secret from everybody. Now he chooses his ladies in Hollywood and that is very expensive, for they expect mink and ermine coats and showers of jewels—I am repeating what this elderly sewing lady says.

I ask, "I am supposed to be cheaper?" and she answers, "No, it is not that. You could have the furs and jewels too. There is nothing cheap about him, because he does not have to earn the money, unless you count his having to spend some time with his aunt, and to agree with all her ideas, and to pay her compliments and make her happy. Then he gets a check or a bundle of bonds, and away he goes." I am bitter and ashamed and say, "I do not feel flattered to be one of so many." This sewing lady who was working for the family in Philadelphia before my lady was born answers that nobody here is ever to be flattered, only members of this family. Says she, "It is something I have learned from watching very rich people most of my life; it is hard for any of them to have real friends, and impossible for them to escape the power of their money; they think they own it, but it owns them and makes them its slaves, and the richer they are, the tighter are its chains. They are fed flattery until they cannot live without it, and there is no dose too strong for them to swallow. They have dominated the lives of other people until they think that they are gods. Arrogance is the word for them, as persons and as a family." It is a word that I have never heard and that I have to look for in the dictionary; I can't always find the words, because I am not sure of the sounds, but I got that one. She tells me to watch and I will see this, even with a person as kind and good as my lady. I answer, "I am upset by such ideas, for when I came here I never meant to pass judgment on my employers." She says, "You will not be able to help seeing what they are."

I have been thinking about it ever since. Mrs. Harries is what people call a radical; she wants everybody to be that, but I have an idea she would be shocked if she heard the opinions of this quiet old sewing lady. I hope that you will not be shocked by hearing such things from your loving Sister

Pamela

LETTER XII

Dear Mother:

I have been owing you a letter. It would be hard for you to realize how busy I am, being an errand girl for this big house. But I do not mind it, for everybody is kind and it is always interesting. It is like being in college, only the teachers do not know that they are teaching.

Mrs. Harries is so very good to me. I think it is because I am her own discovery and am so respectful. She is kind, but she likes people to do exactly what she says. She has taken me twice into town with her, and the last time she did not put me in the front seat with Pietro but took me into the back part with herself and another lady, Mrs. Fearing, who is visiting her. The back seat is wide for three but those two great ladies almost filled it full. There are two little seats that unfold from the back of the front seat and on one of them sits me, listening to my betters converse and not saying a word. It is a strange thing being a servant; it is supposed to be as if you did not exist; the masters go right on talking about their affairs, the most intimate, just as if you were not there. I am embarrassed to be there, but of course since I do not exist why should I worry? Mrs. Fearing has a married daughter that is expecting, and the things that have happened to her are most alarming to me. My own mistress does not approve of having babies; she thinks it is a mistake of nature, and there are far too many people in the world for their own good.

You ask what I have been reading in my Bible. I have decided that under God's Providence there can be no such thing as an accident, and if I ask Him to guide me and then open the Book with my eyes shut, it will be what He wishes me to read. So last night I read Leviticus 20, which is about some awful things the Jews were not allowed to do, and as I do not want to do any of them I felt safe. The night before I read Psalm 51 and it is beautiful language; I learned some of it and addressed the Lord in that way before I went to sleep. I am grateful that from earliest childhood I have heard such noble words, and it must be that I have learned to speak in that way, for now and then I see the help look at each other and smile. I lose no chance to tell them how the Word of God has been given to them and they cannot but respect it. Even to the Papists I have told it, and they may have been set to thinking about their salvation.

Rachel has sent me two new pamphlets, one about Baptism and the other about the First Angel's Message; they help me, but I fear they would not be appreciated by people here. Miss Lucy is still reading "The Great Controversy," and I continue to answer her questions and pray God to help my uncertainties. I am so glad about Jennie's having two kids; that is a kindness of Providence, perhaps to make up for Grampa's illness. I wish I could be there to milk her; there is something warm and friendly about milking and I miss it. If ever I should be unhappy in this too grand place, I could come home and never miss it in our tiny ranch. Such is your humble Daughter

Pamela

LETTER XIII

Dear Sister:

Well, I have news to report this evening! Miss Yvette is back. She drove in about lunch time, her and the young lady who is her friend and always goes about with her, and my, such elegant persons you never did see the like! I did not see them come, but I saw her go through the drawing room and run up the stairs without bothering with the elevator. I don't know if she saw me, and I doubt if she will ever, being much too grand. She is in her thirties, but looks much less, and the other lady about the same; she is Miss Carol and, my dear, you will not believe it, she is a rodeo rider; she comes from a ranch in Montana, and rides the wildest horses, and even steers, and has won prizes at shows and is known as the Queen of the Quinta, whatever that is, nobody has been able to find out. I don't suppose she does that any more now; she is driven by Miss Yvette in a fancy car and wears sport clothes, as they are called. They have been in high wild mountains where there is a great hotel and you pay about fifty dollars a day for each person, and Miss Lucy swears that is so. I am so ignorant that I find it hard to believe such things, but she shows me the pictures that Miss Yvette has sent home. It seems that these rich people are not content to wait for winter but must find it in summer by climbing into mountains where they can go about on what are called skis, which are long things that you slide on and sometimes break your leg.

Well, I got a good look at Miss Yvette and Miss Carol, more than I ever expected to see of any women alive. It was quite shocking to me. I think I have told you that the telephone is in a big closet off the drawing room, and there are extensions in the rooms, but people can shut the extensions off, or maybe they are not in their rooms when it rings; my orders are that if I hear it ring a third time I am to go quickly and see who is wanted and go and tell them, or if they are away, write down the message. So I answer, and it is a man named Mr. Chisholm, asking for Miss Yvette, and I know that she is out in the swimming pool, and I tell him to hold the wire, and I run there. The pool is the most beautiful thing you could imagine, alongside the loggia and with a wide walk all around it, and canvas chairs and seats with striped awnings. The pool is big—I think you could put four houses like ours into it, or maybe six—and it is painted blue inside so that the water looks blue; it must be that you can see the mountains while you swim; and when the water is run out it runs down into the orchards so that it is not wasted.

Well, there are the two ladies swimming, and all they have on, I blush to tell, is a little tight thing with no arms and very little legs. I suppose they think it is all right because there are no men about, and if the gardener were to come he wouldn't exist. My young mistress has lovely blond hair, but now it is in a little rubber cap which matches her suit. She is gliding through the water like she was born there. I tell her the message and she doesn't stop her graceful swimming, but says, "Oh, bother! Tell him I'm out." I have the idea to protest, but I think better of it and run back, and there is Stella, the dining-room maid, and I say, "Stella, will you tell the gentleman on the telephone that Miss Yvette is out?" Says she, "Why don't you tell him yourself?" and I explain, "It is against my religion to tell a fib." "What cheek!" says she. "And besides, she is out of the house, isn't she?" I hadn't thought of that, so I go to the

phone and say, very polite, "Miss Yvette is out," and he
gives me his number. Later, when I try to give it to Miss
Yvette, she says she does not want it, and that is all. She
does not ask who am I, or even my name. She never says
anything friendly; so different she is from her sister.

Well, I talk about all this with Miss Lucy when I have a
chance. I remark that this Mr. Chisholm had a very nice
voice, but Miss Yvette only said "Bother!" Miss Lucy replies that she does not care for men, she thinks they are all
after her money, and maybe they are. I say, "But she is a
lovely young woman," and the answer is, "Yes, but she is
more interested in Miss Carol." I say, "But that does not
make sense. Does she never mean to marry?" Miss Lucy
says, "I doubt it very much. It is more important to her to
keep her money." "But," say I, "would her husband take
her money? He might make more." She explains about the
laws in California; there is something called a community
property law, that she is not very clear about herself, but
the husband can claim ownership of half the wife's property, or perhaps it is of her income after the marriage; anyhow, Miss Yvette doesn't want to part with half of anything, she would rather take her rodeo-riding lady and be
off to any part of the world that strikes her fancy. Now they
have a lovely speedboat all varnished and shiny and it rides
on a little trailer cart, and they have it hitched behind the
car and are off to the beach or to some bay where the speedboat can run. Miss Yvette has a house of her own there, and
the two young ladies take one of the servants, and maybe
someday it will be me, and then I'll have a new story to tell
you. This evening they have dressed up and gone to some
dinner party, we do not know where, but maybe they have
told Mrs. Harries.

I must stop now. I have opened to Daniel 7 and see it is
full of strange prophecies about the Ancient of Days, and

the beasts that are kingdoms, and I could maybe know which they were if I knew more about the kingdoms that have been on earth since Daniel's time. Good night and best love from your devoted

Pamela

LETTER XIV

Dear Sister:

Wonders never cease in this home of them. I have met a Papist priest, and after that a movie queen! If anybody had told me a year ago that such things could happen in my life, I would have thought them crazy.

Well, first the priest; he came to the Sunday afternoon, and there was a poet reading his verses, and if he is not crazy then I am, take your choice. He was tall and thin, wore spectacles, and had long hair; he came from a place called Greenwich Village, which is no village but a part of New York City. He is famous and that is apparently enough, for if he is famous people want to hear him and more important to look at him. My lady paid him a hundred dollars—I saw the check. But she surely paid him no compliments. She is so frank that she is funny. She said to the company, "I hope you understood this, I didn't." They all talked about modern poetry and why it was different from old-style, and pretty soon they got off on politics and social justice and what is to be done about the poor, which is where all the roads lead to in this millionaire home.

The Papist is a Frenchman, but he lives in Los Angeles, and is called Father Dupre which is pronounced Do-pray, and I suppose means that he does. He is little, round and rosy, and is kind in manner, which I suppose is one of Satan's wiles. When he was called upon to speak he talked about modern French poetry and said nothing about religion, and this I preferred since his is merely idolatry. I was not introduced to him, of course, but I offered the tray with fruit juice to him and he said, "Thank you, my dear." He wore a black suit with a white collar that had no opening, so I don't know how he got into it. That is all about him, but I never expected to meet one of them and it gave me a strange thrill. He was not at all what I imagined.

There is rather more about the movie queen. Master Charles brought her to lunch, and they were motoring to the beach called La Jolla, but you pronounce it La Hoy-ya. Her name is Lotta Lane and she is very popular; perhaps you have seen her name in front of theaters. Miss Lucy insists that she earns two thousand a week, no less, and I am past ever being surprised by anything in this world. The help were all abuzz, for they have seen her pictures and know all about her from the magazines. She has had three husbands, and before that she worked at a soda fountain. She plays what are called "sexy" parts and her principal stock-in-trade is heaving her bosom; Miss Lucy knows, because she has to go to the movies when Mrs. Harries invites her, but I suspect that she is not so bored as she makes herself think.

The women help all wanted to wait table, but I did not enter that race; I have learned the household pretty well by now and I can manage to think up an errand that will take me into the drawing room, so I got a good look at her. She was painted, but that does not fool me any more; her hair was like a golden crown of ringlets. I would guess her to be thirty-five or even older; Master Charles is only twenty-one, so they do not match, and if she earns so much money, why does she want his? The thought came to me that maybe he had brought her here in order to show me that he was getting along all right without any help from me; but perhaps that would be attaching too much importance to myself.

Sister dear, it is a most awful and wicked world; I am realizing it more and more. This woman who portrays evil women, "vamps" they are called, gets paid much more than the President of the United States, and maybe a hundred times as much as one of our reverends. Her face and her heaving bosom are shown on the screen to millions of people all over the world, and if that is not a triumph of Satan, who can imagine one? I see this pair go off together, and Miss Lucy tells me that she stays quite openly in his apartment in Hollywood, and he in hers; it seems wicked to even think about it, but what can I do? If I mean to combat Satan I have to know what he is up to, it is no good for either you or me to shut our eyes and let the evil one have his way. I wonder about this and think, well, she is famous, so maybe he is proud to be seen with her; he is rich, he has made himself known for wasting money fast, and maybe that is a kind of fame in her eyes; he is young and handsome, and I suppose in their world it is expected that her life should be the same as what she shows on the screen— her role, it is called.

What puzzles me most is that he should bring her here to his aunt's home and show her off. Does he not know this will hurt his aunt? Or does he think that it won't hurt her, that she too will be proud to have Lotta Lane to lunch and will tell her friends about it? Surely it is my duty to understand my mistress, so I ask Miss Lucy, who tells me that Mrs. Harries is sad about it, but what can she do? She cannot change him, and she must not quarrel with him, for she has adopted him as a son and her heart is bound up with his; she makes excuses for him, she might even have been willing to change her moral code to excuse him. It is indeed a strange, a dreadful thing, and oh, how I thank God for the faith that binds our family and keeps us from having to change our moral code!

I tell you little but dreadful things in this letter; but do not worry for me. I think I am stronger for knowing what this world is. Truly, our "adversary the devil, as a roaring lion, walketh about, seeking whom he may devour"— I Peter, 5:8. Your steadfast Sister

Pamela

LETTER XV

Dear Mother:

I am so glad to hear of your approval of what I am doing, and how much my monthly contribution has been a help to you. Truly, our Heavenly Father knoweth what we have need of.

I have been trying to do my duty here and to make myself useful to my employers, and there are signs that I have been succeeding. Something that happened today will give you pleasure, I am sure. Miss Bascom has been called home by the illness of her mother, and Mrs. Harries is left without a secretary; when I came to her room to dust she said, "Oh, dear, what shall I do? The postcards for next Sunday's meeting should be got into the mail today." I made bold to say, "Could I do them for you, Mrs. Harries?" "What sort of hand do you write?" she asks, and tells me to go to her desk. So I sit and with her gold fountain pen, which I have been scared even to look at, I write, Mrs. Margaret Harries,

Rancho Casa Grande, Junipero, California. She looks at it and says, "Why, that is quite plain; it will do." So I am sent to Miss Bascom's room, where she has the cardfile, and I spend a couple of hours addressing the printed postcards, and feel that I am a regular secretary. Not that I would try to take Miss Bascom's place, but it might be that she will get married someday, being such an elegant person.

Then after lunch my lady wishes to drive to town and takes me with her, also an old lady, Mrs. Stokes, who is a guest, and was a friend of her mother. They talk about the families in Philadelphia and who has married who and the names of their children, and I try to look as if I was not listening. We drive to the bank and she tells me to go in and cash a check, and not to let them give me higher than twenties because it is a bother getting change. The check is for a thousand dollars—just think, all she has to do is to write, "Cash, one thousand," and her name—she doesn't even bother to put the date, I doubt if she knows it. I hand the check to the young man, and he does not blink an eye but takes a package of new bills that have not a wrinkle. I wonder, does the bank print them? Is it what Mrs. Harries says should be done—only they do not give them to the poor? Well, he counts out fifty of those bills and it is quite a wad and I stick them quick into my pocket and run to the car, for I am scared that some bandit may be watching. But Mrs. Harries is never scared and does not even bother to count the bills but just sticks them into her handbag and I doubt if she ever will count them.

Then we drive to the stationer's and I buy her a magazine, and then to the candy shop and I buy the kind of chocolates that she likes, three kinds, and that she will nibble all day and wonder that she is stout. Then they go into a show, and she takes a box and will nibble there. Pietro drives me to the grocer's, and there is a long list which Mrs. Jessup has prepared, and the grocer will pile all the stuff into boxes and put them into the trunk of the car. I mail the postcards, and go to a bakery and buy the special kind of buns that Mrs. Harries likes, and then my duties are done. Pietro goes in to the show, and I sit and read the magazine, and there is an article which tells why it is not as some people say, that the rich are idle; their money works for them and is used to pay the labor which produces goods, and it is the best system in the world and is called the American way. I try to figure it out and I can see that Mrs. Harries' money paid the man who sold the chocolates, and may pay the man who will make some more; but it seems to me it is a question of who is to eat the chocolates when they are made. Mrs. Harries eats too many, and I am sure that has never been the case with the dear washerwoman whom I love. I would send you a box paid for out of my own money, only I know it would give you more fright than pleasure to see me spend my earnings like that, so instead I send you the best of love from your dutiful Daughter

Pamela

LETTER XVI

Dear Sister:

It is a sad letter that I have to write today. I have shed many tears, not for myself but for my kind mistress and for her wayward nephew. Alas for both of them, that have been offered the help of the Lord and have rejected it!

I went in this morning to take her orange juice, and I

take one look at her and see that she has been crying; her eyes are red, and no doubt she has wiped the tears out of them but they are coming back. Perhaps it is too bold of me, but I have learned to love her and to be sorry too; so I say, "Oh, Mrs. Harries, is there some bad news?" She says, "Yes, it is very bad." Miss Lucy has told me that almost always the rich people hide their troubles and lock their family skeletons in their closets, as she puts it; but this is not true of Mrs. Harries, who will always say what is in her mind. Now she says, "It is Charles; he is drinking again." I say, "Oh, I am so sorry!" and you may be sure that is true. Says she, "I just had a telephone call from a friend in Hollywood who says he is in a bad way and needs help—but what can I do? His uncle will have nothing to do with him, and I cannot control him any more." Now the tears come and run down her cheeks and she is kept busy wiping them away. Can you think of anything more strange than the story of this lady who has so much money she can stuff a thousand dollars' worth of bills into her handbag, but she cannot buy the one thing that she wants most, which is the love and companionship of the young gentleman she adores.

What can I say except that I am sorry again, and then, "I wish so that I could help you!" She looks at me through her tears and says, "They tell me that he took you out one evening." I say, "Yes, Mrs. Harries," for I surely will not ever tell her a fib. "Tell me what happened," she says, and I am blushing very red, I can feel, but still I tell the truth. "It was my hope," I say, "that I might be able to influence him, by telling him about the faith that I hold and convincing him that it was based upon the word of God. But I fear that I did not get very far with him." I stop, and she says, "He tried to make love to you?" "Yes, Mrs. Harries, I am afraid that he did. He kissed me several times, and I was frightened and begged him not to, and so he stopped. He was gentlemanly, I admit." "Indeed yes," she says, "he is a good boy at heart. People tell me that I have let him have his way too much and have spoiled him. Evil people know that he has money, and they gather round him to try to get it away from him. I try so hard to interest him in my ideas, but I fear I bore him, and what can I do?" The tears continue to run down her cheeks, but she does not sob or cry. She is a very quiet person, and Miss Lucy has told me that nobody has ever heard her raise her voice or lose her self-control.

Now she has asked me a question, and it is the opportunity I have been thinking might someday come, and I have the firm purpose to meet it if it does. We have been told in Scripture to be bold in Christ and to be His witness to all men; so I say, "If you will permit me, Mrs. Harries, I think the mistake was to bring him up without the help of God. We are all of us but weak mortals, and when we rely upon ourselves alone we are as broken reeds." Says she, gazing at me, "You really believe that, don't you!" So I answer, "Indeed I do, and I have had many proofs of God's goodness, not the least of them your coming to my poor home." "So," she says, "I have been a messenger of God without knowing it!" "Indeed, Mrs. Harries, you have been that, and if you will but hear what I tell you, it may be that a poor parlormaid can be the same to you. For in the sight of God we are all equal, and it was humble fishermen who were chosen to become the disciples and to spread the word all over the earth."

Well, she takes it most graciously. She says, "I know you believe all that sincerely." I answer, "I believe it with all my heart and soul, and so might you and Master Charles also, if you would but study God's words in His Holy Writ." "I tried to read that old book," she says, "but I was just too bored. It is full of crimes and slaughters and horrible things that I couldn't endure." "It is the story of the ancient Jews," I say, "and what God revealed to them in His own time and His own way. It has all been studied and interpreted. But I think it might have been better if you had begun with the Gospels, which deal with the life of Christ." "I tried that too," she says. "I began at the very beginning, and it was about how somebody begat somebody else and it was all begat and begat, and I got sick of so much begatting. It is a messy business, and I got through with it long ago. What do I care about all those Jewish names? It is supposed to be the ancestry of Jesus' father, but he wasn't supposed to have any father. Can you tell me how a man who was born of a virgin can have a line of fathers going back to Abraham?"

Forgive me, dear Sister, for writing these words. It is what she said, and I am telling you the truth no matter how much it hurts to write or to read. I said to her, very humble, "I am not a learned person, Mrs. Harries, and God's Word does not stand or fall by the ability of such as me to explain it. This I can tell you surely, the people of our faith do not drink, they do not smoke, they do not gamble, and they do not go a-whoring. If Master Charles could be persuaded to join our church, he would be saved from all these evils which distress you so greatly. That would be a proof of God's goodness and His power that would mean far more to you than anything I could tell you about the ancient Jews." To that she says, "You are a good child, Pamela, and I would be glad if you could convince him." "Is that really true, Mrs. Harries?" I ask, for of course it is very important. "Indeed it is true. Try your best and see if you can help." "But," I say very serious, "it is no use to try if you will undo my efforts by saying things such as you have just told me." At that she cannot keep from smiling in spite of her tears. "I will put a seal upon my lips," she says.

"I will say nothing about the subject in his presence—nor, if you wish, in yours." To that I say, putting on a bold front, "I would rather that you told me the truth, for my own faith cannot be shaken, it is built upon the Rock of Ages."

Is not that a strange thing to have befallen a humble servant? She says that she knows a doctor who has influence with the young master, and she will pay this doctor to go and bring him home and help to take care of him. She says, "Do what you can to help keep him entertained, Pamela. It is too bad that you do not play cards, because he likes to play, and surely it is no sin if it is not for money." I tell her that it is a strict rule of our church, but that I can read to him. She says that he can read to himself, but after he has been drinking he is very nervous, and he wants company and wants above all things to be diverted. I say, "I have never known anybody that drank liquor, Mrs. Harries, but of course I will do the best I can, if that is your wish." She explains, "He seems to crave female society, and of course it is much better that he should be in the company of a nice girl like you than those Hollywood women who think only to get furs and jewels from him." I tell her that I would surely not know what to do with furs or jewels. Then she says something that gives me a great start: "If he should kiss you, do not take it too seriously, for it will not really hurt you." I say, "Oh, Mrs. Harries, but it can lead to worse things!" She says, "It need not, if you are careful, for you are a good girl and he knows it. There are some men who are very susceptible to a woman's influence, and the right one can control him and lead him away from bad company."

So there I have a new set of duties! I think, was there ever anything stranger? My sister is studying to be a nurse and working hard at it, but here it seems that I have been made into a nurse without any studies whatever! I say, "But what about my other duties, Mrs. Harries?" She answers that she will tell Mrs. Jessup to have some of the other girls do them. "They are idle half the time," she says. I think to myself, Oh, dear, how jealous they will be of me and my new job! I am frightened about it, for I have no sense of being equal to such a duty, and cannot think how to set about it. But be sure that I shall be conscientious and that no harm will come to your devoted Sister

Pamela

LETTER XVII

Dear Mother:

I have two quite wonderful pieces of news for you this week. First, that Miss Lucy has read enough to convince her that we are right in keeping the Sabbath as the Lord's day, and so from now on I shall have company in my worship. It makes no difference to the household, since her work is of a kind that can be done the next day as well; but it has made a great impression on the help, who begin to think that my ideas may not be so foolish after all. The second is that my mistress has given me permission to try to convince the young master to have faith, and has promised that she will not say anything against it. Nothing has given me such joy since my coming here. Truly, righteousness shall go before Him and set us in the way.

We have had the first good rain here, and already the mountainsides are beginning to show green. Soon the ground will be soft, and the disking for the barley will begin. The

climate here is not so different from our own, but being
higher I think it is a bit colder. As you know, all climate in
California is always unusual.

I am glad to hear that Grampa is improving and that the
kids are thriving. You should begin now to take more milk
for yourself and let the kids learn to forage for themselves.
They will not do it unless they have to. I have observed it
in this place; the people here work only because they have
to and they are careful not to overwork; the masters don't
have to and they don't, especially the younger pair. They
are our kids; they stay young, and admire themselves for it,
but I do not admire them. Best love to you and Grampa,
from your hard-working

Pamela

LETTER XVIII

Dear Sister:

The young master is home. The doctor brought him; it
was night, and nobody saw them; now he is in his room.
The doctor is young and good looking; he eats with the
family, so we have seen him. To Master Charles' room
there are taken pots of hot coffee and milk and fruit juice.
I suppose those are the things that people have when they
have been on a "bust"—that is what they call it in the
kitchen. Truly, wine is a mocker, strong drink is raging. I
thought it was forbidden to be made or sold; but Miss Lucy
tells me that rich men have their bootleggers and get all
they want.

Well, I have been told to help him, but I have not been

told when or how, and surely it is not up to me to seek him out. I will wait until he appears and see if he still has any interest in me, and then I will continue this letter. . . .

He was two days in his room, and then in mid-morning he came down in the elevator, and he saw me dusting the drawing room, as before. All the color is out of his cheeks and they look like clay; he has scraped himself on the chin while shaving, and he looks very melancholy and walks slowly. The doctor is gone, which I suppose means that he is cured, but he does not look it. He sees me and says, "Hello, Pam." I say, "Good morning, Master Charles. I am glad to see you." I have thought it over and made up my mind to fib, which I hope will be forgiven; I say, "The flu is a terrible thing." He says, "Is that what I have?" and I say, "That is what they tell me." "Yes, it's very bad," says he, and he will play the game—I not knowing if I have fooled him, but anyhow, it is easier this way. He says, "Come out into the sunshine," and since that is my new duty I put down my dusting rag and go with him, and since he is sick I suppose it right for me to take his arm and steady him. We go to the lawn swing which is by the swimming pool, facing it, and has a canvas top, all red and gold color, very gay. I have sat in it once, after dark, just to see how it feels; now I sit in it by day, like any lady, and he sits beside me and says, "Do you know how to swim?" I tell him that I have never had the chance, there is no water near the ranch where I was brought up. He says, "I will teach you," and you can imagine my panic at the idea that he might expect me to wear something like I saw on the two ladies here.

Well, he asks me about my home, and I tell him, hiding nothing, for I am surely not going to learn to be ashamed of our poor condition, and anyhow, he might take the notion to come there someday. It is my hope to convert him,

and that means he will see me with the eyes of God and
not those of a young millionaire. And besides, last night I
was reading James 5: "Go to now, ye rich men, weep and
howl for your miseries that shall come upon you." I read it
and it startled me, because it sounds so much like what
people here call radical, and which I hear sometimes on the
Sunday afternoons. It tells the rich about the evils which
are to come to them; but this one, poor fellow, has them
now, I think, for I see that his hands are trembling and his
eyes are restless and wander here and there while he talks,
so I know that he has only half a mind on me.

I tell myself that I am going to be a nurse like you and
must learn about such matters. I say, "Could I fetch you a
glass of orange juice, Master Charles?" He bursts out in a
wild way, "What I want is a good stiff shot of whisky!" So
I see my duty and say, "Oh, no, Master Charles, you must
not take that! That is against the law and would be terrible
for your flu. Do, I beg you, have some orange juice or milk,
that will give you the nourishment you need. Don't you
know that there are minerals in them that your system has
need of in illness?"—for I have not forgot the lessons I have
learned in our Dr. Kellogg's health book. I am no ignoramus, and he is not to think so. He says, sort of surly, "Oh,
all right," so I run quick, for fear that he will disappear before I get back. I bring him a glass of orange juice and one
of milk, and both are cold and look very nice to me. He
takes a few sips of the milk and makes a face. He says, "You
drink the orange juice," and I set a trap for him, saying, "I
will if you will drink the milk." So I match him, sip by sip,
and he gets it down, and I think I am clever and making a
very good trained nurse.

I have been told that I must keep him entertained, and I
think probably he will enjoy talking about himself, as most
people do, so I ask him about his life in military school, and

he tells me that it bored him greatly, and this I can believe, because they would make him work and he had never had to take orders before. I pretend that I am very much interested in military ways, and for an hour I keep him busy; but I know that he is a shrewd young gentleman and has learned to be suspicious of people. So I try Europe, and he tells me about Paris, which he says is the most beautiful city in the world, and the people there know how to get happiness out of life. I have decided not to talk any religion until he is feeling better, so I do not say anything about the wickedness of Paris, but hear about its wonderful buildings and parks, and about the Huns who could not take it. He is not like his aunt, who is always for the underdog and hates war so that she blames the side that insists upon winning—at least that is the way I have come to interpret her. But Master Charles, I think, hates the Germans more and loves the French; I ask him and he says that both sides are to blame for that war. It was stupid and greedy politicians that made it, and now he says they were fooling President Wilson and making a mess of the peace settlement and there will surely be another war. He says that nobody in power is honest or can be trusted, and I think, oh, dear, if I believed things like that I might want to go off and get drunk myself! But don't worry, dear Sister.

I think there could not be a better chance to bring in the subject of our Heavenly Father and His care and guidance; so I do, but alas, it does not help, he only argues with me that no merciful God would have let all those humans be slaughtered, poor peasant lads who had no idea what they were fighting for. He does not believe there is any God, or at least if there is, He does not care for us, or how many of His children are killed by earthquakes and avalanches and plagues and floods and hurricanes. He thinks that life is some kind of blind accident, and that we have to take our

chances and learn to protect ourselves the best we can, and
so far we have done very badly. There is no use arguing
with him, I fear; he does not accept the Bible as a Holy
Book, but says it is Jewish history and legend; he says
maybe there was such a man as Jesus, and he got a raw deal,
as so many others have done who tried to help the ungrateful human race; you get no thanks for it. I stopped trying
to argue and instead I prayed for him in my soul. Maybe
it did good, we shall see.

I saw him getting restless again, and this time I got him
orange juice. Then he wanted to know if I played pingpong
and I told him, alas, I knew no games. He offered to teach
me checkers, and I hope that is not the same as cards; I let
him do it, and of course it wasn't much fun for him, but he
laughed over my blunders and I laughed too, and it kept
him busy for a while. I think that I am making a very successful young gentleman's nurse. But every now and then I
see that wandering of his eyes. It has been explained to me
that he is suffering terribly for lack of the poison he has
been taking, and I am afraid to leave him for fear he may
have some hidden and may get it. The wine closet is locked,
but he might demand the key, and none of the help would
dare to oppose him. Could I do it, and would I, and what
would happen? I did not ask my lady those questions; I
have just been turned loose on my own, and to say that I
am scared would be putting it mild.

Well, I stick by him, the whole day. There is a victrola
in the house with plenty of records, and I fetch it, and he
picks out the music that he likes, and it is jazz, and I know
it is dance music, but I do not have to think about dancing
while I listen. Then he picks up a newspaper and reads the
headlines, and comments on the mess the world is in. I do
not say much, because I am so ignorant, but not nearly so
much, Sister, as when I first came here. I have been busy

picking up bits of conversation, and speeches on Sundays. I do not tell him that we have no newspaper in our home and that I seldom saw one. I listen, and admire his knowledge, and that pleases him, and I see that helps.

Presently he says he will take me for a drive; but I am afraid to let him do that, because his hands are not steady, and I tell him I have heard that after the flu one's heart is bad and it is better to rest and not strain it. He says I may drive him; and when I tell him that I have no idea how to drive, there is a new game to play; he will teach me. Of course I am excited, and that is a good thing, because it interests him; I see that what he likes is to be superior to somebody, even if it is but a poor parlormaid. I tell him that I am terrified of his car that is so powerful, and he agrees to teach me with one of the smaller cars that is in the garage; the gear shifts are the same, he says. He promises to drive very slow, so I get in, and he drives to one of the big barley fields that has not yet been planted. There are piles of rock here and there in it, but plenty of room between, and he gives me a lecture on gears and how to start and to stop, and then I take his place. I have never been worse scared, but I do exactly what he says, and after I have killed the engine a few times I get the car going, and I find that I can steer it here and there. I don't run into the rocks, and little by little I get used to it and feel myself tremendously smart. I make sure that I can stop whenever I want to, so I get over my fright, and after I have started about twenty times I no longer kill the engine.

We go rolling here and there over the barley stubble, and he plays a game with me, tells me there is a red light, and now there is another car coming, and what will I do; there is no other car, but I move over to pass it, and then he tells me there is a parking place by the pile of rocks and I have to learn to back into it, and when I am not close enough he tells me I am out in the street and will be getting a parking ticket; when I get too close he tells me I am scraping my rear tire on the curb, and so on. He is patient and of course I thank him, and try my best, because I know that if I am stupid he will get bored with me, but if I am quick to learn he will think that he is a good teacher and be satisfied with himself. I did not know what a man who has been drunk would be like, but now I discover that he is like a child, and I begin to think that maybe he is that way always, because he has had everything handed to him and has never had to make any serious effort.

So he tells me that I am a driver now and we can go on the road; and after I have changed my clothes we go. The first time a car comes toward me I am in terror, but I keep to the right and it goes by without any trouble, and so gradually I get up courage. He says, "Let's go to town," so I drive. At the crossings I am scared again, but he has taught me the signals and it is all easy. He says, "Let's have a soda," and on a side street I find plenty of room and draw up by the curb and park. We walk around the corner to a drugstore and he has a chocolate ice-cream soda, and I figure this is good for him. He buys me a big box of chocolates, and I see that it makes him happy to spend his money, and I decide that it is not the same as a mink coat or a diamond brooch. I am afraid that he may know of some place where he can get some liquor; but no, he must realize how it would shock me and I should shame him by my tears. I decide that he is enjoying what his aunt has called "female society," and I give him plenty of it. I am so proud that I have learned to drive a car, all in one afternoon; I laugh and chatter, and he knows that I am very young, and that he is older and wiser.

Well, I drive him back, and I tell him that he should have a nap, and it amuses him to have me pretend to be his nurse and give him orders. He asks if I will read him to sleep, and I think fast and say that I will provided that he will promise not to think about another drink of whisky or anything of the sort. He promises, and I go up in the elevator with him. He has a lovely big room with fine furniture in it which I do not know how to describe; I have been in it dusting before he came, so it is not strange to me. I am careful to leave the door open and he does not close it. He has been reading what they call a crime story, and I take it up and read to him, and of course I don't understand it very well, but I read, and he lies on the bed and presently I can tell by his breathing that he is asleep; so then I stop and steal out and close the door softly. I go to my lady's room and report to her what I have done, and she is very happy and says it is wonderful. I tell her about the box of candy that cost two dollars and I think I should give it to her; but she says, "Keep it, child, for heaven's sake!"—that is a way of speaking, even though she does not believe there is a heaven. I tell her I will pass it round among the help and she says, "They get too much to eat anyhow." I keep to myself the thought that there is no one of them that weighs as much as the mistress.

I go to the kitchen where dinner is being prepared. They have all seen me in the lawn swing, and getting a driving lesson, or have been told about it, and they are crazy to hear from me. I tell them about the candy, and how I will distribute it, but after dinner, so as not to spoil their appetites. Mary, the kitchen maid, says, "And will you pay the price?" I say, "There has been no price asked," and she answers, "There will be." I wanted to ask how she knew, but I thought that might be spiteful, and I am trying to speak only love to the people in this house where it is so much needed. Keep a share of it for your loving Sister

Pamela

❦

LETTER XIX

Dear Mother:

Your letter telling how you pray for my welfare touches me deeply. Please do not worry about your spelling, as I am not so good myself and better not take me for a model.

You ask about the people I meet here, those of the quality. I do not often meet them, exactly; I see them and wait upon them. While doing so, I pick up bits of talk and then ask the help about them, those who have been here longest and have found out. This place belongs to my lady, and Mr. Harries sees his friends at the club if he sees them anywhere; he does not seem to have any relatives, at least they don't come here. Mrs. Harries has many relatives and they travel a lot; they visit here and then go and come again. There is an old gentleman, Uncle Walter, who has a round red face and seems to know about horses and dogs; when he is not talking about them he is telling funny stories, and I find it provoking because I hear the beginning of the story but miss the end; it would not do for me to linger in my duties. There is her brother, Mr. Tom Egbert, who is also stout and jolly, and she said that he is kwizzical; at least that is the way it sounded but I cannot find it in the big dictionary. He said to me, all of a sudden, "You are a pretty girl, Pamela." I was confused and said, "Oh, thank you, sir!" and went as fast as I could, for I am afraid of these gentlemen that I might have to give them offense. His wife is a tall thin lady who wears jet beads and sits very stiff.

As to the friends, there are ladies who come to the Thursday luncheon, and three of them are old friends who were at school with Mrs. Harries in the East, and two are very rich widows and she says they have no idea what to do with their money, but they say that they invest it and it is put to use. I hear them argue, they scold each other but don't seem to mind it a bit; they all call the mistress "Maggie" and they come back next week. Sometimes they play cards, but mostly they discuss what she calls current events; she will read them something out of a newspaper that she finds disgraceful; or perhaps it will be a begging letter from some poor person. She says, "How can such things be, and here we sit and eat filly minyong and green peas and never think about the sufferings going on in the world." Then Mrs. Hauser, whose husband manufactures pianos, says, "You could have given us a cheaper cut if you had thought." Mrs. Armstrong, whose husband owns several newspapers around here, says, "But maybe the story is not true, the woman may be a fraud." My lady replies, "I shall make it my business to find out. All of you leave everything to me." "The old refrain," says Mrs. Robbins—she too is kwizzical. I hear all this because I am waiting table and am passing the filly minyong, which is a French name.

Well, Mother dear, someday I will tell you many more things about these great rich people, whose ways I am learning, but I don't want to take too long from my devotions now. I am getting an education of a sort. I am learning how to meet them and to take care of myself, and after Rachel has become a doctor I will be able to save some money, and perhaps go to college myself, who can say? Best love to you and dear Grampa from

Pamela

LETTER XX

Dear Sister:

A strange, strange lot of people your little sister has fallen among! Would you believe it, Miss Yvette came today with friends, stayed a while but did not even see her nephew, to say nothing of trying to help him, and then she went off again. She telephoned that she was coming, so a special good lunch was got ready for four extras; she came with her rodeo rider and a very sporty married couple. They ate lunch, talking about dog races the while, and after lunch they played the game called pingpong; it is little balls they knock back and forth with wooden paddles, and they are amazing skillful; they bang and slam and I was not supposed to watch but I got a glimpse between some porteers. After that they have a swim in the pool though it is cold, and oh, my dear, would you believe it, the three young ladies wore in front of the man those same so-scanty bathing suits, and the man wore only a pair of trunks. I did not steal any looks at that but talked about it with Miss Lucy, who says it is the custom and they all do it when the young people are at home, and they do it at the beaches and wherever they are. She says the missionaries taught the savages to put on clothes and now the smart people have gone back to where the savages were. "Well," I say to her, "it is not for me."

The four young ones went away in Miss Yvette's fancy car. I have just come from Miss Lucy's room, where she told me that Miss Yvette went up to greet her sister for a few minutes and she may have asked about Master Charles but she did not see him; they do not like each other and stay apart. Miss Lucy explains that Miss Yvette is very conservative, having her brother-in-law's ideas, while Master Charles has some of his aunt's ideas, and they might make two pairs of friends, except that the young master is bored to death by his aunt and Miss Yvette doesn't really care very much for anybody but Miss Carol and some other young women who make what is called her "set." It seems that these fashionable people have a saying, "God gave us our relatives, thank God we can choose our friends," and so it is in this strange family. There are four sets, and it seems that I am in one of them—young master has chosen me for his latest friend, and I am wondering what is going to come of it for me.

He did not come down until his younger aunt was gone. I had been worried, for fear he might have got hold of some liquor, perhaps from some of the men on the place. But no, he looks some better and has a little color, and when he sees me emptying the ash trays from the visit—for they have smoked, all four—he says, "Well, you have been seeing the social whirl, and how do you like it?" I say, "I did not see much, sir, and that little I did not find so good." Says he, "It is as rotten as that devil you believe in, but it does not show in public and so it is to be set over me." I say, "I do not know what that means, set over you, Master Charles." He answers, "Have you not been told that she is to be the heiress, and will have the fortune, and will control me?" I am shocked and say, "No, I have not heard that." I wish that he would not tell me such things, but he has his wish, not mine. Says he, "Oh, yes, she is to have full charge of me and tell me how much I should spend. I would get drunk, you see, and gamble it all away the first chance I had!" "Oh, sir!" I exclaim. "How much better it would be if nobody could say such things about you—if you did not

ever drink or gamble. Both those things are evil, nobody
can deny, and you have far too much good sense not to
know that in your heart." "And you are going to convert
me and make a good religious man out of me!" he says.

When he was speaking of his young aunt there was fury
in his voice, but now I know that he is making fun of me.
I say, "You know in your heart that I am right and that you
would be a happier man if you believed what I do." He
says, and this time means it, "Yes, my dear, you are right,
and I would give a lot if I could believe it, but unfortu-
nately I can't. This world was not made to please me, but
is something very stubborn that I could not change if I
would." I tell him, in the words of John, "I can of mine
own self do nothing; I seek not mine own will, but the will
of the Father which hath sent me." But he does not wish
to believe that or to hear about it; says he, "It would be
the greatest comfort to think that, but I don't seem to hear
the call. Would you like to play a game of checkers and see
how much you have managed to learn?"

We play for a while, and of course he is bored, because I
am no good. He says, "I am all right now, and let us go for
a ride." I have no clothes fit to go with him in the daytime,
and I want to say it, but I check myself because it might
sound like a hint for him to get me some better, and may
God help me never to make that mistake. I decide that I
will just take no thought, according to the words of Jesus.
He gets his fine car and we go without a word to anybody;
the housekeeper will have to make of it what she can, or
maybe the mistress has told her that I am promoted. There
are most wonderful roads all about us, and he knows them,
and we roll along and there is one fine sight after another,
and since I know he is not in the mood for religion I talk
about the beautiful world God has made, and he says, "Yes,
but man has defaced it with advertising signs." I can see

that he is like his aunt, he is not disposed to admit anything good about the human race, and I suppose I should agree with him since we are told that man is a fallen creature and that the devil is the prince of the world.

He wants to be kind, and he likes to tell me the things he knows, so I show interest while he talks about the history of this state; how, long ago, the Spaniards came in by the way of Mexico, and found the Indians ignorant and dirty, and set up missions to teach them to live better. We come to one of these old missions, built of adobe, and there is a great vine that was planted by the priests. Young master says he has never seen inside the place and it might be interesting, so we get out. I know that it is Popery but resolve not to say a word. A young priest comes, wearing a black robe which I find ugly; but he is handsome. He takes us around and shows us everything; there is an altar with images and paintings, and I know that this is idol worship, but I do not speak against it, and I think perhaps it may have been better than what the poor Indians had. When we leave, Master Charles gives the priest a dollar bill for his trouble and tells me that is one of the ways the old mission is supported.

We start driving again. I see that he is still nervous and restless, and the driving keeps him satisfied. He has no special place to go, and I do not ask him; he just drives, and I admire the scenery and talk about it. The Merseedys is a wonderful car, and just flows along, and when I comment on that he tells me I may drive it, and I need not be afraid, it will behave like the small car, only more quickly. So we change places, and I drive, and I find that the car obeys my lightest touch, and I exclaim about it and can understand what a pleasure it is to own. Then I wonder if I am being corrupted, and if the first thing I know I will be liking fur coats and jewels. Yes, the devil is a roaring lion, and goes about ravening the prey! But I tell him in my heart that he will not rule me, and that I would surely not be driving this foreign car which cost six thousand dollars if it were not that I am trying to save the soul of an unhappy young man.

He says that he is hungry, and we come to a cafe beside the highway, and I know that I am not dressed for a fashionable place, but he says to hell with it and we go in. He will have fried chicken, and he tries to tempt me, and can hardly believe that I have never tasted meat. When I say that I would not have a chicken killed for me, he says, "The chicken is dead already, and anyhow, I am going to have half of it and the other half cannot live alone." We have fun with jokes; he gets me a vegetable plate with an egg on it and says I am killing what would have been a chicken. I say, "Yes, but it isn't yet, and it doesn't know what it might be." He watches me eat and says, "It is hard to believe that you can have such a lovely color on such a diet." I answer, "I can tell you how to have just such a color if you will let me." He does not ask how, for he knows, of course. He is having a large glass of lemonade, which I am told is a help to poor victims of the demon rum.

Well, we drive again, and I make myself entertaining by asking him about himself. He talks more about Paris, which he loves. He talks about Hollywood and says it is a bad place indeed; that everybody there is putting up a bluff and trying to be greater than somebody else and few indeed are happy. He talks about Lotta Lane, and says she is a bitch; I ask if he is in love with her and he says, "How could I be?" I say, "Then why do you go around with her?" and he says, "I have to go around with somebody. But she is a dummy; she just goes through the motions which the director teaches her. She does not know anything herself." I say, "I do not know anything, either," and he answers, "Yes, but you will learn." I say, very earnest, "I am honestly trying to, Master Charles," and he says, "Stop mastering me; I don't want to be your master, I want to be your friend. Call me Charles." I tell him, "I am afraid to, I might get the habit and say it before the other help." He says, "To hell with them!" and I do not rebuke his language, because I am trying to help him, and I am thinking that it is much worse for him to get drunk than to use swear words. Tell me if you think that is right.

He puts one hand on mine as he drives, and this time I do not draw it away. My mistress has told me to try to keep him happy, and I have prayed over it and asked God what to do. I like his hand, and a lovely feeling steals over me when he takes it in mine. But also I am frightened by my feelings, and I think, what is he going to do now, and can this be right? I have never in my life been so mixed up about anything. I say, this is temptation; this car is temptation, and this lovely ride; the devil is after me. But if I can save this young man from getting drunk again, will not that be a victory over Satan? I try to put myself in Satan's place and guess which he would prefer, to have me being kissed or to have Master Charles drunk. I fear I am not very good at taking Satan's place, for I never wanted to hurt anybody in my life, and it is hard for me to imagine such an attitude as malice.

We are in a quiet spot and he parks the car under a tree where the moonlight is not so strong. He takes my hand in his and says, "How is it going to be this time, Pam? If I should kiss you, will you have hysterics again?" I say, "Master Charles, that is, Charles, I want so much to be good to you and help you, and I am willing to do whatever my conscience permits." "And you are not sure if your conscience permits you to be kissed by a young man?" "Yes, sir, that is the truth!" "You have never been kissed before?" "Oh, sir, surely not!" "You have never even thought of it?" "Oh, sir, I never have!" "Well, I don't know, I had the idea that girls sometimes think of it." "No, sir, I never did. I lived very much alone on our ranch." "But you went to school, didn't you? And no boy ever offered to kiss you?" "I guess it was my faith, which is very strict. My mother warned me."

He sits a while and holds my hand and plays with it, and I am no less frightened, but I see that he is trying to reassure me, and I want so much not to displease him. I have thought it over and guessed that perhaps the reason he went off and got drunk was that I had repelled him so severely, and I surely don't want to have that on my conscience a second time. He says, "You are really a good girl, aren't you, Pam?" and I say, "I really am trying to be, that I can assure you." He says, "You are the first really good one I have ever known." "Oh, sir," I cry, "don't say that!" But he says, "You're telling me the truth, and why shouldn't I tell you the truth?" To that I have no answer; he thinks for a while and says, "You talked with my aunt about this, didn't you?" I say, "She asked me, and it was my duty to answer." "She asked you to help set me straight?" "Yes, sir." "She told you that you might go driving with me?" "Yes, Master—I mean, Charles." "And she told you that I might kiss you?" "Yes." "Did she say how many times I might kiss you?" "No, she did not say." "Did she say how far I might go?" "No, sir, I think she left that to my judgment."

He is leaning toward me, looking into my eyes; there is enough moonlight for me to see that he is smiling; he has a funny little chuckle, like a baby's. He says, "Let us try a little experiment, Pam." I say, "What, sir?" and he says, "First, leave out the sirs. We are not in the Army. Second, I will kiss you, very, very gently, and see if it hurts." I am afraid to speak, but he is holding my hand, and I suppose it is trembling; he leans closer and puts a very gentle kiss upon my lips, and then he draws back and says, "There! Did that hurt so much?" I have to admit that it did not; more than that I would not say, but I know that it made me strangely excited, and every moment I grow more distressed by uncertainty. But he, apparently, has none; he is as gay as a child and takes it as a game. He says, "Let us try it again," and he touches my lips once more, but this time he lingers a bit longer. "You see," he says, "it doesn't hurt a bit, but on the contrary is a very pleasant feeling. And all the time you have the knowledge that you are giving me the same sensation, only more so. Love is a delightful thing, and has never harmed anybody in this world if they are wise and careful about it."

His arm has stolen behind me, and now he is drawing me to him, and he says, "You are the sweetest child I ever dreamed of, and I would not harm you for all the treasures of the world. I am happy with you, and this can be the happiest time of my life. May I kiss you once again?" I am ashamed to admit that I murmured my consent, and he put both his arms about me and drew me to him, and pressed a kiss upon my lips that was different from the others, it did not come to an end, but stayed there; and such a feeling came over me as I had never imagined, a trembling of my whole body, and it seemed like my heart was going to break out of where it is. But a great fear came with it, and the fear increased, and it was as if I heard an alarm bell clanging in my soul. I could not get free from his embrace, but I turned my face away from his kiss, and said, "Oh, no, sir, that is enough! We must not go on!" But he would not give up, he held me fast, and where before he had kissed my lips he now kissed my neck with force that terrified me. I cried again, "No, no, Master Charles, it is not right!"

Well, we had quite a struggle. I began to cry as before

and to be beside myself with fright. It was a strange set of emotions, Sister, for I knew at the same time that I liked to be in his arms, and half my fright was that. I was alone with him in this lonely place, but my greatest fear was that I might give way and let him do what he wanted. I was ashamed of myself, and still am, but I am being honest with myself and with you too. My fear became terror, and I had a great fit of weeping and trembling, and that annoyed him, as it did before. He said, "Are you going to make a fool of me again?" and I cried, "Oh, do not say that! I am trying to be honest and good to you, sir, but it is not right, I know it is not right!" "What harm have I done you, girl?" And that I cannot tell him, I can only say, "I am a poor country creature and I cannot argue with you, sir, but I cannot let you do it." And so it is all spoiled. He is angry, and calls me a fool, and it only makes me weep the more. "Oh, sir, I have tried so hard to help you, and I have failed! You must take me home." So he starts the car, and as I go on sobbing he says, "Stop it, for God's sake. I am not hurting you now, am I?" To that I said, "It is not the hurt, it is that I wanted so to help you and I have failed so miserable." "Forget it," he says. "It is my fault, I should have known that you were too ignorant." "Yes, sir," I say, "I know I am ignorant and I told you so. I do not know the sort of things that movie actresses know, and I cannot behave like one of them."

"What is it that scares you so?" he asks after a while. "Is it that you are afraid you will become pregnant?" I had never expected in my life to hear a man use such a word to me, unless perhaps it was a doctor. But here I am, and I don't want to make things worse than I have already, so I say, between my sobs, "I did not think of that, I only think it is wrong." "Because if you did," he goes on, "you should be told about birth control, which makes all the difference in the world in our attitude to love. Do you know about that?" I can only tell him that I do not know what he is talking about, so he goes on—oh, Sister, do not be too shocked, maybe you have heard about this, I cannot guess. I cannot bring myself to put it on paper, only to say that it means you need not have any babies if you don't want them, even though you are married. And here I sit, and he tells me exactly how it is done, and I am as if paralyzed, I cannot make one sound, only just sit and shudder. Of course I could jump out of the car, and I think of it, but it is going very fast and I don't. He says, "So you see, it is perfectly safe and you have nothing to fear. That makes all the difference in the world, and turns what might be a danger to you into a harmless pleasure. Can't you see that?"

I have to try to find a voice; and I manage to say, "Oh, sir, I have studied the Word of God, and I have never anywhere read that the reason for not being sinful is that you might have a baby. Sin is sin, and it is forbidden in place after place, and it is because it is against God's will. It is one of the ways by which the devil brings men and women to ruin, and to lose their immortal souls." "I don't know that old book the way you do," he says. "I cannot out-quote you, but I am sure it says a lot in favor of love." "Yes, but that is the love of brothers and sisters, it is not the love of man and woman. For that there is a special word which I do not like to repeat to a young gentleman." "Even though it is the Word of God?" "Yes, sir, even so." "Well, we call it making love nowadays, and it sounds much pleasanter." "No doubt, sir, but that does not change the fact that God has forbidden it." "But then why does he make it so pleasant that everybody wants to do it?" "That I cannot tell you, sir, for I do not know all the ways of God. It distresses me so that I wish you would not talk about it any more."

So for perhaps half an hour he does not say one word,

and I think that he must be in a rage, and that perhaps I have lost my position. But then he says, very mild, "All right, Pam, let's call it a night, and I'll let you alone. It is not my fault or yours that we were brought up in different worlds. We can still be friends, can't we?" I brighten up and say, "Oh, yes indeed; and I do hope you will let me help you." "Help?" he says. "Nobody can help me; I am a lost soul." It is dark and I cannot see his face, and I do not know if he is sad or if he is joking. I say, "You must not say that, Charles"—I get the courage to call him what he has told me. "There is a hymn that says, 'While the lamp holds out to burn, the vilest sinner may return.'" So he begins to chuckle and says, "That's me, for sure!" And he goes on chuckling for some time.

Well, Sister, this is the longest of letters. I have sat up late for two nights writing it. Do not worry about me, I have not lost my place and all is well. I know that you will wish me never to go out driving with him again, and I have taken that resolve. I have become the parlormaid again and am doing my duties. Do not fear for your devoted Sister

Pamela

LETTER XXI

Dear Mother:

I have not written much because there is not much special news. I do my work and have every reason to think that I am giving satisfaction to my mistress. She does me special favors, such as to offer me a candy when she is eating some, or to ask me how my mother and sister are getting along, and of course I have only good reports to give to her. She talks to me about the problems of her nephew, which of course she would not do if she did not have faith in my discretion. He is not very happy, and I have ventured to tell her that it is because he does not have to work; she admits that I am right, but alas, I fear she lacks the will to refuse to give him money.

She is a lady of the kindest heart that ever I knew. There are some workingmen on strike, and she had been told that they are mistreated by the police and others, and she is in a dreadful state of mind about it. It seems that the world is a more cruel place than you or I have ever dreamed. My good lady who has everything is not content to help those she sees about her, but wants to help everybody all over the world, and that is something that I fear cannot be done in this life. But it is not for me to argue with her, and I don't think God will expect it of me.

Give my best love to Grampa and tell him he is not to work too hard, he has sure done his share. Tell him he can count upon my twenty dollars regular, for I am surely going to hold onto this place that has been a gift of Providence to my family. What we have done to deserve it is hidden in the mind of the Lord. Your dutiful Daughter

Pamela

LETTER XXII

Dear Sister:

I have read and studied your dear letter, and it is kind of you to take so much time from your studies; but pray do not worry for I am in no danger, really. Of course I know that you would be willing to get along without my earnings, but I am sure it would be a mistake to give up this position. I may do some good here, and I know I am doing good to myself. I can get a better position someday if I understand the ways of educated persons. I would go back to tending goats if I had to, but I much prefer to meet such people and learn from them.

A week has passed since my ride with young master, and he has not bothered me. When he passes me in the house he says, "Hello, Pam," very cheerful, as if nothing had happened. He is letting me alone, and perhaps thinks he is teaching me a lesson. I am willing to learn it. Very nice to ride in the fine car, and learn to drive it, but the price is higher than I guessed. I find that I am thinking about him a great deal, and wishing that I could help him, for I know that he has good in his soul, if only he had not been mistaught and accustomed to idleness and pleasure-seeking. But he will not hear me, and I have to leave him to God.

Miss Yvette had been here, and they seem friendly, but that is the way of these elegant ones, they do not show what is in their hearts, except now and then when it bursts out like a volcano. She went with her brother-in-law to a show of some sort, and stayed the night here, and then off she went again. Such a smart young lady—you hardly ever see any of these people in the same clothes twice, or at least so it seems to me. They are always so fresh and clean, with never a spot or even the smallest wrinkle. Poor me, I question my wicked soul, is that one of the reasons I am so impressed by Master Charles? I have to admit that it is—and also that my heart bumps in a most uncomfortable way whenever I catch a glimpse of him. I say, "Get thee behind me, Satan!" But who am I that Satan should have to obey me?

Today he brought another actress in his car. This time she is really beautiful; she is young and has deep rich coloring which I think is her own, and she speaks with a quiet ladylike voice—or so it seems to this goatherd who is getting to be so knowing. It is my day to wait table, and though I am asked I refuse to give it up, I am so curious about her. I wonder again, is he bringing her here to show me what I might so easily be? Or just to spite me—but no, I don't think that is fair, for he is not a mean person. I have decided that he is well meaning but weak, and needs somebody to guide him.

Well, I pick what scraps of conversation I can while I bring them pieces of the leg of a lamb spread on a silver platter, and then mashed potatoes and green peas in a dish that is divided in half and holds both. It seems that she has learned to act in the place called Greenwich Village, and now she has come to Hollywood and it is hard for her here, because the type that is favored is a little cutie, and she is not that but is what young master calls the Greek goddess type. He has promised to help her get a job in spite of this, and I wonder if she is paying the price which he has so carefully explained to me. I would much prefer not to have such a thought about beautiful young women, but he has put it into my mind and there is no way to get it out that I know. I think, oh, yes, he is putting me in my place, and showing me that he can get much better ones than poor me, and I cannot for a moment doubt that she has many more charms than I can offer. Afterwards I talk with Miss Lucy about it, and she gives me a strange idea, that it is the nature of men to value more what they cannot get than what they get too easily. If that should be true, then the ranch girl who believes in God may have something over the Greek goddess named Sylvia Sloane. Too bad that I do not want it!

I have a sad story to add to this. There has been a terrible quarrel between the master and the mistress. Oh, my, I never heard the like! He had gone to her room, which is upstairs in front, at the head of the stairway which curves in a half circle as it goes up; he has not bothered to shut the door, he does not care if all the help hear and maybe he wants them to. I must tell you that there are workingmen called IWW that are radicals, and they are trying to organize the ranch workers; they are supposed to be terrible people, only my lady insists it is not so. Some of them have been beaten and some put in jail, and she is very indignant about it and defends them. She has two of them come to the house to talk to her, and now she is talking of inviting them to come on Sunday afternoon and tell the story of their troubles, and the master is wild about it; he roared and shouted and said God-damn and bastards and other awful words that I will not put on paper. I did not hear a word from her for she never raises her voice, but she must have defied him, for, oh, dear, he got worse and worse, and I feared that he might strike her or even kill her. He called on Jesus Christ, but he did not mean it in a reverent way, it was just an oath. This went on for a long time, and it was hard to see how a man could stand such rage and not burst something inside, as indeed he will some day, Miss Lucy says. He came tearing downstairs and rushed out of the house and, believe me, I was hidden safe in the telephone closet when he came by. Miss Lucy says he does like this every now and then, but it does him no good whatever; she has never given an inch except to say that she will always give him notice so that he can make his plans to be elsewhere. The trouble is the meetings get into the papers and that is what makes him most angry of all.

Well, you can see that I am in the midst of excitements. Miss Bascom is addressing the cards, and the meeting is to

be, and everybody wonders, will he come there and make a
scene and maybe beat up the wobblies, as they are called?
She has told him that if he interferes she will have him arrested, for it is her house. Will he? And will she? Oh, dear!
Master Charles has gone back to Hollywood and will not
be in the mixup and neither will Miss Yvette who is at her
beach place. But all of us women help are in a flutter, and
those who have to be here wish they didn't, and those who
have leave half wish they hadn't. I go upstairs and read my
Testament to calm my mind. I am sure that God knows
whether these wobblies are as bad as they are painted, and
He is the one to deal with them. I shall have my Sabbath,
and go to church if the weather permits the walk, and am
sure that all will be well, so have no worry for your devoted
Sister

Pamela

LETTER XXIII

Dear Sister:

Well, the terrible Sunday has come and gone, and the
earth did not open up and swallow us. Mr. Harries did not
come as he had threatened. The company came, and I laid
out the food for them and did my many duties that I have
learned well. The two wobblies came. They are quite young
fellows, one fair-haired like me and the other darker; they
seemed very decent to me, and they told terrible stories so
that I could not keep the tears out of my eyes. It seems
that they are beaten and driven out of the great ranches
where they try to get the men to join them—it is called

organizing. They are accused of all sorts of crimes such as setting fire to haystacks and driving copper nails into fruit trees to kill them; that is what you see in the papers, but Mrs. Harries had written a letter to the government in Washington, the Forestry Service it is called, and she read aloud their letter saying that there is no possible way that copper nails could hurt fruit trees.

There were many speeches, and some people agreed to write to the newspapers and call upon the editors to protest; that was the worst that happened, except that my lady shed tears and so did some of the others. I have no doubt that she gave the men some money, which would make her husband still more angry. I have been made to see that I have been very ignorant about what are called social questions; for if I had read these stories in the papers I would have believed them but now I do not. I went to my room and read James 5 again: "Behold, the hire of the laborers who have reaped down your fields, which you have kept back by fraud, crieth; and the cries of them which have reaped have entered into the ears of the Lord of Sabaoth."

Among the people that come to the Sundays there is a preacher, at least he is called that; he is a Unitarian, and Miss Lucy tells me that these people do not believe that Jesus is the Son of God, which I suppose makes him worse even than the Papists, for he has had his chance and has rejected it. He is a tall, scholarly-looking gentleman with iron-gray hair and spectacles, and he and his wife have been twice invited to dinner, which means that they are special people, and so I have to be polite to them and keep my opinions of Unitarians to myself. His wife is a little woman, very quick and lively, and as usual I am troubled that I have to think evil things about persons who appear to be so good. She often says what she thinks at meetings, and Dr.

Clark is always called upon by my lady, who has a high opinion of him. I suppose she gives him money for his church; she gives it to everybody she likes, except the rich ladies who of course have their own. She rarely lets a Sunday go by without saying, "It is the state that should print this money and put it into circulation. It is absurd to tax people, or to let anybody be in want in a world where there is plenty of everything."

I tell you about the Clarks because now there is another adventure. My lady sends for me and tells me that some of the wobblies have committed the offense of singing in jail, which they do, and they have been put in solitary confinement, each one in a cell with nothing but bread and water; they have been there for two weeks, and my mistress cannot sleep for thinking about it, and now she will drive up to San Quentin prison to protest to the warden about it. Mrs. Clark is going with her, and she would take Miss Bascom along only she has a cold, and so I am to be the one to go and wait upon her. Of course I am happy, and tell her so, and we are to start tomorrow morning. San Quentin is in back of San Francisco Bay and we go by the inland route and it is something like five hundred miles, which we will drive in two days and a half, stopping at hotels. Could you believe that your Little Sister was going to see the world like this—the outside of a great prison and perhaps the inside too? I have not done anything so they cannot keep me there, and I hope they do not keep my good lady, but I am scared. I will be sure to write you the news from your devoted Sister

Pamela

LETTER XXIV

Dear Sister:

Well, I have had a lot of adventures and will tell them to you, and if it is too much for one letter I will make it more. I have been inside San Quentin prison, but they were very polite and let me out again, so I did not need to worry. "Sick and in prison and ye visited me not"—the blessed Lord will never be able to say that to me!

To begin with, I had a long, long ride in the big black Packard, which is called a limousine and I am told costs five thousand dollars—just think of it! We passed within a few miles of our ranch, but I could of course not expect that great ladies would delay for me or my mother. We went by Foothill Boulevard and by what is called the Ridge Route which winds through the Tehachapi Mountains and then into the great wide San Joaquin Valley, where you see the High Sierras all the way on your right. It is bright sunshine, and Pietro just sits there all day without a word and drives, maybe forty miles an hour, maybe fifty, my mistress does not seem to care how fast; the great car rolls along so smooth and presently you get used to it and hardly know that you are moving. The two ladies sit in the big back seat with plenty of room to spread and to have their things, and I sit on one of the little folding seats with my back to them; so it is easy for them to forget that I am there, and they go on talking, and I listen and learn all kinds of things which are new to me, some of them pleasant and some frightening.

I learn about the Unitarians; they believe in God, and

they believe that Jesus was a great and good man, which I suppose is better than nothing. Mrs. Clark tells all about God to Mrs. Harries, but my lady has no use for God whatever and will not hear to Him. She says that she could manage things much better, and she tells Him just what she would do; no woman would be allowed to have more than two or three babies, and then there would be plenty of food for all; also the government would print enough money so that everybody could buy what they need. Mrs. Clark doesn't think that would work and explains that if you print a lot of money you increase the prices of goods, because there is more money bidding for the goods on the market; but my lady argues that as the goods were bought up, the manufacturers would see that more goods were required and would make them, hoping to get a larger share of the money. As I listen, I find that each side sounds reasonable to me, and I guess it means that I have not a very good head for what they call economic questions.

I learn that Mrs. Clark is a Socialist, and she is trying to convert Mrs. Harries to her ideas, this being a very good time, since they are alone together (not counting me at all) and she has no way to escape. Miss Lucy has told me how all sorts of people try to put their ideas into her mind, since of course she will give money more freely to the causes she believes in; it has happened more than once that she gives to causes which are contradictory, only because she likes the people who are promoting them. Mrs. Clark explains that many people think that Socialism means dividing up, but this is not so, and no doubt that will help her with my lady, who I am sure would not believe in dividing up the Rancho Casa Grande. What Mrs. Clark believes in is making the great trusts, the big industries, into national enterprises, and my lady says she believes in that heartily. I sit as still as a little mouse, and I wonder, what would she be saying when it came the time to nationalize the Penn Shipbuilding Corporation? That doesn't need to worry me, of course; what I want is to learn the meaning of the long words they use, and someday perhaps I'll be able to have an idea of my own.

Well, we spend the night in a place called Madera, in a very nice old hotel, and I have a maid's room to myself, and a bathroom which I share only with another maid, whose mistress is coming from Seattle, a tremendous long way off, to spend the winter in Palm Springs—so the great ladies travel around. This maid is older than me; and she wants to know how I learned so young, and who is in the family and especially what gentlemen, and I tell her that the master is away a lot and hardly speaks to me, but the young master is very friendly. She asks, "Has he made love to you?" I think, I am never going to see this woman again, and all I know is her first name which is Dora, and all I have told her is Pamela, so what does it matter, I might learn something from her. And so I say, "He kissed me several times, but I would not let him go any further." Says she, "What has he offered you?" and I answer, "Offered me? He has not offered me anything but love," and she says, "Oh, you poor kid! If they are as rich as you say, he should give you a diamond ring at least; and make sure it isn't a phony." I have learned enough about the world to know that it would do no good to be shocked, or to talk to her about my faith, for I suspect that she is a Papist. I just let her talk, and she tells me her experiences, and I will not repeat them, dear Sister, for I doubt if you have ever met any person like that. I say that I am to be called at seven and I am tired, so good night, and I say my prayers. I do not say, "I thank Thee, God, that I am not as Dora," but I say, "I thank Thee, God, that I have Thee in my soul."

In the morning my lady has breakfast in her room, and I

eat in the coffee shop, and Pietro is there and we have a chat; he is a nice fellow and likes me, and he talks about his little ones which he calls bambini. I help my lady to pack all those fifty-four articles which she brings with her, and the dresses which are of very soft and delicate material called chiffon; I learn all the names. Some things are of silver and ivory, and I have never seen any so beautiful, and once or twice I exclaim and she does not mind that. She has a diamond ring on the dresser and I make sure she does not leave that or anything else. I do not have to carry anything down because the boy carries them all, two bags in each hand and one more under each arm. My lady gives me money and tells me to pay the bill, which is about thirty dollars, including the dinners last night, and she says it is not an expensive place. She tells me to tip the chambermaid and the boy, and I have to ask her how much. When I give her the change she hands me back five dollars which is to be for my breakfast and other expenses; when I tell her that my breakfast cost only thirty cents she says that I am not to stint myself. Later I learn that I have pleased her, for she is disgusted with people who travel with her and try to get things they are not used to at home. When she takes a lot of women to dinner she will limit them to one dollar each. For me, that is twice what I ever spent in a cafe in my life.

We drive again and come in the afternoon to the great prison, which is built on a sort of point in the bay and has walls around it. I would say it was beautiful if it was not so terrible; there are several thousand men kept there, and I doubt if they find any beauty. They are Satan's victims; he has got into their hearts and is here with them, I doubt not. I would like to be a missionary and come and try to save them; so I think, and then I learn that this is to come about, at least in part. Mrs. Harries has telephoned to the prison and been told what the visitors' hours are, and that each visitor is permitted to see only one prisoner whom she must ask for by name, and those prisoners who are in solitary are not permitted to receive visits. My lady has a list of the wobblies, and it is her idea that she will ask for one of them, and Mrs. Clark for another, and me for another, and that way we will bring some comfort and support to three of these oppressed workers. I do not know the names of these men, except two or three that I have heard have been abused. "What on earth shall I say to him?" I ask, and Mrs. Harries says, "You have heard some of the talk in our home and you are sorry for him, are you not?" I answer, "Indeed, yes, Mrs. Harries." "Well, then, tell him so. Speak to him as a human being, and let him know that you understand what he is trying to do for his fellow workers and the sacrifice he is making. Say that we are trying to awaken the public to what is going on and that they are not entirely forgotten in this dungeon. Can you not say that?" I tell her that I can; and she adds, "Don't say anything about religion, because they don't believe in that, they call it pie in the sky." I have never heard those words and naturally they puzzle me; she explains that they have a song in which they mock the preachers, saying, "You'll have pie in the sky when you die." She does not know how that hurts me and I do not tell her; I will see the man, and if I say something about my faith, it will surely not hurt him.

We have to sign our names when we go in by the big gate; then we are taken to the office, and each of us has a list of men to ask for, and we read down the list until we come to one who is not being punished. We are taken into the room where the interviews are to be and we are told to sit on a bench and wait until the men have been brought. It is a long room and down the middle from floor to ceiling is a screen with small mesh, very strong no doubt. That is so that we cannot give the prisoners anything but only speak to them; there are stools that we are to sit on, and stools for them on their side. We wait, and are alone, and there happens something so funny that I laugh whenever I think of it, and I have no doubt it will be so the rest of my life. I must explain that my lady does what she calls facials, which are exercises of the muscles of her face so that they will not get flabby and sag. I do not know if she invented these or if they have been taught to her; anyhow, she lets her jaw way down and then snaps it up sharp; she twists her mouth first to one side and then to the other; she wiggles her cheeks, she sticks out her lips, she turns her eyes this way and that. These facials she will do at odd moments, such as I take for prayer; and as our wait turns out to be long, she thinks this is a good moment. She is making the most extraordinary faces, but she is so used to it that she forgets how she looks to others. I look around the room and discover that at one end, high up, there is a small hole, and at that hole there is plainly to be seen an eye; I realize that there is a guard there, keeping watch to see that we do not break any of the regulations. I whisper to my lady, "There is a man watching!" I expect that she will be embarrassed, but it goes to show that I do not yet know her. She says, "Well, what of it?" and goes right on with her facials.

Well, the prisoners are brought, and after that I cannot think of anything funny. My man is young and has fair hair like me. I have been expecting somebody dangerous and wicked looking, but this boy might be my older brother if I had one. He has bright blue eyes and a frank look, and it gives me a shock to see him here in a cage like some wild animal and with a guard standing behind him. He is looking at me, as if to say, "What is this?" so I tell him that I am maid to Mrs. Harries and that she is a friend of the workers, and I tell him of the two who came to speak at her home, and how she has come here to plead with the warden. So he knows that it is all right, and he says, "We are not criminals but political prisoners, and we do not recognize the class justice which has put us here." I say, "I thought you might like to know that you have friends outside," and he says, "Sure thing, and thank you ever so much, and I am glad it is a working girl that can understand her own class." He tells me that he is the son of a poor farmer, and has become an agricultural worker, and an organizer of them, and will go on as long as he lives, and nothing 'the class enemy can do will weaken him. I promise to take that message out for him, and he tells me of one of the wobbly songs that says, "Remember, you're outside for us while we're inside for you."

Paul Darrow is his name, and he tells me that he is in for eight years, and they will give parole to burglars and hold-up men for good conduct, but never to politicals. I know that I have only a short time to talk and when I have heard his story I tell him, "I want you to know that I am a religious girl, but it is not the pie in the sky sort, but the kind that believes in the brotherhood of man now." He says that kind is okay by him. I tell him that the rulers who crucified the Savior have taken over His churches, but that the humble people have Him in their hearts, and they have His promise to cast down the mighty from their seats and to exalt the humble and the meek. I tell him, speaking fast, that God is in his heart and will give him courage to bear all oppression. I tell him to ask for help and he will find that it comes. He sees that I have tears in my eyes and knows that I am speaking from my heart. He says, "All right, Miss, I'll think about it and maybe give it a try."

Then the guard tells us that the time is up and the boy is led away.

There are the other two ladies, also with tears in their eyes. Mrs. Harries has asked to see the warden and takes us with her. The guard leads us to the office, and there is the man. He is polite, but hard and cold, and you can see that he is not going to let himself be weakened by anything we women can say to him. Mrs. Harries does the talking, and I have never heard her speak so well. She tells him of these men she has met and what their ideals are, and that they are in no way criminals, and that every civilized country except America has special regulations for political prisoners, and gives them special treatment because they are known to be well-meaning men, idealists, not wishing to do harm. "There is no place for such people in America," says the warden, "for this is a free country and they must obey the law, and if they break it they do so at their own risk. As for this prison, there can be no exceptions. I have no choice but to enforce discipline." So they go, back and forth, and you can see that they live in different worlds, it is as if they spoke a different language. Mrs. Harries begs and pleads, but she gets nowhere, and when she goes out she breaks down and weeps, and there are Mrs. Clark and me, one holding one side of her and one the other, and all three of us weeping in each other's arms. Partly it is sorrow for the prisoners, I know, but also I think it is partly that she is not able to have her way, that some man should have the power to say No to her, and it stays No and she cannot help it. She has taken this trip for nothing. That is all for tonight, from your loving Sister

Pamela

LETTER XXV

Dear Sister:

Your little one is seeing the world. We crossed the bay in a great ferryboat, which took perhaps fifty or a hundred cars, besides all the passengers; I got out and stood on the upper deck and looked at the bay with all the docks and ships, and San Francisco which is hills and tall buildings standing up. We stayed in a great hotel where my lady paid thirty-five dollars a day for just the rooms with nothing to eat. The streets are lined with store windows where you can see every sort of wonderful goods, and it would be easy to forget one's faith in God and want these things. But we did not do much shopping, for my lady was mad about those boys "in the hole," as they call the solitary. She has friends here, and one is a newspaper man, and she invited him to lunch and told him about it; also there was a very sweet young woman who is the sister of one of the boys, and she had the heartache, and they did not talk about anything else. The newspaper man will write about it, and meantime your Pamela is learning about what is called the "radical movement," which I thought was wicked, but I have decided that it is not as bad as the rich people who think only of piling up their millions and care nothing about the sufferings of the poor.

Well, we drive home by the coast route, which is some wonderful scenery, and when we have turned into the interior my lady says, "Would you not like to see your mother?" I give a little cry and then choke up, and she says, "All right, we will stop, but not for too long." She tells Pietro, who knows the way, having not forgot the broken connecting rod; now the weather is not so hot and it will not happen again. So we go, and pretty soon there is the house with a new tarpaper roof, and our sign by the road which amuses my lady: "Washing done. No Saturday visits." Grampa is bringing in cabbages to be safe from the frost. I get out and run up to the house, and there we have a scene, with hugging and some tears. Oh, how happy we are! We talk fast, for the time is short, I dare not keep my great lady waiting. I tell them where I have been, and I quote the psalm to them, "Let the sighing of the prisoner come before thee," and they are almost without speech. I say, "I must go," and Mother makes a quick shift to her Sunday dress, and ties a band about her hair, and down she goes to the car; Grampa will not come for he cannot be made fit so fast.

So Mother tells Mrs. Harries how grateful she is, and hears from my lady's own lips that I have been dutiful and good; and then we go, and I wave and am both sad and happy. My lady never leaves anywhere without making some present, and always has the car half-filled with goods, some of which will never reach her home. This time she has given a fine box of candy, the like of which Mother never saw, I am sure. It is only later I learn that she has tucked under the wrapper one of those twenty-dollar bills which she gets fifty at a time from the bank. "Lady Bountiful," somebody has called her, and that has pleased her.

She says, "Since we are so late we may as well have dinner at the Rancho Conejo." I must tell you that she knows all sorts of eating places, all over Southern California, where you get special things to eat, such as rainbow trout, or borscht, which is Russian, or tacos, which are Mexican, called Spanish; or where she can buy special kinds of candy, Turkish called halvah, or Danish of which I forget the name; or tropical fruits called cheremoyas or sapodillas. At all these places she knows the people, and will talk about what they have, and ask questions about themselves and their families and how they are getting along, and if it is not good she will talk about it afterwards and say it is a disgrace to the country. If she is driving into a town and sees dirty messes by the road she will point it out and write a letter to the mayor or the city manager and tell him to clean up. She calls this being "civic-minded," and if there are vermin in the jails she will write the newspapers; one official called her a "sob sister," and she has never forgiven him for that unkindness.

Well, at the Rancho Conejo, which means rabbit, you can have them, or you can have guineas, which is a kind of small chicken which are half wild and you hear them making a tremendous racket. The place has an inner court, very pretty, and there we sit waiting for our dinner to be prepared and talking with the lady. It is a bit chilly, but Mrs. Harries does not mind, being well padded; Mrs. Clark gets up and walks about. I listen to the conversation, and learn about this little place, and that it does not pay, and why they do not advertise, and enough about the business so that I shall never want to run one. At last our meal is ready and I have three guinea eggs which are small and had to be hunted for out in the desert. All this trip I have eaten with the two ladies, except my breakfast, and I am glad that I have learned how to hold my knife and fork and do everything proper. I run all the errands, pay the bills, do the telephoning, and try every way to make myself useful. When questions are asked, I answer if I can, and when I am not wanted I pretend that I am not there.

At last we get back home, and Charles is there. He did not get drunk, which is a great load off my mind. Perhaps I helped. There is more about him, but it will have to be in another letter, for I have duties to catch up with, and I have promised to tell Miss Lucy my adventures. That is a sort of rule here, everybody who learns anything about the family shares it with the rest; it is passed on and nobody is left out. I can be sure that tonight Pietro is telling his family all that happened on the trip, and tomorrow it will be known even to the Portygees—that is what the American help call them, and are polite to them but do not mix socially. Goodnight and best love from

Pamela

LETTER XXVI

Dear Mother:

Oh, what a joy it was to see you both, and to find you well and the roof fixed. What a joy it will be to hear the first rain beating on it and not have to run for pails and pans!

This is just to tell you that we got home safe, and that my lady had only kind things to say about you and your bringing up of me. That twenty dollars is wonderful and is only a sample of how she works. No one who comes near her is allowed to suffer, but sometimes she does not give as wisely as in this case. I shall not mention that I know about it for fear it might seem like hinting for more.

Do not be worried about my taking up with radicals. My lady says that is used as a bad name; it really means people who want to go to the root of our social evils. She says the newspapers do not always tell the truth, and she can prove it to anyone who will listen. Believe me, my religious faith is unshaken. I can speak up for God, even in the state prison, and I did. Best love to both, from your devoted Daughter

Pamela

LETTER XXVII

Dear Sister:

This is another story about Charles—he has told me again to call him that. You ask me to promise to tell you everything that happens, and I do promise—it will be a good way to make sure that nothing bad can happen.

He is polite and friendly, and always as if he was having a little laugh at me. I play a game of checkers with him, and he says, "I want you to know, Pam, I have not touched a drop of liquor for a week, and it has given a great surprise to all my friends." I say, "I am so glad to hear that! You may not know it, but it is the power of God." "Maybe you prayed for me," says he, and I tell him, "I did indeed, and have my answer." "Well," he says, "let us celebrate what all my friends recognize as a miracle. I have not forgotten that I promised to teach you to swim." "Oh, sir," I say, "the water is much too cold now." He says, "I know that. I would not teach you here, there would be too much gossip. I know a place where there is a pool that is warm, and this is a lovely sunshiny day." "Oh, sir!" I say, and do not know what else to say. "You will come?" he insists, and I am blushing furiously, I can feel. "Charles," I say, "I have to speak honestly. I cannot do again what I did that last night." "This," he says, "will be a swimming party. I give you my word that I will not kiss you." "Nor try to, sir?" "Nor try to." "And you will not be vexed with me?" "I will be as cheerful as a cricket is supposed to be. I have not felt so well in a long time." I say, "But I have no suit," and he answers, "It will be possible to find one in a shop." I, playing safe, persist, "And you will let me pick it out?" He knows what I mean and says, "It will be the most modest outfit in the great emporium." I object, "But my duties?" and he says, "Don't worry, I can fix it, and it shall be the best duty you ever did or thought of."

So I pack the little bag which the mistress has given me for trips, and I put on my poor best dress, and my coat for the night which will be cold, and he brings the Mercedes— I have learned that I am spelling it wrong—and away we go. What Mrs. Jessup will think of the undusted drawing room I do not know, and I just have to tell myself that the help do not exist. The wind is whistling by and the scenery goes the same way, but silently. The young master starts telling me about a movie that he remembers; it is by a comic actor called Charlie Chaplin, whom he knows well. It is called "Shoulder Arms!" and is about the war and all the funny things that happen to a new recruit and how terrified he is in the trenches. I have told him that we are not allowed to attend shows, and he asks if we are allowed to be told about them, and I tell him I have never heard that this would be a sin. He tells me how this scared soldier hides in the hollow stump of a tree during the battle; and how there is a German spy who has a tree stump made of paper, so that it is light and he can walk around in it; and how these two get mixed up, and the recruit gets among the Germans. It is so funny that I cannot stop laughing. He asks if I would not like to see such a picture, and I wish I could; then I realize that it must be sinful to be brought to such a state of mind. But I have done it and it is too late.

Well, we come to the beach, and it is all so lovely I am lost in wonder. We park the car and go into a shop and he tells the saleslady that I am to have a suit. She looks me over and takes my size and then holds up one of those scanty things such as I have seen Miss Yvette wearing. I say, very quick, "I want something that is more suit than that." She tells me, "This is the latest thing, Miss," but I say I want something earlier. So she gets me another that is of very fine material, a lovely pale gray color, but alas, where the legs should be is very little, and where the arms should be is nothing, and where the back should be too. I do not quite know how to say it in the presence of a gentleman, especially one who I know is chuckling to himself over my plight. I ask for something with more cloth, and she tells me they do not have them, they are not made any more, it is what everybody is wearing; it is plain that I am showing myself to be a country goose. He says, "Come on, you will be late for the party," and grins; he says that suit will do, and he pays about fifteen dollars for the bit of cloth, and when I protest outside, he says, "You are paying for the style." I am in a panic, because I know I am doing wrong, and the panic is double because if I do not please him he might go off and find a bootlegger here at the beach.

We get into the car again and he tells me, "Really, dear Pam, don't you see that what part of your skin you show is a matter of convention purely? There are parts of the world where you may bare your whole body but not your face. Here nowadays you have to cover your breasts, but if you were in the South Seas you would be perfectly modest in a grass skirt and no more." I feel driven to say, "Back in the hills where I was brought up I had to patch my dresses, but I always had one on." "Of course," he says, "but now you are not in any hills but at the beach, and what is in the shops is what people are wearing, and if you wore your mother's bathing suit, they would think you were a comic character out of a movie."

We are going to what is called a beach club and is a very elegant place—you must learn the word swank, which he calls it. There are bellboys in uniforms with brass buttons, and there are game rooms and tea rooms, and outside are tennis courts and croquet grounds and loggias with deck chairs and striped awnings and all the things I have got used to at Casa Grande. There are two great pools; one is sea water, cold, and one is fresh water, warmed, and for lessons it will be warm, I hope. Apparently Charles belongs to this club, and he registers me as a guest, and I am shown to a dressing room where there are ladies in various stages, and I have a locker. I grit my teeth; I am going to pretend that I am in the South Seas, or worse, and do what the others do. I put on my suit, and I do not dare to look down at myself, to say nothing of a mirror; I flee out to the pool and hope that it will be better when I get into the water. I see ladies of all sorts and sizes, old ones and young, fat ones and lean, and some very pretty, and there isn't a single one with any more suit than mine.

Well, he comes, and he has only trunks on. He leads me into the lovely warm water, the part that is shallow. He has told me a lot about swimming and the strokes, so I am prepared. The first thing I have to learn is that my body will float, so he lets me back and tells me to lie straight and flat, and to breathe natural and not be afraid. He holds his hand under my back and gradually lowers his hand and then takes it away, and I am surprised to discover that I am floating alone. I smile at him and he smiles back and then he bends over me and says, "I am not kissing you!" He is teasing, of course, making as if he almost was, and he is.

Well, now I am turned over and learn to paddle. He holds me up and gives me courage and is very kind and patient; so presently I learn that I can keep myself up and I get over my fright of the water, and have fright of the devil instead, for here I am with this handsome blond young gentleman, and I am half naked or a little more, and he is holding me in various ways, and is making love to me just as much as he ever did before, only he is not kissing me, as he promised. He is holding to the letter of the promise but not the spirit, I should say, and I have been taught that it is the letter that killeth and the spirit that giveth life. In short, he has found a way to outwit me, or perhaps it is Satan who has given it to him. He is not making the least pretense not to be in love with me, but is telling me with his eyes and also his hands, and I am in three kinds of panic, because I am trying to swim in three feet of water, and he is the handsomest man I ever saw and the smartest I ever talked to, and at the same time I have the fear that if I do not keep him happy he might order a drink right at this place. (You can get it here, in spite of the law, only it is served in teacups.) In short, it is the awfulest confusion I have been in yet.

We come out of the pool to rest for a while, and he tells me to lie in the sun as other ladies are doing, and he sits and looks at me and says, "Don't you know that you are perfectly lovely, and that you belong in places like this?" I answer, "It would take me a long time to get used to such an idea as that." Says he, "You are a lady, and maybe the best of the lot." "Until I open my mouth," I say, and he answers, "Well, keep your mouth closed for a while, as when you are swimming." So he sits and pays me compliments, and I see that he is devouring me with his eyes, and I realize too late that I am pleased. In short, I fear I am in love with him, and I want so to save him, but I know that I cannot, and I think, Oh, but I must try! I think, What if he should order a drink, or threaten to? I am in a panic, and I realize exactly how his poor aunt feels, and how her will turns to water in his presence and she cannot deny him anything. But I can, and, oh, I must!

He is looking at me with his desire in his eyes, and he says, "You know you love me, Pam." I say, "Oh, sir," and he says, "Can the sirs! Say Charles, or better, say Dear." I prefer Charles and I say, "This is not the place to talk of such things." He answers, "This is exactly the place, it is what it is built for." "Is that really so?" I ask, and he says, "Here you can see exactly what you are getting. Look me over and see if I please you." His face is all one smile, and if I did not know he was wicked I would think he was an angel. I say, "You are making it hard for me, and doing it on purpose, I fear." "With all the purpose I possess. I am in love with you and you are in love with me, and we can be marvelously happy together."

I have thought about it, oh, a lot, and am resolved to fight it out with him, for he has a good mind, and if I score a point he gets it. I say, "For how long?" and he answers, "Forever and then a night." I tell him, "Be honest to your- self and to me. How long would it be before you were tired of me and wanted some other girl?" "I will see that you never want as long as you live," he said, and I told him, "That is not what I mean. I am earning my living now and can always do it. I am talking about love. If I love a man, it will be for good." Said he, "You are so serious, Pam!" "That is just the difference between us, Charles. To me love is something serious; to you it is play." "It is the loveliest play in the world, my dear; and you are throwing it away." He is leaning over me, murmuring in a soft voice, which sets me to sort of tingling all over. "Darling, you can have anything you want; we will set out in the car and drive to New York; we will go to Paris and see the world. There are so many wonderful sights and so many lovely things I can give you!" I am listening, and all of a sudden I am saying, not to him but just to myself, "The devil taketh him up into an exceeding high mountain and sheweth him all the kingdoms of the world, and the glory of them; and saith unto him, All these things will I give thee, if thou wilt fall down and worship me."

So up I start, and say, "You were teaching me to swim, Charles, and for that I am grateful." I step down into the pool; he has been showing me the strokes, and now I am no longer afraid, I am sure that I can do them, and I start out into the deep water, away from him. I get some water into my mouth but I cough it out and grin at him and say, "How is that?" He sees that I am being game, and he likes that, and says, "Hooray!" So I go on swimming and try the strokes he has shown me, and he follows along the side and watches and corrects me. Pretty soon I get tired, not because it is hard work but because I am so excited; I am proud of myself and at the same time I am frightened, for I know that I have got the best of him, but I am not sure how long it will last. When I come to the steps I climb out and sit by the edge of the pool near other people, so that he will not be able to make love to me too much; but the devil is in him now, and working hard; he sits between me and the others, so that he can look all his feelings at me, and he murmurs, "I love you, I love you, I love you!" So I wait just long enough to get my breath and then I am up again, saying, "We must dress now; it is getting late."

I run to the dressing room. I have had a little rubber cap over my hair so the hair is not wet, and soon I am all ready and wait in the big main room for him. He says, "You can dress faster than any other woman I ever knew," and I would like to tease him about his vast experience, but I don't want to make the kind of jokes that he does. He says, "We will have tea," and leads me to a table, and presently the tea is brought, and I am being served, not serving. He says, "You need never serve anybody again while you live." I say, "Only you?"—for I have listened to smart conversation and learned about how it goes. He says, "How I wish I could take you to dinner and then to a show." But I have had enough of the devil for one day, and I tell him, "You must take me home now, or no one will believe that I am a good girl." He says grudgingly, "You always know exactly what you want, don't you?" I answer, "You have taught me that I am no longer to call you Master."

So we go to the car and he starts to drive, and when he is out of the traffic he lays one hand on mine, and presently he takes mine; I think, he did not promise not to do that. I realize that it is a danger, because those shivery feelings are going all over me and I do not like them; so I say, "You have taught me to swim and I am grateful. Would you be willing to give me another driving lesson?" Says he, "Oh, you kid!"—for of course I do not fool him. He gets out and I slide into his seat and he goes around the car and gets in on the side that has been mine. "Shoot," he says, and right away I forget and kill the engine, and get confused so that he has to tell me all over again. It is just as well, for it takes his mind off his bad thoughts, and I drive slow and careful. There is no handholding now, because when he tries it I say, "That is dangerous," and I am no longer impolite, just teasing. So I drive, and again I am proud of myself, and he watches—he is a careful driver himself and has never had an accident, he tells me. How he does it when he has been drinking I do not ask. I talk about the wonderful car and how it behaves, and he tells me about the other foreign cars he has owned, the Daimler and the Fiat and so on, and I learn more of the things that are elegant and smart. If only I can keep his mind on cars and the places he has driven to and the people he has met, I

will get home safe with nothing bad on my conscience—
and I do. And so, Sister, that is one more day of your
devoted

Pamela

LETTER XXVIII

Dear Sister:

A week has passed, and I have not written because I have
been a hard-working girl again, and no special adventures.
Charles has gone on a trip, I have not been told where;
perhaps he has taken some lady for a vacation. I have come
to suspect that when he tries hard with me and is disappointed he goes away; I hope it is to forget me and not to
spite me, for I hate to think that he might be mean. I
surely wish him no harm, except that of not getting what
he wants from a poor country girl.

I suppose it is foolish of me to worry about him, but I
cannot help it. Whenever I think that he may be drinking
I have a heartache. I cry out to God, why has He allowed
such things to be, and the only answer is that each of us
makes his own fate, chooses his own bed to lie on. But
then I say, "No, this boy's bed was made when his mother
and father were killed in an avalanche, and his uncle and
aunt started to quarreling over him." I try to learn the
right lessons from life, and I hear Charles himself say that
you cannot change the world or the people in it; but I
know that is no doctrine for a Christian. Jesus came into
the world to change men's fate, and He has bid each of us
to strive earnestly to change those about us. The harvest is

plentiful and the laborers are few. May I be a good and earnest one, as I have been in the household of my earthly mistress.

Last night she took part in a most extraordinary scene. I must tell you that she has never stopped fretting about the wobblies and their mistreatment. She reads newspapers both morning and evening and learns what is going on, and when she reads about some IWW "den" being raided or some of them being beaten up, she is very unhappy. All the time that things are being done to her, her orange juice being brought and served or while she is getting her Swedish massage and her oil rub, and while she is giving the day's instructions to Mrs. Jessup and Miss Bascom and even to me, she remarks upon the wicked things that are going on and how hard the hearts of men are. She does not talk to me about God, having promised Mother not to, but I hear her say to others how impossible it is to believe that a good God would permit such things to happen. I have heard her saying it even while she is doing her rolling, which is on the floor, because of her worry that she is growing stouter, and this she has read is a way to prevent it. Another is to take her cane and walk half a mile every evening before dinner, and for this she likes to have company, and twice for lack of it she has invited your humble Sister, and all the way has told me her ideas, which I am learning to understand and to agree with so far as has to do with earthly affairs.

Well, now she has two house guests, or did have until last night. One of them is a poet who has come from San Francisco and whom she met there on our last trip. He is rather young, has lovely wavy hair which is cut long in back, and he wears a black bow tie; I have been told that he is a Communist, and he has been to Russia and is giving lectures telling about it; his picture has been in the papers,

and there have been large headlines and scoldings of him
for having advocated that the workers should do the same
thing in America. The other person is a pretty little lady
who is called his wife, but she keeps her maiden name and
I have learned by now that you cannot always be sure, for
some of these people do not believe in marriage and don't
bother with it; you just call her Miss Creevy and ask no
questions. Whether my lady has asked I do not know.

But my master perhaps knows about it. He comes driving
up in his car just as his wife and her two guests are coming
in from her walk. I was not there, but Miss Lucy was in her
room, which is upstairs at the front, and she heard loud
voices and ran to her window. The most awful thing, the
master has reached into his car and got a pistol and there
he stands pointing it at Mr. Kingman, the poet, and shouting at him the most awful curses that any woman's ears
ever heard. It seems that the master has forbid him the
house, but the mistress has told him to come nevertheless,
and now he is being ordered out. My lady steps in front of
the gun and says, "If you are going to shoot, shoot me,"
and the poet says, "You don't have to shoot, we will go."
The master shouts, "Then go! Go now!" and seems to expect them to start walking. My lady says, "They have a
trunk in their room," and my master says, "If this traitor
crosses my threshold again I will shoot him like a dog. I
will get his belongings." So he calls a gardener who happens
to be near, and the two of them go into the house, and upstairs, and they throw the things of the couple in their
trunk and some bags and shut them, and the master himself helps carry the trunk to the elevator, and when they are
down he comes lugging one end, which I suppose is heavy
with poetry books—anyhow, the master is purple in the face
and the veins are swollen in his neck and he looks like he

will have a stroke of apoplexy, as Miss Lucy says he surely will if he goes on like that.

Well, my lady has had Pietro called and a car is there that has a trailer in back, and the poet and his wife have got in the car. Pietro runs and carries one end of the trunk and they lay it in the trailer. My lady says, "Take them to the train, Pietro," and the master, who is standing on the steps with the gun, shouts, "Take them to hell!" Mrs. Harries says to the guests, very quiet, "I am so sorry and ashamed." The poet says, "It's quite all right, Mrs. Harries. We should not have come." Pietro tells us afterwards that Mr. Kingman was pale and somewhat shaky in the knees; he will have something new to write a poem about. My lady goes to her room and locks herself in, and when I see her later I can tell that she has been weeping. But of course I say nothing, and she says nothing to me. But what a strange world I am living in! I am all a-tremble, wondering what will come next out of this. Your loving Sister

Pamela

❧

LETTER XXIX

Dear Sister:

I can understand that you are worried at my being around where people may be shooting guns; but do not take it too serious, for I promise you that I will duck if I happen to be near. Miss Lucy tells me there has been an agreement about it. Dr. Clark, who is a minister—if you can call a Unitarian that—came out here at Mrs. Harries' request, and she talked of a divorce; but he went to see the master at his club, and there has been a settlement that she is not to have Communists and anarchists and wobblies as her house guests; they can come to the Sunday afternoons along with all the other sorts, and the master will stay away on that afternoon, as always; but if she wants to meet the dangerous kind it will not be at the home but at some outside place where he will not run into them and lose his temper. So they are on speaking terms again, but never in her room, only in front of company. Poor man, he is another soul without a religion, and I am busy with the thought that I might some way find a chance to win him to the Lord. I have been in this house more than half a year, and never has he spoke to me except to give me an order and to say "Thank you" when I do it. He is really a kind man, I believe, and I am praying that God will give me some chance to tell him of our faith. He must know that I have it, on account of my Sabbaths so carefully kept.

There is a great difference in gentlemen, I am learning. There is a college professor who comes to the Sunday afternoons; he is radical and makes sarcastic remarks about the way the country is run and the way the newspapers tell only such news as suits them. He pays attention to me, looks me over, and I am sure would like to be alone with me, but after a while I decided that I did not want that to happen. Also there is a cousin of Mrs. Harries, younger than she, who helps to run the business in the East and comes here now and then; he has a wife but does not bring her along, and I could tell her that she had better be watching out for herself. He is rosy-faced and round, and at the table you can see that he enjoys his food; several times when he has seen me at my work he stops to talk, and the last time he said, "Did anybody ever tell you that you are a very pretty girl?" I suppose I blush, and I say, "Oh, sir, I do not think about that." Says he, "Well you should, for it might be worth a lot to you. I should like to meet you some time." I say, "Meet me?"—for I am taken aback. He says, "You might come to my room and find out." I see then what he means, and say, "Oh, sir, I could not do that." He says, "I would pay you generously." I say, "No, sir, I am sorry," and go on with my work. I say nothing more, for I have learned a lot in this half year; I wish to make no enemies, and I do not think it would do much good to talk to Cousin Andy Morrison about the Lord and His commandments. I have heard Mrs. Harries say that he is a "sporting man" and that he bets on the races; so I leave him to that kind.

But all the gentlemen are not like that, I am glad to say. There is Mr. Mackenzie, who is literary editor of one of the newspapers. He has a wife and brings her with him to the Sunday afternoons. He has bright blue eyes and is always smiling, even when he is being sarcastic. He has a quick nervous manner, and I am sure knows a great deal. For all the time I have been handing him food, I have never heard a word from him only "Thank you." But I hear him talk, and he said it took them a long time to get here, for he never drives faster than twenty miles an hour. I think to myself, "Oh, dear, I have driven the Mercedes faster than that!"

Well, last Sunday we had talk for the first time. He was out on the loggia, looking at our barley fields which are turning green and are fitted so close to the mountains all around. I go to tell him that the talk is about to begin, and he says, "There is too much talk in the world!" Then, as I smile, he says, "I hear that your name is Pamela." I say, "Yes, sir," and he asks, "Any relation to the famous one?" I say, "I didn't know there was such a one, sir," He tells me, "She might be—let me see"—and he figures in his mind—"she might be your great-great-great-grandmother."

I say, "Indeed, sir?"—not knowing anything better. He looks at me gravely and asks, "Tell me, has anybody ever tried to make love to you in this establishment?" I am taken aback and say, "Oh, sir!" He fixes the blue eyes upon me and commands, "Tell me the truth!" Of course I don't want to lie, and I don't want to offend him, so what can I say but "Yes, sir." Then he says, "I hope it is some one of your own station in life." As I delay he says again, "Tell me!" So I say, "No sir, it is not." "It is some rich and powerful person?" "Yes, sir," "I hope he is not old." "No, sir." "Well, well, how extraordinary!" says he. "You are indeed the great-great-great-granddaughter of your great-great-great-grandmother!"

I see that behind his pretended sternness there is his usual smile. "I will tell you," he explains. "Pamela is the heroine of a famous novel. Apparently you have not read it." "No, sir," I answer; "my church does not approve the reading of novels." "Indeed?" says he. "That is a mistake, for if you know which novels to choose you can learn a great deal about life from them. And anyhow, you might say that Pamela is not exactly a novel, for it is a long series of letters." "Oh," say I, "that might be different, for I am permitted to read letters, and to write them also. I write long letters to my sister." "And you tell her what is happening to you?" "Yes, sir." "How interesting! I should like to read one of the new Pamela's letters." "Oh, sir," I say, "that I could not permit, not for all the money in the world." At this he laughs and says, "You do not realize how much you are telling me. Your cheeks betray you." And at that I decide that I had best keep quiet.

Says he, "I will tell you the story of Pamela. She was a serving maid in a wealthy household in England; her mistress died and the young master took over this country estate. Pamela was only sixteen. How old are you?" "I am seventeen," I tell him, "but I was sixteen when I came here." "Very curious! Well, the young master sets out to persuade the serving maid to part with her virtue, and she tells about it in letters to her father and mother. It is a long-drawn-out story, reciting all the details of the master's efforts and the poor girl's resistance. It was published nearly two centuries ago, and was the beginning of English prose fiction. It set the fashionable world on fire, all the great ladies read it and wept over Pamela's sufferings and trials. The master was violent; he had her kidnaped and kept under guard for a long time. I trust that nothing like that has happened to you!" "Oh, no, sir," I say, and know that I am covered with blushes. "Everybody has been polite to me." He has been smiling but now becomes serious. "You did not mean to tell me this," he says, "but don't worry, I know Charles well and what to expect of him. He has not had his way, I hope." "No, sir, he has not." "Well, do not let him have it." "No, sir, I shall not. I have God on my side." "Indeed, Pamela! And so did your great-great-great-grandmother. She was a deeply pious girl, and her virtue was more important to her than anything else in the world." "It is so with me, sir," I tell him, and he says with another of his smiles, "I must go in and hear the talk, or people may begin to think that I am parting with mine."

He tells me that he has this book in his library and will bring it if he can remember to. I wonder what you will think, dear Sister. If it is letters, I suppose it is not the same as a novel, and he assures me that it is the most virtuous book that could be imagined and will strengthen my resistance; so I have told him that I should like at least to see it. I hope that you and Rev. Strayker will not feel that any evil is intended by your devoted Sister

                                                                    Pamela

LETTER XXX

Dear Mother:

I have been living a very quiet life here. I do my duty
and try to please people, and I keep my promise to my
Mother and do not neglect my Testament a single night.
My lady has a great deal of company and it makes extra
work, but I do not mind for I see new people and try to
understand what they say and so improve my mind. At the
last Sunday afternoon I had some talk with Mr. Mackenzie,
who is a literary editor, and he tells me there is a famous
book called "Pamela." I am wondering how you came to
give me that name. Surely not from the book.

One never knows what is coming here. There have been
heavy rains; I suppose you have had them too, and it will
mean pasture for the nannies. Here the great wash which is
below this place has become a river, and last night there
must have been a cloudburst far up in the mountains, for
we had what people tell me is the worst flood in memory.
The houses are placed high, and this great house is always
warm with a big oil furnace; but below are cowsheds, and
among other things a chicken yard. I have said my prayers and am just getting into bed when I hear the roaring
of water and shouts of men. I look out of my window but
it faces the mountain and the flood is in front; so I slip on
my dress and run to Miss Lucy's room, and there she is
looking out, and we hear the rushing water and see that the
men have flashlights. She says, "The chickens will be swept
away!" and I say, "I will go and help." She cries, "Oh, no,
you may be drowned!" I say, "I have learned to swim and

I am so proud of it." She says, "It is not woman's work," but I say, "I have done hard work at home and why not here?" She says, "You will ruin your dress," and I say, "Well, they will not mind washing it."

So I run downstairs; I am barefoot, and I think, they excuse that at the beach and they will here; I would hate to lose my shoes. The master is away, but the young master has just come back and he is in charge. In the hall I see Mary, the kitchen maid, and I say, "Come along," but she is afraid. I run out, and truly that great rush of water in the darkness below is frightening; but I see the men with flashlights and run along the bank to them, and there is Master Charles. He sees me and is pleased and says, "Good for you, Pam!" The pens which are full of laying hens are set up on trestles, and the water is up into the pens and the hens are all up on the roosts and making a tremendous cackling; they are scared and so am I, only I do not make any noise. The water is up to my chest and the footing slippery. I take one end of a pen, and it is all I can do to lift it; I lift, and the young master lifts the other end, and we stagger up the bank and set it on higher ground, and then go down for another. As fast as we lift one off a trestle the flood carries the trestle away, but they are not so important as live chickens, some of which have already gone. More of the men have come running, the Portuguese, and we save most of the pens, and also get the milk cows up to the high ground. The gardens have not yet been planted, and I suppose all the mud that will be left is good soil.

When we have saved everything we can reach, we stand on the bank and watch the flood by the light of a car that has been brought up, and it is indeed a terrifying sight, all that mass of water swirling, and we hate to think of the poor people in the valley below who will lose so much. Master Charles sees that I am shivering and my teeth chattering, and he says, "You should go in and get dry." He himself has on his fashionable clothes and has ruined them, I fear; it may be they cost more than the chickens, but it was natural to try to save living things. I am the only woman that has helped, so I am thought to be something of a heroine; but really it was not dangerous, because if I had been carried away by the water I could surely have got hold of a trestle or something. It did me no harm, and I have learned what it means to live in a canyon in California; I am glad that our poor home is on a hillside. Your loving Daughter and Grampa's loving Granddaughter

Pamela

LETTER XXXI

Dear Sister:

You will see my letter to Mother about the flood. It is gone in the night, and when I look in the morning there is a sad sight all over our valley. The barley will all have to be resown. I don't take much time for looking, because the furniture has to be dusted just the same as if I had not been a heroine. I am working dutifully when Charles comes and stands to watch me. He is pleased with me, and when that happens it means trouble, alas. He says, "Let's take a walk, Pam." I do not say that I have duties, for there is no duty higher than to keep him happy at home; I know that my mistress is pleased this morning, so relieved that he shows no signs of having been drinking again. I have been afraid too, that what I have done to him might be the cause of his going off. I say, timid like, "Will you behave, Charles?"

and he promises, but what he means is not so easy to be sure.

The rain has stopped and there is bright sunshine. Along the side of the mountains runs a road that is not much more than a bridle path. It was used for that, but nobody rides horses any more; it serves to get out to town when the main road is flooded, or is all mud and silt, the way it is this morning. The water has not reached this path, and it is what is called decomposed granite, which hardly holds water at all, so it is firm to walk on. We go until we are past the canyon mouth, and there we sit at a place called Inspiration Point and look out across the wide valley, and see where the water has been and what damage it has done. We talk about our adventure last night; we only saved chickens but we are as proud as if it had been people.

But presently we have said all there is to say; and then he takes my hand. I know what that means now, and I say quickly, "You promised to behave!" He answers, "Look, Pam, how long are you going on tormenting me?" Most humble and proper I reply, "Never have I failed in duty and respect for my masters." "Masters?" he says. "Are you kidding me?" To that I say, "I called you Master until you forbade it. I will resume it if you wish." "Do, for God's sake, stop that nonsense," he says. "I am crazy about you, and you know it well. I don't want you for a servant, I want you for a friend. I go away and try to forget you, but I can't." "I am your true friend," I assure him, "and I promise to remain that as long as I live. That is more than you have ever said to me." "I say it now, Pam. I want you the worst way!" I take advantage of his expression, and say, "That is just it; but you do not want me the best way, and that is the way I have to be wanted." "Tell me," he says, very mild, "what is the best way?" I say, "I have told you so many times, Charles; it is the way of the Lord. I believe in Him, and you do not, and that is a barrier that must always stand between us. I could not be happy, not for one day, with a man who believes what you believe about God. I should forever be trying to save your soul and boring you with arguments and appeals." "And so you are going to sit and watch me go to hell!" "I am surely not going to do it without giving you every chance. I have tried again and again. I have begged you to humble your heart and pray for guidance. God will forgive your sins and wash you clean if you ask Him to. His mercy endureth forever."

He sits for a while, and then says, "So that old God is what stands between us and our happiness!" I tell him that He is indeed an old God, He is what Daniel calls the Ancient of Days. "But be careful how you speak of Him, for He has ways of punishing those who blaspheme Him." "So, you think He will punish me for not believing that He exists?" "I am absolutely certain that He will do that." "Well," he says, "old dear, why not find out? Why not settle the question once for all? Here I am, a vile reprobate, trying to seduce an innocent virgin; worse than that, I am trying to destroy her faith and make her into an atheist like myself. Surely there is no more shining target for God's anger, there is no one more deserving of hell fire—and right now, before I have gone any farther with my wicked schemes! Surely you admit that they are wicked!" "Indeed, yes, Charles, and that is why I am terrified for you." "All right then, we are going to make a test; we are going to put it up to God. Surely He will come and save an innocent virgin from the agent of Satan who is seeking to destroy her soul! Surely God, if You exist, You will not permit this blasphemy to be spoken, or this betrayal to be accomplished! Strike down this evil-doer, here and now, as a proof that You are, and that You live, and that Your words are the truth!"

I am so horrified I start to my feet and scream, "Oh, Charles, do not speak such words!" He rises also. "I have spoken them," he says, "and I stand by them; they are on the record against me till the Judgment Day. I say, 'Do not wait until that day, God! Do not permit me to tamper with the faith of this child! Prove it to her now! I am no good and everybody knows it. I don't care very much about living, and I am willing for You to take my life now, and show her that I am wrong and she is right. I say that You do not exist and never have existed. I say that You are a fantasy in the minds of superstitious Hebrew peasants. You are a delusion out of a stupid old book. You are an insult to the intelligence of every thinking man. I tell You all that to your face, and I dare You to do anything about it!' "

It is in vain I cry, "He is a good God! He is a God of love!" That only starts the madman off again, shouting to heaven, "If you are a God of love, why did You send that flood last night and wipe out people's fields and gardens? Why do You send floods in China every spring and drown tens of thousands of helpless peasants? Why did You send the Lisbon earthquake and kill sixty thousand people in a few seconds? Why did You send an avalanche and kill my mother and father, two happy young people having a vacation they had earned? My father was a doctor and did good to people, but You destroyed him—You good God! You have put a billion or two of people on this earth, most of them in misery and all of them in ignorance, and You leave them that way! You have left them all through the ages, tormented by disease, by murder and lust! If you really love them, why don't You help them, why don't You tell them the truth in such a way that all can understand it? Why do You put it in old Hebrew books that are full of contradictions and absurdities which any child can perceive? Why do You leave Your truth to be got from fat and lazy priests and shouting hillbilly fanatics? Why do You leave Your church to split up into hundreds of sects? Why do You set them all warring and making confusion for people who want to do right? If You want the truth to be known, why don't You come down and show Yourself, and give Your orders, plain and clear?"

"Oh, Charles," I plead, "stop! stop!" But he says, "It is for your God to stop me if He wants it done! He has the power, He knows how to do it. Let Him send a thunderbolt to knock me down! Let Him send a bear to devour me, a devil to drag me to hell—any way that is easiest for His Omnipotence! One flick of His finger and my heart stops beating; and then this pious girl will have a miracle to tell about all the rest of her days. Satan will never again be able to sow doubts in her heart. If ever in all time You had reason for a miracle, it is now! Strike, for Your glory!"

I am so horrified I cannot stand any more, and I cry, "I am going!" But he catches me by the wrist, and I discover that he is strong. "You are going to see this through!" he says. "This is the test that will settle it, and never again will you be able to threaten me with this heathen idol of yours." With his other hand he takes out his watch and holds it. "Now!" he shouts. "Now, Lord of Sabaoth, Rock of Ages, Ancient of Days, or whatever You call Yourself, Jehovah of the Thunders, Lord God of Battles, here is my defiance. I don't believe You exist, but if You do I hate You, I despise You, I defy You to do Your worst. I give You one minute to take me to hell and to save the soul of this deluded child. I will count the seconds while You get Your thunder ready, and if You don't take the chance, You will never again be able to persuade this child that You exist. Now then"— and he starts to count—"one, two, three, four," and he is looking at his watch. I am shaking so that my knees are almost giving way. When he gets to the last numbers, "fifty, fifty-one, fifty-two," I can stand it no more, I give a mighty heave and tear my arm free and start to run, run, run as I never did before in all my life. I don't want to be there when the thunderbolt strikes; I don't want to have anything to do with his awful blasphemy, the most wicked thing I ever heard in all the world.

But I am like Lot's wife, I cannot help but look behind me. The time is up, I know; and there I see him, stretched flat on his back, not moving. The most awful horror seizes me; God has taken him at his word, and his soul is gone to hell, and is even now in everlasting fire! At that moment I know that I loved him, and that I should have saved him, I should have done whatever was needed to save him; but now he is lost and gone forever. I run back, as fast as I had come; I fall on my knees by his side and have just breath enough to whisper, "Charles! Charles!" At that moment his eyes open and up he pops, with such a grin on his face as I never could have imagined on any devil; he bursts into a laugh and cries, "Well, here I am! Back from the grave! Snatched from the jaws of hell!" I realize that he has been mocking me; he knew I would look around and would come back when I saw him dead, as I thought, poor me! I have so many different emotions that I am torn to pieces; I am furious with him, and at the same time so glad that he is alive, and also I am in terror because God has been mocked, whereas I have read in Scripture, "Be not deceived. God is not mocked."

I do not know what to make of it, but he does; he is still laughing, but before I realize it his arms are about me and he is kissing me, as I have never been kissed before and never dreamed to be; he is kissing my lips, my cheeks, my throat. And again the terror seizes me. I cry, "No, no, you must not!" "What?" he asks. "Is it not settled now? Are you still afraid of that old God?" he cries "That old God who does not exist, or who does not care enough for you to save your soul?"

I am all but overcome by the emotions which have swept over me, that are like the flood of last night; but just as I managed to keep on my feet then, so now I exclaim, "You promised to behave and you are not doing it." He pretends to be surprised and hurt, but when I think it over I decide that he wasn't really, he was just trying to take advantage of me and to sweep me away; he pretends that because God did not strike him dead, therefore I am to surrender my virtue to him. But amid all the confusion I have sense enough to doubt that this follows, and I remember my promises to you, and to myself, not to mention Mr. Mackenzie. I keep saying, "No, Charles, no!" and push his hands away. He grows terribly vexed—I think he had his mind made up that this defiance to God was to be his great stroke, it was to roll over all my opposition and submit me to his will. But I do not give up my faith quite so easily; I say, "It is possible that God may have plans for you that you do not dream, Charles." At that he is in a fury and cries, "Oh, damn God!" And without waiting for reply he springs up and walks fast away.

He does not look back as I did; and I have clenched my hands tight and made up my mind that I will not call him. My heart is aching, because I know that I shall not see him again for a time. I know by now that he goes off in anger, and that he gets from other women what is not to be had from me. And perhaps he will start drinking, as he did before; and, woe is me, I cannot save him! "O Jerusalem, Jerusalem, how often would I have gathered thy children together, even as a hen gathereth her chickens under her wing, and ye would not!" You will see that this paper has been wet with my tears; I am so sorry for this tormented man. I cannot save him from himself, alas; it is all I can do

to save myself from him. Give some advice to your unhappy Sister

                                              Pamela

Dear Mother:

I have not much news these days. I work hard and earn a
good word now and then from my mistress. She has much
company and that makes a lot of work; but it is what her
great house and all the people are for, and I do not see anybody working too hard. They put things onto me because
I am one of the lowly, but I do not mind. I see many ladies
and gentlemen and sometimes have a chance to hear what
they say. There come gentlemen with brown skins from
India, and they are not the same as colored; my lady is
interested in freedom for their country, and also for the
Irish, and for all the oppressed peoples—there are many
such in the world, it seems. She does not believe in charity
but in justice, she explains, and I am sure that God would
approve of this, but it would succeed better if she did it
in His name.

The young master is away, and young mistress Yvette
comes but does not stay long. She is a most fashionable
person but not what I would call warm-hearted. This place
is supposed to be her home and she has her room here, very
lovely, but she is not often in it. She drives up with her
friends, stays to a meal, and kisses and pets her much older
sister enough to justify her being the heiress. But she does
not share her sister's ideas, and if there is company she

thinks it her duty to assert herself; it may be some learned gentleman who has spent his life studying the world's problems, but Miss Yvette will tell him what is what while finishing a chicken patty. From this you will guess that I do not like her very much, but that is not necessary; when she gives me an order I say, "Yes, Miss Yvette," and do it and that is all. Her sister so craves affection, and I wish that I were an important enough person so that I could give it to her.

I am sorry indeed to hear about the frost, but then, Providence has been so good to us in so many ways that we cannot complain. We have health, and you have love from your devoted

Pamela

LETTER XXXIII

Dear Sister:

I have prayed over it, but I shall not take your advice to give up this position. It is true that I am not certain of my own strength, but I am certain of God's and He will help me. My faith has not been shaken. There is much that I do not understand, but I have studied the story of the temptation and how the devil challenged Jesus to prove that He was the Son of God by casting Himself down from the pinnacle of the temple, and Jesus said, "It is written again, thou shalt not tempt the Lord thy God." I think it is a clear answer to Master Charles. Of course God was not under obligation to strike him dead if He did not wish to, and no doubt He has plans which will be revealed in His own good time. My only thought about this is sorrow for the unhappy young man, who can hurt only himself, and does.

I am staying here because I am able to help Mother and you. You may say that you can get along, but there are only so many hours in the day and only so much strength in your body, and what you give to earning your keep you cannot give to study. Someday you may be able to pay me back, but now you need the money that my mistress sends you, and I only wish it were more. I have taken Miss Lucy into my confidence in this matter, because she is so much older than I and knows the family better; she says I am in no danger if I pray and strengthen my resolve. She is able to help me, by pointing out how selfish the young master is; he says that he needs me, but what does he mean by that? He needs me for his pleasures, but never does it cross his mind to say that he will make an honest woman of me. I am good enough to be his partner in play, but nowhere near good enough to be his partner in earnest. Miss Lucy has heard him say to one of the rich ladies who come here, "Why should I marry when I can get what I want without it?" You can rest assured that I shall not forget these words. I am not being so silly as to take up the notion that a parlormaid might become his wife; but I am no longer so ignorant as I was when I came here, and have taken note what it means when an elegant rich gentleman professes love to one so humble in station. When he got tired of me he would give me some money and then be sure he had done his full duty.

Miss Lucy says that this is what she means by the arrogance of this family. It is their money that gives them power, and they hold on to it, excepting Master Charles when he is drunk and no longer knows what he is doing. Miss Lucy says that our mistress is one of the most generous of the rich, but she gives only of her income, never of her capital. She owns stock in the great company, and every year it pays what are called dividends, and in the war years much more; the rich keep the stock and spend only the income it brings them each year. They know well that this money means their ability to command the services of others. You will see that your little Sister is becoming what the Socialists who come here call class-conscious. It is interesting to watch the few rich persons who become class-conscious for the poor, and so they have two consciousnesses that make war inside them. Miss Lucy says that our mistress will give checks to the people whose ideas she agrees with, but nobody that knows her has ever seen a share of stock in the shipbuilding corporation, and nobody has the slightest idea what her holdings are. Someday this stock will be passed on to Miss Yvette, and after that there will be no more talk about social justice and not even about charity.

There will be no change in the religion, but as you see there may be change in the politics of your Little Sister

Pamela

⋘⋙

LETTER XXXIV

Dear Mother:

I am sorry to have seemed neglectful, but I have so much work to do, and you have always insisted that my devotions shall come ahead of my family. You ask me to tell you more about these people I live with. It seems like gossip, but I suppose you worry not to know more about them. Well, there is a new Portuguese baby, something that happens often; and Master Charles, who has taken a trip to San Francisco and is now back in Hollywood, has let somebody persuade him to buy some fancy sort of sheep called caracul, and they were brought here in two big trucks, and now pens have been built for them, and one of the Portuguese men will take them out on the mountainside to graze, and we all hope that the coyotes who howl there will not get them. When Master Charles takes up a notion, his aunt pays the bill. I am told that in the garage there is a huge desk for which he paid eight hundred dollars but has no use for it; also I am told that he bought an electric sewing machine for Miss Lucy, but she was afraid to use it, and now it has disappeared; somebody knew somebody who had use for it and it will never be missed. The watchful master of this household cannot keep up with it all.

Also I will tell you about Miss Bascom, the secretary, who is a fine young lady. I get along with her because I let her be as grand as she pleases and do exactly what she asks. But the trouble with young lady secretaries is that young gentlemen come along, and my mistress laments that she has had more than her share of such trouble. Now there is a young gentleman who is called a buyer for the Penn Shipbuilding, and he came to one of the Sunday afternoons, and since then he has come three times to take Miss Bascom driving, and so we are all making jokes about Mrs. Harries having more trouble ahead of her. I will confide in my dear mother that I am working hard to educate myself, so that someday I may become a secretary, which is a much higher station than a parlormaid and a bold thing for me to dream. Wish luck to your dear Daughter

Pamela

LETTER XXXV

Dear Sister:

Oh, my dear, the most terrible time I have been having, and the most awful story I have to tell you. Charles has been drinking again, and has come home, not drunk, but just a little way, and with a man called Regis who is his companion, and I suppose takes care of him and drives for him when he needs it, as he does now. The household is upset but nobody shows it, and the mistress looks calm and dignified, but her eyes show her weeping. Mr. Harries is away, or perhaps he stays away because he has been told. Now I see what God has done to my poor young master, and how His name is not to be taken in vain.

Well, that is the way it stands, and when my work is done I go to my little room and read my Testament, and write a cheerful letter to Mother, and then I kneel and pray. Never did I pray more earnestly than for this strayed lamb; I tell God that it is not his fault, it is his upbringing, and the fact that his father and mother died. Of course God knows all that, but I beg for mercy in our Savior's name. Then I go to sleep; and I don't know how much later I wake with a start for I hear a sound and feel the bed move, and I start up and the next moment there is a pair of arms about me and the smell of liquor in my face. I cry out, and he says, "Hush, it is only me," and I say, "Oh, Charles, no, you must not be here!" He whispers, "I love you!" I suppose he has made up his mind that it does no good to argue with me and that he will say nothing but that; he says it over and over, "I love you! I love you!" All the time I am folded in his arms and he is kissing me again and again, on my lips and my eyes and my cheeks. I am terrified, and if I have ever been the least bit tempted it could not be now, for I am as it were drowned in the smell of liquor which I abhor.

I don't want to scream for I know it will mean a scandal; but I know that I am in danger, and I don't know whether to fight him or not, for that may enrage him and he is stronger than I. After every kiss he says, "I love you," and of course I know he does not but only wants to have his way and is provoked because I have denied him. I try to reason with him; I say, "No, no, Charles, you must not do this! No, no, this is not fair to me! You will be ashamed if you do it!" He goes on saying, "I love you, I love you!" and I say, "I do not love you, and if you do this to me I will hate you forever. I will only have to kill myself, and what good will that do you?" But he goes on trying to overwhelm me with his kisses. So then I try to fight, and I discover to my horror—I can hardly bear to put this on paper— the man is naked, and he is trying to overpower me and has torn my nightgown. So there is nothing for me to do but scream, and believe me I do it, "Help! Help! Help!" I am no weakling, and since he has to have both his arms about me he cannot stop my mouth. So I scream, and then he cries, "Damn you, little bitch!" and sort of throws me down onto the bed and rushes away.

I start up, because I cannot be sure but that I may have to fight some more; but no, he is gone, and has left my door open. I have to think quick, for there are voices; Cookie has opened her door, and then Mary, and they are calling, "What? What is it?" I have scared them, and I say, "Oh, I am so sorry, I had a terrible nightmare." That is true in a way, and how I wish it was true all the way! I say, "Forgive me, please," and calm them down. When I go back to my room and close the door and turn on my light I find Charles' dressing gown lying on the floor. That would be a terrible thing to be found so I hide it in my closet. I am afraid to go to sleep again, for he might come back; I am still trembling all over, and I go to Miss Lucy's room; she is awake and I make her promise to keep the secret, and then I tell her what has happened. We talk for a long time and then we lie in her narrow little bed and sleep.

In the morning I wait until my lady has had her orange juice and toast and is reading her mail and morning paper, which are brought every morning by one of the men who live in town. I say most humbly, "May I interrupt, Mrs. Harries?" When she asks, "What is it?" I say, "I am dreadfully sorry, for I have been so happy here and I love you truly, if you don't mind my saying so; but I fear that I cannot stay any longer." "Why, what is this?" she asks, and I tell her, "It is very sad and hurts me to say it, but Master Charles came to my room and tried to force himself upon me, and I had to fight him to save myself." "Oh, dear!" she says. "How unfortunate!" But I think she is not as much shocked as I am to tell her. "I hope he did you no harm," she says, and I answer, "No, Mrs. Harries, only to tear my nightgown. He did no more because I did not let him." She says, "Oh, Pamela, men are terrible, they are like mad bulls; they cannot control themselves and nobody else can control them. I dislike them, but they are here and they run the world; that is why we have wars and all the misery." "Yes, Mrs. Harries," I reply, "and it is great misery for me, for I have been so happy here." "Oh, mercy me!" she exclaims. "Tell me how this happened. Have you given him encouragement?" "Quite the contrary, he has pursued me and I have told him No, many, many times." "It is most unfortunate," she says. "It upsets me greatly. I cannot let you go, for you have been so helpful, and I have had plans for you."

"But what can I do, Mrs. Harries? I would not dare to sleep in my room again." "I will tell you how to fix it," she says. "We will have one of the men put a strong bolt on the door of your room and you can make yourself safe." "Well, I suppose that could be done," I admit. "It would be better if I put on the bolt myself though, for if one of the men does it he may guess the reason and it would be better not." "Can you do carpentry?" she asks, and I tell her, "On a little place like ours I learned to do everything. It needs only a bolt and some screws and a screwdriver." "Very well," she says. "I am going to town today and will take you and you can buy them. I will increase your pay to sixty dollars a month, because you have been so attentive to your duties. I had hopes that you might be able to help Charles, but it seems that he is like all the other men, and I suppose you could not give him what he wants. Too bad, too bad!"

She picks up her paper and I bow myself out. I think over her last sentence and realize that I have much to learn about the world and especially its portions which are called higher. The thought comes to me that my honored mistress would have been willing for me to become the concubine of her nephew and to live in her home with him on that basis. Well, it was done in the old Bible days, and I suppose elsewhere. But God has changed his law in such matters, and I am sure it would be sinful and not meet with the approval of our church. That means nothing to her, for what she is thinking about is to keep him happy and entertained, and not drinking. If men are like that, and cannot control themselves, she will say that it is most unfortunate; if later on he gets tired of me, she will say that it is too bad and will pay me some money. Now I am to have more money to pay for my fright and my torn nightgown and the inconvenience of having to bolt myself up. Of course, I am glad to have the money, and so will stay and take the risk; but I will not fool myself with the idea that it is because I have been so attentive to my duties.

Well, Sister, you need the money too, so you must not scold me. Both of us have to learn about the world which belongs to the men, as my lady says. Miss Lucy tells me that it could have happened just as well in an office, many girls are pursued there. It could happen also to a nurse, so watch out. And do not fail to tell me about it, because we have to help each other and it is part of our education. But, oh dear, what a shock it has been to your innocent Little Sister

Pamela

LETTER XXXVI

Dear Sister:

Well, not all news is bad. Young master has gone away. He went that night with his friend Bill Regis, and where they are now I have not been told; but the good stout bolt is on the door, ready for their return. Also, I keep the door of my room locked and the key in my pocket, lest any gentleman should be waiting in my room, say in the clothes-closet. The gentleman's dressing gown which was on my floor has been put back in his clothes-closet, and nobody will be the wiser.

What I have to tell you is about a different sort of gentleman, the nice Mr. Mackenzie, who has come to another Sunday afternoon. This time it was an Irish lady, telling about the struggle of her country for independence, and about the dreadful things the Black and Tans have been doing, and my lady says it is just like Southern California, where it seems they have a Red Squad that does very bad. Mr. Mackenzie doesn't seem very eager to go in to the lecture, and when I am passing him he says, "I have brought what I promised you, Pamela," and takes a book from the pocket of his coat and gives it to me. "Oh, thank you, sir," I say; and then, "It is but a little book." He says, "It is on thin paper and has about five hundred pages; also it is small type, so it is a great long story." "I thought it was an old book," I say, and he tells me this is a modern edition, it is reprinted from time to time, it is what is called a classic. I thank him again and promise to read it, and he says, "Do not begin it at night, for you may get no sleep and you will weep your eyes out." I tell him, "I could hardly weep for a woman that I know has never existed." But he says, "Don't fool yourself, she will exist in your mind."

He asks me if I never liked to pretend when I was a child, and I say, "Yes, sir, I had a doll that was made of rags but I pretended it was alive." "Well, then," says he, "pretend that Pamela was your great-great-great-grandmother. We will call her Pamela One and you Pamela Two, and you will learn a great deal from her letters, which come to you from nearly two centuries ago." I say, "Oh, sir, I am so glad that they are letters, so that it is permitted for me to read them." He smiles kindly and tells me, "You are a good girl, and I will let you keep this book, if you like." I am quite overwhelmed, for it is such a pretty book; but he says it is the inside that counts, and he is very curious to see what I make of a story so old and out-of-date as this.

I do not take his advice, but when my work is done and I am in bed, safe behind my bolt which I have put on good and tight with long screws, I take the little book and start to read. There is an introduction with many long words which I skip. I am interested in my great-great-great-grand-mother—as I am pretending, for I am sure it can do no harm. I have figured up that I have sixteen of these, and as our family came from England, it is easy to fool myself. Mr. Mackenzie has told me that a writer usually has some model in mind, and it is quite possible that this writer named Richardson knew a serving maid named Pamela and that he used her; it is surely not likely that our family has been other than poor. So why could it not be?

The letters are to the mother and father and tell how the mistress died and left a few of her belongings to this humble maid; and how the young master took charge and how he began paying most evil attentions to her. And, oh, it was just as Mr. Mackenzie had said, it was all as if I was there in the room, and I became excited and was set all to trembling. The place was quite different from Rancho Casa Grande, and the help were different, but the heart of the story was like mine, and when the young master started to kiss the poor child it was so real to me that the tears came to my eyes and I had to keep wiping them away in order that I might be able to read at all. I will copy one of the scenes, so that you may see for yourself.

"I broke off abruptly my last letter; for I feared he was coming; and so it happened. I put the letter in my bosom, and took up my work, which lay by me; but I had so little of the artful, as he called it, that I looked as confused as if I had been doing some great harm.

" 'Sit still, Pamela,' said he, 'and mind your work, for all me. You don't tell me I am welcome home, after my journey to Lincolnshire.' 'It would be hard, Sir,' said I, 'if you was not always welcome to your honour's own house.'

"I would have gone; but he said, 'Don't run away, I tell you. I have a word or two to say to you.' Good Sirs, how my heart went pit-a-pat! 'When I was a little kind to you,' said he, 'in the summer-house, and you carried yourself so foolishly upon it, as if I had intended to do you great harm, did I not tell you you should take no notice of what passed, to any creature? and yet you have made a common talk of the matter, not considering either my reputation or your own.' 'I made a common talk of it, Sir!' said I: 'I have nobody to talk to, hardly.'

"He interrupted me and said, 'Hardly! you little equivocator! what do you mean by hardly? Let me ask you, have not you told Mrs. Jervis for one?' 'Pray, your honour,' said I, all in agitation, 'let me go down: for it is not for me to hold an argument with your honour.' 'Equivocator, again!' said he, and took my hand, 'what do you talk of an argument? Is it holding an argument with me to answer a plain question? Answer me what I asked.'

" 'O, good Sir,' said I, 'let me beg you will not urge me farther, for fear I forget myself again, and be saucy!'

" 'Answer me, then, I bid you!' says he; 'have you not told Mrs. Jervis? It will be saucy in you, if you don't answer me directly to what I ask.' 'Sir,' said I, and fain would have pulled my hand away, 'perhaps I should be for answering you by another question, and that would not become me.' 'What is it you would say?' replies he; 'speak out.'

" 'Then, Sir,' said I, 'why should your honour be so angry, I should tell Mrs. Jervis, or any body else, what passed, if you intended no harm?'

" 'Well said, pretty innocent and artless! as Mrs. Jervis calls you,' said he; 'and it is thus you taunt and retort upon me, insolent as you are! But still I will be answered directly to my question.' 'Why, then, Sir,' said I, 'I will not tell a lie for the world: I did tell Mrs. Jervis; for my heart was almost broken: but I opened not my mouth to any other.' 'Very well, bold face,' said he, 'and equivocator again; you did not open your mouth to any other; but did you not write to some other?' 'Why now, and please your honour,' said I (for I was quite courageous just then), 'you could not have asked me this question, if you had not taken from me my letter to my father and mother, in which, I own, I opened my mind freely to them, and asked their advice, and poured forth my griefs!'

" 'And so I am to be exposed, am I,' said he, 'in my own house, and out of my house, to the whole world, by such a sauce-box as you?' 'No, good Sir,' said I; 'and I hope your honour won't be angry with me: it is not I that expose you, if I say nothing but the truth.' 'So, taunting again! Assurance as you are!' said he, 'I will not be thus talked to!'

" 'Pray, Sir,' said I, 'of whom can a poor girl take advice, if it must not be of her father and mother, and such a good woman as Mrs. Jervis?' 'Insolent!' said he, and stamped with his foot, 'am I to be questioned thus by such a one as you?' I fell down on my knees, and said, 'For Heaven's sake, your honour, pity a poor creature, that knows nothing of her duty, but how to cherish her virtue and good name! I have nothing else to trust to; and, though poor and friendless, yet I have always been taught to value honesty above my life.' 'Here's ado with your honesty,' said he, 'foolish girl! Is it not one part of honesty to be dutiful and grateful to your master, do you think?' 'Indeed, Sir,' said I, 'it is impossible I should be ungrateful to your honour, or disobedient, or deserve the names of bold-face and insolent, which you call me, but when your commands are contrary to that first duty which shall ever be the principle of my life.'

"He seemed to be moved, and rose up, and walked into the great chamber two or three turns, leaving me on my knees; I threw my apron over my face, and laid my head on a chair, and cried as if my heart would break, having no power to stir.

"At last he came in again; but, alas! with mischief in his heart, and raising me up, he said, 'Rise, Pamela, rise; you are your own enemy. Your perverse folly will be your ruin. I tell you this, that I am very much displeased with the freedoms you have taken with my name to my housekeeper, as also to your father and mother; and you may as well have real cause to take these freedoms with me, as to make my name suffer for imaginary ones.' And saying so, he offered to take me on his knee, with some force. O now I was terrified! I said, like as I had read in a book a night or two before, 'Angels and saints, and all the host of heaven, defend me! And may I never survive, one moment, that fatal one in which I shall forfeit my innocence.' 'Pretty fool!' said he, 'how will you forfeit your innocence, if you are obliged to yield to a force you cannot withstand? Be easy,' said he: 'for, let the worst happen that can, you'll have the merit, and I the blame; and it will be a good subject for letters to your father and mother, and a tale into the bargain for Mrs. Jervis.'

"He by force kissed my neck and lips; and said, 'Who ever blamed Lucretia! All the shame lay on the ravisher only: and I am content to take all the blame upon me; as I have already borne too great a share for what I have deserved.' 'May I,' said I, 'Lucretia-like, justify myself with my death, if I am used barbarously?' 'O, my good girl,' said he, tauntingly, 'you are well read, I see; and we shall make out between us, before we have done, a pretty story in romance, I warrant ye.'

"He then put his hand in my bosom, and indignation gave me double strength, and I got loose from him by a sudden spring, and ran out of the room; and the next chamber being open, I entered it, shut to the door, and it locked after me: but he followed me so close, he got hold of my gown, and tore a piece off, which hung without the door; for the key was on the inside.

"I just remember I got into the room; for I knew nothing further of the matter till afterwards; for I fell into a fit with my terror, and there I lay, till he, as I suppose, looking through the keyhole, espied me upon the floor, stretched out at length, on my face; and then he called Mrs. Jervis to me, who, by his assistance, bursting open the door, he went away, seeing me coming to myself; and bid her say nothing of the matter, if she was wise.

"Poor Mrs. Jervis thought it was worse, and cried over me like as if she was my mother; and I was two hours before I came to myself; and just as I got a little upon my feet, he coming in, I fainted away again with the terror; and so withdrew; but he staid in the next room to let nobody come near us, that his foul proceedings might not be known.

"Mrs. Jervis gave me her smelling bottle, and had cut my laces, and set me in a great chair, when he called her to him.

" 'How is the girl?' said he: 'I never saw such a fool in my life. I did nothing to her.' Mrs. Jervis could not speak for crying. 'So,' he said, 'she has told you, it seems, that I was kind to her in the summer-house, though, I'll assure you, I was quite innocent then as well as now: and I desire you to keep this matter to yourself, and let me not be named in it.' 'O, Sir,' said she, 'for your honour's sake, and for Christ's sake!' But he would not hear her, and said, 'For your own sake, I tell you, Mrs. Jervis, say not a word more. I have done her no harm. And I won't have her stay in my house; prating, perverse fool, as she is! But since she is so apt to fall into fits, or at least pretend to do so, prepare her to see me to-morrow after dinner, in my mother's closet; do you be with her, and you shall hear what passes between us.'

"And so he went out in a pet, and ordered his chariot and four to be got ready, and went a visiting somewhere."

That is the way it goes, dear Rachel. I could not stop and I read on and on, even though it was my sleep time and I knew I would be sorry next day. In the end my eyes were red and aching, but even so I had to do something that I suppose was very wrong; I was supposed to read straight through, but I couldn't endure it, I had to turn to the end and see what happened to Pamela One. If this cruel master had his way with her, I thought that I just could not bear it; but I read that he married her, and of course that made it all right, and I could cry myself safely to sleep. I was late for my work in the morning, the first time that happened since I have been here. I did not tell anybody what a bad thing I done, but have hidden the book as my secret.

It has set me to thinking all day; two things, first that I will never so misbehave again but will set myself one half-hour to read, and always after my Testament and prayers. When the half hour is up I will stop, no matter what is happening to my great-great-great-grandmother. The other thing is the question, would I be satisfied to end like her and marry the cruel man who had pursued me? I admit to myself that I have sometimes dreamed that Charles might ask me to marry him, though he has never spoken that word. I know that I would never marry a man who did not take the pledge against liquor, and I cannot see how I could marry a man who did not believe in God and keep the Sabbath. It is hard for me to imagine Charles doing these things; the second would be harder than the first, for he would have to humble his pride and I think he would rather go to hell. He might change his mind there, of course, but it would be too late.

Another thing, I try to imagine myself becoming a member of this great family. None of them would like it, and would I be able to make them like me, and could I be happy if I failed? Truly I would not, and the only thing that could tempt me is that I am so sorry for poor Charles, in whom I have seen so much good. Alas, I am afraid that I should do just what his aunt has done, which is to love him more than is good for him! Forgive this foolish dreaming, which I should never have mentioned if it had not been for peeking into the end of the book. I wonder if anybody ever did such a foolish thing as this—except your devoted Sister

Pamela

LETTER XXXVII

Dear Mother:

I have most wonderful news for you. My lady has told me that because I have been so attentive to my duties I am to receive ten dollars more each month. I am sure you cannot be more proud of me than I am of myself. The laborer is worthy of his hire! I am going to keep the first ten, as I am in need of a pair of shoes, since what I have are not fit to go out with Mrs. Harries in. There are many little things, like bus fare to go to church. After this first month I will send four dollars more to you and four to Sister and keep two more for me.

There is something else very interesting that I have learned about in this wonderful place. My lady reads a great deal in the papers, and goes into the shops and learns things there. She has brought home a little box that is the strangest trick you have ever heard of; it is an invention that is called a radio, or sometimes a crystal set, and with it you can hear voices and music out of the air. There is a little rubber tube that has two prongs and you stick them in your ears; my lady let me do it and she turned a little wheel, and there came music that you could hear plainly, and she says that music was being played in Los Angeles, which is almost a hundred miles away. It was what is called jazz, which is music for dancing, very ugly, I thought, but she says that on Sundays there is better music, and every morning there is a man who tells you the news so that you do not have to wait for the paper, and maybe soon there will be no more papers. Did you ever hear of anything so wonderful? In back you can see into the little box, and it has batteries which have to be changed now and then and I am to be shown how to do it. Mrs. Harries says they are now planning to invent bigger boxes, so that then everybody in the room will be able to hear what is going on. This little box is a great comfort to my lady, for she is fond of lying down, and with this by her bedside she can have company all the time.

There is something else that will interest you and Grampa. A gentleman here has given me a book which is called "Pamela," and it is letters written by a girl of that name in the year of 1740, and tells all about life in England and is most instructive. You tell me that I was named for your Aunt Pamela, and I am wondering if you know who she was named for, or anything about our family a long time back. Somebody may have had a family Bible and you may know where it is. I have never thought to ask, because then I did not know about this book which is said to be famous and the gentleman calls it a classic.

Well, that is a lot of news from your loving Daughter
Pamela Two (so the gentleman calls me, joking)

LETTER XXXVIII

Dear Sister:

You will see my letter to Mother telling about the wonderful radio set. It is being shown to everybody that comes to the house, and as soon as they hear it they say they will have to have one, so there will be lots of them to be made.

Well, the young master is gone to New York, his aunt has had a postcard from him, which Miss Bascom read before she took it to Mrs. Harries; she told Miss Lucy about it and so it has come to me. Our poor lady does not know what he has gone for or what he will be doing, except that he will surely ask her for money and she will send it. She studies his writing to see if he is still drinking, and then she goes out to a lecture or a picture show or whatever, trying her best to not think about him, but not succeeding, I am sure. It is my fear that in her heart she thinks that if only I had been willing to do what he asked of me, he might be safe now and happy in her home. I do not know this, I only fear it, and it troubles me, and makes me think, how mixed up this world is, its goodness and its badness. How fortunate I am that I have the Rock of Ages on which to take my stand! Be sure that no one will ever tempt me off from it.

Well, I have stuck to my resolve regarding "Pamela"; I

have read only one half-hour every evening. I read fast as
I can, and look at my alarm clock and then at the book to
see how far I am going to get; it is like a race. The book is
going to last me a long, long time, and keeps me in a tumult; I think about it all day, and would not think it a
wholesome thing except that it is such a pure and pious
girl, from whom I can learn so much and get courage and
fortitude. She writes about her faith, and of course it is not
like ours; since ours did not exist at that time it is in no
way her fault. I am flooded with tears for this poor girl who
is so much like me and yet different. Her persecution was
much, much greater than mine, her master far more wild
and less polite at all times. If that is the way men behaved
in those days I do not wonder that my mistress says they
are mad bulls. Apparently a poor girl then had no way to
earn her living unless she got a letter of reference from her
former employer. Her parents owned no land, and at least
our dear Mother has four acres, and while there is not
enough water it will keep some goats alive and grow vegetables if they are irrigated. I have talked with Mr. Mackenzie, who is very amused that I am crying so over the
story, and he has explained to me what he calls the English
land system. It seems that in the very old days every village
had what was called a common, where the people had the
right to graze their animals; but little by little the rich took
possession of this land and the poor were helpless and their
chains grew tighter, and if you protested you were thrown
into jail. You could be put into jail for being in debt and
you could not get out again.

Now I have got to that part of the story where Pamela
fears so greatly for her virtue and is so terrified by her master's importunities that she is resolved to leave this wicked
house, whatever the cost may be; so she writes some verses
to the people she is leaving behind and who have helped

her secretly as much as they dared. I will copy the beginning for you:

> My fellow-servants dear, attend
> To these few lines which I have penn'd.
> I'm sure they're from your honest friend;
> And wisher-well, poor Pamela.
>
> I, from a state of low degree,
> Was plac'd in this good family:
> Too high a fate for humble me,
> The helpless, hopeless Pamela.
>
> Yet though my happy lot was so,
> Joyful, I homeward from it go,
> No less content, when poor and low,
> Than you here find your Pamela.
>
> For what indeed is happiness,
> But conscious innocence and peace?
> And that's a treasure I possess;
> Thank Heav'n that gave it Pamela.

There are fourteen of these stanzas, and I have not time
to copy them all, only one more, the last:

> On God all future good depends;
> Serve him. And so my sonnet ends,
> With thank ye, thank ye, honest friends,
> For all your loves to Pamela.

This will be enough to show you how excellent the lines,
and how edifying the book, which someday perhaps we can
read aloud together. I have copied these so that you may
see how like the story is to my own, and that I am not wasting my time. If ever it should happen that I would have to
say farewell to Rancho Casa Grande, I will copy all this
lovely poem and leave it with my honest friends. I will
hardly need to tell them that I did not write it, for they will

not imagine me capable of anything so eloquent. That is the word Mr. Mackenzie used, but he was smiling and I am never sure what he means, because he finds the book old-fashioned, and with these learned gentlemen everything has to be exactly up to date or it is nothing in their eyes. But to me it is as if Pamela One were my real ancestor, and her sufferings were happening to me day by day, and I am almost suffocated by the emotions I feel. Read this, for example, and imagine me thinking about Master Charles:

"But see the lordliness of a high condition! A poor body must not put in a word, when they take it into their heads to be angry! What a fine time a person of an equal condition would have of it, if she were even to marry such a one; his poor dear mother spoiled him at first. Nobody must speak to, or contradict him, as I have heard, when he was a child; and so he has not been used to be controlled, and cannot bear the least thing to cross his violent will. This is one of the blessings attending men of high condition! Much good may it do them with their pride of birth, and pride of fortune! say I: all it serves for, as far as I can see, is to multiply their disquiets, and everybody's else who has to do with them."

What change would I have to make in all that, save of the one word aunt instead of mother? So you can see why the book is so real to me, and why I could not get to sleep for thinking about her if I did not know that it will all turn out right in the end, and that her virtue will be rewarded as the title of the book says. May God guard and spare such sufferings to your Sister

Pamela

☙❧

LETTER XXXIX

Dear Mother:

I have delayed to write, for I have not much news. I am
having a very peaceful life and little to tell. On Sunday I
had a chance to hear parts of a talk about the Japanese by
a missionary who has just returned from that country. I
have learned that the women there are very oppressed and
in need of God's word, for the religion being taught to
them is no religion at all but a kind of idol worship with
the emperor as God. I have thought how wonderful it
would be if I could prepare myself to be a teacher to those
people, and what a strange outcome that would be to my
service as parlormaid!

Yesterday Miss Bascom was away and so I had a chance
to take an automobile ride with my good lady. She does not
like ever to ride alone, but must have one or more of her
friends to talk to, and one person who is not rich and will
run errands for her; that was me. We drove a long way—
that is, Pietro drove, of course—and came to a canyon in
the mountains, and there is a camp, mostly of tents, and a
sort of school for children from Los Angeles, very poor
children who do not see much of the country, and my lady
has helped this school with money. The people are some of
them Russians and some Jews, and they work part of the
day and grow vegetables, and the rest of the time they
study. They are people who think that what has happened
in Russia that is called a Revolution is a good thing for the
poor and will help the peasants there and the workers. My
lady is very certain about that and indignant with the peo-

ple who call them Reds; she talked about it all the way on the drive and she seems to know, for she reads a great deal and marks the pages and cuts out this article and that and sends it to people who are misinformed, as she says. She wishes to educate even poor me and tells me about things that I should know.

Those at the camp seem very good people to me. There was a bright young girl named Nella Brodsky, who is one of the teachers, and is very pretty, but dark and foreign looking; she showed us all over and told us about the work. She was nice to me, just as if she took me for one of the family, but maybe it was because I am a worker, and I surely do work. I did not fail to tell her that I hoped they were doing it in God's name and that they could have no abiding success if it was not so. I take the chance to spread the Word wherever I go, and trust that some of the seed will fall upon good soil. This you may be sure of, having properly taught your devoted Daughter

Pamela

LETTER XL

Dear Sister:

What a strange world Providence has seen fit to put me in! Today in came the young master. No word of warning— not to me, anyhow. In he walks, with a lovely gray overcoat that is what is called tweeds, and a hat that is Homburg—I learn these things from Miss Bascom, who is all for the fashions, and likes to show a humble maid that she knows all the latest and best.

Well, he comes, and he says, "Hello, Pam, how's the old

girl?" It seems that you are only called old when you are young. Miss Bascom is in the room, and he gives her a smacking kiss and gives me one, and then upstairs he goes, two at a time, laughing. She says to me, "He is not drunk, for when he is that he is surly." I am glad, and realize all of a sudden that there has been something lacking in the house. That has been true of Miss Bascom also, for her handsome big gentleman, the buyer, has been away on a buying trip.

I knew Charles would return, of course, and I had never one night failed to bolt my door. I have made up my mind that I will take no more walks or drives or swims with him, but will be strictly the servant of his aunt. Let him be angry, but he will not be so angry as if I give him encouragement by trying to be kind. I am all in a terrible flutter—oh, dear, oh, dear! I cannot tell whether it is what has happened to Pamela One or Pamela Two, they are all mixed up together in my mind, and that terrible night when he was in my room is all a part of the long siege of my great-great-great-grandmother. Last night I was reading how she had been kidnaped and was in the hands of the dreadful treacherous Mrs. Jewkes, and I closed with the letter that she sent to her "strange wicked master," as she calls him:

"Sir, if you but knew the anguish of my mind, and how much I suffer by your dreadful usage of me, you would surely pity me, and consent to my deliverance. What have I done, that I should be the *only* mark of your cruelty? I can have no hope, no desire of living left me, because I cannot have the least dependence upon your solemn assurances, after what has passed. It is impossible they should be consistent with the dishonourable methods you take."

This might be to Charles from your devoted
                                                        Pamela

LETTER XLI

Dear Sister:

Something unusual has just happened. I received a letter that is not from you or Mother, the only ones who write to me. It is on prison stationery, and is from that young fellow, Paul Darrow, that I talked to in San Quentin. He is only allowed to write once a month, he says, and that is why he has not written sooner to thank me for my visit. He says that I am allowed to write to him, and there are little printed directions at the top telling me the rules about it. He has a number, 423718; my, that is a lot of men, but I suppose they are not all there now. Even so they are very lonely, he says, and a letter from the outside is always a great event. He is working in the jute mill, and says that is not a job a free man would choose. I suppose that is as much as he would dare to say.

I remember him as a very nice boy, and I suppose it is my duty to reply, but I do not know just what to say. He would not be interested in my affairs, I being almost a stranger to him. I would like to say something that would give him hope, but I do not know what it can be. I thought he would be glad to know what my lady is doing to keep the persecution of the IWW in people's minds; I asked her about it and she said, "Tell him, by all means. I write that myself." I cannot be sure that the prison people will let such a letter come in, but I wrote it. Also I looked up prisoners and captives in the Concordance and I have given him texts to read; I do hope they let him have a Bible. Do you think so?

I showed Miss Lucy the letter, and she has told others, and so they tease me, asking, will I wait for him? Well, it would be quite a wait, eight years, and then some more while he was getting a job to take care of himself, to say nothing of your devoted

Pamela

LETTER XLII

Dear Mother:

I have the most amazing story to tell you. It may come true and it may not, I cannot be sure, and you must not count on it too much or be too disappointed if it doesn't; but this is what: there is a chance that you may have a water-well drilled on your place. The kindness of my dear mistress has made the chance. For fear of disappointing you I might be wiser not to mention it, but I am afraid not to, for some day a rig might show up and you might send them away, thinking it was a trick of some sort.

All this came about through Mrs. Fearing, who is a rich friend of my lady and comes to the Thursday luncheons and other times. She and her husband own land and houses and do a lot of trading, and there was talk of young master buying from them a tract near Junipero and developing it with low-price houses. I made bold to say, "Be sure there is water on it, and plenty, because if not you will be stuck. That is what is the matter with our ranch, we have barely enough water for drinking and washing and a tiny garden patch, but if we had a well drilled and got water we would be comfortable." I had no idea of giving a hint, but out of it came the remark that a well wouldn't cost much, and why not get one? I said, "Oh, no!" more than once, but Master Charles said it should be done and my lady said she would pay for it. I kept saying it was too much and objecting that even if we had water neither Grampa nor you could work four acres now; but the answer was that if we had plenty of water we could sell three one-acre lots with water rights and be well off. Mrs. Harries said, "Of course," and that is where the matter stands now. I don't know what will happen, and would never so long as I live speak of it or hint at it; but it might be that tomorrow a rig will show up and all you have to do is to let the man pick out the most likely place and go to work.

You see how it is with rich people like this, whatever they want they do and you can never tell what is going to happen next. My good lady likes to have people happy around her, and of course it is plain that they are better company that way. Well, that is all tonight from your happy Daughter

Pamela

LETTER XLIII

Dear Sister:

What a story I have to tell you this time! I have already written some of it to Mother, so you do not have to send her this or say anything about the matter. It is a mixed-up situation, as you will see.

The beginning was that Mrs. Harries, poor soul, is trying so hard to think of some way of saving her adored nephew from himself and the bad people who are ruining him. Everybody tells her it is because he has no work to do, so she thinks, Oh, if only I could find something that would interest him! She had hopes of me, but I failed her, and he goes back to his movie stars and wild parties, as they are called. Now there came a suggestion from Mrs. Fearing, one of her friends, who has a tract of land on high ground just above Junipero. She persuaded my lady that it would be a wonderful site for what is called a housing project; it will all be laid out pretty with little streets wandering through the trees, and there will be a playground for the children and a school and church and everything nice, and model houses will be built and sold to working people at a price they can afford, and it will be something most useful. My lady thinks so, and has been to look at the place. She has talked to Charles and tried to get him pepped up, for it would be a way for him to make some money for himself and at the same time be busy. I believe she would give half her fortune if she could be sure of getting him saved by it.

First I must tell you about this Mrs. Fearing, who is a large lady and fills half the back seat in the big car and my lady the other half. I find that the help do not trust her but say that she is a shark; she is very determined to have her own way and is always ready to sell some real estate to any rich person she meets, or to sell anything else for a commission. She dresses elegant, and Cookie says that when she comes into the room it is like a ship under full sail, which is something I have never seen. This I do know or pretty nearly know about her: she has a little shrimp of a man for a husband, and she was mad at him when they came to the house one day; I was just outside the drawing-room door and heard her, though I couldn't make out what it was about. Well, later in the evening there are refreshments, and here comes little Mr. Fearing—Buster, she calls him—bringing a tray of fruit juice to the ladies, and he passes his wife and I saw her plain as day stick out her foot and trip him. He almost falls on his face, and the tray goes crash, and I have to set down what I am carrying and run quick and get cloths to mop up the juice and a dustpan and brush for the broken glass. I have observed that when anything like this happens these fashionable people do not show any alarm or excitement but act just as if nothing had happened and leave the mess to the servants. But I do wish I might have been in the car to hear what Buster and his lady said to each other on the way home!

The way I came into it was that Charles invited me to go for a drive with him, and I said, very formal, "Master Charles, I am sorry, but I am not driving any more." He says, "You are going to hold what I did against me?" I say, "No, not that, but I am afraid of you." "Oh," says he, "did I ever do you any harm, except once when I was drinking, and then, honest, I didn't know what I was doing." He did not say he was sorry or ashamed—I do not think he would ever stoop to apologize to anybody, surely not to a serving maid. I say, "I am afraid, because I can never know when you have been drinking or will be." Says he, "You can look at me and see for yourself. I have not had a drink for a week, and I tell you the truth, it was so that I could come home and invite a nice girl to have a drive."

I couldn't help but be touched by that, he can be such a sweet gentleman when he wants to, and, oh, what can I think of but to help him? I say, "You will start making love to me again," and he answers, "I will always be making love to you every time I look at you; but I will promise to make only the sort that you approve of." I tell him, "You know the sort I approve of, it is the love of God. I see that you are two different men, and one of them I hold in honor, and to the other I tell God's words, that wine is a mocker, strong drink is raging." Says he, "Those old birds did have a lot of sense, didn't they!" I answer, "Indeed they did, Charles"—for since he is being decent I take him for a friend again, though with caution. "I only wish that you would let me quote you some of the words from that old Book, those that apply to you, instead of those you pick out to make fun of." "All right," says he, "I promise to let you. But come now and drive and I will let you have another lesson, so that you can fit yourself for a lady chauffeur's job, which is much better paid than a parlormaid's. I will take you and show you the tract which I am thinking of buying and turning into a model community."

I am sure you understand, dear Sister, I couldn't possibly say No to that. Above all things it is important to keep him interested in that idea which has become his aunt's dream. I say, "I will take your word, but if you do not keep it I will have to say never again." So he grins and says, "I am on probation." I get into the car, and am very proud that I can drive it away, and I drive to the town and past it, and all the time he is paying me compliments about how I look and how smart I am and he insists that that is not love-making, that it is just telling the truth—which is God's will, is it not?

I say, "You know I cannot believe all this, Charles, and I try to figure out why you should be interested in me and keep it up. I am wondering, is it because I am the first girl that has ever said No to you and meant it?" "Who put that idea into your head?" he asks, and I say, "Nobody, but I try to think, and I wonder, is it the nature of men that they want what they cannot get, and grow tired of any conquest that is too easy?" "You are getting to be a psychologist as well as a chauffeur!" says he, and I say, "You are teasing me again. Is that because you are afraid to give me an honest answer?" "It could be," he says. "It is hard to face the truth about one's self, especially when it is unpleasant. I think it is because you are happy, and I am unhappy, and I think perhaps I can beg or buy or even steal some happiness from you." I say, "Ah, that is a fair answer; and can you blame me that I hold on to my happiness? I know that if I loved a man I should love him deeply and truly, and if he was not true to me I should never have any happiness again." He has one of those moments of goodness that come to him, and he says, "You are right, and I am a rotter." I answer quickly, "No, you are not that, you are a man who has had things too easy in this life, and you have never learned to use the abilities you have. What makes people happy is to set themselves a task and accomplish it and have a sense of pride in it. I came to your home with my mind made up to try to make myself useful, and I have done so, and that is why I am happy. I see you with nothing to do and I know that that is why you are not so."

Well, that is a little sermon that leads up to the tract of land to which we come. It is high and dry, and we get out and walk around, and the dryness is what worries me. I say, "What are you going to do for water here?" "We will drill an artesian well," he says. "But suppose you don't get water?" "You can always get it in this country if you go deep enough." "Yes, but can you get enough for a whole settlement, such as you would have here?" "If we don't get enough from one well, we can have two or three." I tell him, "I hope you have made sure about it, for it would be too bad to build a lot of houses and sell them to people and then have them find out that they couldn't get enough water for their lawns and gardens. So many people get caught that way; it was what happened to us when we came to California. We saw a spring on the land and thought it was wonderful; that was in the winter, and nobody told us that it might dry up in summer. That is why we have always been so poor; we can only plant things that are full grown by June, and by September we have to pay somebody to bring us water in barrels for washing and drinking." "But that is a shame, Pam! Why didn't you have a well drilled?" "That would have cost hundreds of dollars, maybe a thousand, we couldn't tell until we tried; and we never had such money."

He thinks for a minute and then he says, "Your mother is still living there?" I tell him, "And my grandfather." He asks, "What would she do if a rig showed up there someday and started to drill a well on the place?" "She would know there was something wrong and she wouldn't let them." "But suppose they told her it was paid for?" "She wouldn't believe them; she would be sure it was some sort of trick to get a lien on the place and take it away from her." "Well, then," he says, "you had better write and warn her, because somebody will come." "Oh, Charles," I cry, "I couldn't let you do that!" "Why not?" he asks. "It might be the first sensible thing I have done this year." "Oh, but I could never repay you!" "You have repaid me by being a good friend and giving me a lot to think about; and you have kept me on the water wagon for several weeks, and you might do it some more if I supply you with enough water."

I am so flustered that I cannot think what to say. I try to be honest and I say, "It may not be so sensible, because Grampa is too old to farm land, and Mother could not do it alone." "How much land did you say you had?" And when I tell him four acres, he says, "If you had water on it, you could divide it into one-acre tracts and sell three of them; then you have the money and the water too; also you would have neighbors and not be so lonely. Isn't that sensible?" "Yes, Charles; but I dare not be under such obligation to you!" "Don't be silly," says he; "I am not a blackmailer. And anyhow, it isn't my money, it's my aunt's, and

I know she'll be glad to do it if I suggest it to her. You've seen how she gives money away, and why shouldn't you be one of the lucky?" I tell him, "I know lots of people feel that way, but I never thought to be one of them." "Of course not; and that's why I suggest it. I see the money going to grafters and cheats, and why shouldn't some decent people get a share? Write your mother about it tonight."

So that is how it is; and he says, "What do you think of this land for a settlement project?" I tell him, "What I think is that before you buy it you should ask Mr. and Mrs. Fearing to drill a well and see what they get, and you should put on the property only as many houses as you can be sure of having water for." "By God, Pam," says he, "you are a witch!" I cannot keep from being pleased, even though he takes the name of the Lord in vain. I do not say any more about the matter, because I know that Mrs. Fearing has been sort of motherly to him and he thinks a great deal of her. I think he needs friends so bad, and I don't want to say anything to take one away. But tell me, Sister, what am I to say about this—and what shall I do now if he asks to kiss me again? Oh, dear, oh, dear, could he possibly mean it for that? Your frightened Sister

Pamela

LETTER XLIV

Dear Mother:

Oh, what wonderful news about the well and the windmill, and oh, I am so happy! When your letter came I took the liberty of going to my mistress's room and begging her pardon to thank her, and she said, "That is all right and I am glad it turned out so. I know that your mother is a good woman, or she could not have trained a daughter so well. And those of us who have too much owe a duty to those who have too little." I thought it was a good time to put God's words into her mind, so I said, "It is written, 'But seek ye first the kingdom of God, and His righteousness; and all these things shall be added unto you.' " She smiled and said, "You really do know that old Book, don't you!" I said, "I scarcely know any other, Mrs. Harries; only that and a few school books." She takes it kindly, and little by little I hope that God and His righteousness will steal into her mind.

I think how wonderful the ranch will be, with water in plenty. You can set out some fruit trees, which do not need too much care. I insist that you must get pipe and run the water into the house. Let me pay for the pipe, me with my riches! It will not need a plumber, who will charge high to come out there. Grampa can get a pipe wrench, and measuring carefully have the pipe cut where he buys it. How I should like to be there to help! My back aches to think of all the tons of water that I carried from the spring since I was a child. But I suppose I can count it good training, for I am strong and can take care of myself. There is a Portuguese boy that I think would like to walk out with me; he seems very shy, and I do not help him any. It gives me a pleasant feeling to know that somebody is adoring me from a long way off. But never think that I will present you with a Papist son-in-law! Your most happy Daughter

Pamela

LETTER XLV

Dear Sister:

Mother says that she has written you about the well. Is it not marvelous! I shall never be content till I have seen it with my own eyes. When I thanked my lady for it she said, "It was Charles's happy thought"—giving him the credit, you see. I told her, "I know that," and, says she, "Be as kind to him as you can, and help us to keep him at home." I said that I would, but not without misgivings in my heart; for what could she mean by that remark? She must know that I have done everything in my power save one thing; and can it possibly mean that she would wish me to do that, and is hinting that she would permit it in her household? This question puzzles me as nothing ever in my life before. A strange world that I have come into, and everything is topsy-turvy—one can no longer be sure what is right and what wrong. I am used to the idea that people should desecrate the Sabbath and worship the Lord on Sunday; but that they should not know that sin is sin, that confounds me. I torment my poor head and think, can it be that this so good lady really wishes me to become the concubine of her nephew? Then I tell myself, No, it cannot be, it is a stupid thought; it is because my own mind is no longer pure as it was. But then I say, what else can she mean? And why can she not say it in plain words that a poor maidservant can understand?

There is something else that puzzles my wits, and that is Miss Yvette and her rodeo rider. I notice that whenever the help speak of this pair they have a sort of smile as if they know something they are not saying to a child like me. And not long ago I was taken riding with my lady and her friend Mrs. Aronson, a very elegant lady who is married to a Jew, though I don't think that she is Jewish herself; she was in school with Mrs. Harries and so they are old friends and she comes visiting now and then. They are in the back seat and I am in the little seat, with my back to them, and as usual they give me no heed. Says Gretchen, as the lady is called, "What is this I hear about Yvette?" and my lady answers, "Yes, isn't it strange!"—in a helpless sort of way, as if she could think of no more, and they say no more. I sit there and think, what can it be? I have the idea that maybe the rodeo lady is getting money from Miss Yvette, but there would be nothing so strange about that, for everybody gets money from all this family, except perhaps from the master. I think, it must be something else, and it must indeed be true, or else my lady would have said, "Oh, no, there is nothing to it."

The master is not here very often; he has kept the agreement not to be in the way. I hear talk that there is great excitement in the stock market, the prices change suddenly and he has to be at the board room to see it. Then he plays golf a lot, which as I have told you is knocking a little round ball around a field; I have never seen that and cannot say that I wish to. Charles does it too, and has a bagful of sticks that are called clubs. A strange thing indeed that men who have no work to do should have to invent work! They keep the score carefully and make bets and are proud of their skill; I have heard them bragging. I should indeed be sorry for myself if ever the time came that I could think of nothing better than this to do. Miss Lucy named to me a dozen games that have to do with balls big or little, either knocking them or throwing them or kicking them. I do not remember all the names. I have my Concordance, and read that the Lord "will surely violently turn and toss thee like a ball," and I do not want anything like that to happen to me.

I have just been told that there is to be a swimming party here for the young people tomorrow afternoon. Charles, who has been away, is to bring Miss Sylvia Sloane. My lady has told me that I am to wait upon them, and that is supposed to be a pleasure and so I will take it. I am happy that I shall be in a black costume with white apron and cap—and not in one of those almost-nothing suits! Thus nobody will be tempted to mistake me for one of the guests. Your devoted Sister

Pamela

LETTER XLVI

Dear Sister:

Well, we have had the bathing party, and it was surely most elegant. Miss Yvette came with her friends, and young people came from nearby and others from afar; some I knew by name and some I had not seen before. All the men are handsome and all the ladies young and beautiful; I cannot deny that Miss Sylvia is both of these. They are all as brown as fallen chinaberry leaves, but I suppose not in those places which the strips of cloth cover. The pingpong table was brought out, and some played while others sat in the lawn seats and watched. There is a springboard and they dived in fancy ways, and swam, and then lay around baking in our sun which they do not seem to mind at all, though a few put on dark glasses, which make them look strange. I had plenty of time to watch them, for I was coming and going with ices and iced drinks and little cakes; they had no liquor, I am happy to say, but they would go to their cars now and then and I guessed it was for that. They seem to know ways to keep one another laughing, but what I heard were things that meant nothing to me because they had to do with the different persons and things that had happened to them. I gather that it is easy to laugh when you have nothing else to do.

Well, they all had what I have learned to call a buffet supper, and Mr. Carmichael, the butler, very elegant, helped to carry the foods, and after they had eaten everything— they have good appetites—the party was over and they all went roaring off in the fast cars. Only Charles did not go, but Sylvia went in one of the other cars. I wondered if maybe they had had a fuss; anyhow, I guessed it might mean trouble for me, and I planned to get away to my room. But Charles said, "Can we have a talk, Pam?" and of course what could I say to that but Yes. He has given us a well and a windmill, which is more than he promised, and I dare not guess what it has cost; my lady has told me again and again to be kind to him, and help to keep him at home, and here he is.

So we are sitting out in one of the lawn swings, one that faces the west, looking out over the valley. It is one of those warm evenings of which we have only a few in the whole summer, as you know. There is a new moon in front of us and a bright star, and the scent of orange blossoms comes up from the orchard below, and everything is as lovely as anybody can imagine. But not Charles, alas; he is in one of his sad moods, and he says, "You saw that bunch of idlers." All that I can say is Yes, for they were surely idle unless you count pingpong and diving, at which they were amazingly skillful. He says, "There isn't one person there that is doing anything useful, or has any idea of it; there isn't one that is thinking of anything but his own pleasure." Say I, "Why don't you get a different lot of friends?" And he answers, "They are the ones I was brought up with." I am not sure it would be polite to agree about them, so I say, "But now you are going into a business, and you will have work to do." "Will I?" says he, "or will I just be fumbling? I don't know about the job, and it will just be a question of hiring people who do know, and they will not want me to meddle with them." "You are much too modest," I tell him. "You have a good mind and can learn quickly. If people see that you really want to learn, they will be glad to tell you what they know." "You are a trusting soul, Pam," says he; "but you are a darling, and how I wish you could be happy with me." "I am happy at this moment, sir," I say. He has forbade the sir, but I put it in to remind us both of my humble station.

It does not serve, for he lays his hand on mine, and right away I feel that trembling that disturbs me, and I am no longer entirely happy but only partly so. It is a regular proceeding that I have come to know. First he lays his hand on mine, then he takes mine in his, then he takes it over to his, and pretty soon he kisses it very gently. Then I have to say, "Now, Charles, that is enough," and of course he will have to ask, "Why?" and "What harm am I doing?" I say, "Dear Charles, don't let us go through all that again. You frighten me, and then I start crying, and then you are vexed with me." "What a little prude you are, Pam! But you are a sweet one, and I would not have you otherwise." "That is kind of you," I say, "and if I can be sure of that, then you will not be taking my happiness away, as you said." "If I said that," answers he, "it was not a fortunate phrase. Happiness is not something limited, like a piece of cake or a dollar bill that might be taken from you. Happiness can be made at will, and there is no limit to it. You and I have everything that it takes, if only I could get you to see it." He begins a long speech to me, about how I have been mistaught and am a victim of superstition; how nature has made me for love, and him to love, and how I fear where there is no cause for fear, and no harm can come to me. He says, "Try to be sensible, and look at the facts of life. I have held your hand, but what harm can you show that I have done to it? I have kissed your lips, but is there any brand on them, or scar, or sign of evil?" I say, "No, but that is not the end; you are not satisfied with that, and one thing leads to another."

Well, what this leads to is, he proposes a bargain. We will have what he calls a petting party; I do not like the name, but he tells me I am the only one among young people who does not. He will put his arms about me, kiss me very gently and properly, and will do no more. I say to myself, I wish so to save him and to help him, and to bring happiness to his aunt, and if that will do so much I may call it my duty. So we sit, and look at the moon slowly sinking behind the mountain far across the valley, and at the still white star that follows it; and the smell of the orange blossoms is something to make you dizzy; his arms are around me, and now and then he kisses me very gently, and I think, oh, this is nice, and if he can be happy this way, so can I, and it is all right, as he says. He whispers sweet words, tells me that I am lovely, and how much I have taught him, and how happy I have made him. I suspect that he doesn't mean quite all of it, but it is pleasant to hear, and he has told me this is to be play, and that is what all love is, or ought to be; so I play that it is true. My head lies against his shoulder, and I am warm and comfortable, and I think, yes, this is right, this is the way love is meant to be, and there is no harm in it; if I am good to him, I can make him be good, and he will no longer go after the bad women.

He says, "Put your arms around me, Pam," and I do so, and feel still nearer to him; he is such a wonderful man, handsomer than any I have ever spoken to in my life, and he knows so much more than I. I think of something I have tried to keep out of my thoughts, which is that he might ask me to marry him, and if he did, what am I going to say? Miss Lucy has caused me to think about it and has said that he will never do it. She says, "It is like royalty in England, he will not think of marrying a commoner." I say, "But what is royalty in this country? Is it just having a lot of money?" "It is having a great lot," says she, "and meaning to hold onto it." "But has he not got enough for two?" She says, "Nobody ever has enough, there is always a lot more. He will talk love to you, but the word marriage you will never hear."

Now I think, perhaps she is mistaken; perhaps his feelings are as nice as mine at this moment, and he will forget that he is a young prince. And what will I answer him? I have made up my mind in secret. I will say No. I cannot marry a man that does not believe in God and His Providence. I will not demand that he shall believe everything of our faith, that he must keep the Sabbath and not smoke or eat meat; but two things are necessary to my happiness, that he believe in God and Christ the Redeemer, and that he shall promise to let liquor alone. For how could I be happy with a man that I was sure was destined for hell-fire in the next world, or for misery and shame in this one? No, a thousand times; I have said it I know not how many times to myself in scenes which I imagined.

Now he kisses me, and asks me to kiss him, and I do, for I want more and more to please him. He says, "You know you love me, Pam," and I do not answer, for I want to talk

to him about God and I know that if I do it will only start
an argument. He says, "Look, what a wonderful chance we
have. You don't have to say a word to anybody, just step
into the car and away we'll go. I can telephone Aunt Maggie
in the morning and make it all right. We'll go up to the
Yosemite and see that grand scenery; we'll go to Canada
and see the Rockies. We'll go to Chicago and New York
and visit the museums—you're allowed to see museums,
aren't you? We'll hear the music and meet a lot of famous
people. And then we'll take a steamer to England—we
can get the passports right away. We'll go to Paris, and
tour all France, the loveliest places you ever dreamed of. I
can get the gas—it costs a lot, but I know how to get what
I want. And more than anything else I want you; you are
the girl who can save me from myself and make a new man
of me."

But still he does not say, "Marry me," and of course I
would die before I would say it, for it would be asking for a
share of his money, or so he would take it. No, if it is to be
said, he is the one to say it; and I need not suppose that he
does not know the word. His smart friends may try to forget
it, but it is somewhere in their heads, I am sure.

I see that I have to divert his mind, so I say, "Charles
dear, your aunt has brought a tract of land for you, and you
are going to take an interest in that." "Oh, hell!" he says.
"You know that means nothing to me. I'm trying to please
the poor soul, but it bores me stiff." "But what sort of gratitude would I be showing her, Charles, if I led you astray?"
That amuses him greatly. "Whoops!" he cries. "Who is the
devil here? She will know, never fear!" "Maybe so, Charles,
but she will know that I should not have consented." "Don't
fool yourself with that, kid. She would pay you any price if
you would put me on the straight path and keep me there.
She knows that she has no power to do it. And as for the

price of a windmill and a well, good Lord, we'll spend more than that in a week!"

We are having a petting party, and I must not say anything to annoy or rebuke him. I say, "Look, Charles, one of the reasons I love you is that you have a kind heart, and have been thinking of building homes for poor people and making life easier for them." "And do you suppose they would thank me for that?" "I have been hoping they would." "They'd complain that the doors were made of green lumber and holler for me to come and repair the plumbing. They'd fall behind on their payments, and if I turned them out they'd call me a Shylock and want to shoot me." "Oh, dear!" I cry. "So that is the way you feel about it!" Says he, "I want to please my aunt, who loves me dearly; but heck, what do I know about building projects, and how many years would it take me to learn? She will be swindled everywhere she turns, and how can I help it? There is a chap that calls himself a landscape artist and has a great reputation, and he will make the place all over; she trusts him because he is the son of one of her old friends—but I know that the fellow has a pottery plant where he makes ollas and such things, and he has a way to stain them and pit them and make them look old, and they are being sold for antiques all over this state. He will tell you that he doesn't sell them for antiques, so that puts him in the clear; but he knows perfectly well that the dealers are selling them for antiques and paying him double prices for that reason. That's the sort of thing you run into, all through the business world; it's rotten as hell, and why does anybody want to get into it if he can stay out?"

So this is the end of our petting party that was to be an experiment. When he starts kissing me again my heart is dead; and when he starts pressing me more closely I say, "No, Charles, that is enough now; you promised you wouldn't do that; you must stop now." When he tries not to heed me, I start to weep, and he says, "Oh, God, that crybaby stuff again!" I say, "You promised not to go any farther," and he takes the name of Jesus in vain and says it is a way to drive a man crazy. I say, "I am sorry, but you told me the opposite of that, you told me to try the experiment, and now you tell me it is a failure." Up he starts and exclaims, "I know where to find a girl that will not turn me down!" I say, "That I do not doubt. I will go into the house now," and I go. He follows me, for he still cannot bear to give me up. He catches me in the entry and tries to hold me fast, but I say, "You will make me scream again, Charles!" —and of course he does not want that. He lets me go and I run up to my room, and you may be sure I am glad for that bolt that I have put on with long screws.

The end is sad. In the morning he is gone, and without a note or word to anybody. I see that my lady has been crying, and there are tears in my heart too. I guess that she may ask me what happened, but she is too proud. The less said the better, for I feel sure it would offend her that I had presumed to turn down a request from her royal nephew. It would do no good to tell her about the sin of fornication, and very certainly I shall never speak the presumptuous word marriage in her presence. You will see that I am somewhat bitter in my thoughts, even mixed with my gratitude. It is strange how one can have two such contradictory sets of thoughts, but I have them, and so does she, I am certain. She loves me and wishes me well, but only on the terms that I shall be obedient, not merely to my old mistress but to my young master. Be sure that there will not soon be another petting party for your devoted Sister

Pamela

LETTER XLVII

Dear Mother:

It is so wonderful to hear about the water. Do write me the details; I can imagine everything and it makes me so happy I have tears in my eyes. I am grateful to my good lady and mean to do everything in my power to repay her for this kindness, so beyond all I could have imagined.

There is much talk here about the new housing project, as it is called. Different people call to see my lady with their plans and she hears them all. Master Charles being away, she attends to it herself. Already they have started what is called landscaping; they lose no time, knowing of course that they will be well paid. How I wish that I knew more, so that I could help to make sure that she gets good value. But perhaps she does not care, since it is her idea that she keeps the money in circulation. You see how many new things I am learning; it is strange to think how the same dollar is spent over and over again and makes it possible for all sorts of work to be done.

I think my dear mistress has noticed that I try to hear what is going on at the lectures, and that pleases her, because she wants everybody to be educated, even the lowliest. Last Sunday she had a newspaper gentleman who has been traveling in Europe, and he says that the war has settled nothing, that Germany is going to make another try for mastery as soon as she gets a chance, and sooner or later there will be another great war. This is what my lady herself has been saying ever since I have known her: wars never settled anything, and there was never any good war or bad peace. I don't think she wanted the Germans to win, she just wanted everybody to stop where they were. I don't think she wants there to be any police or jails either; she says that if you did justice and paid people good wages they would not have to steal and they would not. She makes a lot of enemies by such talk but this she does not seem to mind.

This is not a long letter, but is longer than you write to your devoted Daughter

Pamela

Dear Sister:

There is nothing in this world too wonderful to happen to this luckiest of all parlormaids. I am a parlormaid no longer, I am a secretary—or at any rate a halfway secretary, a sect'y-to-be, a sect'y-on-trial. For Miss Bascom's buyer has at last made up his mind—hers has been made up for a long time, we have all been sure. There is going to be a wedding in this house, and you may be sure it will be a bang-up one —Miss Alma Bascom says it herself.

I was hoping it wouldn't happen for another year, for I had the idea that I might educate myself, and was trying as hard as I knew. But no such luck, I thought, when I heard of the goings on. But then my lady sent for me, and I thought it was to be a shopping trip, perhaps for the wedding, and that would be fun. But no, she says, "What's this I hear, Pamela, about your practicing on Miss Bascom's typewriter?" I say, "Well, Mrs. Harries, she was kind enough to let me when I am off duty; and I thought I might be able to help you on her off days, or when she has one of her headaches. I hope it is no offense." "Of course not. I notice also that you look up words in the dictionary." "Well, Mrs. Harries, I try not to be ignorant, and when I hear a word I want to know what people are talking about. Sometimes it is too long a word and I cannot get it straight." "You should ask me," says she. "I know that you are a bright girl as well as a good one, and I wish to help you. I have been wondering if it might not be possible for you to take over Alma's work."

Well, I thought I would just about pop out of my shoes. I can hardly say anything, just, "Oh, Mrs. Harries!" She asks, "Would you like to try?" and then I do not miss another chance. I say, "Oh, I would try so hard! And I believe I could do it if you would be patient with me for a little while." "I have spoken to Alma about it, and she has agreed to explain things to you, if you wish to learn." "Oh, Mrs. Harries, I would work so hard! I ought to tell you that I have thought about it and have watched what she does and how she does it. I will surprise you." "You little monkey!" she says, but that is a compliment, for she smiles. She says, "You will have to learn to do typing, and to take my letters on the machine the way Alma does. You will have to learn who are the people I want to see and who are the ones I want to get rid of." "That will be the hardest part, Mrs. Harries, for I have the idea that sometimes you are not sure yourself." "That is true," she admits; "it is not easy for me." I would have liked to add that sometimes Miss Bascom makes up her mind for her; but it will be a long time before I know her that well.

The short of it is that I am to have seventy-five a month, and if I do well it will be increased until I get what Miss Bascom is getting, a hundred and twenty-five. I cry, "Oh, I couldn't take that much, Mrs. Harries!" She says, "Don't worry, I won't give it to you until you earn it. In the meantime you will be on trial, and I expect you to put your mind on it and learn. You will have to have different clothes if you are going to be a secretary. I will get you some to start you off."

That is the way it was. In the afternoon Miss Bascom drove me in to town in a little car that is used for errands; and, oh glory, I'll be able to use it sometimes, and will I be scared all alone! No, I won't, for I am not going to be a boob. All the way in, Miss Bascom gives me advice and instructions; she is very kind, and of course has to be, for she is getting a lovely wedding as a gift, and will get other things, and I am not turning her out or doing her any harm. She tells me, and be sure that I listen! When we are in the dress shop—I shiver as I tell it, she spent more than a hundred and fifty dollars for dresses and all that go with it so that I would be fit to be even a half-secretary to so great a lady. It took about fifty dollars more for a hat and shoes and stockings and the other things. She has told me to be quiet and calm and dignified, and I try my best, and manage not to shout when I look at myself in the mirror of the shop. I am good-looking, I must tell you.

One thing I said to my lady, "There is a mátter that may trouble you—that you will not have any secretary from sundown Friday until sundown Saturday." She says, "I have thought of that and will adjust myself to it; but I will work you extra hard on Sunday." That I know is true, for I shall have to receive all those visitors and find out the names of new ones and remember everything. I am shaking in my new shoes, which fortunately have not very high heels—I resisted Miss Bascom on that. Pray for your promoted Sister

Pamela

LETTER XLIX

Dear Sister:

The long letter is so that you can send it on to Mother and Grampa. This is just to add something that is not for them. Driving me home in my new clothes, Miss Bascom said, "Now you will get more kisses from Charles." I tried not to look startled, for that is something you never do in the fashionable world; you take everything for a joke and smile over it. I said, "Do secretaries get kissed more often?" and she answered, "They get more opportunities." I would like to ask what she had got, and I was sure that would have been smart conversation; she would perhaps have told me her stories in exchange for mine. But I am not that well educated yet. I said, "You know, Miss Bascom, I am a country girl, and my religion is very strict." She said, "I know that, and you had better hold fast to it." For that you can trust your devoted

Pamela

LETTER L

Dear Mother:

We have had our wedding, and it was the loveliest and excitingest thing. Miss Bascom, that is now Mrs. Denby, looked so splendid, and her gentleman is so stout and stately!

The new secretary that is me has a dress made of light green lawn with little white flowers on it and is the finest I ever dreamed to have on. It was my duty to receive the guests and show them to their seats, many of them people I had never seen before, and Miss Bascom had told me not to be scared, and if I did not know what to say I need not say anything, but just look pretty and nobody would expect me to have much sense. I guess I did it all right and they didn't. The reverend was Dr. Clark, and they tell me he has a right to do it, but be sure if I ever come to get married it will be somebody of our own faith that I can trust to do it right. But he is a kind gentleman and I am sure is acting according to his lights.

Well, I am the secretary; the "half" part of it applies only to the pay, I think, for I do all the work. I cannot type fast enough, so I take my lady's dictation in longhand, writing as fast as I can and if it is too bad I type it in my room. I have moved into Miss Bascom's room that was; it is on the second floor in back and near my lady's; it is so big that I feel lost in it. Now I am Miss Andrews and no longer Pamela, except to my lady and old friends. It is all so strange I can hardly believe it. I practice the typewriter every spare moment, and I have a small dictionary in my room so that I can look up the long words my lady uses. She writes letters to the newspapers and to important persons and tells them what they are doing that is wrong, and she says that is the duty of every citizen. Did you know that? Pray for your fast-improving Little One

Pamela

LETTER LI

Dear Sister:

You will get my letter to Mother telling about the wedding and about my new state of life. Now I have had my first Sunday afternoon and am told that I did all right. The guests had seen me always in a black maid's dress and now must have been surprised to see me in light green and doing the elegant; most of them didn't know my name, so they were the ones to be embarrassed. Now for the first time I had a chance to sit and listen to the speaker, who was a member of Parliament from New Zealand and told how the government there does much more for the people than ours does; my lady sits presiding, and when she agrees with the speaker she nods her head all the time, which is her kind of applause; all know what she thinks, and would not come here often if they did not agree. When it came time for the eats I poured the tea, and, oh, dear, my hands shook, but I soon got over it, for after all it does not take much cleverness to say "One lump or two?" and "Lemon or cream?" and I had been well rehearsed. So I did no spilling, and smiled at everybody, and said something pleasant if they spoke to me. I have found that it makes the whole world different when you have on a ladylike dress instead of a black uniform. I am glad that I did not know it before, or I should have been less happy.

The nice Mr. Mackenzie came, and I had a chat with him—it is proper now, since that is permitted to secretaries. He is much amused that I am so excited over Pamela One, as he has taken to calling her. I have not written you much about it, in view of your fear that it is really a novel in spite of being in the form of letters. I assure you that I have never once permitted the reading to cause me to neglect my devotions; it has been something of a test for me, for oh, it is so thrilling, and when I see that my last minute is almost past I have to take a peek ahead to make sure that the poor soul is going to survive—although I know perfectly well that she has to, for how else could the rest of the book be? What she went through is almost beyond belief, for her master was both cruel and treacherous; I have never met such a man, and am glad indeed that I can say it. The things that he did in the effort to deprive her of her virtue! They were so unendurable that she gave up her place and was to be sent back to her parents, but instead he had her carried off to a remote property that he owned, and there he has her guarded by heartless and wicked servants—oh, the most awful creatures. I will copy for you what Pamela wrote to her parents:

"Now I will give you a picture of this wretch. She is a broad, squat, pursy, *fat thing*, quite ugly, if anything human can be so called; about forty years old. She has a huge hand, and an arm as thick as my waist, I believe. Her nose is flat and crooked, and her brows grow down over her eyes; a dead, spiteful, gray, goggling eye, to be sure she has; and her face flat and broad; and as to colour, looks as if it had been pickled a month in saltpeter; I dare say she drinks. She has a hoarse man-like voice, and is as thick as she's long: and yet looks so deadly strong, that I am afraid she would dash me at her foot in an instant, if I was to vex her. So that with a heart more ugly than her face, she frightens me sadly; and I am undone, to be sure, if God does not protect me; for she is very, very wicked—indeed she is."

Did you ever, in all your life, read of such a dreadful creature? Her name is Mrs. Jewkes, and Pamela calls her in these secret letters "the wretch." She forbids the maids even to talk to Pamela, and when a poor clergyman called Mr. Williams tries to help her she tells dreadful falsehoods about him, and he is arrested. All this goes on and on until you can hardly bear to read it; and every night when I pray, I find myself wanting to pray for poor Pamela One, along with my Mother and Sister and kind mistress and poor misguided young master. I will copy one of the dreadful scenes for you.

"Good Sirs! good Sirs! What will become of me? Here is my master come in his fine chariot! Indeed he is! What shall I do? Where shall I hide myself? O! what shall I do? Pray for me! But O! you will not see this! Now, good God of Heaven, preserve me! if it is Thy blessed will!

SEVEN O'CLOCK

"Though I dread to see him, yet I wonder I have not. No doubt something is resolving against me, as he stays to hear all her stories. I can hardly write; yet, as I can do nothing else, I know not how to forbear! I cannot hold my pen— how crooked and trembling the lines! I must leave off till I can get quieter fingers! Why should the guiltless tremble so, when the guilty can possess their minds in peace?

SATURDAY MORNING

"Now let me give you an account of what passed last night; for I had no power to write, nor yet opportunity, till now.

"This vile woman held my master till half an hour after seven; and he came hither about five in the afternoon. And then I heard his voice on the stairs, as he was coming up to me. It was about his supper; for he said, 'I shall choose a boiled chicken with butter and parsley.' And up he came.

"He put on a stern and majestic air; and he can look very majestic when he pleases. 'Well, perverse Pamela, ungrateful runaway,' said he, for my first salutation. 'You do well, don't you, to give me all this trouble and vexation?' I could not speak; but throwing myself on the floor, hid my face, and was ready to die with grief and apprehension. He said, 'Well may you hide your face! Well may you be ashamed to see me, vile forward one as you are!' I sobbed, and wept, but could not speak. And he let me lie, and went to the door, and called Mrs. Jewkes. 'There,' said he, 'take up that fallen angel! Once I thought her as innocent as an angel: but I have now no patience with her. The little hypocrite prostrates herself thus, in hopes to move my weakness in her favour, and that I'll raise her from the floor myself. But I shall not touch her. No,' said he, 'let such fellows as Williams be taken in by her artful wiles! I know her now, and she is for any fool's turn that will be caught by her.'

"I sighed as if my heart would break! And Mrs. Jewkes lifted me up upon my knees; for I trembled so I could not stand. 'Come,' said she, 'Mistress Pamela, learn to know your best friend! Confess your unworthy behaviour, and beg his honour's forgiveness of all your faults.' I was ready to faint; and he said, 'She is mistress of arts, I'll assure you; and will mimic a fit, ten to one, in a minute.'

"I was struck to the heart at this, but could not speak presently; only lifted my eyes up to Heaven! And at last said, 'God forgive you, Sir!' He seemed in a great passion, and walked up and down the room, casting sometimes an eye upon me and seeming as if he would have spoken, but checked himself. And at last he said, 'When she has acted this her first part over, perhaps I will see her again, and she shall soon know what she has to trust to.'

"And so he went out of the room; and I was quite sick at heart. 'Surely,' said I, 'I am the wickedest creature that ever breathed!' 'Well,' said the impertinent, 'not so wicked as that neither; but I am glad you begin to see your faults. Nothing like being humble! Come, I'll stand your friend, and plead for you, if you'll promise to be more dutiful for the future. Come, come,' added the wretch, 'this may be all made up by to-morrow morning, if you are not a fool.' 'Be gone, hideous woman!' said I, 'and let not my afflictions be added to by thy inexorable cruelty, and unwomanly wickedness.'

"She gave me a push, and went away in a violent passion. It seems she made a story of this; and said, I had such a spirit, there was no bearing it.

"I laid down on the floor, and had no power to stir, till the clock struck nine; and then the wicked woman came up again. 'You must come down stairs,' said she, 'to my master; that is, if you please, spirit!' Said I, 'I believe I cannot stand.' 'Then,' said she, 'I'll send Monsieur Colbrand to carry you down.'

"I got up as well as I could, and trembled all the way down stairs; she went before me into the parlour; and a new servant that he had waiting on him, instead of John, withdrew as soon as I came in: and, by the way, he had a new coachman too; which looked as if Bedfordshire Robin was turned away.

" 'And so you say,' said he, 'that she had another project, but yesterday, to get away?' 'She denies it herself,' said she; 'but it had all the appearance of one. I'm sure she made me in a fearful pucher about it. I'm glad your honour is come; and, I hope, whatever be your honour's intention concerning her, you will not be long about it; for you'll find her as slippery as an eel, I'll assure you.'

" 'Sir,' said I, clasping his knees with my arms, not knowing what I did, and falling on my knees, 'have mercy on me, and hear me, concerning that wicked woman's usage of me.'

"He cruelly interrupted me, and said, 'I am satisfied she has done her duty; it signifies nothing what you say against Mrs. Jewkes.'

" 'Well,' said the aggravating creature, 'this is nothing to what she has called me; I have been a Jezebel, a London prostitute, and what not! But I am content with her ill names, now I see it is her fashion.'

" 'Well,' said I, 'since I must not speak, I will hold my peace; but there is a righteous Judge, who knows the secrets of all hearts; and to Him I appeal.'

" 'See there!' said he: 'now this meek, good creature is praying for fire from Heaven upon us! O she can curse most heartily, in the spirit of Christian meekness, I'll assure you. How happy it is, that you can, at will, make your speaking eyes overflow in this manner, without losing any of their brilliancy! You have been told, I suppose, that you are most beautiful in your tears! Did you ever,' said he to her (who all this while was standing in one corner of the parlour), 'see a more charming creature than this? Is it to be wondered at, that I demean myself thus to take notice of her? See,' said he, and took the glass with one hand, and turned me round with the other, 'what a shape, what a neck! what a hand! and what a bloom on that lovely face! But who can describe the tricks and artifices that lie lurking in her little, plotting, guileful heart! 'Tis no wonder the poor parson was infatuated with her. I blame him less than I do her; for who could expect such artifice in so young a sorceress?'

"I went to the further part of the room, and held my face against the wainscot; and, in spite of all I could do to refrain crying, sobbed as if my heart would break.

" 'Come hither, hussy,' said he, 'you and I have a dreadful reckoning to make. Why don't you come, when I bid you?' 'Fie upon it, Mistress Pamela,' said she; 'what, not stir, when his honour commands you to come to him? Who knows but his goodness will forgive you?'

"He came to me (for I had not power to stir), and put his arm about my neck, and would kiss me; and said, 'Well, Mrs. Jewkes, I believe in my heart, so great is my weakness, that I could yet forgive this intriguing little slut, and take her to my bosom.'

" 'O,' said the sycophant, 'you are very good, Sir, very forgiving, indeed! But come,' added the profligate wretch, 'I hope you will be so good as to take her to your bosom; and that, by to-morrow morning, you'll bring her to a better sense of her duty!'

"Could any thing in womanhood be so vile? I had no patience, but yet grief and indignation choked up the passage of my words; and I could only stammer out a passionate exclamation to Heaven, to protect my innocence. But the word was the subject of their ridicule. Was ever poor creature worse beset!

"He said, as if he had been considering whether he could forgive me or not, 'No, I cannot yet forgive her neither. She has given me great disturbance; has brought great discredit upon me, both abroad and at home; has corrupted all my servants at the other house; has despised my honourable views and intentions to her, and sought to run away with this ungrateful parson. And surely I ought not to forgive all this!' Yet, with all this wretched grimace, he kissed me again, and would have put his hand into my bosom; but I struggled, and said, I would die before I would be used thus. 'Consider, Pamela,' said he, in a threatening tone, 'consider where you are! and don't play the fool: if you do, a more dreadful fate awaits you than you expect. But, take her up stairs, Mrs. Jewkes, and I'll send a few lines to her to consider of; and let me have your answer, Pamela, in the morning. Till then you have to resolve: and after that your doom is fixed.' So I went up stairs, and gave myself up to grief, and expectation of what he would send; but yet I was glad of this night's reprieve."

What I cannot understand about all this, Sister, is that I had always thought of England as a good country, even two hundred years ago, and I cannot imagine why Pamela One did not smuggle out a letter to the police. I ask Mr. Mackenzie about this, and he tells me that in those days the landlords of the district would control whatever squire or constable there was, and it might be that the law would not trouble itself on behalf of a poor child. I notice how everybody in the book writes great long letters back and forth, and Mr. Mackenzie smiles and says that is the way of the story; even the wicked master writes long letters to the poor maidservant that he is persecuting, and if a man did a thing like that nowadays, says Mr. Mackenzie, he would get himself in for a pretty breach-of-promise suit. He asks with a grin if Charles has ever made that mistake, and I say that I have never had a line from him. "Wise boy!" says this editor, and I am left to wonder about it, whether that is just an accident, or whether my young master really has the thought that I might do such a thing to him. Every day I decide that this world is even worse than I thought it the day before. Pray constantly for your innocent Little Sister

Pamela

LETTER LII

Dear Sister:

I have not had much to tell about the master, a very
bitter and unhappy man, by his looks. He comes and goes
and has seldom spoken to a parlormaid; it was my duty to
be sure that he had no fault to find, and when he had orders
they were given to Mrs. Jessup. But now I am promoted to
be secretary, and when there is no company I eat with the
family, and now and then the master is here for a meal, and
I suppose has been told that I am promoted. So he calls me
Miss Andrews when he speaks, but that is rarely. I see that
he looks at me now and then, and I wonder, is it going to
be as with young master? I am learning to know the difference in men's looks, and very soon I see that I have nothing
to worry about from Mr. Harries. He loves his wife; Miss
Lucy says it might be better for him if he did not, for then
he could go elsewhere, and perhaps find some happiness; as
it is, they differ so in their ideas, and quarrel so bitterly, that
she will no longer have anything to do with him, and often
stays away from the table when she knows that he is there.
It is a strange thing, the like of which I have never heard
before. A great rich gentleman he is, and so stern in his look
that I dare to open my mouth only to put food into it, and
then but a little at a time, as Miss Bascom taught me was
proper. I cut a piece of food, then lay down my knife, take
the fork into my right hand, and put the piece of food into
my mouth with that. It seems a lot of extra motions, but
it is right, and I labor earnestly to do right in all things.

I think to myself, I will be a wise girl and keep out of

this family quarrel very carefully. I could have no idea how difficult this was going to be, but I learned yesterday. At lunch the master was there, and my mistress in her room. The master says, "Miss Andrews, I wish to speak with you after lunch," and my heart gives a jump—what have I done that is wrong? I say, "Certainly, sir," and when he rises I rise too and follow him into the drawing room. He says, "Miss Andrews, I understand that Mrs. Harries is giving a dinner party at the Riverside Inn this evening." I answer, "Yes, Mr. Harries." "Who are the guests?" he asks, and what shall I say? I have no way to know whether my mistress would wish me to give that information. It could be that if they are proper persons he would wish to attend, and it would be very rude indeed of me to say No to his request. I have never been told to say No, so I tell him the names, which of course I know, having arranged the affair for Mrs. Harries. When I name Mr. Berriman he asks, "Peter Berriman?" and when I say, "Yes, sir," I see his jaws clamp and a gleam in his eye, and I know there is trouble. I am no longer ignorant of what is going on, and I have heard that "Pete" Berriman, as they call him, is a young preacher who was a conscientious objector, as they are called, and has just come out of jail and is denouncing what the Allied governments are doing in Germany. There has been a lot about him in the papers, and now, according to the agreement, Mrs. Harries is not bringing him to her home but is entertaining him outside; there will be Dr. and Mrs. Clark and several other radicals there.

As soon as the master has gone out, I go to my lady's room and tell her what has happened, and how I did not know what it was my duty to do. She says, "What you did was right; I should have given you orders. In future, when Mr. Harries asks you questions about me, just tell him that I have instructed you to tell him to ask them of me." And when she sees the look on my face she says, "Do not worry. He knows that you are my employee and not his, and that you take my orders, not his." I am not so sure of that, but all I say is, "Yes, Mrs. Harries."

So now I know the fat is in the fire, and in my mind I can hear it sizzling. I know that I am to go along, because my lady is going shopping and then to a show before the dinner; and she will surely not change her plans. She does not say a word and I do not. We drive to the bank and I get money; then I run errands and gradually load up the trunk of the limousine and part of the back seat and the place beside Pietro with packages. Then while my lady goes to see an actress playing what is called the younger generation, of whom I hear no good, I sit in the car and study my Testament—I have never let them see my "Pamela" book, for they would make jokes about the two of us. And then, a little after seven, we go into the Riverside Inn, which is a famous hotel, with fine gardens in front and in the basement a museum with California relics in it. In the lobby, which is big and wanders round in several rooms, we find some of the guests, who are of the pacifist sort like my lady and all invited to meet their hero Mr. Berriman who has been to jail. I am all one bundle of shivers, but nothing happens and we go into the big dining room where there is a special table set. I learn later that the master intended to get there early, but he got a flat tire on the way.

Well, we have what is called a fruit cup, and then soup, and then chicken for the others, and for me and Mr. Berriman, who also is a vegetarian, a vegetable plate with an unhatched chicken, as Charles calls a poached egg, on top. We have just got started on this when the thunderbolt falls. My lady is at the head of the table, and the guest sits at her right; next to him is Mrs. Clark, and then is the new secretary. Suddenly there is like a big red-faced ghost standing behind the guest of honor, and a voice growling, "Are you Peter Berriman?" "I am," says the guest, and looks around to see who this may be. Having been arrested once, he may perhaps think it is the law again. Then says the voice, low but terrible, "Get up and get out of this dining room, and if I ever catch you in public with my wife again I'll break your jaw." Oh my, oh my, I am so scared, but if Mr. Berriman is he does not show it by the flicker of an eyelash; he takes another forkful of his spinach, or maybe it is his carrots or peas or potatoes, and puts it into his mouth and chews steady.

I do not know if perhaps my lady has warned Mrs. Clark about what might happen and has placed her on the other side of the guest on purpose. Anyhow, she rises quickly, and says, "I beg you, Mr. Harries." He growls at her, "You keep out of this!" But he knows who she is and does not touch her. She is a frail little body, and I think one of him would make two of her; she has squeezed in between him and the guest. "Stop for one moment," she pleads, "and realize what you are doing to your wife. You are making a public scandal for her."

You understand, they are almost right behind me, and I hear every word they say, even though they are speaking in low tones; you may be sure that both my ears are busy. Says he, "There is no scandal worse than being seen in public with this traitor." Says she, "You are mistaken, Mr. Harries. If you attack this man in public, the world will put only one interpretation on it, and it will not have to do with public affairs. You may explain all you please, but you will never be able to remove the stain that you have put upon your wife's good name. You are man of the world enough to know that; not even your friends will believe you, no matter how much they may pretend to. I beg you to think twice before you take this dreadful step that can never be retraced."

There is a vacant table behind us, and she persuades him to sit there with her, and they talk, and after that I cannot hear all they say, but I can make out that she does most of the talking and he only growls a few words now and then. Meantime I steal a glance at the guest of honor, and I see that he is still putting away his spinach and carrots and peas and potatoes, getting them chewed up, I suppose, before his jaw is broken. All the others, including my lady, are acting as if nothing has happened. I have learned that that is the way well-bred persons are supposed to behave, and I desire to be one of them and this is my chance to practice. Mr. Harries is a gentleman, and apparently he cannot be rude to a lady, nor answer her arguments; he gets up and stalks out, and that is the end of the affair. We finish our dinner, and then we go into one of the parlors or whatever they are, and sit and chat. Mr. Berriman tells about how the conscientious objectors were treated, some good and some bad—his was fairly good. My lady repeats what I have heard her say a hundred times, about how wicked it is to put people in prison for saying what they believe. From first to last I did not hear anybody mention Mr. Harries, and I doubt if they did until after the party broke up. I am sure they will go off and talk about it, but it will not get into the papers and so it will not be a scandal.

Such is life among the great and wealthy. Among the poor I suppose there would have been a fight, but it wouldn't have got into the papers unless somebody was hurt bad. When I told Miss Lucy about it she says it was what is called a situation, and that when husbands and wives are quarreling there may arise a situation at any time, and it is a good thing that I have had a chance to see how to deal with it. A lady never raises her voice in public and never shows excitement of any sort; she can be sure that a gentleman will never lay hands upon her, and that gives her an advantage which she must know how to use. It is useful to me to have this old lady, who has been in the family most of her life and has seen all sorts of situations. Enough tonight from your fast-rising

Pamela

✥

LETTER LIII

Dear Mother:

I am getting along very well and if I do not write often it is because I have no special news. Last Sunday was very hot and we had a lecturer that would have interested you; he is a colored man that is a doctor, and has been a missionary to his people that are savages in Africa. My lady is not much interested in religious doctrines but is strong for doing good to people here and now, so she has given two hundred dollars to this man for his work. That will buy him an x-ray machine, he says, and he is so grateful.

I know about this because it is one of my duties to make out the checks for my lady to sign. Imagine, I have a list of forty-two people that she pays an allowance to, anywhere from fifty up to two hundred dollars a month, and the last day of each month I have to make out all those checks and address envelopes and put stamps on them and see to getting them mailed. There is a big check book, and I number each check and put the records in the stub in the check book. All that is what a secretary is for, and she also answers

the telephone and receives the visitors and has to know who
has a right to come in, and who has to be told please to
write to Mrs. Harries, and who is crazy and has to be got
rid of quick. Some of them sound crazy to me, but maybe
they will not to her, so I am on pins and needles as the saying is. I say, "Mrs. Harries is very busy today, but I will go
and see." That is in a little anteroom, and there he or she
sits while I run upstairs to where my lady lies in her lovely
pink silk bed—she lies all the time when she is reading or
listening to the little radio set—and I tell her who it is, and
if it is a stranger she says, "Oh, dear, oh, dear, what are
charity bureaus for?" Or if it is somebody she has already
helped she will say, "Oh, dear, oh, dear, he will never have
enough." Then she will say, "I suppose I have to see him.
Show him into the drawing room."

You can see how all this is an education for your daughter. I am told about the different people, and the causes
they work for, and the ideas they hold, and what my lady
thinks about them. She may not always be right, but what
is right for her is what I have to do, so it is my job to understand her mind. I am like the man that I saw a picture of,
walking on a tightrope; I have to balance myself and keep
just so. At first I thought, I will do nothing but agree with
her in everything; but soon I noticed the fact that she seems
to have a contempt for such people, she decides that they
do it only by way of flattery and to get something from her.
She respects more people that oppose her, provided they
do it just right and not too far. She has a sort of scale of
what she will take from this person and that; she admires
most people that are famous and she will take almost anything from them; then come the people that are rich, they
can argue and fight it out with her and they do. But the
poor and humble have to be careful, and you can be sure I
watch my step. As she comes to know me better I can ven-

ture a little more. I say, "Are you sure, Mrs. Harries, that those people are spending the money as they tell you? They don't seem to me to be sincere." Or I say, "It seems to me, Mrs. Harries, that you could save yourself a lot of trouble if you would tell these people to write instead of seeing you." She says, "You are a smart girl, Pamela, and are going to be a great help to me." Wouldn't it be funny if someday I was telling this great lady how to spend her money? Then, indeed, would you be proud of your devoted

Pamela

LETTER LIV

Dear Sister:

I have a choice piece of gossip tonight. I feel like a scandalmonger when I write it, but then nothing is ever confidential in this family. I am always taken aback by it, for I had the idea that rich people would be silent and exclusive. Mostly it is so. Miss Lucy tells me that Mrs. Harries is the only rich person she knows who does not care what she says to anybody or what they say about her. She will tell her family secrets over the telephone, and while I am sitting there with my pad waiting for instructions.

What it's about now, she has decided to divorce her husband. She is indignant with him for his behavior in the hotel, which was a breaking of their agreement; she is going to put him out of her house and out of her life. To do this she has called a conference of the family tomorrow evening. Her brother Tom Egbert is staying in Santa Barbara, and she called him and told her decision, and he will come; these people think nothing of driving miles each way, whether it be for family business or just a bridge party. She tells him the whole story over the telephone, and with me listening. Charles is to come, and Miss Yvette, and my lady's lawyer that is in Riverside, a nice rosy-faced gentleman that is always telling her that she will get into trouble but she pays not the least attention to him. Also there will be Dr. and Mrs. Clark, I suppose because they were in the hotel, and because Mrs. Clark was so clever in keeping the master quiet.

Well, that is the news, and there is a great to-do. She seems quite calm herself, I still have never known her to raise her voice, anywhere or about anything. But I am excited, mainly because I am so sorry for Mr. Harries. I am sure that he is a good man and that he loves her. I wish that I knew him better and that I was not so young; I would try to reconcile them. What do you think I should do? Ask Rev. Strayker about it, please, and help your devoted

Pamela

LETTER LV

Dear Sister:

Well, there has been the family conference, and this is the funniest story I have yet had to write.

They all came, and I was told to be there with my pad and pencil, to make notes, at least the outlines of what everybody said, but what was to be done with it afterwards I was not told. My lady likes company, and also, she likes people to talk about her, and others to hear it, and perhaps she thinks there will be some sort of family archives. She tells them shortly that she has had all she can stand; no agreements are kept, and there is nothing left to the marriage. She asks Dr. Clark to tell the lawyer what happened at the hotel, and he does, only Mrs. Clark is so eager she takes the word away from him and tells her part; the lawyer, Mr. Kelly, who I think is an Irishman, nods his head and listens. Then the jolly Brother Tom Egbert is asked what he thinks, and he talks about scandals and the family reputation, and says it is too bad, and things ought to be patched up, and at any rate let the divorce be got in some place where there are not so many newspapers and where Maggie has not been so much in them. Then Charles is asked, and he has had some drinks, I fear, but he doesn't talk much; he says that whatever suits Aunt Maggie suits him; he can certainly testify to the rudeness and harshness of his uncle. And then Miss Yvette, who thinks it is too bad, and that both sides have a share of wrong, and she wishes they had called her in to discuss their settlement. She is positive as always, but rather vague, and her older sister brushes her aside very soon.

Then the lawyer starts. He uses many long legal words, and discusses the property settlement, and community property rights in California, and what Mr. Harries will claim, and that it will be necessary to talk with him about it; Mrs. Harries will have to make up her mind what sort of proposition she is willing to make and what she expects from him. That is the sort of thing I am there for, or so I figure, and my pencil is flying and my head is bowed over the writing pad. But then I notice Mr. Kelly is hesitating and seems to be stumbling; then I hear a sound, and look up, and look about, and oh, horrors! Mrs. Harries is asleep! Her head is leaning back and her jaw has dropped down and she is snoring in a very gentle, ladylike way. So the lawyer stops, embarrassed, and everybody else is embarrassed, and finally he says, "Well, that is the way it is," and I don't know whether he means the law or the sleeping. So they talk for a while about other things, using low tones; and when my lady opens her eyes again they all stop, and she says, "So that is the situation and you may go ahead and prepare the papers, Mr. Kelly." She makes no apology, and I doubt if the idea of doing such a thing has ever occurred to her in her life.

Well, that is that; and after the company has gone and the other members of the family have gone to their rooms, Charles says to me, "Well, Pam, you have been rising in the world, I see." I say, "I have got some new duties," and he says, "And new opportunities. Are you still keeping your heart in the refrigerator?" I don't want to have any discussion, so I tell him, "You will always have a friend when you need one, Charles." "I need one tonight," he comes back, and I answer, "Say your prayers, and ask God to be your friend, and He will." Then I run upstairs, and you may be sure that I use that good bolt that I have put on my door.

There is just one little bit more and then the story of the divorce is done. In the morning I come to my lady's room to get my orders for the day, and she is talking on the phone. She has told me that I am not to back out but just to sit down and wait until she is done; so I do. I cannot help listening, and I guess that it is Mrs. Clark she is talking to. She says, "I have decided to call it off; it is too much trouble, and besides, I need him to manage the servants."

That is all so far, and if there is more you will get it from your devoted Sister

Pamela

LETTER LVI

Dear Mother:

It was certainly the great kindness of Providence which brought me to this wonderful position, and I do not fail to thank Him on my knees every night. By the way, Dr. Clark has told me that in the time of Jesus it was the custom of the Jews to pray standing up and with arms uplifted to the sky; that Jesus himself undoubtedly did this, and so all the painters have been wrong. But he is a Unitarian and perhaps I should not heed what he says. It is the one defect of this position that I do not meet people of our own faith. So I am careful to go to church every Sabbath that weather permits. The Reverend is very kind to me, and I have met a young grocer's assistant who is a proper young man and asked if he might call on me, but I dare not have him come to this grand place, and besides, my duties leave me no time; that is, I have free time but never know when it will be because it depends upon whatever notion my lady may take.

Her kindness is beyond belief. Cold weather has come, and of course my coat is old and poor by her standards. She says, "I must get you a coat that is fit for you to wear." And when I say, "Oh, Mrs. Harries, I cannot let you do that!" she says, "You cannot help it, it is a part of your job." She is going to lunch at a friend's house and she says, "You come along and Pietro can drive you into town and you get lunch there and get yourself a coat." When the time comes she hands me three of the twenty-dollar bills which she is always getting from the bank, and she says, "Don't get a cheaper one." I ask what sort and what color, and she says, "Suit yourself, but take the time to try some on and get one that becomes you." Oh, how I wish that Miss Bascom could be here! But she is a Mrs. Denby now and is living in Los Angeles.

Well, I go into the place, and because I look poor the young lady has not much use for me; but when I say I want something better she has more. There are rows of coats on the racks, and she tries to show me this and that, but I say "Let me look." It is a great event in my life and I make the most of it. I try on several and I look so fine I can hardly see the difference. You would be surprised if you could see me, for there is fifteen pounds more of me and some of it is in my cheeks, and I promise you I shall never use what they call rouge; neither do I have to have my hair waved, because it does it of itself, and Miss Bascom (that was) told me it was worth a hundred dollars a year to me. You will not understand that, so I tell you that they go to a shop and have it done, and it is called a permanent but it isn't; it is uncomfortable having it done, and you put it up in about forty hair pins at night. Oh, the things I could tell you that the fashionable ladies do! You can read it all in Isaiah 3; it is exactly the same except for the nose jewels and the tinkling ornaments about their feet, and maybe these will come next season.

However, it is nice to look pretty. I have this lovely coat, made of camel's hair, of a light brown color; and Miss Lucy has made me a cute little hat. I see people turn to look at me, and I am pleased, and then I know that the devil is tempting me, so I turn it into a prayer and thanksgiving. Praise the Lord with gladness and come before His presence with a song! So does your loving Daughter

Pamela

LETTER LVII

Dear Sister:

What lovely news you tell me about John! If you really love him and if he loves you, that is the greatest happiness that can come to my darling Big Sister—but I believe I am bigger than you now! I am so glad that he is one of us and is studying to be a doctor, for then you can both be together. As for me, do not worry, for while I meet many men, I am a long way from wishing to fall in love; I have too many other things that keep me interested.

I find that I have Charles on my hands again, more than ever since I am secretary, or half one; I am supposed to carry responsibility—that is what my lady says—and he is one. The poor fellow has been drinking, but not so bad as last time, and I think in his heart he is terrified lest he will go off and do worse. It seems that people become slaves to the habit, and I suppose they start because they are ignorant and do not realize what it will do to them. Now he is nervous and restless, and there is my lady worried, and I think afraid of him; she gives him money because she is afraid of what he might do if she refused. She is not so worried but that she goes off to shows and to lectures; she invites him, but he is bored by her and refuses. This is the sad part of it, he knows all her ideas, and agrees with some of them, but the idea of printing all the money and giving to those who need it he says is nonsense, and when she keeps saying it he explodes with irritation. I have been here long enough now to know that she says the same things over and over; he tells her it is like a phonograph that has got stuck in one groove. I do not mind, because all this world of ideas is so new and strange to me that I can always learn something from any argument, even if it is only what the words mean. But he goes wild and cries, "Oh, for Pete's sake!"

Underneath all the disharmony in this family is the money, which is a terrible power. The mistress has more than the master, and so she can defy him and do as she pleases. The young master has to agree with his aunt, or he will not get what he wants; and he has hanging over him that cruel threat that she will leave her money to his younger aunt and thus put her in charge of him. As for Miss Yvette, all she has to do is to come and kiss her sister once in a while and then go off to her pleasures. Charles blurts out that she drinks too, but does not show it; she does worse things, but who can prove it? So they wrangle, and each wishes to dominate the others but cannot, and they live with fury in their hearts. My lady, very sad, goes about to forget her troubles; and I have observed this strange fact, that when Charles is here she does not take me with her, but leaves me here to entertain him; it is apparently one of the duties of secretaries, whole or half. I have been instructed that at any time Charles wants my time, to walk or to talk or to play checkers or pingpong, I am to drop all other duties, no matter how important. "Do anything you can to keep him at home," she says—and she will not say it but I believe that in her heart when she says "anything" she means just that. I feel quite sure that if I were to leave my door unbolted and let her nephew come in she would not put me out of the home, but on the contrary would promote me from half-secretary to half-member of the family and would give him money so that he could buy me whatever my heart might desire—even one of those diamond rings which she leaves so carelessly on her dressing table and which I am told have cost a thousand dollars each.

This is indeed a strange situation for a girl that is virtuous and means to remain so. I have made up my mind exactly what I intend to do; I am going to talk to my young master about God. Whether it pleases him or not, whether it drives him away or not; God shall be my refuge and strength, a very present help in trouble. When he talks to me about love, I shall tell him about the love of God, which will make us as brother and sister; blessed are the pure in heart, for they shall see God. I have been doing this for several days now, and watching the results with attention. At first it irritates him, and he gives his cry, "Oh, for God's sake!" I say, "Yes, Charles, exactly so." He goes off and sulks for a while, but then he comes back; he has to, because he craves female society. He cannot be interested for very long in looking at his caracul sheep, his fancy chickens and pigeons and pheasants and other creatures he has got here. He has a very lovely German shepherd dog that adores him and would play with him all day, but that does not last. I ask why he does not invite friends here, and he says, "Damn them, they all have to have liquor, and I am an unfortunate wretch that cannot stand it, or the sight or smell of it. Why can I not take just enough, like other people?" I answer him, "None is enough, and that is what I take, and get along so nicely with it."

So here I am in this strange position, as nurse to what they call an alcoholic, and the more I succeed and the more kind I am, the more determined he becomes that I shall sleep with him—as they phrase it in their horrid language which I cannot help hearing. I go to my room and read Pamela One, and she is kidnaped and held prisoner, whereas I am free, but am held by the power of money, which my

Mother and Sister need, and which I am determined to get so long as I can do it honestly. For my protection I have what my great-great-great-grandmother had, which is God; "His rod and His staff they comfort me, and though I walk through the valley of the shadow of death I will fear no evil." I tell this to my patient, and he starts to argue, and cannot let it go, but gets hotter and hotter, and says most terrible things about both God and poor me; but I have read the literature that you have sent me and have sharpened my wits upon it, and am more ready for him now than when I first came here. When I tell him that the pure in heart shall see God, he asks, "And have you seen Him?" I tell him the things I have got from the pamphlets you have sent me. I say, "You are ignorant, Charles. You think that by God a Christian means an old man sitting on a throne and wearing a long beard; but God is Spirit, and He is within you, and you see Him with the eye of faith." "He gave me no such eye." "Oh, yes, He did, but you have kept it closed. God lives in you and works in you, and without Him you would not be. You have the idea that you are an accident, the result of the meeting of atoms; but patterns and forms do not come by accident, they are made by mind, and your mind should know that. You are the superstitious one, who believes that the millions of millions of atoms that compose your being all fell into their patterns by accident. Apparently you believe that all your thoughts are making themselves by accident; but I know that you are a spirit, and that you are making your thoughts, in the same way that God is making you." "Why is He making me so unhappy then?" "He is giving you the chance to make yourself, with the power that He gives you; you can make yourself happy or you can make yourself miserable. If you believe that God is in you, giving you power, you have it, and if you believe that you are nothing but a bunch of atoms, then you don't have the power and you are miserable. You laughed at me for believing that Heaven is up in the sky, where the astronomers haven't been able to see it; but Jesus taught us that the Kingdom of Heaven is within you. You make it there, or you make hell. You love people and you have love, or you hate people and you have hate; God lets you choose."

Well, that is the way it goes, hammer and tongs. This much at least I accomplish, I keep his mind busy and he does not go and get liquor, nor does he try to break into my room. When my lady comes back from whatever it is, maybe the opera which is in Los Angeles and she doesn't get in till two o'clock in the morning—she finds that I have helped. She doesn't know how I have done it but she will not call it God. She does not say "Thank you," for that is not her way, but presently she will think of something that I need and will give it to me or give me the money and tell me to get it and not argue. She is made up about half and half of goodness and of what Miss Lucy calls arrogance; of wish to help others, and of determination to make them conform to her ideas. If I were to convert her nephew and save him from becoming a drunkard, she would be half grateful to me and half cross because I had done it in the name of the Lord, against whom she has set her head. The Jews, as you know, were called a stiff-necked people, but there is plenty of that among the gentiles also. Imagine such wisdom from your timid Little Sister

Pamela

LETTER LVIII

Dear Mother:

I suppose you are interested in all that goes on in this unusual place. My lady has bought the tract of land from her friends Mr. and Mrs. Fearing and I have made out a check for $37,500. Of course I did not write the important part, the signature, which is "Mgt Harries"—that is how she writes it and says "Margaret" is too long. Imagine being able to pay that much money just by making a few wiggles of the pen! I am more than half a secretary now and am getting one hundred dollars. My happiest duty will be to make out checks for thirty dollars each for you and sister; the rest I will keep, for I have to buy more things and look nicer. All the people who knew me in the old days still call me Pamela, but new people call me Miss Andrews, and I try to be as gracious as I remember Miss Bascom was.

There is a well being dug on the property, and there will be streets laid out. The contractor comes, and is a Jew. When I was young I saw the pictures in our church paper of old-time Jews with white robes like they were angels; but this Mr. Heiman is dressed like other men, and is very smooth and businesslike. They have made a contract and Master Charles has gone in to talk it over with a lawyer. My lady wants very much to get him interested in this work, so when I have a chance I talk to him about it, how important it is for the poor people to have comfortable homes with running water and such that we lacked so long. But he is discouraging, he says there is a slump coming soon and the people will be out of work and not be able to pay for their homes. I don't understand what this slump is or why, but everybody talks about it here and some predict it and sound as if they were glad because it is an evil system which is breaking down. I listen to the arguments which sometimes get hot, and my head is in a whirl, but someday I hope to make up my mind. I am getting an education and getting paid for it, and be sure that I am not forgetting to thank God for all His blessings. Your dear devoted

Pamela

LETTER LIX

Dear Sister:

I am having arguments all the time with Charles. All his love-making now takes him straight to Heaven and it makes him cross for he does not want to be there. I load him up with arguments, most of which come out of the pamphlets you have sent me. How fortunate that we have in our college educated men who can see through the sophistries of the worldly and unbelieving and speak on behalf of the Lord! I have not given Charles the pamphlets, for he would not read them, but he gets the arguments from me, and I think he is getting for the first time an idea of what it means to have a spiritual view of life. Yesterday he said, "If that is what you mean by God I might come to agree with you." My heart gave a leap and I was wondrous happy; but later he said, "If I became one of your converts, would you love me, Pam?" My heart sank, for the dreadful thought came to me that he might pretend to believe, just in order to get what he wants from me. I do not say that he would, but I shall never be free from that suspicion.

He can be such a charming person when he wishes to! He is so good looking, and has such elegant manners, and has a sense of humor, but always at the same time sad! How can it be that there is so much evil in him? I cannot believe it and struggle against it, and I take that as a part of the religious life, and what we are put on earth for. When he asks me if I would love him as a convert I tell him that I would give him the love of a dear sister—which does not please him. He says, "Then you do not believe in the love of man and woman at all?" I say, "Yes, I do, but I take it as something serious, and something that will abide, and last for life, and not for a kind of play, as you call it. You were put on this earth to play, it seems, but I was not."

There is a word that is missing in our talk. It makes me think of the man called Joe who takes care of all the machinery on this ranch; he is an oldish man and has one tooth missing right in front, and when you look at him it is hard not to think about that gap. It is the same between Charles and me, there is a gap in our talk, and that is the word marriage. He does not ever speak it, so of course I do not. These smart rich people have decided to take marriage as of no importance, but at least they cannot have forgotten that it exists in the world, and when Charles does not speak the word, that must be deliberate. I wonder, is he trying to tempt me to say it, in order that he may have the pleasure of spurning me, or is he trying to keep from saying it in order to spare my feelings? I grope in the dark about it, and will not come near the subject, for that might seem like hinting. I just put him off abruptly, "There is no use talking about love, Charles, for it does not mean the same thing to us. We speak a different language."

Another in my language is that word arrogance which

Miss Lucy has taught me and which I have looked up. I think that word describes his attitude and his aunt's. I am plenty good for a concubine but not good enough for a wife. I ask myself why, and decide that it is the money they have and I haven't. To be sure, I lack the graces that he has been taught; but I am no fool, and I can learn whatever he wishes to teach me, as I did to drive his car and to swim. But no, I came out of a rural slum—that is their name for our sort of home. I was, as they say, born on the wrong side of the railroad tracks. Not one of them has earned what he has, and that is what makes a person great in their eyes. Mr. Mackenzie, the magazine editor, said to me, with one of his grins, "They are a bunch of snobs, and don't let them fool you." I said, "You must be a Socialist," and he answered, "Worse than that, I am an Anarchist." "That sounds terrible," said I. "What does it mean?" He said, "It means that I don't want to be pushed around." Do not be frightened, dear Rachel, for I have not got any label yet.

I am doing my work and earning what I get and well pleased with it. When Charles had one of his cross fits and said it was hard for him living in the house with a girl whom he admired so much and wanted to love and was denied, I made bold to ask him very quietly if he would prefer that I should not stay here. He said, "Good God, no! You are like a light in this place; you make it endurable." "All right then," I say, "let us be friends. I am being honest with you, as perhaps not many women have been. If you are in trouble, I will do my best to help you and I will give you the love of a sister." "Leave out that phrase," he says, "for it is silly. I know brothers and sisters who hate." "All right then, I will give you the love of an honest friend; but if you want the play that you talk about, you will have to go to Hollywood for that."

This last was sort of mean; but I am tired of being asked

to take the place of these ladies of the screen. I felt sorry next day, for I looked at the newspaper and read that Sylvia Sloane had taken her own life; she locked the door of her hall bedroom and plugged up the cracks and turned on the gas. She really was beautiful, and I thought kind. Charles had already heard about it before I saw him, so I did not see his emotion, if he had any. He said to me, I thought coldly, that thousands of good-looking girls come to Hollywood from all over the country, and only a small part of them ever break into the movies. I asked what became of the rest, and he said, "Some of them marry, but it is a hard place to get husbands in. Some take jobs in the stores and some become B-girls, or ladies on call." I did not ask the meaning of those phrases, but later I found out. When I said that I had liked Miss Sloane, he said, "She was a good kid but she lacked what it takes." I asked what that was, and he said, "Oh, you have to be cute, or you have to be slinky—something so that all the men who sit and watch the screen will imagine you in their arms." Said I, "And do you wonder that our church forbids such conduct?" "No," he admitted, "not if you want to be religious." I never lose a chance to quote Scripture to him, hoping that some of the wonderful words may echo in his mind; so now I said, "Oh, worship the Lord in the beauty of holiness; let the whole earth stand in awe of him." "You little nun!" said he, but not unkindly.

Neither you nor I have ever met a man like this, so it is hard to be sure, but I think I am making progress. His aunt sends him on errands having to do with the housing project, and I try my best to make him see these as worth while. Sometimes he invites me to go along, and I say, "I must ask Mrs. Harries, for she has given me duties." Never once have I been told anything but to go with him, so I lead quite a pleasant idle life. Never once has he failed to put one hand on mine while he is driving, and never once have I failed to restore it to the steering wheel. I quote the police, who are telling in the papers that petting parties while driving are one of the causes of accidents. I am amazed to discover how a man will never give up; it is like a siege between us. I tell him so, and that I am going to win, because I have an ally on my side; victory is of the Lord. Charles says he cannot stand it, and every now and then he goes off, I know not where; but he comes back, and pays me extravagant compliments, which are pleasant but are not entirely swallowed.

Meantime I go on reading my Pamela book, and the terrible scenes which make me think how much more fortunate I am. Here is a description of the man or creature in the form of man whom the cruel master did select to keep stricter guard over the object of his desires. He is some kind of foreigner and is named Monsieur Colbrand, and he bows and puts on foreign grimaces, and speaks in broken English, like what he says of the master: "I was happy in de affections of de vinest gentleman in de varld." I will copy for you the description of him, so that you can see how I weep for the troubles of this poor child:

"He is a giant of a man for stature; taller by a good deal than Harry Mawlidge in your neighborhood, and large-boned, scraggy, and has a hand!—I never saw such an one in my life. He has great staring eyes, like the bull's that frightened me so; vast jaw-bones sticking out; eyebrows hanging over his eyes; two great scars upon his fore-head, and one on his left cheek; two large whiskers, and a monstrous wide mouth; blubber lips, long yellow teeth, and a hideous grin. He wears his own frightful long hair, tied up in a great black bag; a black crepe neckcloth about a long ugly neck; and his throat sticking out like a wen. As to the rest, he was dressed well enough, and had a sword on, with a nasty red knot to it; leather gaiters, buckled below his knees; and a foot nearly as long as my arm, I verily think."

And what part does this dreadful man play in the book? He is called upon to terrify poor Pamela, and does so. These awful scenes go on—I will copy another for you.

"In an hour's time he called Mrs. Jewkes down to him! And I heard him very high in passion: and all about poor me! I heard her say it was his own fault; there would be an end of all my complaining and perverseness, if he was once resolved; and other most impudent aggravations. I am re-solved not to go to bed this night, if I can help it. Lie still, lie still, my poor fluttering heart! What will become of me?

ALMOST TWELVE O'CLOCK, SATURDAY NIGHT

"He sent Mrs. Jewkes about ten o'clock, to call me to him. 'Where?' said I. 'I'll shew you,' said she. I went down three or four steps, and saw her making to his chamber, the door of which was open: so I said, 'I cannot go there!' 'Don't be foolish,' said she; 'but come; no harm will be done to you.' 'Well,' said I, 'if I die, I cannot go there.' I heard him say, 'Let her come, or it shall be worse for her. I can't bear,' said he, 'to speak to her myself!' 'Well,' said I, 'I cannot come, indeed I cannot;' and so I went up again into my closet, expecting to be fetched by force.

"But she came up soon after, and bid me make haste to bed: said I, 'I will not go to bed this night, that's certain!' 'Then,' said she, 'you shall be made to come to bed; and Nan and I will undress you.' I knew neither prayers nor tears would move this wicked woman: so I said, 'I am sure you will let my master in, and I shall be undone!' 'Mighty piece of undone,' she said: but he was too much exasperated against me, to be so familiar with me, she would assure me! 'Aye,' said she, 'you'll be disposed of another way soon, I can tell you for comfort: and I hope your husband will have your obedience, though nobody else can have it.' 'No husband in the world,' said I, 'shall make me do an unjust or base thing.' She said that would be soon tried; and Nan coming in, 'What!' said I, 'am I to have two bed-fellows again, these warm nights?' 'Yes,' said she, 'slippery one, you are, till you can have one good one instead of us.' Said I, 'Mrs. Jewkes, don't talk nastily to me. I see you are beginning again; and I shall affront you, may-be; for next to bad actions are bad words; for they could not be spoken, if they were not in the heart.' 'Come to bed, Purity!' said she. 'You are a non-such, I suppose.' 'Indeed,' said I, 'I can't come to bed; and it will do you no harm to let me stay all night in the great chair!' 'Nan,' said she, 'undress my young lady. If she won't let you, I'll help you; and if neither of us can do it quietly, we'll call the master to do it for us; though,' said she, 'I think it an office worthier of Monsieur Colbrand!' 'You are very wicked,' said I. 'I know it,' said she; 'I am a Jezebel, and a London prostitute, you know.' So she went on a while. 'You're a wicked woman, that's certain,' said I; 'and if you thought any thing of another world, could not talk thus. But no wonder! It shows what hands I'm got into!' 'Aye, so it does,' said she. She came and took me in her huge arms, as if I was a feather. Said she, 'I do this to shew you what a poor resistance you can make against me, if I please to exert myself.' Then she set me down and tapped me on the neck: 'Ah!' said she, 'thou are a pretty creature, it's true; but so obstinate! so full of spirit! if thy strength was but answerable to that, thou wouldst run away with us all, and this great house too, on thy back— But un-dress, undress, I tell you.'

" 'Well,' said I, 'I see my misfortunes make you very

merry, and witty too; but I will love you, if you will humour me with the keys of the chamber-doors.' 'Nan,' said she, 'pray pull off my young lady's shoes and stockings.' "

Such is the scene I read last night, Rachel; and do you wonder that it troubles the sleep of your devoted

Pamela

LETTER LX

Dear Mother:

If I do not write as often as I used to it is because I am kept very busy; and also because I am sometimes delayed in mailing letters which are private. There is a great lot of curiosity in this household, and gossip traveling on wings; I have been told that it is possible to open a letter by holding it over a steaming kettle. I am not accusing anybody but just making sure.

The job of being secretary in a home is not the same as in an office; there you have hours from nine till five, but here I am at call from seven until any hour of the night. In my room there is what is called a buzzer, and when I hear it up I jump and go across the hall to my lady, and it may be anything from taking a message to the housekeeper or helping my lady to pack for a trip to El Centro, where we have just been and spent nearly two weeks sitting in a court-room every day, watching the trial of some farm workers for what is called criminal syndicalism, but which my lady insists is nothing but an attempt of the police with the backing of the great land companies in the valley to keep the workers from forming a union and demanding better

working conditions. You must not be shocked by this, for
it is really very cruel what has been done to these men, as I
have heard the testimony. It is charged that they wish to
overthrow the government by force and violence, but they
deny this, and the way they are treated, it is only natural
that they should have bitterness in their hearts. Mrs. Harries has taken three of her rich friends with her, and they
sit, thinking that this will make the court ashamed to be
too unfair. She writes letters to the papers which they do
not publish, but the wobblies as they are called manage to
get them printed and circulated, even when they are beaten
up for it.

Just now there is another case which is causing my lady
great distress. You remember I wrote you about the camp
where some Russians and Jews have a summer school for
children in the mountains. Now the police have raided it
and arrested those in charge, and have broken up the place
and sent all the children back to the hot city. Arrested is
the girl Nella Brodsky that I liked so much, and the idea
that she is in jail made my lady quite wild, and she sent
Master Charles to bail them all out, and now she has had a
meeting in her home and told all her friends about it. You
may be disturbed about all this, but do not be, for they do
not arrest secretaries, and especially not when they are
pretty and elegant—so says Mr. Mackenzie, the editor who
comes here Sundays and pays me such compliments. He is
the one who told me about the old-time Pamela book, and
I told him what you said about your not knowing who our
ancestors were, and he said it is safer not to know, for you
would be likely to find out things that would shock you.

It is very good news about Rachel getting along so well.
You now have two hard-working daughters on their way up
in the world. Since you ask, I tell you that I have no steady
company. One of the Portuguese boys casts looks at me, but

by now has decided that I am too far above him. The foreman of the ranch, who is a widower with two children, seeks my company now and then, but I have not encouraged him. An old gentleman of Mrs. Harries' family has given me smiles, and so has one of the smart friends of Miss Yvette, but my heart remains intact. I love my family; my best to you and Grampa from your devoted

Pamela

LETTER LXI

Dear Sister:

I am so happy to hear about your being engaged; happier than if it was me, for of course you come first and if I was ahead of you I would think it was not fair. From all that you tell me I am sure it is the right choice. You have been more fortunate than me in meeting the sort of people that you can trust. A common faith is the most important thing in marriage, at least for serious believers like us.

That being so, I fear that I am destined to grow up an old maid, as old as Miss Lucy. What a strange position I am in, to be in daily friendship with a man that I half want to love and the other half distrust and fear. Can there be two beings inside one body of a man? Mr. Mackenzie has told me about a story called "Dr. Jekyll and Mr. Hyde," where it happened that way, but of course that is only some man's imagining. But maybe he saw it before he wrote it.

Charles pursues me all the time; he says he will not give up, and this I do not doubt since he has always had his way, except with the Army, and I am not so powerful as that.

He makes love to me in little whispers, sometimes laughing, sometimes full of misery, and that disturbs me more; I could love him with pity more than with admiration. He takes me driving, and I make him promise, no love-making, and he keeps the promise by beaming on me and saying, "I am not making any love, but oh, what a lot of love I would if I were!" He will say, "Do you feel the car shake? It is because I am trembling so with a desire to do what I am not allowed to do!" I discuss it with him, why he prefers me when there are so many other women, far more beautiful, and more obliging. He says, "You are superior to them." I tell him, "That is very flattering, but my only superiority is that I say No, and the moment I say Yes I have lost it." He denies this, but I know it is so; it is just unendurable to him not to have his own way. He admits that he can go away and forget me, but to live in my presence is perpetual frustration. I had never heard that word, but I looked it up, and it is what he is getting.

We talk much of the time about God, because I tell him it is God that is defeating his wishes. He will curse God, but I tell him, "That will surely not bring you any nearer to victory." So he calms down and tells me that I have brought him to realize the possibility that there may be a Cosmic Consciousness or Universal Mind or something of the sort; he must give it some fancy name like that, but I tell him it is God all the same, and his loving Father, and the only thing that will help him is to realize and admit that. He says he will find it easier to realize that the Father is loving when His daughter shows more signs of having inherited His disposition. So you see how all the talk leads to one thing. I am learning to be matter-of-fact about it, and not to be cross or what he calls prudish. It is a different world I have come into, and I learn to live in it and do my job, of which he is a part. I tell myself that he is a sick man, and if I were being a nurse like you I would have to do more disagreeable things than letting a young gentleman make love to me, especially when his talk is so elegant and he teaches me new words and new ideas about the world.

Every night I read my Testament and discover things which I quote to him during the day. Also, I have my half hour with my great-great-great-grandmother. The story goes on and on and torments me with that uncertainty which you tell me is bad. But I do not think so; I believe that it makes me more contented with my lot, for her persecution was so much more terrible than mine. Hers is more of the body, while mine is of the mind and soul. I remarked that to Mr. Mackenzie last Sunday, and we had quite a talk. He has told his wife about my interest in that old story; she is a stoutish, very sweet lady, and said I must by all means follow the example of my virtuous ancestress. I told them, "There is one thing I cannot understand; I have peeked to the end, and see that she marries her persecutor. How can it be possible that a girl would be willing to marry a man who has shown himself so wicked and so treacherous?"

Mr. Mackenzie gave me a little lecture on the way things were in England two centuries ago. It was a time of worldliness, of business and trade; money was the measure of success. The class system was rigid, and it depended upon property. "A girl like you," he said, "can rise from parlormaid to secretary in a year; but your unfortunate ancestress might have expected to remain a slavey all her days, carrying in scuttles of coal and carrying out jars of slops until she was worn out, and then perhaps be turned off with no hope but to starve. But in this story she had a chance to become the mistress of a fine mansion, and to bear children who would inherit it, and nearly everybody who read the story would consider that she was the most fortunate of maidservants. The great ladies who wept over her persecu-

tions would perhaps judge that her future lord and husband
was not much worse than the one whom they had wedded
for the same property reasons. In those days marriages were
made that way, and love matches, called romantic, were
considered as folly, to be found only in poems and stage
plays."

So you see, Sister, how I am gaining knowledge. A kind
gentleman who has been reading books all his life takes the
trouble to explain something which I might have puzzled
over and never understood. That is why I am sure this book
cannot harm me. It takes me out of one time and into another, and is like history; at the same time it does not fail
to strengthen my virtue, being full of moral sentiments
most uplifting. Someday I may persuade you to read some
of it and see. If once you start, I promise that you will have
as hard a time laying it down as ever I did. Oh, dear, oh,
dear, it is so monstrously terrifying, it would deprive me of
sleep if I did not say my prayers and put my trust in God.
I will copy another long scene for you:

"For the future I will always mistrust most, when appear-
ances look fairest. O your poor daughter! what has she not
suffered since what I wrote on Sunday night! My worst
trial, and my fearfullest danger! O how I shudder to write
you an account of this wicked interval of time! For, my
dear parents, will you not be too much frightened and af-
fected with my distress, when I tell you that his journey to
Stamford was all abominable pretence; for he came home
privately, and had nigh effected all his vile purposes, and
the ruin of your poor daughter; and that by such a plot as
I was not in the least apprehensive of; and oh! what a vile
and unwomanly part that wicked wretch, Mrs. Jewkes,
acted in it.

"I left off with informing you how much I was pleased that I had one night's reprieve added to my honesty. But I had less occasion to rejoice than ever, as you will judge, by what I have said already. Take, then, the dreadful story, as well as I can relate it.

"The maid Nan is a little apt to drink, if she can get at liquor: and Mrs. Jewkes happened, or designed, as is probable, to leave a bottle of cherry-brandy in her way, and the wench drank some of it more than she should: and when she came in to lay the cloth, Mrs. Jewkes perceived it, and scolded her sadly; for she has too many faults of her own, to suffer any of the like sort in any body else, if she can help it; and she bid her get out of her sight, when we had supped, and go to bed, to sleep off her liquor before we came to bed. So the poor maid went muttering upstairs.

"About two hours after, which was near eleven o'clock, Mrs. Jewkes and I went up to bed; I pleasing myself with what a charming night I should have. We locked both doors, and saw poor Nan, as I thought (but, oh! it was my abominable master, as you shall hear by-and-by), sitting fast asleep, in an elbow chair, in a dark corner of the room, with her apron thrown over her head and neck. Mrs. Jewkes said, 'There is that beast of a wench, fast asleep, instead of being a bed! I knew,' said she, 'she had taken a fine dose.' 'I'll wake her,' said I. 'No, don't,' said she; 'let her sleep on; we shall lie better without her.' 'Aye,' said I, 'so we shall; but won't she get cold?'

"All this time we were undressing ourselves. And I fetched a deep sigh. 'What do you sigh for?' said she. 'I am thinking, Mrs. Jewkes,' answered I, 'what a sad life I live, and how hard is my lot. I am sure, the thief that has robbed is much better off than I, bating the guilt; I should, I think, take it for a mercy to be hanged out of the way, rather than live in these cruel apprehensions.' Being not sleepy, and in a prattling vein, I began to give a little history of myself, as I did, once before, to Mrs. Jervis; in this manner:

" 'Here,' said I, 'were my poor honest parents; they took care to instil good principles into my mind, till I was almost twelve years of age; and then comes my late dear good lady and takes a fancy to me, and said she would be the making of me. And this was her lesson—My good Pamela, be virtuous, and keep the men at a distance. So I was, I hope, and so I did. But then, what comes next? Why it pleases God to take my good lady; and then comes my master: and what says he? Why, in effect it is: Be not virtuous, Pamela.

" 'So I have lived about sixteen years in virtue and reputation; and all at once, when I come to know what is good, and what is evil, I must renounce all the good, all the whole sixteen years' innocence, which next to God's grace, I owed chiefly to my parents, and my lady's good lessons and examples, and choose the evil; so, in a moment's time, become the vilest of creatures! All this for what, I pray? Why, truly, for a pair of diamond ear-rings, a necklace, and a diamond ring for my finger, which would not become me: for a few paltry fine clothes which, when I wore them, would make but my former poverty more ridiculous to every body that saw me, especially when they knew the base terms I wore them upon.

" 'So, Mrs. Jewkes,' said I, 'here is my history in brief. I am a very unhappy young creature! And why am I so? Why because my master sees something in my person that takes his present fancy, and because I would not be undone. I, therefore, must, and shall be undone! and this is all the reason that can be given.'

"She heard me run on all this time, while I was undressing, without any interruption; and I said, 'I have a good mind to wake this poor maid.' 'No, don't,' said she, 'I charge you. I am very angry with her, and she'll get no harm there: and if she wakes, she may come to bed well enough, as long as there is a candle in the chimney.'

"So I looked into the closets, and kneeled down in my own, as I used to do, to say my prayers, and this with my underclothes in my hand, all undressed; and passed by the poor sleeping wench, as I thought, in my return. But, O! little did I think it was my wicked, wicked master, in a gown and petticoat of hers, and her apron over his face and shoulders. What meanness will not Lucifer make his votaries stoop to, to gain their abominable ends!

"Mrs. Jewkes, by this time, was got to bed, on the farther side, as she used to be; and, to make room for the maid, when she should awake. I got into bed, and lay close to her. I said, 'Where are the keys! Though,' said I, 'I am not so much afraid to-night.' 'Here,' said the wicked woman, 'put your arm under mine, and you shall find them about my wrist, as they used to be.' So I did, and the abominable designer held my hand with her right hand, as my right arm was under her left.

"In less than a quarter of an hour, I said, 'There's poor Nan awake; I hear her stir.' 'Let us go to sleep,' said she, 'and not mind her: she'll come to bed when she's quite awake.' 'Poor soul,' said I, 'I'll warrant she'll have the headache to-morrow for this!' 'Be silent,' said she, 'and go to sleep; you keep me awake: I never found you in so talkative a humour in my life.' 'Don't chide me,' said I, 'I will but say one thing more: Do you think Nan could hear me talk of my master's offers?'—'No, no,' said she, 'she was dead asleep.' 'I'm glad of that,' said I, 'because I would not expose my master to his common servants; and I knew you were no stranger to his fine articles.' Said she, 'I think they were fine articles, and you were bewitched you did not close with them: but let us go to sleep.' So I was silent, and the pretended Nan (O wicked, base, villainous designer! what an unexpected plot was this!) seemed to be awaking; and Mrs. Jewkes, abhorred creature! said, 'Come, Nan! what, are you awake at last? Pr'ythee come to bed; for Mistress Pamela is in a talking fit, and won't go to sleep one while.'

"At that, the pretended she came to the bed-side, and sitting down in a chair, where the curtain hid her, began to undress. Said I, 'Poor Mistress Anne, I warrant your head aches most sadly! How do you do?' She answered not a word. Said the superlatively wicked woman, 'You know I have ordered her not to answer you.' And this plot, to be sure, was laid when she gave her these orders, the night before.

"I heard her, as I thought, breathe quick and short: 'Indeed,' said I, 'Mrs. Jewkes, the poor maid is not well. What ails you, Mistress Anne?' And still no answer was made.

"I tremble to relate it! the pretended she came into bed, but trembled like an aspen-leaf; and I, poor fool that I was! pitied her much. But well might the barbarous deceiver tremble at his vile dissimulation, and base designs.

"What words shall I find, my dear mother (for my father should not see this shocking part), to describe the rest, and my confusion, when the guilty wretch took my left arm, and laid it under his neck, and the vile procuress held my right; and then he clasped me round the waist!

"Said I, 'Is the wench mad! Why, how now, Confidence?' thinking still it had been Nan. But he kissed me with frightful vehemence; and then his voice broke upon me like a clap of thunder, 'Now, Pamela,' said he, 'is the dreadful time of reckoning come, that I have threatened.' I screamed out in such a manner, as never any body heard the like. But there was nobody to help me; and both my hands were secured, as I said. Sure never poor soul was in such agonies as I. 'Wicked man!' said I, 'wicked abominable woman! O God! my God! this time! this one time! deliver me from this distress! or strike me dead this moment!' And then I screamed again and again.

"Said he, 'One word with you, Pamela; hear me but one word; and hitherto you see I offer nothing to you.' 'Is this nothing,' said I, 'to be in bed here? To hold my hands between you! I will hear, if you will instantly leave the bed, and take this villainous woman from me!'

"Said she (O disgrace of woman kind!), 'What you do, Sir, do: don't stand, dilly dallying. She cannot exclaim worse than she has done: and she'll be quieter, when she knows the worst.'

" 'Silence!' said he to her; 'I must say one word to you, Pamela! You see, now you are in my power! You cannot get from me, nor help yourself: yet have I not offered any thing amiss to you. But if you resolve not to comply with my proposals, I will not lose this opportunity: if you do, I well yet leave you.'

" 'O Sir,' said I, 'leave me, and I will do anything I ought to do.' 'Swear then, to me,' said he, 'that you will accept my proposals!' and then (for this was all detestable grimace) he put his hand in my bosom. With struggling and terror I fainted away, and did not come to myself soon; so that they both, from the cold sweats that I was in, thought me dying. And I remember no more than that, when with great difficulty they brought me to myself, she was sitting on one side of the bed with her clothes on: and he on the other with his, and in his gown and slippers.

"Your poor Pamela cannot answer for the liberties taken with her in her deplorable state. And when I saw them I sat up in my bed, without any regard to what appearance I made, and nothing about my neck; and he soothing me, with an aspect of pity and concern. I put my hand to his mouth, and said, 'O tell me, yet tell me not, what have I suffered in this distress?' I talked quite wild, and knew not what; for, to be sure, I was on the point of distraction.

"He most solemnly, and with a bitter imprecation, vowed he had not offered the least indecency; that he was frightened at the terrible manner I was taken in the fit; that he should desist from his attempt; and begged but to see me easy and quiet, and he would leave me and go to his own bed. 'O, then,' said I, 'take with you this most wicked woman, this vile Mrs. Jewkes, as an earnest, that I may believe you.'

" 'And will you, Sir,' said the wicked wretch, 'for a fit or two, give up such an opportunity as this? I thought you had known the sex better. She is now, you see, quite well again!'

"This I heard; more she might say; but I fainted away once more, at those words, and at his clasping his arms about me again. When I came a little to myself, I saw him sit there, and the maid Nan, holding a smelling-bottle to my nose, and no Mrs. Jewkes.

"He said, taking my hand, 'I vow to you, my dear Pamela, that I will leave you the moment I see you better, and pacified. Here's Nan knows and will tell you my concern for you. I vow to God, I have not offered any indecency to you: and, since I found Mrs. Jewkes so offensive to you, I have sent her to the maid's bed, and the maid shall lie with you to-night. But promise me, that you will compose yourself, and I will leave you.' 'But,' said I, 'will not Nan also hold my hand! Will not she let you come in again to me?' He said, 'By heaven! I will not come in again to-night. Nan, undress yourself, go to bed, and do all you can to comfort the dear creature—and now, Pamela,' said he, 'give me your hand, and say you forgive me, and I will leave you to your repose.' I held out my trembling hand, which he kissed: and I said, 'God forgive you, Sir, as you have been just in my distress; and as you will be just to what you promise!' He withdrew with a countenance of remorse: Nan shut the doors, and at my request, brought the keys to bed.

"This, O my dear parents, was a most dreadful trial. I tremble still to think of it; and dare not recall all the horrid circumstances. I hope, as he assures me, he was not guilty of indecency; but have reason to bless God, who, by disabling my faculties, empowered me to preserve my innocence; and, when all my strength would have signified nothing, magnified himself in my weakness."

Can you not see dear Sister, how happy I become, that I live on a beautiful great California ranch, where everybody is reasonably good looking, and is friendly and polite to me, and where the worst I have to fear is that the young master of the household threatens to go off and get drunk if I do not let him kiss me? So in your prayers give thanks for the kindness of Providence to your Little Sister

Pamela

LETTER LXII

Dear Mother:

This is being a busy time for your littlest one and I do not have much chance for letters. It is what is called the lecture season, and it means that I am taken in to Riverside or San Bernardino or Pasadena or even all the way to Los Angeles with my lady and sit and listen to a talk about anything from postwar conditions in Germany to the new school of painting in France. Then we have something to eat, then drive home, and on the way my lady tells the friends she has with her that it was very useful, or else all rubbish and why should anybody waste time listening to it. Also, she has her own lecturers, that she agrees with, and I have to get the invitations printed and addressed and mailed, the refreshments ordered, and the arrangements to meet the lecturer, who may be a man or a woman and who may stay several days if they have time and if my lady likes them. I meet them and talk with them, or mostly listen, which is what they prefer. Once it is a lady who has lectured all over the world about birth control, and has been arrested for it, but that was some time ago, for it is now respectable, or so my lady says. It seems to me right that poor women should not have to have more babies than they want, and the stories that she tells about it brought the tears to my eyes; but I surely never expected to hear talk about such a subject, and before men and women both. I just have to learn that this is a new world, as they all say it is.

Then comes a gentleman that has been to Russia twice and tells about the revolution there and what it means. Mrs. Harries is very strong for the Russian people and says they have a right to make their own world; this gentleman was that way too when he first came here to speak, but now he says he has become less sure. He is short and stocky and wears a little pointed beard, and his eyes twinkle as he tells my lady things that puzzle her and confuse her mind. He says, "Yes, the Bolsheviks have overthrown the old rulers, and the capitalists and landlords that had all the wealth. Now the wealth belongs to the state; but how much difference does it make? What the wealth meant was power, and now a new set of men have the power, and whether they own the wealth or the state owns it makes no difference to them so long as they control it. What I am afraid of is power in the hands of a few men, and what I want is to see power in the hands of the people, and how can they get it and keep it?" My lady is upset by this, and maybe will not be inviting this gentleman soon again.

There is another lady that is a Socialist, and is thin and very keen looking; she has written a dozen books, I am told, and is also a feminist, which means that she is for women's rights and suffrage and so on. Now she is old and looks like somebody's grandmother. She sits and knits and watches everything that goes on, and when she says something it is often sharp and sarcastic. But she is kind too, and likes me because I do my work and keep my wits about me, so she says. I tell her that I often do not understand what I hear, and she explains things to me like a teacher. In fact I think I am at school here half the time. I never heard so much discussing and arguing; all the problems of the world have to be settled, and sometimes people get excited, but my lady never worries; in fact I have decided that the hotter they get the better she likes it, for she thinks that something is really getting settled now. She will invite two people that she knows hate each other's ideas like poison, and she will bring up the subject and get them started and then sit back and watch like it was a boxing match.

The most agreeable thing is that there is now a radio set that no longer needs batteries but is plugged to the electric socket, so now it has plenty of power, and you do not have to stick little tubes into your ears but can hear the voice all over the room. It is really something hard to believe; half a dozen of her friends sit in her room and all can listen to a man that is speaking in Los Angeles, eighty or a hundred miles away. All go off saying they must have a set like that; but it has cost four hundred dollars and not all can afford it. I have learned to work it, and one of my duties is to turn it on and get it going right, then I can listen to more lectures and news of the world. Morning, noon and night, it goes in the ears of your loving Daughter

Pamela

⊱⊰

LETTER LXIII

Dear Sister:

I have had a second letter from Paul Darrow. He tells me that he does not have much news in prison, but that he got my letter and passed it to the others, and it was a great comfort to them all to know that they had friends outside who did not rest but tried to help them. He says that my visit was a comfort to him, and that he thinks of it many times every day. He asks if he might have a picture of me, but, alas, I have none. Miss Lucy and the others tease me again about waiting eight years; I am sure I would wait eight years for a man I loved, but hardly for a man that I do not know. But I give him the knowledge that he does not have to wait for God, who is with him now and will help him if asked. I have written him much the same as I have told to Charles, and hope that he will take it better. I assure him by God's own words that he does not have to count God as a friend of landlords and moneychangers. There have been many religious men who have fought for their rights and won them with God's help. I do not know whether such a letter as that will be allowed to go into the prison, but shall wait with interest to see. Perhaps someday Mrs. Harries will be taking another trip north. When you have time you might write him a letter and bear God's witness to him. He will assume that you, being older, are wiser. I have come to be sure that the wobblies are not the evil men they are painted in the newspapers. Their religion is not ours, but they stand for justice to God's poor.

Well, we have had another adventure since I wrote. Since under agreement with Mr. Harries my lady cannot bring any Reds to the home, she had them hire a hall for a protest meeting against the breaking up of the children's camp and school. Of course we had no idea whether or not this meeting also would be broken up; the papers had reported that the American Legion was threatening such action, so my lady went and sat upon the platform, dressed in her best and looking very magnificent, as much as to say, "Arrest a millionaire if you dare!" But they didn't. She made a little speech, saying that first of all she believes in free speech, in the right of the people to say what they believe to be true, and it is on that principle that our country is founded, and without it we are no better than they say Russia to be. One of the teachers told about the camp and what had been done to it, and then Nella Brodsky made a talk about Russia, and she is quite an orator. I do not know what to think about that country, which is godless, I fear, but it is certain that these people believe in it with all their hearts, and perhaps it is better than the old government that was.

Anyhow, we had an exciting time. Every moment we thought that a group of men with clubs might come marching in. I was afraid that my lady might wish me to sit by her on the platform, but she did not; perhaps I do not look rich enough. Charles drove us and sat with me and Mr. and Mrs. Fearing. Charles believes in free speech, he says, but I do not think that he would be very keen about it if it were not that he has to please his aunt at all costs. He is trying to drink only a little at a time, and thinks he can learn to.

I am learning about drinking people, that they are always figuring out systems to get the better of themselves, and generally they don't. It is the same with gambling, of which he now will do only a little, he says. I point out to him how much time and thought he wastes planning about it, and how much simpler it would be never to think about it at all. He says, "But how can you live in the world when everybody else is doing it?" I invite him to join our church and he would meet people who are never doing it; but he does not think that would interest him. Poor fellow!

I must tell you another story. I have told how many good and kind things my mistress does, and now I will show you the other side of her; she is made up of one-half pity and one-half pride—or maybe only God could tell the exact portions. Anyhow, they had a quarrel at the last Thursday luncheon, where the important ladies come, and the way of it is this. There is one of the ladies, Mrs. Cheevis, and she used to be rich but is a widow and has lost most of her money—by bad management, my lady says. Anyhow, my lady has been helping this friend, but some time ago decided that she wanted too much. Then Mrs. Cheevis borrowed five hundred dollars from Mrs. Harries, promising to pay it back and giving her what is called a lien on a lot of fine furniture that she owns. She did not pay the money back and Mrs. Harries says she never meant to. Now there is a poor woman that needs some furniture, and Mrs. Harries decides that Mrs. Cheevis has more than she needs and claims some of that to which she has a right; but apparently Mrs. Cheevis did not think she would do this and has set up a screech; so now she is not invited to the luncheon, and instead my lady has prepared a paper, what the lawyers call an indictment, a list of all the bad things that Mrs. Cheevis has done and is doing. She has dictated this to me and I have typed copies of it, and it is read to all the ladies at the party and they are invited to sign it and then it will be sent to Mrs. Cheevis.

Well, there is a big fuss. Some of the ladies sign, but three of them will not, and I can hear them from the drawing room where I am waiting. (It is proper for me to hear, because a secretary has to know everything and maybe attend to it.) I only hope I don't have to go with a truck and see to getting that furniture, for Mrs. Cheevis is a very emotional lady and weeps easily. One of the three who will not sign the paper is Mrs. Clark, and she is very positive; I hope this is not going to end a long friendship. She says the indictment is undignified and unworthy of Mrs. Harries. She should send and get the furniture, or send the sheriff to get it if need be, and to drop Mrs. Cheevis from her list if she wishes, but to let her character alone and not drag her other friends into it. I am not yet sure but I think that Mrs. Harries will give up, and if she does it will be the first time that I know. It is surely not Christian behavior, but I suppose it does not have to be, since my lady does not acknowledge Our Lord. Fortunately she has not asked me what I think about this matter. I am a servant and obey my mistress according to the flesh, as St. Paul directs. Your devoted Sister

Pamela

LETTER LXIV

Dear Mother:

I have delayed to write, because I have been so busy with my many duties. I have done my best to make myself useful, and now I have my reward. I am promoted to be a full secretary, and am to have a hundred and twenty-five beginning next month, of which I will send forty to you and the same to Sister, and I will have just a little more—but I get presents too. When my lady told me this she said she did not know how she could get along without me; I shall do my best to keep her from ever finding out.

My lady is kept very busy with the housing project, and that means that I am too. Master Charles has gone to New York on business of his own, and Miss Yvette is visiting in the north. My lady continues to be active in the cause of what she calls "free speech," but you must not let this worry you, for I assure you that I am not being led astray. It is one thing to grant people the right to say what they please, and quite another to agree with what they choose to say. I am listening to all sides and trying to decide what I believe. I can assure you, the more I hear from the godless, the more glad I am that I have an anchor for my soul. I am resolved with the apostle Paul that "I will pray with the spirit, and I will pray with the understanding also." You will be interested to know that the young wobbly whom I met on my visit to San Quentin, and to whom I have written Bible texts, has begun to think about them and to write me with a changed spirit. He has, of course, much time to meditate upon them, and I think the Holy Spirit has begun to work in him. His name is Paul Darrow, and you should pray for him, along with your devoted

Pamela

Dear Sister:

I have had another battle with Satan for the soul of my young master, and the great deceiver has come out ahead. God in His mercy will have some reason for this, which someday perhaps I shall understand.

He started trying to kiss me again, and I told him that they were not sisterly kisses. He was provoked, and went off to Hollywood, and came back with liquor on his breath. Poor soul, I tried to help him, for I know how nervous and wretched he is at such times. Then he told me he was going to New York; he could not longer stand the boredom of this place, and especially all the irritations and futilities of his aunt's housing project. There are shows in New York, and many sorts of entertainment. He urged me to come with him, telling me all the wonderful things we would do, the interesting people I would meet, the luxuries I would have. I have never seen him so moved, he begged and pleaded, and I thought the tears would come into his eyes. He insisted that I loved him, and I admitted that I did with one half of my being, while the other half was fear and grief. It was a violent scene, and in the end he grabbed me in his arms, and I had to push him away.

At last I heard that word which for so long he has been refusing to know is in the English language. He said, "What would you say if I asked you to marry me?" As you know, Sister, I have not failed to think of the answer, and I said at once, as I had promised myself, "I would say, Charles, that you must swear to me you would never touch a drop of liquor again, and you would have to mean it on your honor." "And what else?" "This also, you would have to let me stay as your aunt's secretary and earn my living as I am doing now." "Oh, my God!" says he. "What lunacy is this?" I tell him, "You have too much money, and it makes you hard and arrogant, and far too confident of your own importance. It would not be long before you had decided that I had trapped you, and the only way I know to convince you that I don't want any of your money is not to take it, but to go on as I am and with the duties in which I am happy." "A fine time I should have with a wife that was chained to my aunt's whims and notions!" "You would be a lot happier, Charles, if you would stay here, and interest yourself in this place and in your aunt's work, and give up all those people who are leading you to destruction and who have no thought but to get as much of your money as they can." "And what about this God of yours?" "He is your God also, Charles, and try as you will you cannot get rid of Him. I have prayed for you, and I do not say that you have to believe, for I do not suppose that a man can control his beliefs; but I should expect you for love's sake to humble your pride and study His word with me and try to understand it." "So that is your decision?" says he. I reply, "You have not asked me, but that is what I should answer if you did." He says, "I'm sorry, it's no go," and out he walks and upstairs and packs his things and stows them in his car, and says good-by to his aunt and off he goes. I suppose he figures that by driving he will divert his mind from liquor.

I find my lady with red eyes. Being an endlessly curious person, she wants to know if I sent him away, and I have no choice but to tell her the truth. "Did you have to be so hard with him?" she says, and I tell her, "I could not help it, Mrs. Harries." I say it humbly, for I mean to keep this very good position, and I know that I have dealt a blow to her family pride. It might have been hard for her to accept a former parlormaid as a niece, but this is worse—I have refused to become one of her family. She will not get out of her mind the idea that I drove her darling away. She still thinks of him as the tiny golden-haired fellow that she hugged to her bosom when he became an orphan, and I shall have to work hard indeed to atone for having sent him perhaps to ruin. Such a small thing it would have been to take him into my bed, and her friends would have seen to it that I knew all about birth control!

Don't forget, Sister, he did not ask me to marry him; he only wanted to know what I would say if he did, and now he knows. He will have some time to think it over while driving to New York. I blush for myself, for every time I hear the telephone my heart gives a jump; something in me is saying, "Suppose it is he, calling to say that he accepts my terms!" He does not hesitate to call any distant place, whenever the notion takes him. But he does not call, and I wonder, is it his love of pleasure that controls his decision, or his fear of being chained, or his pride, that will not permit him to be ruled by a woman? I remember those awful words that I heard him say, "Why should I marry, when I can get what I want without it?" He has found out that he cannot get it from me.

A strange, complicated thing love is, Sister! Perhaps yours is not, and I hope it may never be; but mine is. I admit it to myself, and to you only, I am in love with him. I miss him, and there is a gap in my life, an ache in my heart. I wanted so to help him! He is like a child that needs my help. Mrs. Mackenzie warned me, and quoted a poet, saying that pity turns the soul to love. I suppose that is true of every good woman; but pity is not enough; there has to be courage, too. That is what is the matter with my poor dear mistress; she has been able to say No to her husband but not to her adopted baby. I am asking myself, will she ever be able to forgive me in her heart, because I denied her desire and dared to affront the greatness and glory of her family? Shall I tell her that I love him and that my heart aches too? I would learn something about her that way; but suppose she were to beg me to take him on any terms? A hard problem for your dutiful

Pamela

LETTER LXVI

Dear Mother:

I did not say anything about the depression, because I was not sure if it would get to where you are. But I suppose that when the people in town have no jobs, they take to doing their own washing. You do not have to worry about the money from me, for I am sure it will come just the same. I asked my lady about it and she said, "Oh, I could not do without a secretary!" You see how it is, they do not mean to suffer; I have just made out, and she has signed, a check for Master Charles for twenty-five hundred dollars; but she has told him that he will have to be careful, for Pennship—that is what they call the company—has written her that there may be no dividends at the next quarter. She has stopped all the work on the housing project, for, she says, what is the use to build houses when the people have no money to buy them? I think that what is more in her mind is that she has failed to get the young master interested in it as she had hoped. That is the most important thing in the world to her.

It is strange about these depressions. People say there always comes one after a war, and they argue about the reasons. What they say always sounds convincing to me—until I listen to the next one, who disagrees with him entirely. They argue about it at the Sunday afternoons, and often at meals, and they become excited; but my lady says very sadly, "Everybody goes away thinking just what he thought when he came." She herself is tireless in explaining her idea that the government should print more money and give it to the poor, and the poor would spend it at once for goods, and then more goods would be made with the money. Some people who claim to be wise laugh at that and say all we have to do is to wait and the depression will pass; they fail to see that the poor cannot wait because they have to eat. Says my lady, "What will you do, put them in cold storage?" You and Grampa have always been Republicans and I thought that I was, and I thought that since we elected such a handsome and fine-spoken man as President Harding everything would be all right; but it isn't, and so I am wondering if I will be a Republican any more. Here the master voted for Harding and the mistress voted for Debs that is in jail. I suppose that will shock you, but not so much as if it was good times you were in. All this is too far over the head of your darling

Pamela

LETTER LXVII

Dear Sister:

There has been a most terrible quarrel between the master and the mistress; he was in her room, and all over the house we could hear him roaring. We could not hear what she said to him, but doubtless it was enough to keep him angry; she is stubborn and will never give an inch to pressure. What drives him crazy is that Brodsky meeting where she sat on the platform; it was in the papers, and he says that his name is disgraced and he is ashamed to meet his friends. He called the Reds the most awful names and accuses them of every crime. He calls her a fool and a puddinghead to believe what they tell her. They say they are pacifists, but he says it's only so long as they do not have the power to be anything else, and that she is their dupe, their fat cat, and they laugh at her behind her back. Also he is in a fury about Master Charles, calling him a good-for-nothing loafer, a woman chaser, and worse. He is in a fury over the housing project, which he says is a swindle got up by Mr. and Mrs. Fearing, who have sold her land for twice what it is worth, and if she got the houses built nobody could live in them because there are no jobs in the town of Junipero. Of course she will tell him that it is her money and that she will spend it for what she pleases; so he roars like a mad bull some more, and how he does not burst a blood vessel is a mystery. Afterwards she did not say a word to anybody in the house, but we are all sad to know what is in her heart. I asked Miss Lucy if this would mean another family conference on divorce, and she says it has been like this for many years; it is because he loves her that he cannot control his irritation.

It is sad indeed to hear that the hard times have reached the college and that the people can no longer pay you for work. Do not worry, dear Sister, I will raise your share to sixty a month, for I really do not need some of the things that I buy and I do not wish to accustom myself to luxury. It is one of Satan's devices, and I am troubled in my heart that I have such comforts as I never dreamed of while so many more worthy and useful people are in dire want. I am determined not to become soft and depend upon the things which the rich have; I hold myself ready to go back any day to the old shack on the side of a bare hill and to sleep in a part of the shed. I have not forgot what a luxury I would have thought running water to be, and with it I could raise a garden with everything we need to eat, and alfalfa for the nannies. God will be in that garden and that shed, and He will give me strength to be glad that I did not marry a young millionaire that mocks His Holy Word.

Last Sabbath I went to church, for which Mrs. Harries was so kind as to let me have one of the small cars to drive. It must be a temptation to her to ask me to do some shopping or other errands, but she keeps to the bargain she has made with Mother at the start. It must irritate her vastly that I spend my time saying prayers and reading that old Book in which there is so much "begatting," but she never says a word and neither do I. If I do tell it myself, I am a good secretary, and save her a lot of work and worry and especially forgetting things; she needs me as much as I need her, and she knows both. I meant to tell you about church; there are now two young men who would like a chance to have a walk or a drive with me alone; one is the grocer clerk, whose name is Jotham Hanby, and the other is the son of a tinsmith. Neither of them, I am sure, would forget for a moment that the word marriage exists; but it is plain that I cannot think of it, so I evade being alone with them, and speak only of the sermon and such things. I hope they will turn their thoughts elsewhere, but so far there are no signs of this.

The moment the sun goes down on the Sabbath my work begins, and believe me, I have plenty. I keep out of my lady's way until the moment of sundown, which of course she has no way to keep track of; she knows that when the right moment comes I will be at her door, smiling and ready. She rarely closes that door, for she has an immense bathroom and a clothes closet between, so big that she uses that for her dressing room. She is a great lady, not merely in riches but also in avvordupoys, a French word which I do not know how to spell, but you may tell me, perhaps. She has a scales in her bathroom, but I have never seen her on it, and she only refers to the subject to say that she eats so little. She wears whenever she goes out a very tight thing which is called a girdle and which compels her to sit up stiff and straight, and only me and a few intimate friends have ever seen her without. When she gets home, or when company is gone, she retires to her dressing room and takes it off and puts on a penwar, another French word, and she will come out rubbing herself and sort of working herself all over as if trying to get rid of the creases. Twice a week she drives to have Battle Creek water treatments and massage, or if she is busy I will phone for the masseuse to come to her. I could tell you a lot more of these secrets of a rich lady, but I suppose they are part of what every nurse will learn.

What I started to tell you about was Sunday, which was most strange. Mr. Mackenzie was to be the lecturer, and he chose to tell about a new writer that is an Irishman but lives in Paris and his name is Joyce. He has written a big book that is called "Ulysses." It is supposed to be very bad and is being published in a little magazine. Mr. Mackenzie has got hold of a copy, and he thinks he is doing us a favor to tell about it. "Pamela," as you know, tells all about a girl's life, and this "Ulysses" is all that happens to a man during twenty-four hours, but it is what goes on in his mind, and mostly what is called his subconscious mind, his dreams and so on. Well, perhaps it is because I have never been a man that I could not make it out, and I am sure I

wouldn't even have known it was bad if Mr. Mackenzie
hadn't told us so. He read passages, and the man has mixed
up the words so, and made puns and jokes, with so many
kinds of foreign words, that to me it was all a jumble.
When the reading was through my lady gets up and says,
"I know that Mr. Mackenzie is a great scholar and knows
what he is talking about, and this may be a great work, but
I could make neither head nor tail of it and cannot see the
sense of such stuff." Mr. Mackenzie smiles amiably, as he
always does, and says, "I knew you would feel that way
about it, Mrs. Harries, but I thought that some of your
guests might be interested to hear about this new kind of
art work." "Well, that is that," says my lady, "and now we
will hear from a different kind of writer, one that Dr. Clark
has brought with him, and I hope it will be easier for some
of us to understand what he is trying to tell us."

She introduces what seems to be a boy, but I learn that
he is two years older than me; but he is two inches shorter
and very pretty, with wavy brown hair, blue eyes, and cheeks
with down like a ripe peach; he is dressed very poor, but
clean. It seems he is a farmboy from North Carolina, and
was determined to be a poet and read all the poets he could
find or borrow from people who had books, and then verses
began to come to him and he couldn't get them out of his
mind. He found that he couldn't do it after a day's work
behind the plow, so he decided that he would go back to
the days of the old wandering minstrels, which he told about.
He has an older brother who can run the little farm, so he
goes out and exchanges his songs for a meal and a place to
sleep. He walks on country roads, and looks at the sights
and thinks about life, and composes verses, and when sundown comes he picks out the right sort of farmhouse, not
too big or too little, and goes in and tells them that he is a
poet and if they would like him to stay the night he will

recite to them in the evening; mostly they do, and they like his verses and invite him to stay a while, and when he wishes to go they tell him about friends on the way and offer to telephone and tell the friends to expect him. That way he traveled most of the way to California, getting rides only over the mountains and across the deserts; he has made many friends and has a list of people who want to buy his poems when they are published, but he will not take money for them in advance, not being sure that they will ever be published.

He is very modest and friendly in manner and has a nice voice, and he recites some of the poems, which are about nature and the joy of being alive; one of them is about hard times and what they mean to the poor, and that I know will please my lady. They are all quite simple, and there is nobody that cannot understand what they mean. She says this as she thanks him; then, thinking that perhaps she has hurt Mr. Mackenzie's feelings by her lack of interest in his Irishman, she asks what he thinks of Mr. Plowman's work. (I forgot to say that the young man calls himself Piers Plowman, which is the name of an old-time poet of the people, he explains.)

Mr. Mackenzie says there is room for all kinds of poets in the world, and especially for people's poets, of which Mr. Plowman will undoubtedly be one. "If I may make a suggestion," he says, and turns to my lady, asking if he may, and she says, "Certainly," so he goes on, "I would point out to Mrs. Harries that here is an opportunity which may not come to her often, to give support to a genuine talent. A poet cannot go on wandering about forever in these modern days; he ought to have a friend and patron, who would help him to get his work typed and then put into print. If somewhere on this great estate there should be a room where he could live and be quiet, and have no demands made upon him, it might well be that someday he would dedicate to his patron a book which would be the means of handing down her name to posterity."

Well, that sort of puts my lady on the spot, as they say. She would, I am sure, be willing to have her name become immortal, though I imagine she would prefer it to be some other name but Harries. Also, she has said that she likes the young man's verses, and all can see that he is a person who would give no offense. She has been told by Dr. Clark how he has recited his verses in the Unitarian church and pleased the congregation, and now comes this editor to confirm the judgment; so she says that she would be glad if Mr. Plowman would find her home suited to his taste and would spend the night here. Mr. Plowman blushes like a girl and says it is much the most elegant place he has ever been in, but if there is anywhere a room suited to a poor boy he will gladly be her guest, and pay in his usual coin whenever requested. My lady invites both Mr. Mackenzie and Dr. Clark to stay for supper and talk about the matter, and the result is that we now have a poet laureate of the Rancho Casa Grande, so Mr. Mackenzie calls him. He is spending the night in Charles' room, which I am sure would not please that elegant gentleman. More later from your devoted Sister

Pamela

LETTER LXVIII

Dear Mother:

There is always something new and interesting at this place and that makes it pleasant to work in. Now we have a poet; a young man that my lady has given shelter to, and that she thinks may some day make us famous. He is a very nice farmboy, and his name is Piers Plowman; he looks at me with great respect and says, "Oh, you are so pretty, Miss Andrews!" Perhaps some day he will write me a poem, and if so I will send it to you. The first thing I asked him was, "Do you believe in God?" He looked at me in surprise and asked, "How could a poet not believe in God?" I told him, "There has been more than one such here," and he said, "They could be no true poets, because God's wonders are spread through all the earth for everyone to see." I said, "Do you keep the Sabbath holy?" and he answered, "I keep all the seven days holy, so far as I can, and I have never exploited the labor of others." So you can see that he is a good boy and will be a great credit to the place. Dr. Clark, who brought him here, has declared that there should be a state law requiring that every California ranch of more than five hundred acres should keep a poet.

The story of how Mr. Plowman has got his house to live in is funny. I am not sure if I have told you about the cottages, which is where my lady has a home for all the old people that have ever worked long for her family. They are not really cottages at all, but a long building in the walnut grove, made of concrete blocks and divided into apartments, each with one room and a bath; there an old lady or old gentleman can live very comfortable—only sometimes they do not get along together, and when my lady comes to visit them they bother her with complaints, and if she stays too long with one of them the others have their feelings hurt. There is one, old Mr. Burns, an Irishman, that was the coachman long ago and he must be over eighty; he likes to play the fiddle, but the others say he is not very good, and rules had to be made that he should not play after ten or before seven. He does not like the others and wants to be by himself, so my lady fixed up an old adobe house that is off at the upper end of the place, and was built by a Mexican family that she bought out and got rid of because he beat his wife. Well, now Mr. Burns lives there and can fiddle all night if he wishes, and that is how there was a spare room for the poet, and he can recite his verses to the old ladies, or if he wants to sing them he can walk up the canyon as far as he pleases. He has a very nice treble voice and often sings his songs when people ask him to. When we talked about God he told me he had made the Twenty-third Psalm into verses, so that it could be sung like a hymn, and when I said I would like to hear it he sung it to the tune called Absalom; it was very lovely. I think he will be good for this place, which badly needs religious influence.

Well, that is enough for tonight and I am sure it will make you happy for your devoted Daughter

Pamela

❮❮❮⋯❯❯❯

LETTER LXIX

Dear Sister:

I have been very busy of late; besides all my other tasks I have been helping to get Piers's poems into writing for him. He has told me to call him Piers, but my lady, who is formal, prefers Mr. Plowman. Many of his poems he has never written but recites them from memory, and I do them on the typewriter, at which I have become quite good. They are very sweet poems and sensible; he knows what the life of the poor farmer is—his people were tenant farmers and were trying to buy their fifteen-acre place, but this dreadful slump will make it impossible. He writes about the poor, and about nature and God, I am happy to say, though he is not of our belief; he was interested in what I told him about keeping the Sabbath and has promised to study it. Being a poet is a funny thing; it looks like he is idle all the time, but he is not, because there is something going on in his mind. He takes long walks and meditates, and something comes to his mind and he learns it and has a poem. Someday I hope to send you one of them, but I have not yet felt free to do so. They are the things by which he earns his living.

Last Sunday we had a count, that is a kind of nobleman that comes from Hungary. He is tall and thin and speaks English with an English accent, which sounds funny to say, but it is different. It seems that he sympathizes with the peasants in his country and when the revolution came he turned his estates over to the government; but then there was what is called a counterrevolution, and the count now lives in Paris. He was very interesting, and stayed the night, so I sat and listened to him for a long time. It is proper for a secretary to sit and listen, where it would not have been for a parlormaid; so my education goes faster, and I know what a revolution is like, and how much more cruel the landlords' party are when they come back, and I am surely glad I never lived in that Papist country.

Also, I had some talk with Mr. Mackenzie. I have been reading my "Pamela" right along and have got to the part where the cruel master decides that he will marry her; but she cannot believe it and thinks it is one more heartless deception, and that it will be just a make-believe marriage. Oh, dear, such excitements and confusion as those poor people are in, and me too! I will copy for you the scene where Pamela's father is brought to the master's house, and Pamela does not know that he is in the room:

" 'Oh, sir,' said I, 'your goodness will be a cordial to their dear honest hearts!' At that, my dear father, not able to contain himself, nor yet to stir from the place, gushed out into a flood of tears, which he, good soul, had been struggling with, it seems; and cried out, 'Oh, my dear child!' I knew the voice, and lifting up my eyes, saw my father. I gave a spring, and overturned the table, without regard to the company, and threw myself at his feet: 'Oh, my father! my father!' said I; 'can it be? Is it you? Yes, it is! Oh, bless your happy daughter!' I would have said, and down I sunk.

"My master seemed concerned. 'I feared,' said he, 'that the surprise would be too much for her spirits'; and all the ladies ran to me, and made me drink a glass of water; and I found myself encircled in the arms of my dearest father. 'Oh, tell me,' said I, 'everything. How long have you been here? When did you come? How does my honoured mother?' And half a dozen questions more, before he could answer me.

"They permitted me to retire with my father; and when I poured forth all my vows, and thanksgiving to God, for this additional blessing; and confirmed all my master's goodness to his scarce-believing amazement. We kneeled together, blessing God, and one another, for several ecstatic minutes; and my master coming in soon after, my dear father said, 'O Sir, what a change is this! May God reward and bless you, both in this world and the next.' "

For the first time I have begun to think that you may be right that it is not good for me to give myself up to such excitements as these. I talked to Mr. Mackenzie and his wife about it, and he says that I should learn to develop what he calls my critical sense; at the same time that I feel with the characters I should remember that they are the creation of a man's mind, and should watch the art by which he does it to me, and should think what it is that he is trying to teach me, and what it is that he himself believes, and all I can learn about the world in which he lives.

That is a terrible lot to be in one small head, but I am trying it. He points out to me that these people in the story change their natures suddenly and violently, to suit the purposes of the story. The author waves a magic wand, and at once the master of the estate, who has been so uncontrolled and so evil, suddenly turns into everything good and noble, the moment he has decided to raise Pamela One to the position of wife and mistress of his household; she, for her part, accepts the change, and believes humbly and obediently whatever is told to her. Says Mr. Mackenzie, "They tear every passion to tatters, and to our modern taste the thing becomes absurd." I tell him that I must be a poor feeble creature, because I have swallowed every word of it and never had a doubt but that it was all happening while I read. He says, "That is the way most people read, and especially the way they did in the time of your great-great-great-grandmother."

Now I am afraid it is all going to be spoiled for me, and I have hard time trying to make up my mind whether I want it to be spoiled or not. You, I am sure, would wish me to have no more to do with it; but, oh, dear, I could never get along without attending the wedding, and making sure that poor Pamela One is going to have the happiness which she has earned by so many sufferings. I am, as you see, a silly child, but my editor friend tells me that millions of women have been the same, and it fascinates him to discover that this old story can still exert its spell. He says that he has been making a guinea pig of me, and I was ashamed to ask him what he meant by that. Perhaps you can enlighten your so ignorant

Pamela Two

LETTER LXX

Dear Mother:

This has been a busy time for my kind lady and so for her secretary. The long delayed trial of that Russian-Jewish girl and her friends has been held in San Bernardino; Mrs. Harries has taken it as her duty to go there and sit through the trial every day and persuade as many of her friends as she can to do the same, for what she says will be the moral effect. She has employed two high-priced lawyers to defend the case, and it is what she calls civil liberties. People have a right to believe in the Soviet Union if they wish to and to teach it to children if the parents of the children so wish. Five days a week we have driven to the trial, and in the middle of the day we go to lunch at a hotel nearby, and there are about twenty of us, including the defendants who are on bail, and my lady puts up most of the money. I know all about it because I make out the checks and write letters asking others to help and to come and everything. She is terribly stirred up about it, but I assure you that I am not letting myself be drawn into any Red ideas. Because you say people have a right to say what they believe does not mean that you agree with what they say; quite otherwise, because they say so many different things that nobody could agree with any but a small part. There are many places in the world where we would not be permitted to set forth the prophecies of William Miller, and then we would consider it necessary to become martyrs. It is too bad that other people have wrong ideas, but we cannot change them by force; we give them their chance to see the light, and if they reject it, the issue rests between them and God. You and Grampa may be sure that the sound teaching you have given will not be forgotten or abandoned by your devoted

/Pamela

LETTER LXXI

Dear Sister:

You will have seen the letter which I wrote to Mother about the trial. I am not going to tell her about the trouble which has just happened to my lady. It may be that you have seen it in the paper, if you have time to look at one. It seems that she came home and wrote a letter to the judge, complaining about some of the unfairness which she has seen in the court; his honor was very angry and issued a summons for contempt of court, for it seems that it is not proper to write to a judge about a case that is going on. Her lawyers were very much upset, for fear that she might answer him back and make him angry and he would send her to jail, as he had a right to do for as long as he pleased. We were all in a state, and I packed a bag for her so that she would have what she needed if she had to go to jail; at the last minute I had to run to the drugstore because she had forgot her toothbrush. The lawyers upset us by saying that she would not be allowed to take the bag into jail; they laid down the law to her, that she would not argue with the court, nor answer back, and she has promised, but if she keeps it her friends all agree that it will be the first time in her life. They come to court to stand by her, and the place looks like a meeting of the Thirteen Club.

Never did I expect to see anything like this. She was called before the bar, as they call it, and the cross old judge asked her, "Did you write this letter?" She says, "Yes, your honor," and then he gives her such a scolding as she never did hear in all her life, and she stands there fixing those big brown eyes upon him and not speaking. She is trembling, but I am sure it is because she is mad and not because she is scared. When he gets through he fines her fifty dollars and says that if she does it again he will surely send her to jail. So she takes out a fifty-dollar bill—she has got all kinds and sizes so as to be ready. Fifty dollars is nothing to her, of course, and she is secretly pleased, because all the reporters are there, and they have got her letter, and it will be in all the papers, and will cause them to tell much more about the trial and about Nella's ideas. If they had sent Mrs. Harries to jail, it would have gone all over the world, and maybe that is why the judge did not do it. Anyhow, we all had a time, and nobody more than your scared Little Sister

                                                    Pamela

LETTER LXXII

Dear Sister:

I must write again to tell you the terrible scenes we had at home after that one in the court. The master was furious,

I thought he would go wild; he scolded and stormed, but it did him no good; she is that stubborn, she would die before she would give up. I did not know that such things could go on in a home, especially one so fine. More than ever I realize that life without God is meaningless.

Then came the end of the trial and those poor Russian Jews are convicted of criminal syndicalism, as it is called, and they can be sent to jail for many years. My lady wept, and some of the other women with her, and now that it is over my lady can say what she pleases about it and cannot be sent to jail for it, though many would like her to be. I have letters to write about it, and Piers has written a poem which has pleased her wonderfully and which she had him read on Sunday afternoon; it is to be printed so that she can send it to other people. That is what a poet laureate is for, says Dr. Clark, and he explained to me that it is something they have in England, a man who writes a poem when the king is crowned, or when he gets married, or when a great victory is won, or whatever. Our poet laureate of Rancho Casa Grande writes only sad things now, because that is the way we all feel, including your devoted Little Sister

Pamela

P.S. I really feel so, for Nella is a good girl. If only I could persuade her to call upon God!

LETTER LXXIII

Dear Mother:
    There has been company here, one of my lady's cousins, who is very fashionable but does not have any of her ideas,

but they are good friends. The husband, Mr. Starett, is jolly and tells stories, and she keeps quiet and lets him. They have money and they just travel around and enjoy themselves; their children are in boarding schools and that is the way the rich live. Mr. Harries comes in to meals, which he has not done for a long time. As for me, I have less to do, for the guests take my lady to places with them and I am not needed. I stay at home and copy poems for Piers, who is a very nice boy and the best company I have had in this place. I have explained our doctrines to him, but he is not very strong for that side of religion; he says that what counts is the love of God, and through Him of all the things He has created. He says that God is everywhere and in all things and in a way *is* all things. I warn him that that is what is called pantheism, which I have heard preached against; but he says it makes good poetry. So we have plenty of things to argue about. I never knew a poet before and I find that they are very emotional, and at the same time very much set on writing things the way they want them. Piers continues most respectful to me, because I am the secretary to so great a lady; he was not here when I was the maid in cap and gown. I tell him that I came off a farm of only four acres, while his family has fifteen; but he says his is only rented, whereas mine is owned and has a well and windmill, which gives me a higher social standing. So you see we have fun as well as discussing the First Angel's Message. I do not mean to quit until I have converted him. Your devoted Daughter

Pamela

LETTER LXXIV

Dear Sister:

Charles has come back. He has been in New York and
then in Paris. I had no news of him, save the large checks
which his aunt sent to him and the addresses which she
gave me. Once I wrote him a little note, such as a friend
might, saying that I hoped he was well and having a pleasant time; but he did not answer. Perhaps he did not wish
me to have a written word from him; or perhaps he was
bitter against me. I found that I thought a great deal about
him; he has played an important part in my life, and I
prayed for him often. I thought of him with other women
in his arms and tried not to hate him. I have been taking
Mr. Mackenzie's advice and watching my own mind at
times, and I am interested to note how hatred and love lie
not so far apart.

Well, now he comes in, and it is just as if he had been
off playing golf for the day. He is handsome as ever,
browned, I suppose because he drives the car with the top
open. He is smiling and rosy—his sins appear to agree with
him. He says, "Hello, Pam! How's things?" I say, "Fine,"
and that's all. He has brought me a present from Paris, an
embroidered pink dressing gown that I hope is not im-
proper for a secretary. He has presents for everybody,
having plenty of room in the car. For his aunt he brings
perfumes in bottles so beautiful that they are art works, I suppose; also a hat that makes her laugh when she puts it on,
it is so gay. She has set the bottles up in a row and shown

them to her friends; she is so proud, forgetting that they are bought with her own money. Her love is pitiful.

Everything goes on as before. He takes his bag of golf clubs and goes off to play, in a different place from his uncle. In the entrance hall he passes me and says with his teasing smile, "You been thinking it over, Pam?" I say, "Thinking what over?" But of course I know what he means. "Having some fun with me," he says, and I tell him, "I have been praying for you to be well and happy, and I hope my prayers were answered." "The same old God!" says he, and I reply, "The same yesterday and forever." He goes off laughing, as if he thought that was witty; I have observed that any Bible text strikes him that way; it is new to him and perhaps he thinks I am making it up as I go.

The next time I meet him he says, "They tell me we have a poet now." I say, "Yes, and he is a good one, I think. I hope you will be kind to him." "Has he fallen in love with you?" asks he, and I say, "I hope not." Says he, "If he does not, he is a lout." "He is a very decent and earnest young man, Charles." "Then I suppose he believes in that old God of yours?" "He does indeed. When I asked him, he told me that no man could be a poet who did not believe in God." "Oho!" says the young master. "He should come to Paris, where they grow them in all the attics, and if there is one who believes in God I have never heard his name." So you see, dear Sister, he is not changed and will not. I am sad about it, but God has his reasons, we must believe.

Our poet is very happy here and is pleasing everybody. He is modest and quiet and never comes to the big house unless he is specially invited; he has been told to come to the Sundays, and he gets himself in a corner and sits and listens and watches, and then goes away and thinks about it, and perhaps it causes him to write a poem, and if so I copy it and put in on my lady's reading table. She likes it because she understands it; before now the word poetry has meant to her something that nobody can make anything of, and she asks, "What is the use of it?" But to have a poet that says just what she agrees with—except about God—and says it with rhymes that help you to remember, that pleases her, and she will ask him to recite one, and he does it nicely. Twice she has asked him to stay to supper, and he was unhappy because he knew that his table manners were not right. So I gave him lessons, like Miss Bascom did to me, and told him all the things he should do and those he should not. He has told me his real name, which is Ebenezer Bumblefinger, and he says that is not a poetical name; when he read the poem of Piers Plowman that is six hundred years old he liked it so well he decided to take that name.

Last Sunday we had a rabbi, that is a Jewish reverend, from what they call a temple in New York. He talked about the need of a Jewish state in Palestine. He was very earnest, and my lady said afterwards, "I don't see why they have to shout." I said, "Maybe his temple is big and he has got the habit," and that she thought was funny. It seems that other Jews did not agree with him, and they argued, along with the Gentiles. How were you going to get rid of the Arabs? I did not know there were so many complications in this world, and often I am left bewildered because there are so many good arguments on both sides. But here it always ends happy, because no matter how hot they get, my lady soothes them down and they eat the refreshments together. That is all for now from your loving Sister

Pamela

LETTER LXXV

Dear Mother:

There is not much news from your Little One these days. Things go quietly in this great house—that is what Casa Grande means, and it is surely that. The grain is reaped, the fruits ripen, and our poet wanders about, looking at the mountains and the sky, and is very happy writing verses about what he sees, both with his eyes and his soul. It is interesting to see how the working people respect him, and bow politely but do not interrupt him, because they know he is somebody different. The young master has come back from abroad and invites his aunt's secretary to go driving with him, but she is a busy young lady and generally declines. Her efforts to turn his thoughts to God have not been successful. Perhaps someday trouble will come to him, and he will learn. Knocking a little ball about a field hurts nobody, but it seems not very important work for a young and able-bodied man.

I send you a letter which I have received from the young man whom I visited in San Quentin prison. He is one who has trouble, but whether God sent it or Satan I cannot be sure. Anyhow, I have managed to persuade him to look into the Scriptures, and you will see that the texts I have sent him have worked upon his mind and he is getting a better idea of religion. I am answering by telling him that he may think of me as a friend, and to be sure that in believing in God he does not have to cease believing in the working class, or trying to help them to build a world in which there are no more poor and no more rich idlers. It seems that it

is permitted to send such ideas into the prison, and this
rejoices your devoted

Pamela

LETTER LXXVI

Dear Sister:

I have just had an interesting time. My lady took me and
our poet to dinner at the home of the Fearings, and there
we met what I believe is a great man. His name is Debs and
he has been confined in Atlanta penitentiary, where he was
sent for opposing the war. He is a tall, thin old man, entirely bald, and terribly pale from his prison experience. My
lady did not invite him to her home, for fear that it would
be breaking the agreement with the master; but she had the
Fearings invite him, and she gave him money for his Socialist party, of which he is leader. He is a quite wonderful
man, deeply religious in the sense that he loves his fellow-
men and seeks to serve them, but I do not know whether
he does it in God's name—I had no chance to ask. He talks
continuously, as if he were lecturing from a platform, which
is what he is doing ever since his release. He told most
interestingly about prison life, where it seems that even the
most evil men know love when they meet it; even the
warden and the jailers were sorry when he went. I was interested to hear him tell my lady that she makes a mistake to
help the Communists, because they may be all right for
Russia but they surely have no place in America, which is
a land of freedom and they do not understand what that is.
It was a good thing for my lady to hear, for she cannot see

the difference, and when the Communists tell her that they are pacifists, she believes them, and I think she is for any-body that is "agin the government," as the saying is.

Well, we all liked Gene, as they call the old man; he liked Piers, who recited some of his poems, and Gene said they should be known all over America and promised to help make them known; which of course pleased the poet and also Mrs. Harries. We drove back home, so happy; but alas, next day things were not so good, for my master has heard about it and is in a fury. The Fearings came to the house for lunch next day, and barely have they entered the drawing room when he rushes in and orders them out. He shakes his fist in little Mr. Fearing's face, which grows yellow with alarm; he calls him a scoundrel and sneak, and the pair of them parasites, cheats, rascals that have swindled his wife, selling them worthless land for a high price, and if he ever catches them on the place again he will beat Mr. Fearing's face in. He calls Debs a traitor and firebrand, a scoundrel and a dog, and accuses the Fearings of having plotted to sneak him to a meeting with his wife. My lady is there and tries to stop him; she says, "This is my house!" But he calls her a fool and a dupe of these rascals.

Dr. and Mrs. Clark are there too, and my lady takes Mrs. Clark and pushes her in front of the raging man, and says, "While you are putting the friends of Debs out, why don't you put her out too, for they had Debs in their church." But the master says, "I do not wish to put her out, I wish to put out these two skunks," and out they go, and drive home, I suppose. The master goes to his room, and I to mine, for I am too scared to want any lunch. What my lady did and the Clarks did I do not know, for my lady said nothing about the scene to me. I am so sorry for that poor man, for I know he means well, he just cannot understand his wife, and he hates all the people that gather round her and get her money, and encourage her to believe that she ought not have so much, nor him either, and that what they call the economic system should be changed to help the workers and the unemployed. It is all very confusing to your Little Sister

Pamela

P.S. Here is a poem which Piers recited to Debs:

THE PROPHET

The prophet lived
  In a little town,
And all the people
  Cried him down.
They killed him because
  Of his dangerous views,
For I read about it
  In the Daily News.

A few years later,
  When hate was spent,
Somebody built him
  A monument;
And there were those
  Who called him clean.
For I read about it
  In a magazine.

A thousand years—
  And the rulers came
And bowed and prayed
  In the prophet's name.
His praises rang
  Till the heavens shook,
For I read about it
  In a holy Book.

LETTER LXXVII

Dear Sister:

Oh, the most terrible thing, poor Mr. Harries has had a stroke; that is what they call it, he is paralyzed, and cannot speak. He lies on his bed, and the doctor comes but can do nothing for him. They have three nurses that take care of him, each for eight hours; but my lady will not go near him. Mrs. Clark has argued with her but she will not be moved, she says, "No! What can I say to him that he wishes to hear?" Oh, how dreadful, she does not believe in any hereafter! She says, "Nonsense. It is the end, and the sooner it comes, the better for him. He killed himself by his rages." Charles says the same thing and will not see him.

So there he lies; he will go like the beasts of the field that perish. Apparently he too has no faith and wishes none: an awful thing. If I were a man I would go to him and tell him about God, and perhaps he would nod his head. But what can a girl do?

We are all awed by the near presence of death in the house, but my lady will not have it so; she goes out about her affairs, hardening her heart against the thought of the hereafter and its possible dangers. She takes me with her, and of course I have no choice but to go. I dare not talk to her about God, for it only angers her. She has promised to let me alone on the subject, and that must suffice me; if I challenged her the agreement would be broken, and I could not blame her. Alone, I pray for the soul of this unhappy rich gentleman; he did not mean to be bad—quite otherwise. I have talked with Piers about it. We agree that we would not be afraid of death; it is going back to God, he says, and he would like someone to sing a lovely song while he was dying. I thought this was a good idea, and he wrote a poem about it, which he has shown only to me:

> The rich old man lies dying,
>   He dies without a song;
> What he loves he leaves behind,
>   What he fears he takes along.

Your Pamela

LETTER LXXVIII

Dear Mother:

Very sad news, my old master is dead; he had a stroke, and lingered for only about a week. The doctors could do nothing for him. He did not suffer, they said. The undertaker came and took the body, which was shipped to his brother, who is an oil man in Texas.

I do not think that Mr. Harries had any religious faith whatever. It is a dreadful thing to think of; I wake in the night and wonder, where is he now, and what is he suffering? And I can hardly bear it. Is it not a strange thing that men should so reject the truth that is put before them, and should be so indifferent to its meaning for them? They live entirely in the present and give no thought to the vast eternity. This sets a problem for me, for we are told to love them all, and yet we dare not love them too much, for if we do, how can we bear to think of the awful suffering that lies before them? One wishes to go out into the streets and cry to them like the Prophet Isaiah, "Thou hast trusted in thy wickedness: thou hast said, None seeth me. Therefore shall evil come upon thee; and desolation shall come upon thee suddenly, which thou shalt not know." What else is there to do, but to look out for one's self and one's own? Yet that seems too much like the attitude of the Pharisees, thanking God that they are not as other men.

I think that in a way it has been a good thing for me to live among people who do not share our faith, for it has strengthened me in my own. I see that they are few of them happy people. I find comfort in our new poet, who has a firm faith, also a way of expressing it that is lacking to your devoted

Pamela

LETTER LXXIX

Dear Sister:

My lady is now the undisputed mistress of her household; she will invite here whom she pleases, and Casa Grande will become the haunt of all the differing kinds of radicals—until she decides that they have had enough money, and then she will be wishing them all in Jericho. I think that she is not as contented as she expected to be; she misses him, if only to manage the servants, as she said. Now she puts some of that off on me, and I am rather young for the task; but be sure I shall make no complaint, for it is my purpose to become necessary to her, and thus make myself safe in this good position. I am determined to have a doctor for a sister, and one whose education has not suffered.

Charles comes and goes. For a few days it was a novelty
to be back and to see his friends and hear the news, and so
the one-time parlormaid was let alone. But now he invites
me to drive to the beach with him, and I say, "You know,
Charles, I have pleasure in your company, but I cannot see
what pleasure you find in mine." "You are too modest by
far," he replies; "too modest in all ways." "I am determined
to remain that way, in all ways," I tell him; "and while I
enjoy your company, it must be with that understanding."
So we have it, and we drive to the beach, and have a swim
in the pool, and I do not let myself be too much disturbed
by the bathing suit. He tells me all that I have missed in
New York and Paris, the sights and the shows and the people; it is all part of the world, and I listen to it. He wishes
me to have dinner, and I do, being properly dressed for a
young lady now, but he says it is not much use taking me
to a good place, since I will have only vegetables raw or
boiled and a poached egg and a glass of milk—but he takes
me to such a place even so, because he wishes to have fish
prepared as he likes it. To hear him give instructions to the
waiter is most awe-inspiring, and I think is meant to be so.
He tries to tempt me to taste his fish and assures me that
they do not suffer when pulled out of the sea. He jokes
about it as he does about everything, admitting that at
least I shall never get fat like his Aunt Maggie. He says seriously, "Can you not help her to reduce?" And I say, "Not
so long as she keeps boxes of chocolates in her room." He
asks, "Can you not eat them for her?" and I say, "She
would only send me to buy more."

Well, after dinner he suggests a show, and when I say
No we drive up the beach. A full moon is shining and it is
very lovely, and as usual he puts one hand on mine. I draw
it away and say, "You must drive, Charles." He says, "You
have no use for me whatever?" And I answer, "I have all

the uses of a true friend, and someday you will know that. But I have had several months to think matters over while you were away, and I am determined there shall be no more petting parties." "Are you in love with that poet?" he asks, and I say, "I am not in love with anybody, and am determined not to be. You must understand, I am a working girl and have duties that I am determined to do. I have a sister I am helping, and she is going to become a doctor, which is very important indeed to people in our state of life." "Don't you know that I could help your sister?" he asks, and I say, "Yes, but there is no reason why you should. You would expect a return, and what you call 'that old God' stands in the way." "Poor deluded kid!" he says. "That old God is nothing but a creature of your imagination."

And so our evening is spoiled. I do not get angry but just tell him that it does no good for him to talk to me in that way. I say no more, and he takes me home, and says a short good night, and I go to my room and bolt the door, and that is the end of it. I pray for him and hope it may do good. In the morning I do not see him, and later his aunt tells me he has gone to Hollywood. She asks me what happened and I tell her the truth, and she shakes her head as usual, and says, "Too bad! Too bad!" I am afraid that she is going to make me a direct proposition to become his concubine, but she does not; she must know that it would not be accepted, and for that I fear she blames the God whom I worship, and it will be one more reason for hating Him. To me this is something the like of which I never dreamed, and I decide that my position is more like the old Pamela's than I thought.

She gives me something of a shock when she asks the same question that Charles has asked, "Are you in love with Mr. Plowman?" I give her the same answer that I gave to him, that I am not in love with anybody, and Piers is a good friend whose honest heart I admire. Says she, "You will not be able to go on like that for long, if I know anything about men." "Oh, Mrs. Harries," I say, "he has never spoken one word to me about such a matter!" "It may be," says she, "but he will, judging by the way he looks at you. Watch and see."

So I have something new to think about—oh dear, oh dear! Is Piers going to fall in love with me and take to behaving like Charles? I can be sure it will not be quite the same, for he will know that the word marriage exists, and it would be the first word he would speak; but he would not speak any, because he knows that he has no money and I have none, and it would be an impossible thing. Also it would be sad, because it would disturb his work. I must pray that it does not happen; my dear Sister must do the same for her devoted

Pamela

LETTER LXXX

Dear Sister:

A week has passed, and Charles has not come home; and now, oh, my dear, such a dreadful event! I found my lady with red eyes and made bold to ask what disturbed her, and she told me that she had had a bad message from Hollywood again. I feel the reproach in her voice; I have driven her loved one away by the coldness of my heart, and he has fallen into the hands of those evil people who seek his money. He has gambled again, and he always loses. The women plunder him; they work with the gamblers and are paid by both them and him. Later in the morning my lady tells me that she has been able to get him on the telephone, and he is promising to come home; she is to meet him and they will have lunch there and then he will come home with her. She is going, and says, "You must come with me, Pamela, you may be able to influence him." I say, "Oh, Mrs. Harries, I am afraid it may be the other way, I irritate him." "So does everybody when he is this way," she says; "but come, and we will do our best." What can I say but Yes?

Well, Pietro drives us to Hollywood, which is a long way, through much traffic when we get near to Los Angeles. It gets worse every day and is a problem; they improve the roads, but that only causes more people to crowd into the city. We are going to a fashionable cafe and are to meet him at a parking place near the apartment which he has there. We drive into the place, and Pietro pays fifty cents— he has money for all such things and keeps an account in a little book which he turns over to me once a month, so that I can look it over and make out his check to the right amount. I move into one of the little seats, so that the young master may sit by his aunt; and here he comes, he is sober enough to walk straight, but his face is flushed and his eyelids red and I know the signs.

With him is a girl that I have not seen or heard of before; she has hair that is bleached, I am sure, and much paint and powder and lipstick, but then they all do that here and you cannot tell one kind from another. She is pretty in a sort of doll-baby way, and I suppose scared to meet his great and important rich aunt. He says, "This is Mabel Tidbits," and I suppose that is some sort of joke about her name; but my lady, who is not very good at jokes, has no choice but to say in her dignified way, "How do you do, Miss Tidbits?" Says he, "Call her Mabel; the little bitch has been trying to shake me down." I realize that they are in a quarrel, and as I want to keep out of it at all costs I sit looking straight before me and am not introduced. He puts her into the car, and I think he must have pinched her arm as he did so, for she cries, "Ouch, Charles! You are hurting me!" He says, "I'll hurt you plenty and teach you your place."

I dare not look around, and I cannot see how she is taking this. I suppose that she is paid to take it; it is her living, just the same as sitting here and listening is mine. I hear a stream of foul words. I know it is the liquor, of course; he is not himself, and has told me so; it is that other, the evil creature that rises up and takes possession of him. I sit, and I feel the blood climbing up my neck and throat into my face. I am blushing, not merely for myself, but for my good lady, knowing the agony of embarrassment she is in. I say to myself, "This is more than I am paid for." I remember that I am here because my lady says I may be able to influence him, and surely that means to try; so I turn and say, "Charles, you must not talk this way in front of your aunt." And then right away the fullness of his fury is turned upon me. "Oh!" he cries, "so you are going highhat on me! The little prude, the goody-girl! So proud you are that you are better than everybody else—you with your little tin Jesus! You are going to teach me manners, and what I shall say before my aunt, are you?"—and so on.

All that time there has not come a word from Mrs. Harries, and I realize that she does not dare to speak for fear that his anger may be turned upon her in the presence of us others. No doubt she has heard it before, poor soul. But I cannot think of that at the moment; I have my own temper, it seems, and my thought is, I am paid to be a secretary but not a footmat, nor to listen to blasphemy and obscenity. So I say, to nobody in particular, "I am sorry, but I have heard all of this I can stand," and I open the car door and step out and walk out of that parking lot.

So there I am in that great city of Los Angeles where I have never been alone before. Fortunately I have money enough in my purse for carfare, and I think, I will go back to Mother and help to raise a vegetable garden. Then I think, No, it will be easier to get to Rachel. But I reflect what a sad blow it would be to you to have me arrive with the news that I have lost my job that I was determined to keep. Then I think, have I really lost it? I have not said so, and surely I can wait for my lady to tell me I am fired. What I will do is to go back to Casa Grande and be ready for my duties, but go no more with the young master anywhere. I know that in her heart my lady must know that no decent woman could be hired to sit there and listen to such talk. I think, moreover, that Charles will not pursue the matter, since that has been his way in the past.

I take a streetcar to the railroad depot and there I take the first train to Riverside; from there is a bus to Junipero. It takes me most of the day to make the connections, but I do not mind; I pray for guidance and decide how I am to handle this problem and keep the position which I have earned and am entitled to. I eat a little food in the railroad station, in place of the costly meal which I was supposed to enjoy this day; and when I get to Junipero I pay my last money for a man to drive me to Casa Grande, not wishing to ask any favor or cause any trouble to anybody. When I get there my lady has arrived long since, and I go to her room to report; I have made up my mind to have no argument but to take humbly whatever she may be pleased to say. What she says is, "Oh, Pamela, that was so unnecessary!" I answer, "I am sorry, Mrs. Harries." And that is all, every word! She does not say that *she* is sorry. I have never heard her say that to anybody, and I doubt if she has ever said it in her life, nor has Charles. That is her pride.

She says, "I will expect you in the morning," and I take that to mean that I am not discharged but will go on with my regular duties, and so it proves to be. I learn that Charles is in his room and the doctor is with him—the doctor was out of town yesterday. I say my prayers and thank God for my lovely room, and do not forget to beg forgiveness for the poor young man that is two men inside him and neither can control the other. Pray for him too, and for your dear troubled Little Sister

Pamela

LETTER LXXXI

Dear Mother:

Last Sunday we had a Chinese, and I thought he would have long embroidered robes and a beard like I had seen in pictures; but he was dressed like the other gentlemen and wore spectacles. He spoke slowly so that all could understand him, and he told about the modern Chinese republic that was founded by a Dr. Sun Yat-sen, but you call him Dr. Sun. You see how it is in this place, sooner or later somebody comes and tells you about everything. Dr. Clark says it is what is called a salon; it is a French word and not the same as a saloon, which would not be a compliment.

Master Charles has been sick and has had a doctor here; he is now getting better. Our poet is a very nice young man and works hard though you do not see it. The poets who have been here before have been queer creatures, but this one is our own sort, and very kind. People think that he is falling in love with me, but I hope not. I don't think it would be very good to be married to a man who would be about the house all day, do you? My Pamela that I am reading in a book is getting married, and it is a great excitement, for nobody can make up their mind.

My lady tells me that she is expecting relatives from the East to come, and maybe she will take a trip north with them and will leave me in charge of the house. It sounds scary but really will not be, for everything will go on as it always does, and all I will have to do is to let it. But all the same it will give a thrill to your loving Daughter

Pamela

LETTER LXXXII

Dear Sister:

First I must tell you that Charles is about again. As before, he is nervous and restless, and I do what I can to be company for him. He says not one word about the horrid scene in Los Angeles, and neither do I. I know him too well to think that he would say he was sorry, and it suits me not to have it mentioned.

I keep reading my Pamela One. The poor girl is trying to make up her mind to get married to her great rich gentleman, and you cannot imagine such a to-do. The Mackenzies were here Sunday and I talked with them about it, and he said, "Don't you think it seems rather silly to make such a fuss over a simple matter? Would you do it if you were getting engaged?" I said, "I cannot be sure, for I have seen that people seem to lose their heads when they fall in love. But I would try to be sensible and to think about my future and to decide what was right." "Exactly," says he; "but Pamela is like a chicken with its head cut off; she is one perpetual gush, not of blood, but of emotions. It is done, of course, to keep the reader in a state of suspense and to stretch the story out one or two hundred more pages."

That is one way to look at it, I suppose; but, alas, I am just one more gush of emotions, like my great-great-great-grandmother. Since you too are engaged and may be facing this problem, I am copying some paragraphs of the book, so that you can see what I mean:

" 'This sweet confusion and thoughtfulness in my be-loved Pamela,' said he, 'on the near approach of our happy union, when I hope all doubts are cleared up, and nothing of dishonour apprehended, shew me plainly, what a wretch I was to attempt such purity with a worse intention:—no wonder that one so virtuous should find herself deserted of life itself on a violence so dreadful to her honour, and seek a refuge in the shadow of death. But now, my dearest Pamela, that you have seen a purity on my side, as nearly imitating your own, as our sex can shew to yours; and since I have, all this day, suppressed even the least intimation of the coming day, that I might not alarm your tender mind; why all this concern? Why all this affecting, yet sweet confusion? You have a generous friend, my dear girl, in me; a protector now, not a violator of your innocence: why then, once more I ask, this strange perplexity, this sweet confusion?'

" 'O Sir,' said I, and hid my face in his arms, 'expect not reason from a foolish creature: you should have still indulged me in my closet: I am ready to beat myself for this ungrateful return to your goodness. But I know not what! I am, to be sure, a silly creature. O had you but suffered me to stay by myself above, I should have made myself ashamed of so culpable a behaviour! But goodness added to goodness every moment, and the sense of my own unworthiness, quite overcome my spirits.'

" 'Now,' said the generous man, 'will I, though reluctantly, make a proposal to my sweet girl. If I have been too pressing for the day; if another will still be more obliging; if you have fears that will not then be, say but the word, and I'll submit. Yes, my Pamela; for though I have these three days past, thought every tedious hour a day, till Thursday comes, if you earnestly desire it, I will postpone it. Say, my dear girl, freely say; but accept not my proposal without great reason, which yet I will not ask for.'

" 'Sir,' said I, 'I can expect nothing but superlative goodness from you. This is a most generous instance of it; but I fear—yes, I fear it will be too much the same thing, some days hence, when the happy, yet fool that I am! dreaded time shall be equally near.' 'Kind, lovely charmer!' said he, 'now do I see you are to be trusted with power, from the generous use you make of it: not one offensive word or look, from me, shall wound your nicest thoughts; but pray try to subdue this over-scrupulousness and unseasonable timidity, I persuade myself you will if you can.'

" 'Indeed, Sir, I will,' said I; 'for I am quite ashamed of myself, with all these lovely views before me! The honour you do me, the kindness you shew me!—I cannot forgive myself! For oh! if I know the least of this idle foolish heart of mine, it has not a misgiving thought of your goodness; and I should abhor it if it were capable of the least affectation. But, dear good Sir, leave me a little to myself, and I will take myself to a severer task than your goodness will let you do: and present my heart before you, a worthier offering than its wayward follies will now let it seem to be. But one thing is, having no kind friend, of one's own sex, to communicate my foolish thoughts to, and to be strengthened by their comfortings, I am left to myself: and oh! what a weak silly thing I am!' "

Well, that is the way it goes; and I do hope that I can manage to be more sensible about my own case. Do not be worried, it is not about Charles—he has gone on a fishing trip with Bill Regis to the Gulf of Mexico, where they catch great fish and have pictures of themselves taken. This time it is Piers, for I have been forced to take note that he is interested in me, and not only as a secretary to copy his poems. He has taken to writing about love, very idealistic, far-off adoring love, and I dare not ask him concerning the object of this adoration. I catch him looking at me, and that causes me to blush, and it is very embarrassing; our old friendship and literary interest is somewhat spoiled. Now I have to think seriously, would I be willing to marry a poet, or will I choose to be a far-off star that he will yearn for and worship? It could be that way, for he is a humble young man, and deeply religious, and would, I am sure, never commit the slightest impropriety. But I remember what my lady has said, that they are all mad bulls and cannot control themselves, and fear seizes me; I begin to have Pamela One's emotions all over again. Do tell me how your young man is behaving, and what I have a right to expect.

Living in this place I am forced to keep myself neat and proper, and in my elegant room there is not merely a dressing table with a mirror close before me, but also a full-length mirror in the door of my clothes closet; so I cannot help but look myself over, and be aware that I have become good looking, and I suppose it is natural that the men should see it too. They make it plain that they like to be with me, and there are several who have tried to make what are called dates. I suppose they assume that I have become tied up with Charles, and, indeed, I should be ashamed to have them know to what extent this has been so. Even that poor boy that I visited in San Quentin makes it plain that he is not interested only in God and the working class, but would like to have the thought that I will be waiting for him to come out.

That is the way it is, Sister dear, so I am forced to think about it. At this place people talk about what they call sex, along with everything else; my lady hates it, but there is no keeping away from it entirely, and I have learned what is supposed to be the modern attitude, that you try not to take it too seriously but to be what is called realistic. That is far indeed from what you and I have been taught; but I suppose that we can learn this much from it, that women do not have to be kept in ignorance but have a right to know as much as the men do, and to decide what they want in the way of love. Also, they don't have to be perpetually swooning—I have noted that Pamela does frequently, but I have never done it and wasn't even quite sure what the word meant. I don't intend to be in a tumult of emotion like her, but to try to use what brains the Lord has seen fit to allow me.

Perhaps I should count it as God's goodness that I have met here one man who believes in Jesus Christ. To most of the others the name is something to say when you are angry or surprised. Some of them say they believe in God, but they wrap Him up in such fancy language that I am sure He cannot recognize Himself. When I talk about a loving Father they wonder where I came from, and how I got into the Harries household. I tell them to put the thought of God away in their minds until they are in serious trouble or grief. There is one of the Thirteen Club ladies who is a Christian Scientist, or rather she says she would be only she isn't good enough. She seems to understand what I say, and she quoted a saying of Mrs. Eddy which struck me with force, that "Man's extremity is God's opportunity."

I think that the Mackenzies are the wisest people I have met here, even though they have no faith that they ever mention. They read and think all the time, and are always kind about answering my questions. I am taking his advice to learn to watch my own mind and understand what goes on in it. So with this problem of love, I look back on the way I felt about Charles and the delightful shivers and warm feelings that crept over me; I know now that that is what they call romantic, and I am embarrassed about it, because it was a man I could not respect; yet I was sorry for him too, and hoping to help him, but it could not be done.
Your Little Sister

Pamela

LETTER LXXXIII

Dear Mother:

Today is Sunday, but it is not so busy as usual, because my lady has gone on a trip to the north with some of her relatives. They will take care of her and so she did not need me. Charles has gone back to Hollywood. I was told to look after things, and they seem to be all right so I am not worrying.

Yesterday morning I took our poet to church—our church, as I wanted to see how he would take it. We are allowed to use one of the small cars, and I drove him; he knows how to drive but does not like to, because he is absent-minded, he says. On the way I talked to him about our doctrines. He is not very keen about doctrines, because he says you cannot put them into poetry; when I asked him why not, he could not explain very well, only saying that poetry must arouse the feelings, but that doctrines do not; however, I am sure that they do with me. One thing I have learned is that it is very hard to change one of these poets; if something is so with him, it is so. He will not see any difference between the Sabbath and Sunday; he insists that if you worship the Lord in the beauty of holiness, all seven days are alike. It may not be true for all men, he admits, but for a poet they are; he never knows when God will send him an inspiration. We got into an argument on whether it would be right for him to write down a poem on the Sabbath; he says that if the Lord sends it, it is the Lord's service to write it, and any hour of the day or night will do.

Rev. Tucker preached on the prophecies of the Book of Daniel, and was most edifying, I thought. Afterwards I introduced Piers to him. The Reverend, I think, has been troubled by the idea of my working for Mrs. Harries, of whom he has heard that she attends no church. I assured him that Piers was a good Christian poet and was studying our Advent beliefs. I could not refrain from asking the Reverend about the point we had been arguing. He listened attentively and said that if it was true religious poetry that was written, it might be taken as the same kind of work that he himself had just done on the Sabbath, conducting a service and preaching a sermon. But that was not enough for my stubborn young man, he must have it that all the poetry he writes is religious, whether it deals with God or man or nature. The Reverend, doing his best to be polite, said that it was possible to take that point of view; he thought that perhaps the test would be whether the work was done with reverence or for one's own pleasure. Says Piers, "But do you not find pleasure in conducting a service for God?" Of course the Reverend had to admit that he did, there was a sense in which worship was the greatest pleasure in his life. "So it is with me," says Piers; "my form of worship is writing beautiful poems." Rev. Tucker gives him a pat on the back and tells him he need not worry.

But it was me that was worrying. I can see that he is a very determined young man, and whenever my lady leaves me in charge of him I shall have my hands full. Be sure of the earnest efforts of your beloved Daughter

Pamela

LETTER LXXXIV

Dear Sister:

I have been trying out our poet. I took him to church, as you will see from my letter to Mother. Also, I decided that I would entrust him with the secret of Pamela One. He insists that it is a novel, even though it is letters. This troubled me, but did not trouble him, as he says it is all right to read novels, from the great ones you can learn a lot. He has read one that tells about France in the days of a revolution they had; it is called "Les Miserables," but from the account of it he gave me I could not see they were any less miserables at the end than they were at the beginning.

I told him the story of my great-great-great-grandmother, and the idea amused him, but he said he would not read a story about love, he was afraid of its effect on his own feelings. "It is not so easy for a man to live a virtuous life as it is for a woman," said he. I said, "But you are writing poetry about love." He answered, "Yes, but I am trying to spiritualize it, while this that you tell me is a story of passion and temptation. I wonder that you would read it all." "Oh, but she is so good and virtuous, Piers!" "Yes, but he is not; and as a man I should be thinking of the man." "God forbid!" said I.

As it happens, I have time for reading now, so I am getting toward the end of the story and hardly know whether to be glad or cry. I am reading the scenes with the sister of the master, that is named Lady Davers and is so very proud and haughty. She has come from a journey and will not be convinced that her brother has done the folly to marry this poor girl, and when she meets Pamela she abuses her shockingly. I will copy a part of it for you:

"Well, now I will tell you all that happened in this frightful interview—and very bad it was.

"I went down, dressed as I was, and my gloves on, and my fan in my hand, to be just ready to get into the chariot, when I could get away; and I thought all my trembling fits had been over now; but I was mistaken; for I trembled sadly: yet resolved to put on as good an air as I could.

"So I went to the parlour, and said, making a very low curtsey, 'Your servant, my good lady.' 'And your servant, again,' said she, 'my lady; for I think you are dressed out like one.' 'A charming girl though,' said her rakish nephew, and swore a great oath; 'dear Aunt, forgive me, but I must kiss her:' and was coming to me. I said, 'Forbear, uncivil gentleman! I won't be used freely.' 'Jackey,' said my lady, 'sit down, and don't touch the creature: she's proud enough already. There's a great difference in her air, I'll assure you, since I saw her last.'

" 'Well, child,' said she, sneeringly, 'how dost find thyself? Thou'rt mightily come on, of late! I hear strange reports about thee! Thou'rt almost got into fool's paradise, I doubt! And wilt find thyself terribly mistaken in a little while, if thou thinkest my brother will disgrace his family to humour thy baby-face!'

" 'I see,' said I, sadly vexed (her woman and nephew smiling by), 'her ladyship has no very important commands for me; and I beg to withdraw.' 'Beck,' said she to her woman, 'shut the door; my young lady and I must not have done so soon.'

" 'Where's your well-mannered deceiver gone, child?' says she. Said I, 'When your ladyship is pleased to speak intelligibly, I shall know how to answer.'

" 'Well, but, my dear child,' said she, in drollery, 'don't be too pert, neither. I beseech thee. Thou wilt not find thy master's sister half so ready to take thy freedoms, as he is! So, a little of that modesty and humility that my mother's waiting-maid used to shew, will become thee better than the airs thou givest thyself, since my mother's son has taught thee to forget thyself.'

" 'I would beg,' said I, 'one favour of your ladyship, that if you would have me keep my distance, you will not forget your own degree.'

" 'Did I not tell you, Jackey,' said she, 'that I should have a wit to talk to?' He, who swears like a fine gentleman at every word, rapping out an oath, said, drolling. 'I think, Mrs. Pamela, if I may be so bold as to say so, you should know you are speaking to Lady Davers.' 'Sir,' said I, 'I hope there was no need of your information, so I can't thank you for it; and am sorry you seem to think it wants an oath to convince me of the truth of it.'

"He looked more foolish than I, at this, if possible, not expecting such a reprimand:—and said, at last, 'Why, Mrs.

Pamela, you put me half out of countenance with your witty reproof.' 'Sir,' said I, 'you seem quite a fine gentleman; and it will not be easily done, I dare say.'

" 'How now, Pert One,' said my lady, 'do you know whom you talk to?' 'I think I do not, Madam,' replied I: 'and for fear I should forget myself more, I'll withdraw. Your ladyship's servant,' said I; and was going: but she rose, and gave me a push, and pulled a chair, and setting the back against the door, sat down in it.

" 'Well,' said I, 'I can bear any thing at your ladyship's hands.' But I could no longer refrain tears. I said, 'Pray, your ladyship, let me ask, what I have done to be thus severely treated? I never did your ladyship any harm. And if you think I am deceived, as you was pleased to hint, I should be more entitled to your pity than your anger.'

"She arose, and led me to her chair; then sat down; and still holding my hand, said, 'Why, Pamela, I did indeed pity you, while I thought you innocent. But when you have suffered yourself to be prevailed upon, and have added another to the number of the fools he has ruined' (this shocked me a little), 'I cannot help shewing my displeasure to you.'

" 'Madam,' replied I, 'I must beg no hasty judgment: I have not lost my innocence.' 'Take care, take care, Pamela!' said she: 'don't lose your veracity, as well as your honour! Why are you here when at full liberty to go whither you please?'

" 'I am innocent, Madam,' replied I, 'and willing to keep so.' 'Then,' said she, very mannerly, 'thou liest, child, that's all; and I give thee up!'

"And so she arose, and walked about the room in great wrath. Her nephew and her woman said, 'Your ladyship is very good; 'tis a plain case, a very plain case!' "

That is a long scene, as you see; but it is only a small part of the story. It goes on for pages and pages, but I stopped reading it to Piers, because he is a good boy and she is a very bad woman and uses language which I am ashamed to repeat, and some of it is indicated by d—— and so on. The only way that Pamela One could escape from this terrible woman was by leaping from the window of the room into the garden, and running to her chariot which had been waiting for her. That is surely a funny scene!

While reading it I could not help thinking all the time of Miss Yvette, and asking myself, if I had married Charles, would she have behaved to me like this? I am sure she would have been no less furious, but I doubt if she would have been so stupid. She would have first taken the trouble to make sure whether or not it was a real marriage; she could have done that by the telephone. Strange as it may seem, Lady Davers, once she had made sure that her brother was married, became good and sweet like everybody else; but I doubt if that would have been so in my case. I have observed that these fashionable people go on quarreling after marriage, just the same as before; and that not only in the Harries family. There is a great deal of love lacking in their world. This from your worldly-wise Little Sister

                                                          Pamela

LETTER LXXXV

Dear Sister:

Last night my lady telephoned that she would be home next day; and that I was to have Pietro drive me to Riverside to meet the noon train from the East and get Dr. Archibald, who is a woman and an old friend of hers. This Dr. Archibald is a professor of psychology, and that is a word which I hear all the time and had trouble finding in the dictionary, but now I know it and use it like I was a learned lady myself.

On the drive home this Dr. wants to talk to me. She has gray hair and is tall and dignified, and as she was at school with my lady and knows all the family she asks questions about how everybody is; this as we are driving home. She asks, "How is Charles getting along?" And I say, "Not so well." She says, "You can talk frankly with me, for I have seen him when he was drinking. I tried to get his aunt to get mental treatment for him, but she wouldn't hear of it."

Well, I tell her the story, and she says it is sad, which it takes no great learning to know. She says, "It is a poor way to bring up a boy, to give him everything he asks for and teach him no duties." I say, "That is it exactly." I have not said anything about myself and Charles, but presently she remarks, "I suppose he did not fail to set out after an attractive young woman like yourself," and of course I have to say that he did not fail, and neither did he succeed. She laughs and says she is glad to hear that. In short, we have a nice talk, and by the time we get to the rancho we are friends; she is a wise person. I tell her about the people that have been to the Sunday afternoons to speak and ask if she is going to be one of them; she says, "I doubt if Maggie would want me to speak, for she is a materialist, you know, and understands nothing about the mind; in fact I doubt if she really believes that the mind exists. Does she still say 'bread and butter first'?" I tell her that she says it every day and often several times, and the Dr. laughs and says, "I don't know what she thinks that she thinks with, but it cannot be her mind, for she hates the word, and does not

admit that it is possible to observe it, to say nothing of trying to change it. 'All that is superstition,' she says, and
when I told her that I had been experimenting with hypnotism, it was just as if I had said with voodoo." (That is another word to look up, but I did not tell the Dr. so. I do not
pose as being learned, but then neither do I show my ignorance when keeping quiet will serve just as well.)

All this is so that you will understand what happened
later, which I found very strange and even wonderful. My
lady arrived, and these two old friends, who call each other
Maggie and Bernice, had a long talk in my lady's room, to
which I was not invited; but the Dr. must have said something about me, for I was invited in to dinner, which was
just for us three, my lady's relatives have driven on. Mr.
Carmichael is serving, and we are in the middle of fricas-
seed chicken—and me the egg—when there is loud voices in
the kitchen. Charles has come in, and he has been drinking
so that he staggers. He has gone to his room without letting
anybody know; but there he has got his bottle of whisky
smashed, and has come to the butler to get the key to the
wine closet, and Carmichael has got orders never to give it
up, and will not. So there is the young master, cursing and
threatening, and abusing everybody in the kitchen with
dreadful words; they are used to it and try to pay no attention. The old gentleman—he is that, I think, even though
he is the butler—tries to reason with the young master, but
in vain.

We three sit, hearing the row, and wondering when the
angry young man will burst into the dining room. My lady
eats, or pretends to, and does not move—it is her way in
such a situation, and I have learned why, because she cannot manage him and will only cause him to start abusing
her, as he once did me. Charles has sat down, announcing
that he will stay there till he gets what he wants, and he

will shout, and the company be damned, and so on. So all at once the Dr. rises and says, "Let me see what I can do, Maggie," and she goes into the kitchen. And then the shouting dies down; we hear Charles say more than once that he will not, but whatever it is, he does.

Later on I learn from the help what happened, and it is this: the Dr. took a chair and sat in front of Charles and fixed her eyes upon his and began to talk to him in a quiet voice, telling him that he did not really wish to drink, that he knew he was killing himself, that he thought he could not stop but it wasn't so, he could stop and he would, he had the will power and he would use it, he would not wish to drink any more, he was through for good and all, he would hate liquor because it was poison to him; and so on and on. It must have been half an hour, and the mistress and I just sat there and waited, forgetting our food, and not speaking a word to each other. At last the Dr. came back, saying, "I think he will be all right now, he has promised to go to bed." He went up to his room, and Mr. Carmichael followed and mopped up the whisky and swept up the broken glass and helped him into bed; and meantime Cookie brought us in the dessert; and if my lady ever said "Thank you" to her Dr. friend it was not in my hearing.

I had a talk with the Dr. about it afterwards, and asked, "Was that hypnotizing?" She said, "No, but people are subject to suggestion when they are under the influence of alcohol, as much so as when they are asleep." I took the liberty to say, "I wonder that Mrs. Harries does not ask you to stay and treat him for a while." She answered, "I could not stay because I have lecture dates; but anyhow, Maggie would not ask, for she cannot even admit to herself that it happened; she has walled it off in her mind and cannot bear to face it." "You mean," I asked, "she cannot bear that anyone should have more influence over Charles than herself?" "It is that, and more; it is contrary to her philosophy, and therefore cannot be. Hypnotism and suggestion and all such things are superstition and nonsense."

I asked the good Dr. if she thought her effect would last, and she said there was no way to be sure; a course of treatment might be needed if it was to be a permanent cure. I told her that I had tried to tell him about God, and she said, "That could do it, if you could get him to believe it; but how can you, with his aunt taking the attitude she does?" She added, "Don't let yourself be drawn into this." "I shall not," said your Little Sister

Pamela

LETTER LXXXVI

Dear Sister:

Poor Charles is again wandering about the place, miserable and having to be played with and entertained. And now there is a strange development—one that I never thought of: Charles is jealous of Piers. He hates this kind and gentle poet, because I have been giving time and thought to him! Can you imagine such a thing? That surely is a new kind of psychology for me!

The second day, when he tried to hold my hand and I drew it away quickly, he asked again, "Have you fallen in love with that poet of yours?" I, not realizing the situation, teased him. "He is not my poet but your aunt's." "All right; but answer me." "Would you think he would make a good match?" "He is a country bumpkin." "Well, but what am I—a bumpkiness?" "You would be throwing yourself away, Pam." "Yes, but he believes in God; and you told me to find a man like that." "To the devil with him!" he says. "He makes me sick!" I was worried and offered to play checkers to divert his mind. I have learned to play this game fairly well but have never yet been able to beat him; I am not sure that I would if I could.

He tells me that he is through with liquor for good; it is poison to him. I say that I am glad, and no more. He will not take suggestions from me, and the Dr. has told me not to mention her treatment; she explained that his conscious mind would rebel against it; what good it may do will be in his subconscious mind. This is something they talk about, but I do not understand it. How can there be a mind that is not conscious? How can it know you or you know it? Have they taught this at the College, or is it just one more Godless modern notion?

The more I think about Charles' attitude to Piers, the more it worries me. I am struck by the resemblance to the story of Pamela One. You may remember, in that book is a young clergyman named Mr. Williams, who is kind to Pamela in an innocent way, and the young master is in a rage about him and even has him arrested. I am sure nothing like that can happen here, but it breaks up the harmony which has made me so happy. If Charles goes on hating our poet, it will become impossible for my lady to be kind to him; she will begin finding fault with him, perhaps not even realizing why. Nothing in this world must be allowed to stand in the way of her darling nephew. I think this thing called sex is awful, and I wish I never had to hear of it again. But apparently that is difficult for a woman, especially if she has the misfortune to be young and good looking.

I see that I have to watch every step. I must not take walks with Piers, nor be alone with him; I must do everything that Charles wants, except the one thing which he wants most. I must be kind and friendly, but never too much so, and above all I must keep the idea of God before his eyes; he must know that it is God who is standing between us. He cannot do any harm to God; he cannot discharge Him or send Him away from this estate.

Mr. Mackenzie was here and questioned me about how things were going. He has been like a father to me, so I told him the truth. He startled me by saying that this jealousy might break down Charles' pride and be the cause of his asking to marry me. He went on to say, it is an old story for a woman to marry a man in order to reform him, but it is a most dangerous gamble for her. I assured him there was no chance of such a thing, for Charles is far too haughty to submit to my demands. But Mr. Mackenzie thinks that Charles is humble right now, and he quoted an old saying: "The devil was sick, the devil a monk would be; the devil got well, the devil a monk was he." I recalled how the Rev. Tucker had preached not long ago, we must never any of us forget that the evil one is after us everywhere and all the time. So pray for your loving Sister

Pamela

LETTER LXXXVII

Dear Mother:

I have not much news these days. I have learned all my duties and remember them and do them faithfully; thus I make myself necessary to my lady, and she entrusts me with more and more responsibility. She says, "I don't know what

I should do without you, Pamela." I am determined to let nothing change this.

My lady is her own mistress now and can do whatever she pleases. She prefers that position, and I am sure will never give it up. She likes very few men, and all of them married; I feel sure she will never remarry. She says, "It is a messy business, and I want no more of it." Frankness could go no further.

The weather continues delightful, and members of her family come from the East and stay a while. Also, we have much company. It is a long drive from Los Angeles, but these rich people think nothing of it; they like to be on the move, and this is a pleasant stopping-off place. They bring news of the world; also the people with ideas come—they hope to get money for their causes, and it is rarely they fail. I have to meet them, and sometimes to judge them; this frightens me, but also flatters me. I pray for guidance, and so far I seem to have had it. Even the young master seems pleased with my judgment, and our poet laureate reads me his verses—those he has written and others. There was one about "the desire of the moth for the star," and of course I am careful not to take it as personal. Best love from your devoted

Pamela

LETTER LXXXVIII

Dear Sister:

It is a story full of surprises that I have been telling you; and today came the strangest of all. I was at work at the typewriter, with which I have become fairly fast, when in comes Piers with a manuscript which I am to copy. I tell him I'll finish it before the day is over. He stops to chat for a moment, and as luck would have it Charles is passing the door of the little office, and in he comes, and he looks black. I get rid of Piers quickly, afraid that Charles may say something rude; and when we are alone he wants to know if I am letting that bumpkin make love to me. I give him my word that it is not so, but this does not satisfy him; he says, "You know perfectly well, Pam, that no man can live on the place with you and not fall in love with you."

I answer, "You know perfectly well, Charles, that if I took up a notion such as that, I would be insufferable; so don't tell me such things." He answers, "You are the loveliest young woman I know. You have learned more in two years than most of them learn in a lifetime." "Well," said I, "that is a compliment indeed, and I can only hope that part of it is true." Says he, "That is the reason I came back from Paris." I put a little touch of mischief into it. "You mean because you heard about the bumpkin?" He answers, "I mean that I couldn't bear the thought of your throwing yourself away on a penniless beggar."

So there it is out in the open; he is so jealous that he has to tell me about it. I realize that if I had meant to stir him up, this was the way to do it; but honestly, Sister dear, I hadn't the slightest idea of such a thing! I have dealt with him straight, and I do so now. I say, "Be assured, Charles, I am not going to throw myself away on anyone. I have a position which enables me to help my good mother and my grandfather who is too old to work." "Look, Pam," he answers, "there's no use beating about the bush. I have been a fool, and I am ashamed of myself." I surely never expected to hear that from him and hardly know how to answer. I say, "Really, Charles, the person you need to say that to is yourself."

I was hoping to divert him, but nothing worked. He says, "That sounds profound, but it's hardly to the point. Be honest with yourself, Pam. You know you love me." I answer, "I think it would be right to say that I love you with about half myself. The other half is fear and grief." "Yes," says he, "I have given you cause; but I would like to change. What would you say if I should ask you to marry me?" I say, "You have already asked me that question, Charles, and you have my answer." "It is the same answer?" "Of course. Nothing on this earth could cause me to marry a man who drank liquor; and since I have seen what it does to you, I am a thousand times more determined." "I grant you that, Pam. I have nothing to say for it, and am ready to give it up. But that other idea, that you would stay on and be my aunt's secretary!"

I see that we have got down to bargaining; and I mean to stand my ground, if ever I did in my life. I told him, as I had told him before, that he had too much money, and it had set him apart from humanity. Sooner or later he would take up the notion that I had married him for his money; and for that reason I would never take it. Says he, "If you have to wait on my aunt, what time would you have for me?" I answer that he would be a lot happier if he would stay here and interest himself in this place. We could both work here together. He says, "You mean to stick by that?" I say that I do, and I see the blood mounting to his face and know he is ready to burst. As before, he exclaims, "It's no go!" and rushes from the room.

I go on with my typewriting, since there is nothing else to do. I make some mistakes and realize that I am excited, but I manage to get control of myself by a bit of prayer. I have got Charles and his problems entirely out of my mind when suddenly he comes storming in, crying, "Everywhere I go on this place I run into that damn fool poet! He's a lout! He's a boob! He's a hillbilly nincompoop! I can't stand it, Pam! I go crazy at the thought of your marrying him!" I do my best to calm him down. I say, "Charles, I give you my word of honor, I have not the least idea of marrying him." Says he, "I know, but you will change! You'll decide that his poetry is wonderful and it's your duty to take care of him." I answer, "I am helping to take care of your dear aunt." "You are too pretty," he says, "and the man won't let you alone! You'll find you're in love with him before you know it—he's the only one around. Do, for God's sake, be sensible and marry me, Pam!"

So there it is at long last! I have been through the scene in many imaginary forms, and I tell him, "It's partly for God's sake that I'm not marrying you, Charles. It would be a blunder, because I couldn't help you, and I couldn't make you happy for very long." He has made up his mind, it seems, and he cries, "I give up! I'm in your hands! I'll do whatever you want me to, and I'll believe whatever you tell me." "You say that," I answer, "because you are unhappy. But you can't do it, and you must know you can't. You'd hate me for making you promise such things." Says he, "You've got me licked. Name the price and I'll pay it." "I have told you the price, Charles; it's my self-respect." "Your self-respect requires you to go on working for Aunt Maggie even though you are her niece?" When I tell him that his own respect for me also would require it, he cries out, "Good Lord, deliver me!"

Oh, Sister, we had a hot argument. He was determined to have his way, and I to have mine. He has the habit of having his, but I have the advantage of having God on my side. It was really funny, or would have seemed so to an outsider, I realize as I look back on it. He insisted on pinning me down, fighting for one point after another. "Will your self-respect permit us to have a honeymoon?" I somewhat grudgingly admit, "I suppose we'd have a honeymoon." He demands, "How long would it last?" And I say, "A moon is supposed to be a month, isn't it?" Then he wants to know, "If we had two months, or three—enough to see Europe—would that destroy your self-respect?" When I say, "It would hardly be fair to your aunt," he cries, "Creepers!"—what a funny cry that is, and where did he get it? He keeps insisting that his aunt wouldn't expect her niece to remain her servant, and I tell him, "She would, if that was the bargain." This makes him frantic and he answers, "She'd fry you in oil and eat you if that was the bargain; but I'd hardly enjoy my share of the meal." I rebuke him, saying that he should learn to control his language.

That debate goes on for some time. He wants his own way of life and not his aunt's. The truth is, he is bored by her, and only stays to get her money, I fear. When I make him desperate he exclaims, "All right! All right! You become one of those slaves that every family has! You stay at home and take care of the old folks, while I take the job of major domo, or manager of the ranch, or what have you. I'll see that the citrus trees get properly sprayed and the chicken coops kept clean." I answer, "That might be fun, Charles, if you really loved your wife. If we had a family, you ought to be interested in the home where we were raising it."

So it goes, until he gives up and says, "All right, it's a bargain! You marry me and I'll become house-broke." Then he wants to take me in his arms; but I hold him off and say, "Wait, we're only at the beginning. There is the question of God." "Oh, my God!" he says, and I answer, "Yours and mine! You know I could never be happy married to an atheist." Says he, "I'm not an atheist." "Then what are you?" That drives him to distraction; he says, "I don't know what I am. I am the Frenchman who cried, 'Lord, I believe, help Thou mine unbelief!' " I had never heard that before, and I tell him it might do very well for a start. He pleads that he can't understand God, and I tell him that no man can. What he has to do is humble his heart and ask for guidance. "God who made you and sustains you knows what you need. You have to learn to pray, Charles."

I don't think he had ever prayed before, and it must have been a strange experience for him. I went and shut the door of the room, and then went down on my knees on the rug. I had no idea whether he'd follow me, but he gave another despairing "All right," and there he was by my side. I prayed as I had never done before, "O God, dear God, good God, help two lost children to find the light! Help us to keep our vows of love! And no more drinking of liquor!" I made him say it; I made him repeat every sentence after me, like a child. It could not have failed to touch him, because he saw how much it meant to me. "No more cocktail parties! No more night clubs! No more gambling! No more Hollywood ladies! No more ladies of any sort!" The tears were running down my cheeks, and I cried, "Oh, Charles, you have to mean it! You would break my heart if you didn't meant it!" He swore that he meant it, he swore it on his knees before God. And then, when he got to his feet, I made him promise it on his honor as a gentleman— meaning to bind him both ways, for safety. And when he had said it all, I cried, "Oh, Charles! Charles!" and burst into a flood of tears. He was bewildered and asked, "What's the matter now?" All I could say was, "I'm so happy! So happy!" Then he took me in his arms; and that's the way we got engaged.

Sister, I am so scared about it, and do tell me if it is all right, or what shall I do? Your devoted

Pamela

LETTER LXXXIX

Dear Mother:

This will be the most surprising letter I have ever had to write you. It is to tell you that I am engaged to marry Charles.

I hope you will not be too much shocked. It is true that it is a very rich and great family, but you must believe me that this is not the reason I gave my consent after long urging. He is deeply in love with me, and this gives me strong influence with him. I have taught him to pray, which he had never done in his life before, and he has promised that he will seek God with me. His life in the past has not been what you and I would wish, but he has pledged himself never to touch another drop of liquor, and this I am sure is an achievement which will be pleasing in the sight of God. Please be sure that I have not failed to pray concerning my duty, and am not going to let my head be turned by worldliness and pride. Much against his will, he has agreed that I am to go on working for his aunt, so that neither he nor she can ever think that I married him for his money.

When at last I gave my consent, he went at once to tell her. You can believe that I was scared about what might happen, but she was very nice about it; she came and kissed me on the forehead—the first time I have ever seen her kiss anybody. She is a very reserved person and does not even shake hands with people. She said, "I am glad, Pamela, and you will be the best possible influence for him." She is all wrapped up in him and thinks of me only for what I can do for him. That is all right with me, of course; I am thinking of him in much the same way, that being God's will, I take it. Aunt Maggie—so I am to call her now—told me some time ago that he is susceptible to female influence, and she told me to be that, and I shall.

Later on she told me that my salary is to be five hundred a month, four times what I have been getting. When I protested, she said I would be worth many times that to her, and it would just be pocket money for me. She knew the way to make me yield. She said, "Your mother and grandfather can get out of that shack and move into town and live like civilized people." I will send you half the amount, and also I am going to buy you one of those wonderful little radio sets, so that you can hear voices from Los Angeles and learn what is going on all over the world. You will be invited to the wedding, of course. I will write you about that soon.

God is being good to us, and we must try to repay Him by being diligent in His cause. Your excited and happy

Pamela

LETTER XC

Dear Sister:

Wonders are never ceasing in your Little Sister's world! Rancho Casa Grande is in an uproar, getting ready for a wedding in a week. Charles is impatient, as always, and must have his way. He hates all the fuss and wants nothing but to get away with me; but he has to please his aunt. Poor soul, she craves his company every moment but can never do anything but bore him. He says we must have a trip to Europe, his excuse being that he wants to show me all the wonders he has been telling me about; but the fact is, he wants to escape from his aunt and her ideas, which she repeats endlessly, and generally in the same words. She is good and kind but determined to have her own way and to impress her ideas upon everyone she meets. She has not the least objection to having her niece remain her employee; she will tell me what to do, and at the same time will overwhelm me with favors, and do her best to spoil me as she has spoiled Charles. There is no limit to what I could get from her if I were a money-seeking person. What I mean to do, very tactfully, is to try to weaken the prejudice which she cherishes against the idea of God. I have this great advantage over her, that she could not keep Charles from drinking, while with God's help I can; or so I hope, and she will see it.

She took one of her diamond rings and put it on my finger, but I took it off and refused it. I explained that I did not think it would be becoming for a former parlormaid; people would take it as my showing off my triumph. "Let me stay the simple person they used to know," I said; so she dug out of her jewel box a plain gold ring which is to be my wedding ring. Cinderella will wash the ashes off her but will not put on jewelry.

I am to be married in a simple traveling dress; but even that requires excitement. I was taken to the big shop in Riverside, and my lady-aunt condescended to get out of the limousine and go in and pick out the things I should wear. How the salespeople did smile and kowtow! They know her, of course, and the news of the wedding has spread all over town. I remind myself that the devil is here, putting thoughts of worldly glory into my heart. I hope he is not succeeding too well.

It is a very important thing to be taken into this great family and to become the mother of its future heirs. I try to conduct myself with dignity and do what is expected of me, but not forgetting the faith I have learned. It was my new aunt's idea that we should be married by Dr. Clark, and I did not tell her that I had any doubts about the validity of a Unitarian marriage; I pointed out that I had been attending our own church in Junipero, and that our reverend is a dignified and proper gentleman, who might feel hurt if he was overlooked. She invited him to call, and inspected him, and I am to have my way in this—if not in the clothes I shall wear!

The invitations have gone out, and the makings of the wedding breakfast are on hand. Everybody is excited, and of course me too, but I try not to show it too much. The attitude of the help is interesting; I have tried to win their affection, and believe I have succeeded, and I try to make the change from fellow worker to young mistress as easy as possible. I give them no orders, but only transmit those of the mistress; in short, I remain the secretary, and shall become something else only by slow stages. They would have to be more than human if they did not feel some trace of envy of my good fortune.

I must tell you about Piers. The poor fellow was in love with me, and I think he had the dream that he might have a book published, and win fame and also the girl. Now the dream is dead, but he is very nice about it; he follows me with adoring eyes, and of course I am kind to him, and have made Charles promise that he will no longer be annoyed by him. Piers has written verses which he will not bring me to copy; I suppose they reveal his sorrow. He says that poets write better when they are unhappy—and he has his wish.

Also I must tell you about Aunt Yvette—imagine me having to call her that! I was not a little anxious when I heard she was coming, for I thought of the awful scene with Lady Davers. But it wasn't anything like that. She saw her sister first, and of course heard all about it. All she said to me was, "I am sorry for you, my dear. You will have your hands full." There is no love lost between her and Charles; she is "the heiress," and of course it must have occurred to her that if I should succeed in reforming Charles, she might lose that high position. But she did not mention the subject. It is the fashion of these ultra-smart people to take everything offhand and casual, and that suited me very well—I had been afraid that I might have to jump out of the window, like Pamela One. I forget if I ever told you that she is only a half-sister of Aunt Maggie; their father married twice. Maybe that is why she is so different. I do not expect affection from this elegant lady, but will be content if I can so behave that she does not hate me.

Well, dear, Charles and I will drive over and bring you to the affair; that was his suggestion. I send you extra money —that, too, is his suggestion—and you are to get yourself a proper dress. "Nothing showy," he says—I suppose he fears you might appear in pink lace with spangles. He must have a secret terror of what his in-laws may turn out to be. Do not worry for a moment. We have God with us, now and always. Your devoted Sister

Pamela .

P.S. I am very much in love, but I am not going to show it often.

LETTER XCI

Dear Mother:

The great day is near, and I am enclosing Aunt Maggie's check for three hundred dollars—she wanted to make it more but I insisted this was enough. Here is what you are to do, and remember it is her orders and you must do exactly as she says. So:

Hire a car to take you to the railroad and come to Los Angeles at once. Go to a "decent" hotel—it is her word—and get yourselves each a complete outfit, nothing showy, but quiet, and not too cheap. Also get two bags to carry your things in. Then telephone here. The wedding is to be at eleven on Sunday morning, so the car will be at your hotel at sundown on the Sabbath, and bring you here to spend the night. There will be what is called a "wedding breakfast," which will really be a buffet lunch, and the guests will stay for Aunt Maggie's Sunday afternoon, when the speaker will be a Hindu rebel whom the British have just released from jail; he is a very polished Oxford graduate, so you see what a funny mixed-up situation the world is in.

I want you both to be happy at this affair so important to me. You can be proud of your daughter and you need not be ashamed for yourselves. Everybody here knows where I have come from, and they know that I honor both of you. It is considered to be romantic for a darling of fortune to marry a parlormaid, and I suppose that is what democracy means. Anyhow, you can be sure I am going to hold my head up and always to fight for my rights. I have God on my side, and also our poet, who has promised to write a poem for the occasion.

Do not try to save this money. Spend it as you are told to, and be what these rich people call "right." Your too happy Daughter

Pamela

LETTER XCII

Dear Sister:

Well here we are in what is called an auto camp in Arizona. We drove most of the night through the desert, avoiding the heat. This is a very convenient place—you have a complete little apartment, and alongside is a shed where you park the car, and can bring your things in, or get what you want. It was a nice wedding and I hope you enjoyed it; Mother and Grampa were too cute, everybody agreed. He looked like a diplomat. Charles has been so kind to me, and I am too happy to tell about. We shall be off again in a few minutes, so pardon this scrawl. He liked you—and he is not easy to please. All is well with me. Twentieth-century America is much better than eighteenth-century England! Your married Sister

Pamela

P.S. Send this to Mother.

LETTER XCIII

Dear Sister:

We drove all day and part of the night and here we are
in New York in two weeks. Such a trip—I never dreamed
that America was so big! And now this great city quite
overwhelms me. We are staying at the most fashionable
hotel, and everywhere people run to wait on me. That is
going to be my life from now on, and I can't ever get away
from it. There are so many sights to be seen that I hardly
know which to choose each day and night. I have been to a
great museum of natural history, where there are all the
animals of the world, I think, and many of them are in
groups, set in scenes so that you can hardly believe they are
not alive in their native wild. Also we go to a museum of
art, and there are so many paintings that I was struck
speechless—oh, such beautiful things, such colors, and people in costumes, and scenes of all places and times! It is the
best place to learn what the world is like, and how things
were in past times; I think I could live the rest of my life
here. Charles goes about with me, well content; he knows
so much more than I and likes to tell what he knows, and
needless to say I let him.

Sister, I know that I have married a wild man, but I no
longer have any doubt that I can tame him. I try not to let
him know it, and would not let him see this letter for all
the world. I go everywhere with him, and I let him have
everything he wants, provided it is right; if it is not, he sees
me look unhappy and cannot stand it. We meet a great
many people, his smart friends, and many times a day we

are offered their bootleg liquor, and I see it and smell it and hear all the fancy names for the hateful stuff. Charles says, "I am on the wagon, this time for good." It amuses them, and for the most part they accept it with jokes; they have a theory that there are two kinds of people, those who can "take it"—themselves—and those who cannot "take it," like Charles. Probably they have seen him in liquor and are glad not to have to see him so any more. He and I drink orange juice, which a young doctor has told us has a thing called vitamins in it and is good for us. This I am determined, that if I ever see my husband start to take a drop of the devil's brew, I will put on such a scene of horror and grief as will astonish those present. And I have told him so.

We meet another sort of people also; the intellectuals, they call themselves, the ones he has met through Aunt Maggie. They are older people and more dignified. Some have ideas which I shall never approve, but I do not say so. They are content to have an audience and to do the talking; I listen, as I have always done, and afterwards I let Charles tell me what is right and what is wrong about them. I am a submissive wife, except where my faith is concerned. Among these people I shall meet one now and then to whom I can talk frankly, as I did to Mr. and Mrs. Mackenzie.

One concession I have made to Charles, which I hope will not shock you too greatly. I have been going to shows with him. I find that it means so much to him—it is one of the things people come to the great city for, and one of the ways to keep a restless man entertained. He pays high prices for the best seats and is proud of knowing how to get them. I searched my conscience, and remembered what I had been taught on the subject of the stage and screen; the main point seems to be the corrupting of the young. But I am no longer young in that sense; I have learned the differ-

ence between good and evil, and it can do me no harm to
know how much of the latter there is in the world. The first
thing we saw was a Charlie Chaplin picture, and it was an
amazing experience for me. The figures are so real you are
sure you are in the room with them, and his antics are so
funny that I laughed until it hurt. I still laugh whenever I
think of it, and I honestly cannot see that it did me any
harm.

This is the way I figure it: I have to balance the evil of
breaking our church's rule against the evil of managing my
husband too strictly and so losing my hold on him. I know
it is an awful thing to be living in such luxury as this; but it
is what he is used to, and I cannot change him all at once.
When this honeymoon is over, I hope to take him back to
his home, and interest him in producing something, and
especially in the housing project. Meantime, I read the
Scripture aloud to him every day. These are stories too, and
might be on the screen; I try to explain them to him, and
he becomes interested.

This I know for sure, Rachel, I could never bear to live
in this cruel city for long. It is pleasant to meet so many
rich and elegant people; but you walk a couple of blocks
from the places where they amuse themselves, and you are
in slums that are awful, and see swarms of people with
pinched faces and stunted figures, and there are smells and
dirt and worry and fear. You and I were poor, but we were
in the country and got our full growth and are well and
strong; but these city poor look as if the devil was driving
them. It wrings my heart, and I understand now why Aunt
Maggie with her kind heart is so ill pleased with our society
and so full of radical ideas. I shall come back with a fresh
load of them, and shall do my best to see that Charles and
I do something more than playing with our lives. I brought
the Pamela book along, thinking that it might amuse him

in an idle hour; yesterday I read aloud a paragraph near the end, telling him that it was the principle by which my great-great-great-grandmother had lived.

"All that I value myself upon is that God has raised me to a condition to be useful, in my generation, to better persons than myself. This is, and I hope will be, all my pride. For what was I of myself? All the good I can do, is but a poor third-hand good; for my dearest master himself is but the second-hand. God, the All-gracious, the All-good, the All-bountiful, the Almighty, the All-merciful God, is the first; to HIM, therefore, be all the glory."

These sentiments are also mine, and I know that so long as I hold them, the gates of hell shall not prevail against me. Your devoted Sister

Pamela

Postscript

In the course of a long life the author has had opportunity to observe more or less closely the affairs of a dozen or so of the so-called "great families" of America, that is, the permanently rich. In writing a story such as this, he cannot escape making use of recollected episodes, bits of character and conversation, landscapes and interiors, as well as manners and morals. A thousand such details have been thoroughly mixed up here. For example, I know several gilded youths who got drunk, and one who brought his ladies into the family home; but he never pursued a maid-servant in that home—it was another gilded youth who did that. In the same way, I have known half a dozen ladies of wealth who aided and abetted wobblies, Communists, and assorted "Reds," and I have used details of all these ladies. But if you recognize some episode, some characteristic or feature or remark, and conclude that I am writing about that particular lady, you will be not merely wasting your time but doing an injustice to some living person, or to his or her descendants.

I state explicitly: This is a work of fiction and is to be read as such.

NOTE: The poem quoted on page 268 is taken from a self-published volume of my old friend James Larkin Pearson, a true "folk poet" from North Carolina.

Books by Upton Sinclair

Expect No Peace
Your Million Dollars
Little Steel
Our Lady
The Flivver King
No Pasaran!
The Gnomobile
Co-op: A Novel of Living Together
What God Means to Me: An
　Attempt at a Working Religion
I, Candidate for Governor
The Epic Plan for California
I, Governor of California
The Way Out: What Lies Ahead
　for America
Upton Sinclair Presents William Fox
American Outpost: Autobiography
The Wet Parade
Roman Holiday
Mental Radio
Mountain City
Boston
Money Writes!
Oil!
The Spokesman's Secretary
Letters to Judd

Mammonart
The Goslings—A Study of
　American Schools
The Goose-Step—A Study of
　American Education
The Book of Life
They Call Me Carpenter
100%—The Story of a Patriot
The Brass Check
Jimmie Higgins
King Coal
The Profits of Religion
The Cry for Justice
Damaged Goods
Sylvia's Marriage
Sylvia
Love's Pilgrimage
The Fasting Cure
Samuel, the Seeker
The Moneychangers
The Metropolis
The Millennium
The Overman
The Jungle
Manassas, A Novel of the Civil War
The Journal of Arthur Stirling

THE LANNY BUDD NOVELS

World's End
Between Two Worlds
Dragon's Teeth
Wide Is the Gate
Presidential Agent

Dragon Harvest
A World to Win
Presidential Mission
One Clear Call
O Shepherd, Speak!

PLAYS

Prince Hagen
The Naturewoman
The Second Story Man
The Machine
The Pot-boiler
Hell

Singing Jailbirds
Bill Porter
Oil! (*Dramatization*)
Depression Island
Marie Antoinette
A Giant's Strength